THREE INTO ONE

DOES GO

S. M. Cashmore

SPARSILE BOOKS LTD

For Mary

Gone are the days
When you, and you, and you
And I
Made light of life and time.

But the memories that stay
Of you, and you, and you
And we
Are forever yours and mine.

Contents

Introduction

As noted in the disclaimer a few pages back, this book is not meant to be a memoir, or a work of fiction, but something in between.

A memoir, it seems to me, would be a sort of enhanced diary: today I did this, and then I did that, and afterwards this other thing happened. No doubt this would make interesting reading if the writer led an interesting life, so that 'this', 'that' and 'the other' were interesting events. For most people—myself included—personal involvement in such interesting events doesn't happen very often. So, not just a memoir. I decided early on that I would have to make things up, to keep the reader on the page.

Why focus on a memoir at all? Because this book is written at the request of my first wife, Mary, who wanted me to 'write about us'. It is scarcely a spoiler to explain that I fulfil this promise in Part I: Mary. And once Part I was complete, I felt obliged to go on to write Parts II and III.

All three parts are a mixture of fact and fiction.

Overall, I estimate that about fifty per cent of *Three Into One Does Go* is fact, about thirty per cent is fiction, and the remaining twenty per cent is a combination of the two—either descriptions of real events carried out by fictional characters, or vice versa.

I hope I have interwoven the strands sufficiently well that it is not too obvious which events are real and which are not. In fact, so many years have passed that I am no longer sure myself whether some of the events in this book actually happened, or if I am imagining they did.

Finally, I have an apology to make. Mary's remit for the book, as noted above, was to write about us. This means that many other people have been sadly neglected. This is particularly true of my four children. They feature as bit players in this story, but of course are stars and principal actors in real life. For their apparent diminution in *Three Into One Does Go* I can only apologise, and hope to be forgiven.

Stephen Cashmore
January 2020

MARY

When I saw you
There was nothing else there –
Only you.

When you left
I could see nothing at all –
And even I was lost.

One dull afternoon secretary Margaret—known as Dragon Margaret by almost everybody in the Department—remarked that there was another new student. Upstairs.

–Oh yes? he said, suspiciously.

–On the twelfth floor, Margaret informed him.

The Dragon had done this to him before. She had asked him to collect the post from the mailroom in the basement, and he had trudged down eight flights of steps only to find that it had already been delivered. A man wearing bottle glasses and a cap, looking like a character out of *The Hustler*, told him that it was always delivered, every day, nine thirty on the dot, every day, yes sir.

–The twelfth floor, he said.

–Environment section, she said. –DoE. You need the exercise.

–A new student, he repeated. –What's his name?

The Dragon shrugged.

–There's something you're not telling me, he said.

–There's lots of things I cannot tell you.

–Oh yes? Like the Christmas party?

–What about the Christmas party? What do you know about the Christmas party?

–Like how Jumpers found you under the table with—

–You weren't even in the Department at Christmas.

–I cannot reveal my sources, he said.

–You weren't even in London, said Margaret.

This was true. It was his turn to shrug.

–So are you going?

–What?

–To the twelfth floor?

He stared at her. She stared at him. Rain clattered against the window.

–I suppose, he said. He picked up a pencil, noticed rather moodily that it was an HB, turned it over and put it back down again. He felt that he had been outmanoeuvred.

–Did I tell you about the time the Department tried to ban Christmas? asked the Dragon.

–I'm going, I'm going.

–It was back in sixty-two. Or was it sixty-three?

–I said I'm going. Sheesh.

He picked up his jacket, wrestled it on as he made his way across the office. More rain washed across the window. The day outside was grey.

–If this is another...

Margaret regarded him impassively. He tugged his jacket straight, scowled, and went out. After he closed the door and the sound of his footsteps had faded in the general direction of the stairwell, the Dragon picked up her phone and dialled a number.

–He's on his way. What? Tom. Tom Bradley. Yes. Well, it makes a change from doing the filing, doesn't it?

She put down the receiver, unaware that Tom had tiptoed back along the corridor and had his ear glued to the door. He frowned as he tiptoed away again. What was the old bat up to now?

He went past the lift and turned into the stairwell. He didn't need the exercise, despite the Dragon's acerbic comment, but he didn't like lifts; he didn't like the idea of the long straight drop mere inches beneath his feet. A giant number eight was painted in garish orange on the otherwise grey featureless door which doubled up as a fire escape.

–Are dragons bats? wondered Tom. –Are bats dragons?

He passed a ghostly Nine painted on a door and continued upwards. Then he came to a halt, clutching at the handrail. He had recalled Margaret's shifty expression when he asked about the new student. "What's his name?" he had asked, and she had turned all shifty and not replied. No, no... surely Margaret hadn't sent him on a mission to meet up with a girl? Surely not even the Dragon could be so cruel?

A dull bang sounded from ahead of him, further up the steps, and then the rapid clatter of approaching footsteps. Tom hesitated. Should he stand on the right or on the left? He stepped over towards the outside wall, and then stepped back again to clutch again at the handrail in case whoever it was failed to notice he was there until it was too late and bowled him back down the stone steps. In the event a fair-haired young man with an armful of papers appeared and skirted him neatly. Tom didn't move. The man eyed him as he clattered past, probably wondering why Tom was standing motionless in the stairwell, holding on to the handrail. He nodded briefly—Tom nodded back—and disappeared further down the stairwell. Another distant boom announced that he had emerged into the corridor on a floor below.

Tom resumed his slow trudge upwards.

He didn't know anything about girls. He was frightened of them. He practically never spoke to girls—especially if they were unattached—because whenever he did he became overcome with nervousness and spouted complete nonsense. He had no idea why this should be the case, but he could no more prevent spouting nonsense than he could prevent Monday following Sunday.

As number Ten appeared out of the gloom and vanished behind him, he totted up the number of times he had spoken to a girl. It didn't take long. When he was still at school, there had been Elizabeth, who he had sent a Valentine's card. One of his friends, an utter bastard, had told her who it was from. They had scuffled on the train platform and Tom had stumbled backwards, his heart thudding with shock as his feet met thin air and he hurtled down onto red-brown cinders, luckily between the rails glinting silver in watery sunlight. And when he was a schoolteacher—for three years before deciding there was no future in it and switching to working in a jobcentre—he had plucked up the courage to speak to Jo, a French teacher, although she was English, and Catherine, who was an English teacher although she was French. He could see them both now, sitting across from him in the staff room, heads together, chattering away. He remembered wondering if they spoke English or French to each other.

Unexpected darkness interrupted his memories. Everything faded away, even the Marsham Street stairwell. Tom was momentarily confused, and then he realised that the stairwell lights in between the eleventh and twelfth floors weren't working. He peered up into what looked like a pitch-black tunnel.

–Just great.

He wondered about not bothering. He envisaged turning around, clumping back down to the eighth floor. He envisaged Dragon Margaret arching her eyebrows.

"Well?"

"Well, the lights were out. Er."

"The lights were out," she would say flatly.

He grabbed the safety rail and hauled himself into the tunnel.

–For goodness sake, he muttered.

He found out later that at that precise moment his boss David Pickles opened the door to his office, stuck his head out and, after taking in the sight of Margaret sitting placidly by herself, barked: "Where's whatsisname?"

Margaret arched her eyebrows. "You mean Tom?"

"Yes," barked David Pickles. "Tom. Him. Where?"

"Gone up to Environment," said Margaret. "New student there," she partially explained.

"I've decided to send him on a local audit," said David Pickles.

"Oh?" Margaret thought a moment, and then blanched. "Not with George?" she said.

"With George," said David Pickles with vast satisfaction. "To an RCU."

"An RCU," repeated Margaret mechanically.

"In Milton Keynes," added David Pickles enthusiastically.

"Milton Keynes," whispered Margaret.

David Pickles rubbed his hands together. "Do him good, Tom whatever. He's young. Needs experience."

"There are no good experiences in Milton Keynes," said Margaret firmly.

"Well. Maybe not," conceded David Pickles. "But there you have it. Sort out the accommodation, will you? And find George."

He retreated into his office. The door closed in a self-satisfied fashion.

Tom didn't know any of this was happening. He had no idea that a local audit with George mapped out part of his future. He didn't remember having any presentiments at all, nervous or otherwise, as he shuffled upwards through the darkness. But long afterwards he wondered if a hidden part of him knew that his world was about to change, if some deep part of his consciousness was saying farewell to the Tom that was, in preparation for the Tom that was coming. Why else would his mind insist on replaying past scenes? It was as if part of him wanted to make sure the memories were securely cached in a place that protected them from being seared away by memories of events still to come.

After clambering the last set of steps beneath an invisible string of broken lights, he reached the twelfth floor. Faint vestiges of daylight revealed the outline of a grey door with a mammoth 1 and a slightly smaller 2 painted on it, in what was probably garish orange but looked like the colour of dried blood in the feeble illumination. Tom paused long enough to peer further up the stairwell. He wondered if there was a thirteenth floor, or if it had been missed out in the fashion adopted by many hotels. He had once read a ghost story about a lift which stopped at a non-existent thirteenth floor in a Gothic, haunted hotel. Another good reason for not using lifts, he thought.

He pushed open the fire escape door, let it swing shut behind him. The corridor on the twelfth floor looked exactly the same as the corridor on the eighth. He walked slowly along it until he spotted the Exchequer & Audit sign.

He knocked on the door.

Opened it.

> When first I saw you
> My heart missed some beats.

A young woman turned towards the opening door, hair spilling over her shoulders. For the first time—but not the last—Tom's heart lurched helplessly.

> But made them up pretty soon after.

Tom knew that he would remember this moment for the rest of his life. While their eyes met, his brain somehow noted that outside the windows a giant crane crouched over the embryonic extension to the Tate. Grey sky pressed against the glass. He sensed that one of the fluorescent lights flickered. At the corner of his view, a bag of shopping sat awkwardly on top of a second desk, but of its owner there was no sign.

His memory photographed the office, her questioning eyes. She was unbuttoning a grey cardigan. Her plain brown shoes protruded from beneath a long dress, which looked as if it had been knitted from several different rolls of leftover wool and was a peculiar purple-brown colour.

He opened his mouth nervously.

Her calm eyes continued to look into his.

Nonsense bubbled behind his lips. He fought against it, struggled to stop his mind becoming entirely disconnected from his mouth. On the one hand he wished that this delicious moment might last forever, but on the other he wished that he could sidestep all embarrassments by being sucked instantaneously back into the drab twelfth-floor corridor, the door slamming shut in front of his nervously twitching face. Better still, perhaps he could be sucked back into time, to that moment when he raised his hand to knock on the door. Then he could change his mind, lower his arm, and never enter the room at all, never meet this woman who was sending his thoughts into confused, ecstatic spirals.

Moments dragged by. Her eyebrows twisted quizzically.

His lips said: –I—er, while his brain wondered what he was going to say. He remembered the excruciating morning when he had turned around to see schoolgirl Elizabeth walking behind them on the way to the station and all his instantly confused brain could think of to say was *Are you overtaking?* This became a catchword amongst his friends. They never asked *How're you doing?* or *How's it hanging?* but *Are you overtaking?* Surely he wasn't going to say something as inane as that on this obviously momentous occasion?

He considered telling this story to the woman sitting neatly in front of him, her eyes still connected to his. He considered telling her his whole life story. He considered telling her that if she suggested he jumped out of the twelfth-floor window, he might actually do it just to see her smile.

From somewhere behind him came the sound of a lift whirring into motion and a premonition warned him that this was the owner of the shopping bag coming back into home territory. If he was going to say anything, he'd better say it quickly, because in front of an audience he would dry up completely. He licked his lips.

–Er, he repeated and then suddenly, gloriously, he knew exactly what to say. This knowledge must have shown in his face, because her features aligned themselves into a pleasantly anticipatory look.

–I'm trying, he said seriously, willing her to understand, –not to say any nonsense.

Behind him, somewhere along the corridor, the lift wheezed to a halt and time drifted into those agonising few seconds while everyone waited to see if the doors would open. In front of him, the young woman looked momentarily surprised. Then she nodded approvingly.

–Good, she said.

It was hard to tell on hearing only one syllable, but Tom suspected she had the most beautiful voice he had ever heard, even including Catherine's French-accented husky I've-just-woken-up tones. His heart stopped. He grabbed the side of the door, smiled weakly. His heart started again. The door of the lift whined open.

He noticed a newspaper folded at the crossword page.

–You do crosswords, he said.

–Yes, she said.

–So do I, he said.

Crosswords? he thought to himself. *Are you overtaking?* But unexpectedly her face broke into a smile and he found himself idiotically smiling back.

–And I'm doing the accounting course too, he said.

Footsteps in the corridor echoed away from the room, scurrying away to deep places in the Tower. His premonition had been wrong.

–Come in, she said.

–Is that your shopping?

She followed his glance. –Yes.

He stepped in and closed the door, proud of the way that his hands didn't tremble and his knees didn't buckle. –I'm Tom, he said.

–I'm Mary, she told him. –Listen. Suitable for light sleepers. Seven three. Any ideas?

She watched Tom moved closer, further into the room. For some reason her mouth was dry and the hand which held her pencil trembled.

–Got any letters? asked Tom.

–The fourth one's a T, she said. –Why did you ask about my shopping?

–I thought someone might, um—

–I see.

–Are you doing the course? he asked.

–Yes, she said. –My dad thought it would be a good idea. And by that, he meant he thought it would be a good idea.

–What?

–Never mind. You'll understand when you meet him.

Damn, she thought. *Why did I say that? Perhaps he won't notice.*

–Feather bed, he said before the import of her words hit him. He was standing at her shoulder, peering down at the *Daily Telegraph* crossword. Her long, black hair spilled, unchecked, down her back. He saw that she wrote with her left hand. Suddenly he was sure that he could smell her, a subtle female smell intermingled with the scent of wool. A wave of desire swept over him.

He moaned.

–Feather bed, she mused. –Very good. She looked up. –Are you all right?

He fumbled at a chair at the neighbouring desk and sat down. He couldn't understand what had happened. After all, she was pretty, but not beautiful. Her complexion was slightly olive, her wide eyes were brown, her lips were full but straight rather than curved, and her nose was delicate and small. He had no idea what her figure was like, because she was wearing some kind of smock gathered up below her breasts. His eyes wandered. At least there seemed to be plenty of room there for it to be gathered.

–Tom?

He jerked guiltily, at the same time thinking *She remembered my name.*

–You've gone pale, she said. –No, now you've gone red. Are you all right?

Years later he wrote a short story called The Last and Longest Story. In it, a young man became tongue-tied and confused when he met a girl dressed in white on a summer's day. When he wrote what happened next, he was remembering what happened on that rainswept dreary day in Marsham Street.

His eyes opened wide, he breathed heavily and
he felt his face growing hot and then, just as he

opened his mouth, he remembered what his grand-mother had told him.

'You can't go far wrong if you always tell the truth,' she had said. 'Sometimes you might be thinking of a way to explain something, and usually you'll find it's best just to come right out and say it. You'll feel better if you do.' Now was the time, he thought, to put this advice into operation. It was amazingly easy.

The Last and Longest Story was far in the future as Tom sat, red-faced and guilty in front of Mary, but he suddenly knew that the best thing to do was to tell the truth.

–I don't know what's the matter with me, he said. –Yes I do. You've taken my breath away. Will you come and have lunch with me?

Her hand brushed her lips, suppressing a smile. She gave him a considering look, then smiled anyway. His heart leaped and thudded.

–That would be nice, she said. –Thank you.

He couldn't believe it. He had asked a girl out and she had said yes. He was convinced there must have been a misunderstanding.

–Are you sure? he said. –I mean, lunch?

She continued to gaze at him. She made her eyebrows twist in that quizzical fashion he came to know so well.

–What do you mean, when I meet your father? he said desperately.

–Did I say that? She shook her head slightly. Her eyes met his again in that curiously intimate fashion that he had never experienced before. Then she said something he was quite sure didn't mean what he thought it meant. –Perhaps I was talking nonsense too.

–Oh, he said. –Okay, um. He jumped up and started to back away, towards the door. –Later, then?

She nodded, twisting her pencil round and round in her long fingers. He wondered if it was an HB. He fumbled open the door, but before he went out he held her gaze for a long moment and he was sure—he was almost sure—that an unspoken *something* passed between them.

He didn't remember anything about the return journey down the darkened stairwell. It could have taken five minutes or five hours. He felt as though he had started to hold his breath the moment he had met Mary's steady gaze, but exactly what he was holding it for and the length of time he was supposed to hold it were both shrouded in mystery.

–Don't be so daft, he told himself.

He did remember the stricken look Margaret gave him when he got back to the office.

–What is it? *Oh God, I haven't been fired, have I?* he thought. *Or moved. Oh God, she hasn't rung down to cancel, has she?* This last thought was far worse than the previous two.

–It's David, whispered Margaret. She gazed soulfully at him.

–What about David? Hope surged within him. –He hasn't fallen out a window, has he? Or down Marsham Street's stone steps? Or did the lift break down? *Or drop him off at the thirteenth floor?*

–No, it's you, said Margaret.

Immediate panic. –Me?

–He's sending you out on local audit, said Margaret.

Tom sank down in his chair, overcome with relief. He still had a job. Mary hadn't cancelled.

–Thank God, thank God, thank God.

The Dragon stared at him, perplexed. –Wait till you hear about it, she advised. She told him about it but, at that precise moment in time, he wasn't listening.

Upstairs, Roger B returned from a trip to the stationery cupboard and found Mary staring sightlessly out at grey, damp clouds. Roger B was the twelfth-floor equivalent of Dragon Margaret, except that instead of being an almost-sixty veteran of the Department, he was barely out of his teens and always wore black leather gear as he was a bike enthusiast. He and Margaret got along famously.

–What's up, love? he enquired.

–Nothing, nothing.

Roger B deposited a box of envelopes, twenty-five writing pads and a box of biros in the small cupboard behind his desk.

–Meet the new student, did you? he enquired.

–Um.

–All right, was he?

–Yes, fine, okay. Um.

It didn't occur to Mary to ask how Roger B not only knew that a new student was going to visit, but even knew that he was a he.

–Rotten weather, observed Roger B.

–Is it? said Mary, still gazing out of the window.

That evening Tom went back to his digs in a state of ecstatic disbelief. He lodged with Peter, a maniac living in the guise of a telephone engineer in deepest Cheam. After his first day at Marsham Street, a few weeks before he accepted a lift from Peter in his rusty, dented van, he told Peter, "My boss called me Tom."

"Well, that's yer name, ain't it?"

"And I called him…" He hesitated. Even hours later, in the distant confines of rented accommodation in Cheam, it felt like blasphemy. "David," he whispered.

"Yeah? Well, that's is name, I spose."

Peter slurped tea and flung a biscuit at a black cat called Cosmic slinking towards one of his aquariums of tropical fish. Cosmic squalled.

"Got im."

"Why on earth," said Tom, momentarily diverted, "do you keep fish and cats?"

"I like fish n cats."

"But cats like fish."

"Yeah," said Peter. "Keeps me on me toes, dunnit?"

What Peter had failed to understand was that in his previous job Tom's boss had been a Higher Executive Officer. Her boss had been a Senior Executive Officer.

"—who was, like, God. I didn't even know where he was based."

"Heaven?" Peter laughed uproariously. Tropical fish fled to distant corners of their tanks. "Anyway, wot's that got to do with David wotsit?"

"He's a Principal," Tom had whispered. "The next one up."

"From God?"

"—and he asked me to call him David," said Tom, still not believing it.

Now he planned to tell Peter all about Mary and his eventful day, but as he rounded the final corner a blaze of light met his eyes and he knew instantly that Peter had received a bill.

–Look at this! screeched Peter, as soon as he was through the front door. All the lights in the house were on. The washing machine, tumble dryer, electric cooker, two stereos and three televisions were on. Peter, his hair sticking up wildly as if he too was discharging electricity, was leaping up and down on the spot, waving what looked suspiciously like a telephone bill. –Look at it! Fifty flaming quid! Flaming line charges, flaming VAT, flaming evening costs wotever the flaming hell they are. Look, look, look!

It was hard to look as he was still frantically waving the bill.

–You wanna know wot cost of calls was? You wanna know? He glared at Tom belligerently as if he was personally responsible for making up the bill and pushing it through the letter box. Tom nodded hastily. Peter transferred his glare to the crumpled bill.

–Twenty-six quid! he raved.

Peter had discovered that by loosening a small screw on his electric meter box and thumping it *just so*, the meter stopped running. Now every time he got a phone, electric or gas bill, he would thump the box and use up as much free electricity as he could.

–That'll teach em! he howled.

The first time this had happened, Tom tried to point out that the phone company was not connected to the electric company. "No pun intended," he had said.

"Not connected?" howled Peter. "You flaming mad? They're all flaming *utilities*, ain't they?"

Tom should really have known better than to accept a lift from him, two weeks later, emergency or no emergency. But he didn't know about that yet. Now, he sighed as Peter danced on the spot, gibbering about *flaming utilities*.

–Cook stuff. I've made flaming curry. Ha! Flaming curry! Turn everything on. I'll flaming teach em to— He stopped. Cosmic sauntered out of the living room and calmly ascended the stairs, no doubt en route to the broken bathroom window. –Oh, said Peter. Strains of the Beach Boys from the living room mingled strangely with the Rolling Stones from upstairs and several babbling televisions.

–What?

–Jan's mum n dad. It's tonight.

Jan was the other lodger. She came from somewhere in West Africa and was the colour of burnished ebony. She was extremely self-centred and drove both Tom and Peter mad. She had gone out Friday night, about a week ago, and hadn't come back.

–Sit in, will yer? said Peter. –I mean, you know.

–Okay, said Tom.

–Just in case, muttered Peter.

In the event, Jan's parents turned out to be a very pleasant couple, also the colour of burnished ebony. Tom sat in a corner as Peter launched into a diatribe.

–I know yer worried, he said. –I unnerstand that. But I like to say wot's on me mind. That's the sort of man I am.

–Jan— began Jan's father, but Peter was not to be denied.

–Since Jan's bin ere, he babbled, –we've done all the cleaning n washing, n all me fish died n most of me cacti ain't well, we think—

–Yes, but—

–Jan said she didn't like fish, see, n why shouldn't she do er fair share of the housework?

–I expect she asked, said Jan's mother, a beautiful woman in her mid-fifties, –what your last servant died of?

Peter stared at her.

–She's run away with someone, said Jan's father.

–Probably, said Jan's mother. –Do you know anything about boyfriends?

Peter shook his head. Both parents glanced at Tom, who shook *his* head. Out of the corner of his eye, he saw Cosmic gather himself for a giant leap onto the dining table. An awful premonition swept over him.

–Did she owe anything? asked Jan's father.

–Rent, explained Jan's mother.

–We'll gather her things, said Jan's father.

–She's done this before, said Jan's mother.

–She'll be back, said Jan's father. –She'll come home.

Cosmic, paws splayed and tail flying, landed on the table, instantly took a huge lick of the nearest plate before he could be thrown back off, and then leaped into the air again, squalling horrifically as hot curry burned his delicate feline taste buds. Jan's parents jumped in shock. Their burnished ebony complexions paled. Peter did not even look round.

–Um, no, he said. –Owe me anything? No.

He failed to explain that he always got his rent in advance.

Much later, Tom lay in darkness remembering how the lunatic evening had been preceded by a day filled by his own delicious madness. At lunchtime he met up with Mary in what passed for the Marsham Street canteen, and they both had tea and sandwiches while finishing the *Daily Telegraph* crossword. Mary didn't ask him any questions, and he forgot all those he had meant to ask her. At one point she shifted her chair sideways so they were sitting close to each other. His heart stuttered. At another point, her arm brushed against him. His heart stopped. She flicked her hair behind her ears and her eyes met his. For a moment unspoken words hovered between them again. He was sure of it. He was almost sure of it. Then she looked back down at the crossword and the moment was broken.

He had ham-and-pickle sandwiches. The bread was dry and the ham stringy. The tea was watery and not very hot. He suspected the milk was slightly off. The woman behind the counter coughed and spluttered and called everybody *love*—not that the canteen was exactly full. Two men in overalls drank coffee and smoked cigarettes at one end of the canteen, and a young girl with a spotty face and bright dyed blonde hair sat at the other.

It was the best lunch Tom had ever had.

Afterwards, he took Mary back up in the lift, back up to the twelfth floor, fervently hoping that it would get jammed somewhere. It didn't. She stood in the doorway to her office and he was reminded of the female leads in all the films he'd seen, standing in the doorways to their flats and saying to the male leads—who might be decent characters or duplicitous bad guys—"Care to come in for a cup of coffee?"

"I don't drink coffee," he blurted.

"What?"

"Sorry, sorry. That was nonsense."

"Well, nor do I actually," said Mary.

He meant to say *Same tomorrow then?* or *What are you doing tonight?* but both these questions evaded his grasp of courage, and instead he smiled and nodded and looked vaguely desperate.

"Thanks," said Mary. "For lunch."

"M-my pleasure," stammered Tom. He took a deep breath. "Would, er, would you—?"

"That you, Mary?" called a voice from inside the office. Mary turned around, then turned back again.

"Sorry. Got to go. Boss."

Tom was relieved. "Okay."

He caught a glimpse of someone wearing a bright red shirt as the door closed.

Back downstairs, the afternoon passed in a blur. Margaret asked how he had got on, and he gave a mumbled reply which must have been insufficient because she rapped on the table and asked in a much louder voice, *What's she like, then?* and he had looked up, suddenly suspicious, and asked in his turn, *Her? How did you know it was a her?* Margaret had blushed and muttered something about somebody seeing them in the canteen, but he recalled that there had only been four other people in the canteen, even counting the serving lady, and he didn't think it likely any of them belonged to Margaret's spy ring. He looked at her sternly and said, *How could you?*

"I've arranged accommodation," said Margaret.

"That's nice," he said vaguely.

"For you and George," explained Margaret.

"Who's George?"

"George Fulton, who you're going on local audit with. Also known as George It's On The Department Fulton. You'll need to watch yourself."

Tom stared at her. "You're not making this up, are you?"

"You weren't listening before, were you?" Margaret accused him.

He wondered why he hadn't been listening, and remembered sitting in the canteen with Mary, remembered how she shifted her chair so that they were sitting side by side. One of the crossword clues had baffled them for a while—*timely note changes water level*—and it wasn't until it was almost time for them to go that he looked up at the… "Clock!" he told her, and his heart lurched as she broke into a delighted smile. He admired the way her long fingers held her pencil as she wrote down the answer in her slanted, left-handed scrawl.

"Tom."

"Eh?"

"Never mind."

At half past four his phone rang and a voice said, "You going?"

Margaret had watched with interest as his face at first lit up, then turned beet red, then finally settled on a look of quiet desperation.

"Oh yes," he said. "Oh, you mean now? Oh, well, yes, I suppose I could…"

"I get the Tube," she said.

"Yes," he said. "I've, uh, been on the Tube."

"Tom," she said. "Quit it with the nonsense."

It was funny how his name sounded totally different when she used it.

"I bus and walk. Digs out in Cheam. Mad landlord. About half an hour."

"I'm in a hall of residence in Kensington," she said. "All girls. See you downstairs in five minutes?"

"Oh yes," he said, and stared blankly at the phone after she hung up.

"Who was that?" asked the Dragon.

"It's—it's another student. Same course, comparing notes and stuff."

"Oh yes?" mimicked the Dragon.

Downstairs, Tom hopped anxiously from one foot to the other. Was he late? Had she got fed up with waiting and left already? Had she changed her mind and gone out by another entrance? Was she waiting by another entrance anyway?—after all, 'downstairs' could mean almost anywhere in Marsham Street. A lift wheezed open, disgorged people. Mary wasn't one of them. Two girls, laughing, came down out of the stairwell. One of them had long blonde hair, the other was a stunning Indian girl wearing a figure-hugging sari. On any other day of virtually his entire life up to date, Tom would have admired her as she undulated past, but not today. He barely spared her a glance. Another lift landed with a shuddering clunk, paused. Its doors opened. Tom shifted from his left leg to his right. It was becoming hard to see the North lifts over a stream of people leaving Marsham Street. He could have moved to the other side of reception, but then it would have been equally difficult to see the South lifts.

Mary came out, into the main concourse.

Tom froze, on one leg, oblivious to the curious stares of passers-by.

Mary stopped, somebody else coming out of the same lift bumped into the back of her, she sidestepped—Tom could see that she was apologising—she looked around. In a few seconds she was going to see him. Tom held his breath in an agony of suspense. Then she caught his eye and broke into a smile. She waved and threaded her way through the departing throng towards him.

"Good day?" she said.

Tom pondered. It had been the best day of his life, but he wasn't sure if he ought to say so. "Um," he said, and then they pushed through the swinging doors and somehow the subject was brushed behind them. Outside it was warm but dark and muggy. Most of the cars crawling up the Embankment already had headlights on. Pedestrians hurried off in various directions. One man dived across the road to the accompaniment of indignant horns.

"I go this way. I get the District at St James."

Tom nodded, walking beside her. He noticed that she moved with a long, easy stride. He actually went in the other direction to catch his bus, but he wasn't about to admit it.

"You in tomorrow?" he asked.

"Yes. Here." She passed him a scrap of paper.

He took it and stared at it uncomprehendingly. Why was she giving him a scrap of paper? They had reached the entrance to the Tube station.

"Got to dash," she said. She touched him briefly on the shoulder. "Bye, Tom."

He watched as she joined a mass of fellow travellers. For a moment he stood there, a stationary object dividing the flowing stream of commuters. His lips silently formed *bye*. He stood there, unmoving, for long minutes, until he was convinced in spite of himself that she was not coming back.

He stuffed the piece of paper in his pocket, turned around, and retraced his steps past Millbank Tower to what had become his regular bus stop.

The scrap of paper.

–Damn, he said aloud, in darkness now that Peter had finally consented to turn off all the lights. –Damn damn damn. In the excitement of finding the house lit up like a Christmas tree and the subsequent visit of Jan's parents, he had forgotten all about it. On the way back, on the bus, he had worked out that Mary, in her already familiar left-handed scrawl, had given him her phone number. She wanted him to call. He swallowed nervously. Superimposed on the darkness of his bedroom, he kept seeing her face breaking into a smile. Underneath the blankets, he kept feeling her touch on his shoulder. He wondered if she was lying awake, thinking of him, and that thought led to other thoughts which kept him even wider awake. Perhaps she wasn't thinking about him at all. Worse, perhaps she was thinking that he just hadn't bothered to call, and not want to see him again. Not want to go out to lunch. Why hadn't he arranged to go out to lunch again when he had the chance? Why didn't he think to call? –Damn, damn, he gritted into darkness that slowly became dawn. He wasn't sure if he was happy or not.

Next day, the dragon Margaret refused to tell him the phone number of the section on the twelfth floor until he admitted what he wanted it for. He said, –Look, I just want the number of the section up there. She said, –Is it a boy or a girl? He said, –What does that matter? It's a phone number, all right? She said, –I'm not so sure this is a business call. He said, –I expect I can find out some other way. She said, –Oh yes? You thinking of trying reception? Mm? They'll only put you through to me. He shouted, –Look, Margaret—and stopped, as David came into the office.

Both Tom and Margaret smiled at him politely.

–Morning, David.

–Morning, Margaret.

–Morning, sir.

–Call me David, Tom.

–Morning, David, sir.

They smiled fixedly at David as he collected a file and a pile of correspondence, turning their heads to follow him as he went back to his door. He paused before exiting, glanced at them both with a puzzled expression, shook his head, and went into his office.

Margaret returned her gimlet gaze to Tom, who sighed and gave in. All right, yes it was a girl he wanted to call and yes, he fancied her and yes, he wanted to ask her out for lunch. Margaret smiled toothily.

–Why didn't you say so?

But when he rang, somebody told him that Mary was out on a visit and wouldn't be back until lunchtime, possibly not until after lunchtime. He put the phone down and stared unseeing out of the window in an agony of apprehension. She was out. Why hadn't she told him she was going to be out? He had asked if she was going to be in, and she had said yes. But that was before he hadn't called. So maybe she hadn't known she was going to be out. If that was the case, why hadn't she rung him this morning? That was *after* he hadn't called. On the other hand, why should she? They had only met the previous day, after all. It was hardly as if they were an item. Who had she gone out with? Who had she gone out to meet? Who was talking to her, right this minute?

–Here, said Margaret sympathetically, plunking a mug of tea and a chocolate biscuit on the desk in front of him. Tom gazed at them. He hadn't known Margaret had a stash of chocolate biscuits.

The door banged open.

–Margaret!

A large man wearing a check suit and bright yellow tie strode in, wielding a gold-tipped walking stick.

–George, said Margaret, her tone carefully neutral.

–Good morning young feller-me-lad, boomed George. Tom jumped to his feet, ready to shake hands, but George had already barged across the room. He opened the door to David Pickles' office and plunged in.

–David!

–George. It was possible to note that David Pickles' voice was also carefully neutral. The door closed. Tom sat down again.

–That was George, said Margaret unnecessarily.

–He's… Tom sought for the right word: –flamboyant.

–He's one of the characters, admitted Margaret. Uncharacteristically, she didn't seem to want to say anything more.

Tom did some filing, read a few files. George's voice continued to boom intermittently, and presumably David Pickles was saying something in the intervening silences. Time slowed down to a crawl and almost stopped. Between one stationary moment while Tom wondered what Mary was doing and why she hadn't contacted him and the next eternal moment while he wondered what exactly had happened to him that his thoughts had been thrown into such disarray, he wrote:

> Woman,
> Your smile propels me
> Into lands of uncertainty.

Years later, when time was precious, when he wanted every moment to stretch forever but instead they flew with remorseless speed into the past, he remembered sitting in Marsham Street, doodling, thinking, agonising. The Dragon typed. George's voice boomed. A fire engine blared past, eight floors below. The phone rang and he looked up hopefully, but the Dragon held a murmured conversation with someone and replaced the receiver, not meeting his eye. He sighed and looked down at his poem.

David Pickles' office door crashed open.

–Well young feller-me-lad…

–His name's Tom, barked David Pickles from somewhere behind George's vast bulk.

–Well feller-me-Tom it looks like you and me are headed for God-awful Milton Keynes God help us.

Tom had jumped to his feet and was wondering what to say. George slammed a pile of computer printouts on the nearest desk.

–I'll leave you to it, remarked David Pickles, and disappeared back into his office.

–Cup of tea? asked Margaret.

–Nothing stronger? boomed George. –Gods Margaret I remember when—

–I'll put the kettle on, interrupted the Dragon hastily. George propped his walking stick against another desk, hooked a chair with one massive leg, and sat down beside Tom.

–Sit down sit down, he said. –Vouchers from this print, we want a sample a random sample mind of invoices preferably over five hundred pounds, you know what a random sample is do you?

Tom nodded and shook his head.

–Make a list we'll check them out when we get to God-awful Milton Keynes. Well you will young feller-me-lad there are some advantages to rank after all and a bit of tick and turn never hurt anybody, what d'you say Margaret?

–Just the four sugars still, is it?

–Gods what a memory the woman has.

George slurped mightily.

–Should we ask them to look them out? asked Tom. –The invoices.

–Gods no what are you thinking?

–He's a trainee, said Margaret.

–Explains a lot.

Slurp.

–No we definitely don't tell them in advance. If we did that they could change the numbers, orders, entries well pretty much anything check out Gray's Inn if you don't believe me no you just make the list up young feller-me-Tom and I'll show you how to tick and turn when we get to the God-awful place, okay?

–Okay, said Tom.

–And we are going to want some files for starters when we look for points. David suggests pre-planning correspondence the A67 project we'll use that for starters anyway, can you get on to Milton Keynes Margaret and ask him to have them ready?

Margaret nodded. Tom leaned forward to make a note about the A67 and suddenly realised that his new poem was sitting in plain view next to the printouts. He started guiltily. George followed his gaze.

–What's this? woman your aha hmmhmmm propels ahahmmm I see Margaret have you been smiling at young feller-me-Tom have you been flirting and batting your big blue eyes?

Tom was blushing furiously.

–George, said Margaret firmly.

–Perhaps not, conceded George. –You've booked us in my hotel eh?

Margaret sighed. –Old joke, she told Tom. –The George Hotel.

–I'll give you a lift, said George.

–Downstairs? asked Tom. –What time?

–Don't be such a bloody fool young feller-me-Tom of course not downstairs, you can't claim mileage for going to your place of work can you?

–He's a trainee, reminded Margaret.

–What's your address?

Tom wrote it on his pad, tore it off and passed it over.

–Cheam eh okay half nine on Monday then. See you.

George stood up, grabbed his walking stick, turned to go. Despite the fact that he was facing away from her, Margaret held out her hand. George took something from his jacket pocket and turned back again. He beamed at Margaret.

–A treasure, he boomed. He put a sheet of paper into her outstretched hand, turned again, and barged out.

Margaret sighed and pinched the bridge of her nose. Tom craned his neck to read the piece of paper, which seemed to be a form crammed with tiny writing.

–It's his travel claim, said Margaret without looking up.

–He, er. Tom searched for the right words. –Seems to know what he's doing.

–Oh, he knows what he's doing all right. Claim the mileage to your house. Claim the allowance for taking a passenger. All legal. If George Fulton spent as much time on his work as…

Margaret's gaze flicked over his shoulder. He hadn't heard the door open again. He turned and almost banged his nose on the bunched-up woolly material of Mary's smock.

–Tom?

It struck Tom that he really rather wished that he had bumped his nose on her smock.

–Shall we have lunch?

He shot to his feet, knocking over his chair, and whirled, almost knocking Mary over as well. He grinned idiotically. Mary twisted her eyebrows, then grinned back. –Fool, she said.

As he followed her out of the office, he glanced back at Dragon Margaret. She gave him a thumbs-up and, after the door was closed, dabbed at the corners of her eyes with a handkerchief.

They decided against the canteen for lunch and instead found a sandwich bar on Victoria Street. It was there that they discovered the first astonishing coincidence. As they settled down on bar stools overlooking the street and started to unwrap sandwiches and prise open the tops of plastic cups of tea, Mary said she was sorry she hadn't been in after all.

–It's all right, said Tom. It really was all right. The worries of the morning had vanished as if they had never been. He watched as Mary took a sip of her tea. Outside, clouds bubbled over the City of London and one or two passers-by looked up and tentatively opened umbrellas. Mary explained that her boss had taken her out on a visit first thing.

–It's all right, said Tom. It was better than all right. He had re-alised that *she* had asked *him* out to lunch. The world was a different place than it had been two days ago. He took a sip of his own tea and took a bite of ham sandwich. Rain began to streak the window. Cars going towards Victoria Station had their wipers going, but those coming in the opposite direction did not. Mary said that there had been no chance to call, either before they left or while they were at the interview.

–It's all right, said Tom.

–Is that all you can say? complained Mary. –Will you say something different?

–All right, said Tom, then realised what he had said and turned bright red.

–What made you join Exchequer and Audit?

–A friend, um, recommended it to me.

A few months previously, Beryl—a trainer who had been trying to teach him the art of interviewing—had informed him that "Exchequer and Audit is the last bastion of the eccentric civil servant".

She knew that, she said, because her husband Ralph was already one of them.

"Ralph will get an application form for you," she decided. "It'll be for the best. You'll see."

Which he had, and now here he was, a fledgling and, according to Beryl, eccentric auditor. Tom watched as Mary unconsciously flicked her hair behind her ears. –What about you?

–My father's an accountant, she said, as if this explained everything. Her placid eyes regarded him over the rim of her cup of tea. Ah yes, Tom thought. He was supposed to meet her father sometime.

–Where do they live, your mum and dad? he asked.

–Derry, said Mary. –I was born in London, but my dad has a job in Derry. What about yours?

–Sandhurst, he told her. –Nothing to do with the army—just happens to be where my dad works.

–You got any brothers or sisters?

–A sister—lives down on the South coast. You?

–Three sisters, said Mary. –They're at home. I'm the youngest. Elizabeth is ten years older than me…

The hairs on the back of Tom's neck suddenly stood to attention. *Elizabeth?*

–… and the twins are thirteen years older than me. That's Catherine and… What?

Tom had held up his hand. –Let me guess, he said. His heart was hammering, although he could not quite say why. Perhaps he had glimpsed the normally invisible machinations of fate. –Josephine? Jo?

Mary stared at him, perplexed. Her brow creased. Tom divined that his guess was correct. It dawned on him that Mary might be wondering if he was a crazed stalker who had already researched her background and had joined Exchequer and Audit specifically to engineer this meeting. He waved his hands in agitation.

–It's amazing, he said. –I knew three girls—that is, I didn't really *know* them, but there were these three girls that I…

He looked into her faintly amused eyes, took a deep breath. He would just have to tell her the truth.

While he babbled on about schooldays, falling in front of trains, and then more schooldays except by now he was a teacher, Mary gazed at the water trickling down the window of the sandwich bar and remembered the last time she had been out with anyone. Gregory Updike, rugby player training to be a chemical engineer, had taken her to a dance towards the end of university days. It had not gone well. He had fumbled her into a corner and was trying to work out how to get underneath her layers of clothing, and in fact had undone one of the buttons on her dress before she broke free. She had made a dash for the exit. He followed, moving so quickly that she had half-turned and flung up an arm to ward him off. In the event it had done much better than that.

"I didn't mean it," she wailed to her best friend Christine later. "I caught him under his chin, here"—she demonstrated—"and his head stopped but his feet kept going so he fell backwards and… and he—"

"Knocked himself out," said Christine, having already heard the conclusion to this story.

"He was moaning when I left."

"Well, that's all right then."

"What am I going to do?" wailed Mary.

"I expect you'll get lots of invitations," said Christine. "To join the rugby team."

Mary stopped wailing. She sniffed, thought about it, caught Christine's eye. Next second they both started giggling helplessly. Eventually they quietened down.

"Wish I could have been there," said Christine. "Anyway, Greg's not the one for you."

"No?"

Christine might have been six months younger than Mary, but she was much wiser in the ways of the world.

"No," she said firmly. "Do you feel woozy when you see him? Does your brain turn to mush? Do your legs feel all wobbly? Is your heart going at twice its normal speed?"

Mary shook her head.

"Well then," said Christine.

–So you see, said Tom.

Mary blinked. Tom was staring at her earnestly. Mary realised, a little to her own surprise, that her brain had turned to mush.

–I won't be here at the weekend, she said.

Tom blinked back at her. His face registered a number of emotions, one after the other. Mary could read them as easily as reading a book. First he was surprised at her non-sequitur; then upset and a little worried that she hadn't been listening to his long story about Elizabeth, Catherine and Josephine; then disappointed that she wasn't going to be around at the weekend; finally, tentatively, pleased and excited at the thought that she thought her weekend movements might be relevant to him.

–Oh.

–Family get-together, she said.

He nodded gloomily. –I won't be around next week, either. I've been sent on local audit. Milton Keynes.

–That sounds—interesting, she offered.

–Not as interesting as… He swallowed. His brain had clearly disconnected itself from his tongue again, otherwise he would never have started this sentence. She was smiling slightly, as if she could read his every thought. *To hell with it.*

–as being with you, he said. He looked away, heart beating wildly, then back at her.

There was a long silence, broken only by the chatter and clamour of other sandwich-bar patrons, the noise of traffic from Victoria Street and the distant howl of a siren.

–Well, she said eventually. She wondered what to say. Not only had her brain turned to mush, but her heart was beating at twice its normal speed. –Well, have you ever been to the National Gallery?

Tom, not trusting himself to speak, shook his head.

In the National Gallery that evening Tom, greatly daring, plucked up courage to hold her hand. As he had never done this before, he clasped her fingers in what was virtually a judo hold, and she was forced to stoop forwards to prevent her wrist from being dislocated. She hunched around the National Gallery in this awkward position for almost an hour before gently disengaging her fingers from his. He looked at her with puzzled disappointment until she re-engaged their hands in a more conventional manner.

–Fool, she said.

They ate in the café. They managed to finish the crossword. Mary found herself trembling and passed her pencil to Tom to fill in the squares. He gave her a curious look, but took it without comment. What he didn't know was that, forty-five years before, a man called Graham had bumped into a woman called Evelyn at a tea shop in the fashionable end of Dublin. *And by bumped into,* Graham was fond of telling anyone who would listen, *I mean bumped into.* At which point Evelyn—who was always there because they were inseparable for sixty years after—would say *Best dress. Coffee. Never wore again.* She hardly ever spoke in sentences. *She was going to an interview, but she couldn't soaked in coffee, so I had to take her home, didn't I? Same day I could have told her I loved her and wanted to marry her.* Evelyn would smile slyly. *I knew.* Graham would jerk in surprise—it was only the hundredth time he had told this story—*You knew? Gods, I thought you were still thinking about that damned crossword clue. Union song played back in middle of spread.* He would pause. *Crosswords,* Evelyn would say. *Cross words. Never had any.* They would smile at each other. Graham would say, *Did we do crosswords or did we do crosswords? What was the answer to that clue? I can't quite remember...* And Evelyn would smile, and not answer, and eventually he would say *Oh yes. Marriage. That was it. I remember now.* Their four daughters heard the story every anniversary. They joined in most of the punch lines. Their fourth daughter by some fifteen years was Mary.

As she sat next to Tom, the well-rehearsed story flitted across Mary's mind. She was glad they were sitting down, because her legs felt wobbly and she wasn't sure she would have been able to stand up. Her heart jumped when he gently took her pencil and smiled at her.

Tom remembered to ask some of the questions he meant to ask, and discovered that she went to university to study history. She found out that he had taken a degree in mathematics.

–Oh good. You'll be able to help me with the statistics.

–Death by horse kicks in the Prussian army, remarked Tom.

–What?

–If you plot the number of deaths by horse kicks against time you get a nice curved shape—he described a bell curve with his hands—that's important in statistics.

–I'm sure that'll be very useful, she said, then sighed. –Tomorrow's Friday.

This was true. At the weekend she would be away, and the following week he would be away. Tom already felt a gnawing sense of loss augmented by worry that she would meet somebody else while he wasn't around.

–Come around to my place for a meal, he suggested. It crossed his mind that two days ago he would have thrown himself down a lift shaft rather than issue such an invitation to a girl. When did he—Tom Are You Overtaking Bradley—start asking girls back to his place for a meal?

–Okay, she said. It crossed her mind that two days ago she would have run a mile if any male member of the species had offered to take her out, or two miles if they had invited her back to the place where they lived.

–Meet Peter and Cosmic, he said persuasively.

–Okay.

–Not to mention two hundred tropical fish—no, probably only a hundred and fifty now—and a roomful of cacti.

–Okay.

–And I'll drive you back afterwards. What?

–I said okay.

Because it was Friday, they managed to get away early, Tom was carrying a briefcase ready for Monday's visit to Milton Keynes. Mary, he couldn't help but notice, was wearing a pale raincoat which emphasised her height and shape and contrasted nicely with her long dark hair. They found a pair of seats on the bus, and he took her hand. Holding her hand on the bus was somehow much more intimate than holding hands as they walked along.

They got off the bus under a dark sky. One or two stars were already visible—stars or planets, Tom wasn't sure which. Planets twinkled, stars didn't, or was it the other way around? He felt Mary's fingers entwined with his own. Impulsively he gave them a squeeze. She squeezed back and his heart pounded thunderously.

–A sort of chilli con carne, he said.

–Sort of?

–Pete will be back about five.

But when they approached the house, lights were already on and the front door was wide open. Tom hoped this didn't mean another utility bill had arrived. Then he realised that only upstairs lights were on, and the door was swinging gently, to and fro, over letters and leaflets still strewn over the floor just inside.

–Wait here, he told Mary.

He edged into the hallway, trod carefully past the doors to the living room and dining room, turned at the foot of the stairs. He could hear footsteps upstairs, banging noises. He started. Something had shifted in the darkness opposite the stairs. He froze for long moments until his straining eyes realised it was Albert and Victoria—two bright yellow tropical fish—swimming lazily around their tank, unconcerned that any excitement might be happening in the outside universe. Tom started breathing again.

The footsteps trod above his head, moving out into the upstairs hallway.

He turned to face the stairs.

The world disappeared in a bright flare as somebody turned on the hall light, blinding his night-sensitised eyes. He staggered, unaccountably losing his balance, and threw a forearm up over his face. When he moved it away and managed to open his eyes, it was to the unexpected sight of a pair of legs wearing ragged denims. Skin the colour of burnished ebony was discernible through holes just above the knees and, he could not help but notice, even higher.

–Jan, he said stupidly.

She didn't look too good. She had one black eye and she looked grey. Her right hand was trembling as it clutched at the banister.

–Ah've come for my things, she said. Her voice sounded empty.

–Your mum and dad took them, Tom told her.

They stood looking at each other. Tom compared this girl with the vibrant, if irritating, girl from a few weeks ago.

–You've lost weight, he said, and winced mentally.

Jan's eyes filled with tears and she launched herself down the last few stairs, cannoning into Tom, burying her head in his chest, clinging to him with desperate strength. Reflexively, he put his arms around her. He couldn't help thinking how ironic it was that the first girl he put his arms around should turn out to be Jan.

–Hello?

Mary appeared in the pool of light at the foot of the stairs. Curiously, it didn't even cross Tom's mind that she might be disconcerted to find him in a clinch with another woman.

–This is Jan, he said, nodding his head downwards in case Mary failed to notice who he was referring to.

–Ah, said Mary.

Jan unexpectedly emitted a whooping wail, the equivalent of a human foghorn. She paused, hiccupped, took a deep breath in preparation for a repeat performance. Tom hastily grasped her shoulders and pushed her face away from his chest.

–It's all right, it's all right, he said, although plainly it wasn't. –How about a cup of tea?

–What am Ah going to do? wailed Jan.

–Calm down, calm down, said Tom. He wondered if saying everything twice was any help. Perhaps it was, because Jan took a deep shuddering breath, sniffed and wiped her face with her sleeve. She caught sight of Mary.

–Who's that? It's not Peter.

Tom's imagination served up an image of himself sitting on a bus, holding hands with Peter. He blanched and made an indeterminate sound.

–You laughing at me? demanded Jan with a touch of her old belligerence.

–I'm Mary, said Mary.

–She's here for dinner, added Tom.

Jan's eyes lit up. –Dinner? Ah'm hungry.

–Yes, but what happened? asked Tom. –You went away and didn't come back.

–Ah'm back now.

–You know what I mean. Anyway it doesn't matter, you're back now. He saw Mary quirk her eyebrows at him, and realised he had just repeated Jan's words. –I mean to say, you can phone your mum and dad and—

Jan emitted another wail. –Ah can't!

–What?

–Ah can't! Ah can't!

–Why not?

Jan clutched at his jacket and shook it violently. –Ah can't tell them!

Tom grabbed her hands. –Tell them what?

–That… that…

Understanding bloomed in Mary's face. She stepped forward and put her arm around Jan's shoulders. –Let's go and sit down. In here, is it? Tom, how about that cup of tea?

Muttering to himself, Tom went into the kitchen while Mary led Jan, still sobbing, into the living room. He put the kettle on, then measured out portions of rice into a saucepan and tried to put that on to boil. The gas kept blowing out. He remembered that the front door was still open, so he went to close it, glancing into the living room as he passed. Mary was sitting with Jan on the sofa, arm still around her shoulders. She looked up and gave her head a brief shake. Jan had her face buried in her hands and probably wouldn't have noticed a bus manoeuvring past the doorway.

Tom picked up the post, closed the door, went back to the kitchen and made the tea. When he went into the living room, Mary had removed her arm from Jan's shoulders, and Jan was wiping her eyes.

–Here you go.

Jan honked and wiped her nose. She tried to pass a handkerchief back to Mary.

–You keep it.

–What have you two been talking about, then?

Jan avoided his gaze but grabbed at the mug of tea and held it in both hands. Mary gave him a warning look. –Um, girl stuff, she said.

Tom wondered what this mysterious description meant. He wasn't sure what to say. Jan glanced up and he caught sight of her black eye.

–How'd you get that?

–Door.

Mary reached out and briefly squeezed one of Jan's hands. Jan sighed. –No. Okay, it was a man. Ah run away, okay?

–Where were you? asked Tom curiously.

–Scotland. Ah run away from Scotland.

–You just got here from Scotland? said Tom incredulously.

–No wonder you're hungry, said Mary.

–No, Ah'm hungry cos Ah've got no money. Ah spent it all on the ticket.

Tom exchanged a puzzled glance with Mary. –Okay, but why didn't you—?

–Ah wanted a change of clothes, all right?

–Okay, okay, said Tom. *I'm saying things twice again.*

–Tom's right, you know, said Mary gently. –About your parents.

Jan had bowed her head again. Now she shook it, but it was more in sorrow for her situation than in refusal. They all looked up as a whistling noise sounded from the rice cooker in the kitchen. Tom jumped up. He hesitated, then grabbed the phone and held it out to Jan.

–Phone. Then food.

Jan licked her lips but didn't move.

–They want you back, Tom said. –They're worried sick, especially your dad.

–My dad, whispered Jan. Her eyes started to fill with tears again.

–None of that, said Tom hastily and added, to make absolutely sure: –None of that. Here. Phone. He gestured with the phone and Jan finally took it. She placed it on her lap and looked at it as if it was likely to explode. Tom didn't move. After long seconds, Jan picked up the receiver and hesitantly dialled a number. Mary looked up at Tom, nodded slightly and gave a smile.

He went out into the kitchen. He could hear Jan's voice, at first hesitant, and then more animated. There was a long pause, then Jan's voice again, more subdued, then more silence. Tom judged it the right time to go back with a plate of something resembling rice and chilli con carne.

–Well?

–They're coming to get me.

–Well done, said Mary.

–Thanks, said Tom. –It doesn't look too bad, does it?

–Not you, you fool.

Jan took the plate and started shovelling in the food as if she hadn't eaten in two days. Perhaps she hadn't, thought Tom. He went out and fetched a glass of water.

–Have they got far to come? asked Mary.

–Bout'n hour, mumbled Jan. She scraped her plate.

–More? asked Tom.

Jan nodded and held out her plate. Tom exchanged a rueful glance with Mary, but went out yet again for a refill. Jan tucked in again with apparently undiminished appetite. Cosmic appeared in the doorway, sat down with his tail curled in a neat question mark.

–So, what happened?

Jan froze, then ate more slowly. –Ah don't want to say.

–Okay.

Jan scraped the plate again, sat back with a sigh. Tom thought she didn't look quite so grey as she had earlier.

–He wanted me to do things and Ah didn't want to and anyway Ah couldn't because… because… well Ah jus couldn't.

Mary made a small movement with her hands, describing a rounded stomach, and Tom nodded slightly. Jan, her eyes fixed firmly in the past, noticed nothing.

–an when Ah tole him, you know, why Ah couldn't, then he hit me. He was gonna kick me too but this other guy there, he pulled him off, an Ah jus run away. And Ah didn't know what to do so Ah come back here.

There was a silence. Then Mary said –You did, and she was about to say "right" when Cosmic leaped to his feet at the sound of loud banging noises in the hall.

Tom glanced at his watch. Five past five.

Peter momentarily filled the doorway, larger than life, and then he was in the room, shedding his gigantic raincoat, his hair as usual sticking out in all directions as if his enormous presence attracted some form of static electricity.

–Flaming taxis! he bellowed. –Think they own the flaming road, don't they! They should…

He caught sight of Jan.

–What? he bellowed.

Jan jumped off the sofa and backed away, pressing up against the wall.

–Ah didn't mean it! It was an accident!

–Tobler, choked Peter. –Marmite, all the Grumpies. Flaming hell! he roared, –You killed em all!

–It was an accident, squealed Jan.

–Accident? How can yer kill all me fish by accident?

–Not all of them, Pete, interposed Tom.

–No thanks to er! bellowed Peter. He advanced towards Jan. Tom jumped up uncertainly. –What did yer do, eh?

–Ah fed them, squeaked Jan. –Cos they looked thin.

–They ain't thin! roared Peter. –That's just the way they is. Was. He did a double-take. –What do yer mean, fed em?

Jan pointed a shaking hand. –With–with—

Peter stared. –You fed em cactus food?

–Ah didn't know, whimpered Jan.

Mary made a muffled noise and Tom observed that she had both hands plastered across her mouth.

–You fed Tobler, an the Grumpies an… an… Peter broke down. He collapsed into a chair, legs splayed out in front of him.

–Ah'm sorry.

–Flaming hell, breathed Peter. –Cactus food. What a way to go.

Tears were streaming down Mary's cheeks. Tom moved over and solicitously lent her his handkerchief, given that Jan had appropriated hers. Peter noticed her for the first time and jumped up again. He glanced at Tom.

–Yore Mary, right? You all right?

Mary swallowed, wiped at her eyes, nodded.

–I know, it's a sad business, said Peter, which almost set her off again. This time it was Tom who snorted and turned his face away. –Still, it sounds like—

Peter looked at Jan.

–It looks like it might've bin a mistake. Flaming ell, what appened to you?

–Door.

Peter nodded. –It appens, he said. –Appened to me once. Needed three stitches in me ead because a flaming door wos open when it should of bin shut.

–Jan's parents are coming to collect her, said Tom.

–Good, said Peter. It was hard to tell if he thought it was good for Jan that her parents were on their way, or good for Peter that her parents were coming to take her away. –Sorry about all this, he said to Mary. –Must be bit of a shock.

–A bit, admitted Mary.

–Still, we've got a meal, eh? He caught sight of the empty plate on the sofa. –Wot, you've et it already?

Jan's parents arrived soon after, and Tom never forgot the way Jan flew along the hall into her father's outstretched arms. He never saw her again. Peter had flounced upstairs, so Tom and Mary sat quietly and ate what was left of the meal. Afterwards they cleared up the kitchen together, and then they got into Tom's sports car for the first time, and he found his way back to Mary's residential hall.

–Thank you, Tom.

He turned off the engine.

–It's been an evening I don't think I will ever forget.

He had parked underneath a yellow streetlight. Parts of her face were illuminated, other parts were in darkness. But he could see that she was smiling.

–Me neither.

–I can't ask you in for coffee, because it's a girl's hall. And you don't drink coffee. But if I could, Tom, I would.

She paused, and seemed to be waiting for something. He didn't know what it could possibly be, so he just nodded and shook his head mutely.

–Have a good time in Milton Keynes. See you next weekend.

She leaned forward and pressed her lips against his cheek. Then she turned, fumbled the door open. She jumped out and walked quickly away, almost running. She didn't look back. She didn't close the car door, either. Tom had to unstrap himself and reach right across the passenger's seat to grab the handle and pull it shut. His heart was pounding. She kissed me. The passenger seat was still warm where she had been sitting. Was she waiting for me to kiss her? He put his hand to his cheek wonderingly, then took it away and looked at his fingers as if they would somehow furnish some evidence of what it all meant. He leaned back on the headrest and took deep breaths to steady his nerves. If I could, Tom, I would. It was ten minutes before he felt that it was safe enough to drive away.

Mary watched him from the shadows. She was watching to see if he would punch the air, smile triumphantly and start singing a ribald song—all the sorts of things she imagined Gregory Updike would have done in the same situation. She hadn't meant to lean forward and give Tom that kiss. But she had laughed so much that evening and he had looked so completely bemused and happy at the same time, that she hadn't been able to stop herself.

–And my legs were wobbly, and my brain turned to mush, she told Christine later that night over the phone.

–Oh my God, said Christine tinnily.

–He just sat there. He touched his cheek—you know—where I kissed him.

–You kissed him? Oh my God.

–I thought he was going to float out of the window and drift up into the air, like in a cartoon.

–Good grief, said Christine.

–What am I going to do?

There was a long, tinny pause. Eventually, Christine said in a wondering voice, –I don't think it matters what you do, Mary.

On Monday morning lust briefly fought against avarice when George Fulton saw Tom's sports car, but the lure of the travel claim won out. They climbed into his ancient Austin and set off through a bright, cool autumn morning. George wound his way through the centre of London using roads that looked as if they hadn't changed much for the last hundred years. Some were even cobbled.

–Good weekend? he asked while they waited at traffic lights.

Tom pondered his response, not completely sure whether it had been a good weekend or not. He had spent most of it trying not to forget a single moment of Friday evening and the way it ended under the yellow streetlight, but on the other hand trying not to think about anything that happened that evening, because he knew he wouldn't be seeing Mary for at least a week, and he didn't have any idea what was happening. He thought he knew what might be happening, but he didn't like to put even possibilities into jeopardy by thinking about them, still less by talking about them. So his days had been spent trying not to think thoughts about Mary, even though his thoughts were filled of nothing else. And his nights had been sleepless while he lay there rather selfishly hoping that she was sleeping as badly as he was.

George glanced over and saw that Tom had dozed off.

They got to Milton Keynes at about midday, checked themselves in at the George Hotel, and had lunch in a nearby restaurant: –It's on the Department, remarked George, and then drove a short way to the offices of the RCU. –We'll get ourselves settled and get the files and invoices and so on and so forth. I've done this twice already two years ago and four years ago there's nothing to it you'll see young feller-me-Tom.

Tom, now fully awake, wondered how he was going to concentrate on checking invoices against a printout when two nights ago he had been kissed for the very first time. How was he supposed to be able to read boring road construction files, or check even more boring printouts, when all the time he was wondering what Mary was doing? When he was wondering if Mary was wondering what he was doing? He thought, as they were directed from reception into a nearby waiting room, that this was going to be the start of one of the most dismally dreary drawn-out weeks of his life.

He was wrong.

After ten minutes, George got up from the beige-coloured sofa in the waiting room and started to stalk around like a caged tiger. He swished his cane at a pot plant standing innocently in the corner. After fifteen minutes, he started to growl unintelligibly. Part of the pot plant became disconnected and floated gently onto the beige-coloured carpet. George started for the door, when it abruptly opened and a tall, elegantly dressed woman came in. She and George eyed each other. After a moment she extended a languid hand and said in a distant voice: –And you are?

Tom hadn't known George for very long, but he already knew that this form of greeting was unlikely to improve his temper.

George ignored the outstretched hand and growled: –Am I to understand then madam that you do not know who we are and were not expecting us?

The woman flushed and withdrew her hand. She grew, if possible, even taller and more distant. –You are the auditors?

–We are, madam, and you are?

The woman considered this question for a moment, then gave a brief nod. Whether this was because she had decided that this was an acceptable question, or because she was conceding that George had won the first round, Tom found it impossible to judge.

–Catherine Copeland, Senior Administration Officer.

–Fulton, grunted George. He made no effort to introduce Tom.

–The Director left instructions that you were to be given the use of the conference room. Catherine Copeland's tone of voice made it clear that if she had been left to make arrangements, they would have been lucky to be accommodated in anything much bigger than a broom cupboard.

–Yes Graham usually does, said George. *Round two to the audit corner* thought Tom. Catherine Copeland was clearly nonplussed at George's casual use of the Director's first name. She turned on her heels. George and Tom followed.

–The files, said George.

–Are there, said Catherine Copeland primly. Again Tom got the subtext: as Senior Administration Officer, Catherine Copeland didn't need to be reminded how to do her job.

–We need invoices, got that list Tom?

Catherine Copeland came to an abrupt halt.

–Invoices?

Tom reflected that, for the first time, George had called him Tom. He fumbled in his briefcase and found the list. He made to pass it to George, but he indicated with a jerk of the head that he should pass it directly to Catherine Copeland.

–Of course invoices, growled George. –You never been audited before Ms Copeland? we'll be needing payroll details and other files but they can wait. Have you got a copy of that list Tom?

George knew perfectly well that Tom had a copy. He had made sure that Tom had a copy of everything. Tom realised that for some reason George wanted to make sure that Catherine Copeland also knew they had a copy.

–Yes, sir.

–Where's this boardroom or are we going to stand in this corridor for the rest of the afternoon?

Catherine Copeland had been looking down the list of invoices. Tom thought she had a faintly worried look on her face. Now she looked up, her lips pressed tightly together, and set off up the corridor. George gave Tom an unreadable look. They marched in silence around a corner and up a short flight of steps. As their footsteps echoed, Tom was reminded of the stairwell in Marsham Street, of climbing up to the twelfth floor to meet Mary for the first time. So long ago, it seemed. Was it only last week?

–I'm in here, said Catherine Copeland as they passed a door which carried a notice announcing *Administration and Accounts*. And then, a few doors further down the first-floor corridor: –Here.

The boardroom contained nothing but a gigantic oval table surrounded by chairs. A number of files had been placed neatly at one end of the table. George ignored them. He went to the window at the far end of the room and inspected the view, as if he was deciding whether the accommodation was suitable. Tom put his briefcase on the table.

The silence stretched.

–Will there be anything else? said Catherine Copeland eventually.

George turned. –A cup of tea would be nice. And you, Tom? Tom nodded.

–Four sugars, said George.

–One, said Tom, earning an approving look from George.

–Of course, said Catherine Copeland primly. –I'll see to it.

She turned on her heels again and clicked out of the room, leaving the door open. Tom went to close it.

–It'll be cold it'll have no milk, said George dismissively. –Something.

–She didn't look happy, remarked Tom.

–Serve her right.

–No, I mean when we gave her the invoices list.

–Her little administrative world not as neat tidy orderly as she thought I expect, here you take this one.

George tossed one file to Tom, settled down in a chair, and picked up another one.

–What am I looking for?

George shrugged.

After a few minutes somebody tapped at the door and Tom went to open it. A young man with bright red hair and thick glasses that made his eyes seem twice their normal size came in, carrying a tray. He was wearing a loud check suit that clashed with his pale shirt and red tie. It was so loud, Tom thought, that it would probably clash with anything.

–Miss C-Copeland says you c-can get the invoices t–t–tomorrow.

George grunted. He picked up one of the polystyrene cups from the tray and peered into it. An expression of distaste crossed his face and he put it back down.

–Where's Frank?

–F—f—f

–Berger.

–Oh, you m-mean F-Frank. He's b-been off sick f-for... The young man paused. His enormous eyes glazed as he thought about it. –Easter. Since Easter.

–Since Easter? George glared at the young man as if Frank Berger's illness was his personal responsibility. –He's the senior accountant, Tom: he's been off since Easter? who's been in charge then?

The young man swallowed. –Miss C-C-C. He swallowed again. –Miss C-C-C—

–All right, said George irritably. –Take these cups away will you, come on Tom we'll go find ourselves a decent cup of tea.

The door swung shut behind the young man. George was struggling into his coat.

–It's on the Department they can't expect us to go all day without a decent cup of tea.

That evening Tom lay on his bed and looked at the telephone on the bedside table, wondering whether to call. It was only his first day away, after all. On the other hand, they hadn't spoken since Friday and that was three days ago. On the other other hand, she hadn't called him, so perhaps she didn't really want to talk on the phone. Perhaps she didn't want to talk to him at all. An icy hand clutched at his heart. Perhaps that kiss had been a *farewell* kiss. Tom was fairly certain that this was not the case, but the notion wouldn't go away.

Perhaps she hadn't been with her parents at the weekend at all, but had gone off with a group of friends to… to… well, to do whatever it was groups of friends went off to do at the weekend. Tom reflected that the last time he had done anything like that was when he had gone to the south of France with some old schoolfriends and had spent most of the time lying on the beach, reading and writing under the hot Mediterranean sun.

The hotel telephone swam back into view. Tom knew that his memory was deliberately throwing up reminiscences so that he could avoid having to make a decision. About whether to call.

He groaned.

He sat up, took a deep breath, and picked up the receiver. Dialled. Heard it ringing at the other end. His heart was pounding thunderously, and he suddenly realised that he didn't have the first idea of what he was going to say. He rehearsed a few conversations.

"Hello?"

"Hi, it's me, Tom."

She would be delighted: "Tom! How is it in Milton Keynes?"

"Fine except for the tea. Did you have a good weekend?"

Or she would be non-committal: "Oh, hello Tom. How are you?"

"Fine, except for the tea." No, that didn't sound right. "Fine. How are you? Did you have a good weekend?"

Or she would be positively discouraging: "Tom? Oh, can you ring back, I've got somebody with me just now." More icy clutches at his heart. She wouldn't say that, would she? No, she was in a girl's residence so even if she did have somebody with her, it could only be another girl. Couldn't it?

He realised that the phone was still ringing at the other end and it dawned on him that she wasn't going to say any of those things. She wasn't in. He put down the receiver and stared at it. How could she not be in? Where was she? What was he supposed to do now? How was he supposed to go to sleep? Now Tuesday was going to be a day of eternal torment, one of the most dismally dreary drawn-out days of his life. He was going to spend the whole day wondering where Mary had been the previous night, and wouldn't be able to spend one iota of concentration on invoices, files or anything else to do with the audit. Of course, he had already thought that Monday was going to be a dismal, drawn-out day and it had turned out to be nothing of the sort. But he had no way of knowing that the same was going to be true of Tuesday as well, only more so.

–Sleep well? grunted George over breakfast.

Tom made an indeterminate reply. The fact of the matter was that he had hardly slept at all, but he didn't feel like telling George that. George would only want to know why.

On the way over to the RCU George said, –Okay here's the plan you go through the invoices today it should only take you a day even if you follow them back to the originating requisitions, okay?

–Okay, said Tom gloomily.

–Cheer up young feller-me-Tom tomorrow you can check the payroll stuff that should only take a day as well even if you chase some back to the personnel files mind you they can often be interesting to read, okay?

–Okay.

–Then on Thursday you can look through files on the motorway spur extension project which was overspent by over two hundred thousand for some reason I'm finding rather elusive maybe you can see something I can't anyway it will be good experience for you, okay?

–Okay.

–Friday home. I'll drop you off in Cheam you'll get a half day out of it how does that sound?

–Great, said Tom gloomily. They turned into the car park and it started to rain.

George disappeared in the direction of the staff canteen to sort out the availability of a decent cup of tea. Tom deposited his coat and briefcase in the boardroom and then went to knock on the door of *Administration and Accounts*. He was a little nervous about it, partly because Catherine Copeland was clearly not amused at being audited, and partly because she was a senior executive officer. He remembered saying to Pete that a senior executive officer was roughly equivalent to God. "Don't you fret," George had growled at him. "We're not even civil servants we're officers of the House of Commons don't you forget that young feller-me-Tom." Tom remembered that too as he knocked on the office door, but it didn't make him feel any less nervous.

The red-haired young man opened the door and stared at Tom with his unnervingly huge eyes. He was wearing a light green suit with pale pink stripes and Tom wondered if he had a dreadful suit to wear for each day of the week.

–Er, I'm Tom Bradley. The auditor?

–Oh yes. C-come in. He opened the door still wider and retreated into the office. Tom followed him in and looked around curiously. Computer printouts littered the floor and were piled precariously on two tables by the wall. Two desks covered with smaller piles of correspondence, files and other paperwork faced each other by the window. One of these desks clearly belonged to the red-haired young man. A blonde woman of about forty sat at the other, typing industriously on an electronic typewriter. She didn't look up. Bedraggled pot plants lined the window sill.

–Ah, here, said the red-haired young man.

It was, Tom thought, a miserable and uninspiring office. He thought fondly of Dragon Margaret and chocolate biscuits. He noticed that the red-haired young man had only provided him with two invoices.

–Did you get the full list?

–Um.

Of Catherine Copeland there was no sign. The door to a room off to the right had frosted glass and Tom assumed she must be in there.

–Miss C-C-Copeland said to p-pass on the m-message that the others are in archives and we m-might be able t-to get them by F-F-F… Deep breath. –B-by F-F-Friday.

Tom raised his eyebrows.

–We're very b-busy, apologised the young man. –W-what with F-F-F… Another deep breath. –F-F-Frank being off.

Tom pursed his lips and shrugged. –Okay, I'll pass that on to Mr Fulton.

Holding the two invoices—one was an electricity account and the other was from a company imaginatively called Cement Solutions—he went back out of the office, feeling that all was not going as well as it might. This premonition was soon vindicated.

–Only two not until Friday archives God give me strength. What's the woman playing at?

Tom retraced his steps along the corridor, trailing in George's wake. George didn't bother knocking at the door. He stormed straight in. Both the red-haired young man and the blonde typist looked up in surprise. George intercepted a nervous glance towards the frosted-door office and without saying a word stormed across the office and barged in.

Tom lingered uncertainly in the outer office. The blonde woman was examining him with interest. The red-haired young man, who had frozen in a position half way out of his chair, sank slowly back down again.

–Tom!

He jerked guiltily and scuttled across to join George in Catherine Copeland's inner sanctum.

–How dare you? squeaked Catherine Copeland. She had pushed herself back from her desk as George loomed over it.

–On the contrary how dare you madam? boomed George. –We are here for a week you knew we were coming we asked for those invoices yesterday and expect to see them today.

–But—

–They are not old invoices madam we that is my colleague here specifically selected them from an up-to-date listing provided at Marsham Street. Are you seriously suggesting you cannot find invoices less than two months old madam?

George paused, breathing heavily. Catherine Copeland glanced at Tom.

–Just two months? Well, I didn't know that.

With somebody else this obvious attempt at a compromise might have succeeded, but George was having none of it.

–The dates are on the list madam I seem to recall you reading them while we were standing in the corridor.

–Dick—that is, Mr Jefferson, didn't tell me, persevered Catherine Copeland. Tom presumed that Dick was the red-haired young man.

–I'll speak to Mr Jefferson then.

Catherine Copeland waved her hands agitatedly. –No, there's no need. I'll see to it.

George snorted.

–I'll see to it now, promised Catherine Copeland.

George glanced at his watch. –It's nine thirty Tom here will come back to collect them at ten thirty won't you Tom?

–Ten thirty, repeated Tom.

–Ten thirty? squeaked Catherine Copeland. –An hour? We might not—

–Then give us what you've got and Tom'll come back at eleven thirty for the rest won't you Tom?

–Eleven thirty, repeated Tom. He had to suppress a sudden grin at the thought that he must sound rather like the speaking clock.

–Do we have an agreement madam?

Catherine Copeland nodded wearily. George pushed himself upright, turned and barged back out of the office and out into the corridor, not sparing the blonde typist or young Dick a glance. Tom followed after, closing both the frosted door and the door to the outer office as he went. He found George sitting in the boardroom, glaring at the cups of tea he had inveigled out of the staff canteen.

–Stone cold, he grumbled.

–Does an audit usually go like this? asked Tom.

–Copeland Copeland rings a bell, muttered George. –No no no the last time I can recall was in Luton five years ago. It turned out the manager and his secretary were having an affair.

Tom reflected that the chances that Catherine Copeland was having an affair with young Dick were negligible.

–Don't think that's happening here though eh? come on let's go get another cup of tea it's on the Department.

At ten thirty Tom returned to *Administration and Accounts,* and red-headed Dick handed him more than half of the required invoices. At eleven thirty he went back again and collected all of the others except one. Red-headed Dick apologised profusely and said that he and Dorothy would turn over the office looking for it. Tom thanked him and left feeling vaguely embarrassed.

Silence descended on the boardroom. Tom compared the details on the invoices with the details on the printouts. George read files. Outside a lowering sky blotted the sun from view. The door opened once, to admit Dick triumphantly bearing the missing invoice. –Ms

C-C-…. He gave up. –Had it all the time, he explained. At twelve thirty George suggested they had a break for lunch, and they descended to the staff canteen rather than risk getting soaked outside. Tom found himself remembering the canteen at Marsham Street, with the spotty serving girl and curled-up-at-the-edges ham sandwiches. At the RCU he had hot soup and a crusty roll, and George treated him to a bar of chocolate afterwards.

–How's it going? George asked as they climbed back to the boardroom where their files and papers were scattered all over the big oval table.

–Okay, said Tom. –All matches so far. Sometimes have to add a few up to get to the computer total, like you said.

George grunted.

Tom had got so caught up in the events of the morning that he had scarcely thought about Mary. He felt slightly guilty. He tried to imagine her sitting up on the twelfth floor, with Roger B in his black leathers, perhaps chatting to Red—what was his name? Turner? something like that—who he had yet to meet. He wondered what she did for lunch, whether she made herself sandwiches or ventured out along the Embankment to find somewhere to eat.

The rows of numbers began to blur in his vision. So this is what they meant by tick and turn. Tick something. Turn the page. Keep checking. Does x equal y? Does y equal x? Are the names the same? Do the dates match? Tick. Turn.

–Cup of tea young feller-me-lad I see you've nearly finished.

So he had. Nearly all the invoices were stacked neatly in one pile, with only two or three left to check. He looked at his watch and was surprised to find that it was three o'clock.

–I'll get them, he told George. –I need to stretch my legs.

As he went down the stairs, he found himself thinking not about Mary and what she might be doing at this time of the afternoon, but about young Dick. What had he said? "She had it all the time." Why would Miss Copeland be hanging on to an invoice nearly five weeks old? Why was Catherine Copeland clearly so put out at having her invoices audited, if it came to that? Perhaps George was right. Perhaps she just didn't like intrusion into her well-ordered administrative domain. But Tom recalled the faint look of worry that crossed her face when she first saw the list of invoices, and he wondered.

He bought two cups of tea, remembering to pick up five sachets of sugar, and went back to the boardroom. George was looking out of the window at the miserable weather. Tom sat down and worked his way through the remaining invoices.

–You're keen. George was standing behind him, slurping his cup of tea.

Tom flung down his pencil and shook his head. –One of them's out by five pence. See, that looks like an eight but it's a three.

–Well spotted, said George heavily. –The Department will be proud.

–But why was she so upset?

–I'll tell you lad people don't like auditors, you'll have to get used to it.

–But you said yourself this wasn't normal.

–Maybe I upset her, admitted George. –I don't like being kept waiting.

Maybe, Tom thought, but he didn't think so. He looked at the computer printout and the long list of ticks. George sat back down, sighed, and picked up the file he was reading. He thumbed through a set of photographs showing the gradual development of the nearby motorway extension, which for the most part looked like nothing more than a small expanse of concrete turning into a vast expanse of concrete. Or tarmac. Or whatever it was.

Tom's gaze fell onto the last invoice, the one that young Dick had finally unearthed in the possession of Catherine Copeland. Concrete. He remembered carrying the first two invoices from *Administration and Accounts* to the boardroom. One of them had been for Concrete Solutions.

Tom's brow furrowed.

Something clicked.

He sifted through the pile of invoices, found the one for Concrete Solutions. He put it down next to the one Dick had tracked down, which appeared to be from a company called Office Interiors and Furniture Co. Ltd. Both were for the value of fifteen hundred pounds exactly.

His computer list revealed that there were three other invoices for exactly fifteen hundred pounds in the sample he had picked. He extracted them all and laid them side by side. His heart was pounding with excitement. Carefully, he took some blank sheets of paper and covered up the top part of each of the three invoices, then sat back and examined the results.

He shook his head in amazement. There could be no doubt.

–George.

–Hmm what?

–Come and look at this.

–What hmm? George emerged from his file. –What have you been up to young feller-me-lad?

–Look at this.

Tom indicated the spread of invoices and paper, and George's eyebrows climbed. He got to his feet and lumbered around to survey what was on view.

–Five invoices, he said. –Mmm ah all for fifteen hundred looks like same company those two signed by one person those three by another, pretty eclectic mix of goods I have to say. What's your point Tom?

Without saying anything, Tom removed the sheets of paper to reveal the names of the companies at the top.

Concrete Solutions.
Office Interiors and Furniture Co. Ltd
Signage Ltd
George Broker & Sons
Fleet Maintenance Consortium

–Oh, said George. He hooked a chair closer, sat down. Tom watched him anxiously as he perused the invoices in more detail. At one point he picked up *Signage Ltd* and *George Broker & Sons* and held them up to the light, one on top of the other. He put them down again. After what seemed a long while he sat back and sighed.

–They look the same, ventured Tom.

–They were typed on the same machine look at the lower-case g it's higher than it should be, see?

Tom saw. –What does it mean?

–It means you've found a point Tom. Let me think a minute.

Back in the hotel room that night Tom picked up the phone, desperate to speak to Mary and tell her about all the excitement. But again there was no answer. He stood up and paced around the room, unable to contain himself. He had found a point on his very first audit. But Mary was out. Why was she out? She must know he was going to call even though, now he came to think of it, they never made any firm arrangement. But even so, she had kissed him. How could she possibly kiss him and then not expect him to call in the evenings?

It wasn't until the weekend when he was back in Cheam that he found out the prosaic answer. She called him on Saturday morning:

–Sorry Tom, my phone was out of order. I didn't know.

She had spent all week wondering why he hadn't called. Several times during office hours she had been tempted to find out his number in Milton Keynes. She had even thought about ringing Margaret to find out the number of his hotel. But every time this happened, she thought to herself that he hadn't bothered to call her, so why should she bother to call him? She couldn't explain the hard ball of misery that coiled in her stomach when she reached this conclusion, nor her lack of appetite and general disinterest in the world at large. On Thursday evening the plump Italian girl from the room next to her in the residential hall knocked on her door and said, "Itsa your mama."

"What?"

Rosa frequently mimicked her own accent and she thought Mary hadn't understood her. "Your mother," she said. "On my phone."

"Yes," said Mary. "But why?"

It turned out that her mother had been trying to reach her for several days and had finally discovered that her phone was out of order.

–Oh good, said Tom. –I tried every night.

Magically, the hard knot of worry in Mary's stomach dispersed. If it was possible to feel almost light-headed, that was what she felt.

–I'm ringing from downstairs, she said.

–Lots to tell you, said Tom. –We—

–I'm hungry, Mary interrupted. –Meet me outside, by the—you know—by the lamppost? She wondered if her voice was blushing.

–Late breakfast, early lunch, whatever? Half ten? We could, um, catch up.

Tom, who was still in his pyjamas, clutched at the receiver so hard that it creaked. He struggled to speak. Somehow over the last week he had forgotten how nerve-wracking it was to talk to a girl, but now it came back to him with overwhelming force.

–Tom?

–Yes, he squeaked, and his brain conjured up a sudden unexpected image of Catherine Copeland squeaking at George. He cleared his throat and mustered up a more manly tone. –Uh, yes. Okay.

–Okay then. Bye, Tom.

He put down the receiver and hurtled up the stairs two at a time, narrowly missing a collision with Peter who had emerged from his bedroom, yawning and rubbing at his eyes.

–Yore back then?

–Got to dash! shouted Tom. He showered, dressed, grabbed his car keys and rushed outside. The weather had turned cold and his breath steamed a little as he turned the ignition.

Nothing.

–Come on, come on.

Still nothing.

–For goodness sake! screamed Tom. He had promised Mary he would be there. What would she think if he didn't turn up? He couldn't even ring her to let her know what had happened. He took a deep breath and turned the key for a third time.

Nothing.

He saw Peter standing at the window, watching him curiously. An idea bloomed. He rushed back into the house.

–Car won't start.

–It's bin sat there all week, observed Peter.

–I'm supposed to meet Mary in… in half an hour. Can you help?

–I've got some WD40 somewhere, said Peter maliciously.

–A lift! shrieked Tom, dancing from foot to foot. –Can you give me a lift?

–Well why dint you flaming say?

They dashed out of the house, Peter shrugging on his gigantic raincoat and Tom glaring at his dormant sports car. Peter owned a large green battered van. Tom climbed up into the passenger seat, reflecting that he must be at least as twice as high as when he lowered himself into his own car, while Peter clambered into the driver's seat. The engine started first time with a deep burbling rattle.

–Kensington? shouted Peter.

–Kensington, confirmed Tom. He glanced at his watch. Maybe they would make it.

–Got to get some diesel, shouted Peter.

Damn, thought Tom. They probably wouldn't make it.

The van shot out of its parking place and Peter turned sharply up a hill. He was revving the engine, leaning over the steering wheel. A small white car stuck its nose out from a side road about a hundred yards further up the hill.

–Don't you… shrieked Peter. He revved harder, his whole body leaning forwards as if he could make the van speed up through sheer will power. Tom clutched at the dashboard. The white car edged out still further. Peter's van accelerated microscopically. At the last moment the white car shuddered to a halt and Peter roared past mere inches from its bonnet. Peter was shaking his fist and glaring triumphantly past Tom, out of the passenger window.

–Yaah!

Tom turned around to see the white car pull out of the side turning and fall in behind the van. It blew its horn indignantly.

–What? roared Peter. He slammed on his brakes. Tom, still looking out of the rear window, grabbed at his seat to prevent himself being thrown backwards against the windscreen. He saw the white car screech to a halt. The two vehicles sat motionless in the road for a few seconds, the green van burbling and burping at the smoother sounding white car.

–Did that bugger blow is flaming horn? bellowed Peter. Not waiting for an answer, he put the van into reverse and careened backwards towards the white car. Tom wrapped his arms around his car seat and closed his eyes. –Yaah! bellowed Peter again. Tom opened his eyes to see the white car also reversing erratically down the hill. When it reached the side turning it slewed around the corner, partly mounting the kerb, and stopped.

Peter stopped. He leaned across over Tom and glared out of the passenger window again, although the driver of the white car was invisible behind a reflecting windscreen.

–Peter, began Tom weakly.

–I know I know. I'll get yer there. Just dint want this flaming bugger cutting me up. Wots he think he is, a taxi driver? Dunno wot the roads is like any more. Leave a space, some bugger jumps in. Across the lights—see that! idiot could of waited—traffic, you know when the lights is red, stop across the junction so nobody can get going the other way. Lights change red green red green and not a sod moves. I dunno, here, this'll do.

During this diatribe, he had nursed the van up the hill, through several junctions, and now turned into a petrol station.

–Look at that flaming idiot.

A large blue car had left a gap of two or three feet between its passenger side and the petrol pump. Consequently there was hardly room enough to squeeze in next to it to use the pump on the other side, but Peter was in no mood to be denied. He edged into the gap, slowly but inexorably. The middle-aged man filling up the blue car watched. After what seemed like several hours, the van was ensconced right next to the petrol pump on the driver's side. It was also ensconced extremely close to the big blue car, but Peter was blithely unconcerned. He grabbed the five-pound note proffered by Tom, jumped out, and started filling up with diesel.

Tom sat shaking inside the van and wondered if there was another way he could get to Kensington on time. Reluctantly, he concluded there wasn't. He hoped nobody else tried to pull out in front of Peter. He hoped no traffic snarled up at traffic lights. He had a feeling that Peter might just try to drive straight through or over any cars unfortunate enough to be caught stuck across the middle of a junction.

Peter came back, having spent four pounds fifty on diesel and pocketed the difference. The middle-aged man also came back. As he squeezed into his car, he banged the side of the van with his door. Peter jumped. –What the…?

–Er, there's not a lot of room, Pete.

63

Peter sat back, partly mollified. Tom congratulated himself on avoiding another confrontation, when inexplicably the middle-aged man decided to check that his door was really shut, and banged the van for a second time.

Peter jumped again. –That flaming bmne..er… Tom could not hear exactly what he said because he had opened his door, leaped out, and raced round towards the blue car. The middle-aged man—and the middle-aged woman sitting next to him—saw Nemesis approaching and drove off hastily. Peter made a wild swipe at the retreating backside of the car and appropriated its aerial.

–Yaaah!

Tom slid down inside the van, hoping to make himself invisible to anyone outside.

–See that? Banged me twice! Peter was fuming as he climbed back in. –See this! He brandished the aerial at Tom. –That'll teach im!

Tom slid down still lower as Peter roared off into the traffic, narrowly missing a pedestrian unlucky enough to be walking past the petrol station at that moment. Peter was muttering to himself. They took several turnings. Tom glanced at his watch. Twenty past ten. It was going to be close.

Peter cackled wildly. –Look! Look! It's im, the flaming bugger! It's no good… ahhhaaaaa! … you can't… Peter was roaring incoherently. Tom peered nervously out the front windscreen and saw that they had pulled up in a queue at traffic lights immediately behind the big blue car. He could see the driver leaning forward, fiddling with his radio controls. Suddenly he looked around, as if Peter had made his presence felt by some powerful telepathic force. Peter grabbed up the aerial and waved it wildly, cackling all the time. The middle-aged man's eyes widened in surprise and shock.

The lights changed. Tom slid almost completely under the dashboard, trying to pretend that he had no real connection with Peter and the van. Cars moved forward. Peter seemed disappointed when the blue car turned left and vanished into the depths of London. Tom, on the other hand, was mightily relieved.

The van burbled on for a while, turning this way and that. Tom kept his eyes tightly closed and prayed for survival.

–Where?

–What?

–Where is she?

Tom slid back up and peered out of the side window. –Left here. See that building? That's it. Anywhere will do.

Peter took him at his word, screeching to a halt instantly and double parking alongside a bright yellow mini. Tom half expected someone behind to blow their horn in annoyance at this manoeuvre, with dire consequences. But perhaps it was nothing more than normal driving in the big city, because the traffic merely slowed up and sidled past, facing down vehicles coming in the opposite direction.

–Pick you up later? asked Peter.

–No, no, I couldn't possibly.

–You sure?

–I'll get a bus.

Tom slammed the door. The van immediately bucked and jerked impressively on the spot, as Peter struggled to co-ordinate clutch and brake. Then it barged out into the traffic, which phlegmatically rearranged itself around the van, rather like iron filings lining up behind a magnet. The green roof moved down the road, towering over most of the cars surrounding it, until a bus roared past and cut everything from view.

With a shock, he remembered why he was there. He trotted around the yellow mini and looked about, trying to remember exactly where the momentous Friday evening lamppost was situated. He glanced at his watch. Ten thirty-five. Surely Mary hadn't arrived, waited five minutes, and left in a huff? When he looked up again, she was coming out of the gates of the residential hall, zipping up a thick coat over one of her shapeless woolly smocks. She saw him at the same time as he saw her and veered in his direction.

–Hello Tom, you look… where's the car?

–How do I look?

She looked at him consideringly. He took the opportunity to look back at her. He had forgotten her calm grey eyes and the way in which she quirked her eyebrows. Surreptitiously he reached behind and steadied himself on the bonnet of the yellow mini, as his legs had turned to jelly. He supposed this might be as a result of delayed shock after the events in Peter's van, but he didn't really think so.

You passed, and the world
As usual,
Speeded and swayed alarmingly.

I am only half pleased
I did not fall.

–Rather pale, actually. Are you all right?

Tom mustered up a smile and said, –Where are we going? Let me tell you about it.

As they walked together along the pavement, diffidently linking fingers, turned a corner and skipped across the road to a pizza-cum-coffee shop, Mary listened with half her attention to Tom's story of the Nightmare Trip from Cheam to Kensington, as he put it. She found herself giggling as he described the White Car Confrontation, and laughed hysterically when he told her about the Great Aerial Robbery and subsequent Alarm of the Middle-aged Couple when they found their radio failed to work, and how they found out why when they saw Peter brandishing his trophy.

The other half of her mind could not help but notice that, minutes after meeting up with Tom, she was laughing again. She was also eating again. They had ordered two different pizzas and were each having half of each.

–So anyway the car didn't start. But I won't be taking any more lifts with Pete. How was your weekend, with your mum and dad?

Actually, for the first time that she could remember, Mary had wished that she did not have to go to the family gathering. Rather to her own surprise, she had found herself constantly wishing that she was back in London, walking around museums or doing crosswords with Tom. She hadn't noticed her aunt Maud glance at her mother and tap her nose meaningfully, nor the way her father looked puzzled when she forgot to laugh at one of his jokes, and how her mother had signalled at him with her eyes. She thought she had joined in as usual. She would have been surprised if someone told her that she had spent much of the weekend gazing vacantly out of the window, occupied with her own thoughts.

–It was okay.

–And… and did you have a good week? Tom was bursting to tell her his news, but felt guilty that he had already monopolised the conversation with his tale of how he had got to Kensington.

–I sat in the office, she said. –I read some files. I got textbooks for next week. *I wondered why you didn't phone me,* she thought, but didn't have the courage to say it aloud. –How was Milton Keynes?

–It was great, enthused Tom. –I found a point on my first audit. George was great. There was this dragon woman Catherine Copeland and he faced her down with his walking stick, it was like George and the dragon, really…

Mary was laughing again. Tom lowered his fork and gave her a sober look. –Seriously, he said, –we came back on Friday and I went to a meeting with the Director in Audit House. The Director, he said, "Call me Ken".

–The Director? What on earth for?

–To decide whether to call in the police.

He described how he had found the five invoices, and after a little thought Mary realised their significance. George said they should keep things quiet at first. "No sense in letting on that we know just yet birds coops flying and so forth," he had told Tom. "Change of plan tomorrow I'll drop you off you can check the sample see if there's any more then get payroll stuff as planned."

–Were there any more? asked Mary.

–Just one, said Tom.

"Any more?" asked George when he finally turned up at the conference room.

"Just one. Look. Braithwaite Haulage. Same style. Same letter g. Same everything except for the value. Only a thousand."

"Is that all?" grunted George

–Although whether he meant only the one invoice or that it was only a thousand pounds, I don't know, said Tom. –Mind you, even in my sample we'd found nearly ten thousand pounds.

George had dropped Tom off and then gone back to use the hotel phone to apprise David Pickles back at Millbank Tower of developments. They had discussed it in detail. "Main thing is keep it under our hats," George told Tom.

"Act normal," said Tom.

"Exactly do the payroll do the files do everything we would normally do act normal that's exactly right young feller-me-Tom but…" and here George leaned forward confidentially even though they were the only people in the huge board room, and its door was closed "… but copy the invoices check a few more besides keep a look out for anything amiss. I'll contact the bank about the cheques."

–Cheques? asked Mary.

–That's what I asked, said Tom.

"The invoices were paid by cheque weren't they well who were they made out to Braithwaite Haulage? hmmm I don't think so."

–I see, nodded Mary.

For camouflage, Tom copied all the invoices rather than just the six suspicious ones, and told young Dick that he would be asking for a few more as it hadn't taken as long as he expected to check them. Catherine Copeland had come out to see what was going on. "All okay?" she asked. "Everything ties up with the print," Tom assured her, having practised this response before coming along to *Administration and Accounts*. Young Dick guided Tom to the payroll department where he gathered another pile of computer printouts and a number of personnel files from the personnel office next door. He didn't have the faintest idea what he was going to do with them, but George was right about one thing. They did make interesting reading.

–There was one woman, Agnes somebody or other, she's been off work for—wait for it—four months because of the stress of going through a divorce.

–Was that strictly relevant to the audit? asked Mary, a little disapprovingly.

–Well, no. But the funny thing is, her husband—or rather ex-husband I suppose—also works for the RCU and personnel had written to him, asking if he needed time off, and he wrote back saying no thanks, he'd never felt better in his life.

Mary was unable to resist a smile.

On Thursday George disappeared for a couple of hours. He came back with a small envelope and a thunderous expression. "Damned fools at the bank didn't want to hand them over well I soon told them," he boomed once the conference room door was secured. Tom could imagine the scene at the bank.

George tore open the envelope and succeeded in wrestling open the taped package inside. He thumbed through the cheques. "For God's sake," he breathed.

–What? exclaimed Mary, then blushed and put a hand over her mouth as she remembered where she was.

Tom leaned forward. –Cheques. Four made out to cash. Two made out—if you can believe it—to Ms Catherine Copeland.

–For God's sake, breathed Mary. –That's… that's… She made out cheques to *herself*?

"You better believe it," George told the Director on Friday afternoon. "Tom here he found it not me I just tidied up loose ends."

"Tom," acknowledged the Director. "Well done."

"Thank you, sir."

"Call me Ken," said the Director.

"Yes, sir, Ken."

"We copied everything we could to hand to the police."

"There's complications," said David Pickles, who was sitting in on the meeting.

"When I say well done, I meant it," said the Director. "But it gives us a problem."

–Problem? asked Mary. –How could there be a problem?

Tom scowled. –Politics, he said. –Or tactics, the Director called it. He said I had presented them with a tactical problem.

"How can there be a problem?" boomed George. His face was turning red. Tom momentarily imagined him looming over the Director's desk, waving his gold-tipped walking stick, while the Director backed away and squeaked fearfully. But the Director merely stared hard at George, and it was George who eventually looked away. "Crying out loud," he muttered. "What else do you want? cheques made out to her by name she's been able to order and pay since Easter, the accountant's about as intelligent as a wet piece of seaweed."

Tom thought this an unkind but accurate description of young Dick.

"Ms Catherine Copeland has… connections," said David Pickles. George looked up sharply.

"Copeland Copeland I knew I knew the name from somewhere. Oh gods she's not related to that bedamned Caitlin woman is she?"

David Pickles waved his hands agitatedly and glanced significantly at Tom.

"I think Tom knows that anything we say in here is confidential," remarked the Director.

–Oh, said Tom. –I forgot about that.

Mary, elbows on the table and her chin resting on her clasped hands, merely raised her eyebrows.

–Anyway it turns out Catherine Copeland is the sister of Caitlin Jamison who apparently is an MP and has caused the Department all sorts of trouble over the years. The Director was… Tom paused, searching for the right word –he was *uneasy* about going to the police.

–But the evidence, said Mary.

–I know, said Tom. –It was left that the Director was going to approach his boss, whoever that is. Can you imagine? Even a Director has a boss.

George said as they left Audit House in the late afternoon, "They won't touch it feller-me-Tom you mark my words they'll offload it onto GIA."

"GIA?"

"Government Internal Audit. They'll paw over all the records for ages point out the system failings recommend 'stronger segregation of duties.'" George made quotation marks in the air, almost decapitating a passer-by with his walking stick. "I'll bet a pound to a penny the lovely Catherine gets the chance to pay back what she's made off with or most of it anyway then gets transferred all done and dusted forgotten."

"So nothing more for us?"

George shrugged. "Probably not still you can never be sure better keep a note of everything in case we end up in court, come on I'll give you a lift."

Outside the pizza place the sun tried vainly to heat the autumnal air. Traffic thrummed along the main road at the end of the street. Tom wondered if Peter had made it safely back to Cheam. Mary buttoned up her thick coat and reached out to hold his hand. It was hard to believe that not much more than a week ago they had not even met each other. He held out his hand. They twined their fingers together and headed off into a shopping centre, intent on collecting textbooks for the course work that, starting on Monday, the Department was about to put them through.

Time blurred. The days merged into new patterns as they met up outside the college every morning, sat next to each other during lectures, and worked together in the library long into the evening. They made new friends, notably Derek Worth who bought himself an Amstrad computer and showed off all his printed essays and neatly laid out accounting problems, and Anne Caird who had an uncanny ability to put people at their ease and talk about whatever was troubling them. Tom was not nearly as frightened of girls as he used to be. He had no trouble talking to Anne, who was one of Mary's special friends, and frequently chatted to other girls in the class. The one exception was Jennifer Huntley who was so ravishingly beautiful that Tom always seized up with embarrassment whenever she was nearby, in case anybody—but especially Mary or Jennifer herself—thought that he lusted after her. Which of course he did.

Examinations loomed. Tom recalled sitting for his finals at university, perched uncomfortably on a high stool with a tiny seat, because for some reason the exams took place in the chemistry building. He had thought himself reasonably well prepared and not especially nervous, but when he turned over the paper his mind went completely blank. He couldn't even remember the name of the exam, never mind answer any of its contents. A long time before, somebody he had vaguely known at school had attempted A level physics but realised as soon as he saw the examination questions that he had no chance. So he wrote: "I do not know the answer to these questions, but here is a list of the kings and queens of England." He failed. In the chemistry building, Tom's powers of thought slowly returned to him and he eventually managed to complete the paper successfully. But he never forgot those terrible moments when he could remember nothing.

–Not even my name, he told Mary.

–You'll be fine.

The week preceding the exams was designated revision week, and they spent most of it either in the library or in Cheam, asking each other tricky questions and practising the arcane arts of double-entry bookkeeping. By Friday they had had enough.

–I was thinking of going down to see my mum and dad at the weekend, said Tom.

Mary's face fell. –Oh, okay.

–I mean, would you like to come?

He couldn't believe he was saying it. He listened to his own words and wondered where he had got the confidence to utter them. Since when did he, Tom-Are-You-Overtaking-Bradley, start inviting girls back home for the weekend?

–I'm sorry? he said. He had been so caught up in the wonder of it all that he hadn't heard her response.

–Fool, she told him.

In Sandhurst, they walked in the woods, went to the pictures. Tom's mother insisted on digging out old photographs of Tom when he was a baby, much to his embarrassment. Mary looked at them all with a serious expression, but then burst into fits of giggles when they were alone.

–You were so-oo cute, she smirked. –Especially in the bath.

His face turned red, but he wasn't as nervous as he used to be. –I'm still cute, he told her. –Just bigger, that's all. She twisted her eyebrows. Oops, he thought, and flushed even more brightly. –You wait, he said. –I'll get to see all your baby photos and then we'll see who's laughing.

She shook her head. –No you won't. We had a house fire when I was little, and there aren't any photos left.

At night, she slept in the spare room while he lay awake in his old bedroom, watching the achingly familiar shadows twist and writhe across the wall, although now he interpreted them differently. Mary was only a few yards away, but it might as well have been a hundred miles. He wondered if he ought to knock on her door. He wondered what she looked like, dressed for bed. He wondered if she did dress for bed. He imagined her sleepy head turning towards him, long hair tousled, dark against the white pillow. Suppose he knocked and went in? What would he do? Hold her hand? *Are you overtaking?* he whispered to himself, and turned over, and tried unsuccessfully to go to sleep.

Before they left, his mother took him aside and said:

–Your father likes your girlfriend. So do I. You must bring her again. Does she play bridge?

He was too stunned to answer. Girlfriend. He had a girlfriend. So this was what it was like to have a girlfriend. His face was swallowed up by an enormous grin which stayed in place long after they started back on the road to London.

–What are you grinning at? asked Mary suspiciously.

–Oh, just something my mother said.

–And what was that?

Well, why not tell her? He swallowed. –She said… she said…

–Out with it, Tom.

The radio blared out a new tune and distracted him. –I've never understood this song, he said. –Trees don't move.

–She didn't say any such thing. Mary did a double-take. –What?

Tom swallowed again. –She said, you know, just as we were about to leave, she said that my father said…

–Tom!

–er, that he liked my girlfriend. And that she did too.

He clutched hard at the steering wheel and stared straight ahead. A hundred yards passed. Quarter of a mile. More. He sneaked a look out of the corner of his eye and discovered to his astonishment that Mary was doubled up in the passenger seat, hands plastered across her mouth, holding back hysteria. Her face was bright red.

–It's not funny, he said, hurt.

She nodded frantically. Laughter escaped, was muffled again. –Yes it is, she squeaked. She lost control again, wiped tears from her eyes. –It's *poetry*, Tom. *Poetry.* Not *oh a tree in motion.* It's *poetry in motion.*

He looked at her, and their eyes met. He could tell that she knew perfectly well what he had just said.

–Fool, she whispered, and then bent forward in another paroxysm of giggles.

After the examinations and not long before Christmas her parents came over for a brief visit. They all went out for a meal and Tom was exposed to the Graham and Evelyn double act for the first time.

–He does crosswords, said Mary mischievously.

–What? bellowed Graham. –Crosswords? Did we do cross-words?

–Cross words? remarked Evelyn. –Never had any.

–What was the answer to that damned clue? bellowed Graham happily. –What was the damned clue? Oh yes: *Union song played back in middle of—*

–Graham, said Evelyn.

–What? What? Graham caught sight of Tom. –Well, ah, yes, perhaps you're right. Um. Anyway how did they go, the exams?

Mary emerged from where she had been hiding behind her hands and said, –Tom turned over all the papers very slowly. Tom glared at her. Afterwards, he told her, "If I'd known you were going to say that…"

"Yes? What, you wouldn't have come?"

"What was all that about crosswords, anyway? What was that clue?"

"It's an old family story," Mary said evasively. "Tell you another time."

Tom had turned over all the papers slowly because he remembered all too well the dreadful mind-numbing events of his university examination. "If I turn over the paper slowly," he told Mary as they queued up for Economics on the first day, "and I feel my mind going, I can turn it back again and everything will be all right." Mary rolled her eyes. "Mind you, it's only Economics," mused Tom. "If I assume enough parameters, I can just about assume the solution." He had a mathematician's contempt for economics.

–Quite right, Graham nodded. –Damned stupid subject. Stick to debits and credits and you can't go wrong.

After the meal, Mary's mother took him aside and said, –Glad she's met you. Broad shoulders.

Tom stood as upright and as broadly as he could. Mary's mother nodded, then leaned forward to say confidentially, –Someone to look after her.

Tom gaped at her. A few weeks ago, he had never had a girl-friend, never taken anyone out, and now here was Mary's mother saying how pleased she was that they had—what? Met? Hooked up? Got together? was this—? could it be—?

Tom glanced up as Mary returned from whatever mysterious place women went to, and caught her eye. She smiled at him. With a sudden shock he realised that the answer to all his questions, as far as he was concerned, was yes. Yes, yes and yes. Why he had only just realised it, he wasn't sure. He had descended into ecstatic shock when he first met her, after all, and had experienced a tingling excitement every day he had met her since. But now he realised he was so in love that there was nothing else he wanted in the world except her. Recklessly, he thought *I want to marry her.*

He grinned at Mary's mother, and at Mary's father hovering close behind. At that moment, he felt huge affection for them. *They* had brought him to his senses. *They* had made him realise what he wanted out of life, how he wanted his future to be shaped.

Minutes later, he hated them absolutely, as they whisked Mary off to Londonderry for a family Christmas.

> Yesterday,
> My mask slipped.
> I almost showed through.
>
> Today,
> When we met,
> We talked of the weather.
>
> Tomorrow?
> I am afraid tomorrow
> You may already have forgotten me.

Had she forgotten him? While she was gone he walked the rainswept streets of London. He could not get her out of his mind. Night after night he put on his coat—or sometimes he forgot to put it on—and went out. He walked. He went to the snooker hall and recklessly challenged Beech, the professional at his snooker club, to a match. Which he lost handsomely. –Good game, said Beech untruthfully. He walked home with a cold knot of worry coiling in his stomach. He lost his appetite. Many years later he went through the same experience all over again in unimaginably different circumstances and, recognising the symptoms, he wrote different words. But that lay far in the future. Now, he went out and hardly noticed when he got soaked through, and wondered if he was making mountains out of molehills. They had agreed not to call as it was so expensive, but he wrote to her every day. Mostly she wrote back.

–You know I'm serious about you, Tom eventually said on the phone, when he could resist picking it up no longer.

–Oh? Mary said, and he was seized with misgiving.

But when she returned, she fell against him in the dark, hiding her face. Then they kissed, their first kiss, both of them with lips pursed, and tight, and trembling.

In the new year they went to see Mary's sister in Aberdeen, and found that too awash in cold rain. Tom wrote later about the rain, remembering how it slanted down from a grey sky, as if the weather was shading in the surroundings with bold watery lines. He remembered virtually nothing else about the visit except for ten seconds of magic when they walked the dogs—Mary in a woollen hat, cheeks flushed and eyes sparkling, young nieces and nephews running dog-high around their feet and at one point after Tom had thrown a sodden stick high into the rain—in his mind, in the future, Tom flew apart from the scene, like a genie, and saw himself in borrowed ridiculously large boots losing a tug-of-war with an equally ridiculously large dog, Mary in the background half-bent, laughing—and then flew back to experience what the picture didn't show, the freezing rain plastering his hair to his scalp, mud, the uproarious barking of dogs and screaming of children, Mary's eyes meeting his and—warm and salty and private in the middle of it all, the press of her lips and the length of her body, a promise of times still to come.

After Christmas Tom sat in the office, wondering exactly what he was supposed to do in the couple of weeks before classes started up again. The office didn't seem real. The dragon Margaret looked like a character from a previous life, someone he used to know but whose essential characteristics had been forgotten, swamped by the force of later events. What was real was kissing Mary in the driving rain, holding her hand in the cinema, feeling her arms tight around his chest. The brightly lit office filled with hard, rectangular desks and filing cabinets felt like a hard, rectangular corner of somebody else's dream.

–Good Christmas?

–Great.

It had been a dreadful Christmas. He had spent virtually all of it wishing that it would end so he could get back to London.

–You went home?

He nodded. –Home, then Aberdeen.

–Home, said Margaret glumly, and Tom realised that he had no idea if she was married, or where she lived, or indeed anything about her personal circumstances. It struck him that this was rather remiss.

–Oh, he said. –Where—?

The phone rang and he picked up the receiver. His heart jumped at Mary's excited voice. –I've passed! she said. –Results are here. Anne passed, she called a minute ago, don't know about Derek or Jennifer. What about you?

He swallowed, suddenly nervous. What about him? He hadn't heard anything, that was what about him. Perhaps they sent out all the pass results first, and followed up with the fail results later. Perhaps he was in the second, fail batch. Probably he was in the second, fail batch. He knew he should have concentrated more on Economics.

–You'll be fine, Mary reassured him. –They just haven't come yet. I'll ring around. See you later.

Mechanically he put the phone down. Dragon Margaret eyed him inquisitively.

–Results, he said. –Mary's passed. He remembered that he was going to ask Margaret about her Christmas. –Oh yes, no mine haven't come yet, did you—

The phone rang again and he snatched up the receiver. He was certain Mary had found that everyone on the course except him had passed. She would wish him luck in his future career, and hope they might see each other from time to time. They would probably end up exchanging Christmas cards on alternate years, as he already did with a handful of old school friends. All this because of inconsistent variations in what passed for economic theory.

–Tom Bradley?

It wasn't Mary. It was a man's voice.

–Yes?

–This is Popplewell, over at Audit House. Ken wants to see you.

–Ken?

–The Director, explained the voice patiently. –He wants you over here, in Audit House. Now.

–Oh. Okay. Right.

–Have you had any phone calls this morning?

–Er, well, just one.

–Yes? Popplewell's voice sharpened. –Who was it?

–It was, er, another student about the exam results, I didn't think—

–Okay, interrupted Popplewell's voice. –Get over here immediately, please.

The line went dead. Tom replaced the receiver slowly. Dragon Margaret eyed him even more inquisitively. All of a sudden the brightly lit office resembled the edge of somebody's nightmare much more than the corner of somebody's dream. Perhaps he really was dreaming? Surreptitiously he pinched the palm of his left hand. It hurt, and Margaret was still looking at him inquisitively. It wasn't a dream. It was hard, harsh reality.

–That was someone called Popplewell. He got to his feet and reached out for his coat. –The…

He fell silent. The enormity of what might be about to happen suddenly overwhelmed him. He was about to lose his job because of a stupid economics exam.

–Popplewell? said Margaret. –He's the Department's press liaison officer. What did he want? Tom detected the subtext of this question: *What could the Department's press liaison officer possibly want with you?*

What indeed?

Press liaison? thought Tom. His mood lifted slightly. It was, after all, unlikely the Department would want to advertise his failings in the newspapers. –The Director wants to see me.

Margaret stared at him, astonished. He shrugged on his coat, left the room, and then immediately came back in again. Margaret was staring at the door at the point where he had left as if it could somehow explain why the Director had summoned him. –Phone Mary and tell her what's happened, will you? he said.

For once he took the lift, and he walked briskly up the Embankment underneath a pale, wet sky. A lively wind whipped droplets of water from the tops of railings and leafless branches, throwing them horizontally into his face. Why would the Director want to see him? Had something happened to David Pickles who, come to think of it, hadn't turned up in the office that morning? It didn't seem all that likely that the Director would deal with that eventuality by summoning Tom. Well, perhaps something had happened to somebody else. Tom's heart thudded uncomfortably. Had something happened to his parents? Had somebody, knowing vaguely that he worked for the Department, somehow got hold of press liaison, and Popplewell had got hold of the Director for him to impart the tragic news?

A sheet of water thrown up by a bus ploughing through a deep puddle missed him by mere inches. He didn't notice.

–Oh God, he whispered. This interpretation of events seemed all too possible. Now he even understood why Popplewell had asked about a phone call. He wanted to know if anyone else had already broken the bad news.

At reception he told them who he was, and he was waved through to a meeting room on the ground floor. He was expected to see himself in. He hesitated outside the door, unsure of whether he should knock. –God's sake, he muttered to himself. –The Director's about to tell you that something has happened to Mum or Dad, and you're worried about whether you should knock?

He walked in.

The room was dominated by a huge table. Congregated at one end were the Director Ken—it occurred to Tom that he didn't know his surname—David Pickles, George, and two men Tom had never seen before. One wore a pale yellow suit and purple tie; the other a sober suit and a red bow tie. Everyone looked up at his entrance.

–Ah, Tom, said Ken. –Come in, sit down. This is Archibald Urquhart, junior minister of construction. The man with the bow tie nodded briefly. Tom gingerly sat down next to George, who was looking unusually subdued. The man in the pale yellow suit half rose from his chair and leaned over to shake hands with Tom, who bobbed in place as he wasn't quite sure if he ought to stand up to shake hands.

–Vince Popplewell.

–Sorry, sorry, said Ken. –Thought you'd met.

Tom shook his head mutely, and glanced at George. George evaded his eyes. Tom didn't know what all this was about, but clearly it was nothing to do with his parents.

–At the weekend, said Ken heavily, –Richard Jefferson took his own life.

Tom looked from Ken, to David Pickles, then to George. He didn't understand.

–Wet seaweed, grunted George.

Tom got it. Young Dick and his giant eyes.

–It'll be on the news tonight, said Popplewell. –You might get a phone call. If you do, refer them to me. Here's my card.

Tom remembered young Dick bringing in plastic cups of tea, and George sending them away; young Dick helping him out with the photocopying and stuttering his way through directions to the payroll section. He would hesitate to say that he had become friends with young Dick, but certainly he did not think of him as being tarred with the Catherine Copeland brush. He stared wordlessly at George.

–Sleeping tablets a bottle and a half.

Afterwards, normal rules and timetable suspended, he told Mary all about it. They were alone in her office on the twelfth floor. He had come in, sought out her grey, level eyes, and blurted –Something's happened.

"Here." David Pickles passed a photocopied note. It read:

I didn't do any of it, except for the tea money.

–He photocopied it… photocopied it… Tom had a sudden vivid picture of Dick standing at the photocopier late in the evening when everyone else had gone, saw him drag the sleeve of his jacket across his eyes as the white light at the edge of the machine pulsed and faded, pulsed and faded, counting down the moments of his life. It was too much. His own eyes unexpectedly filled with tears. Mary came across the room and he enfolded her in his arms, neither of them caring if Roger B chose that moment to come back into the office.

–It's all right, soothed Mary. –It's not your fault.

–But if I hadn't found those invoices.

–You weren't responsible for the invoices. That woman was.

Archibald Urquhart cleared his throat, suggesting that taking the time to brief a subordinate member of staff might be acceptable to the Director, but it certainly wasn't acceptable to a minister, junior or otherwise. Ken ignored him.

"He sent at least five copies of that note that we know of. Audit Office, Catherine Copeland, local newspaper, girlfriend and parents. There may have been others which we don't yet know about."

Young Dick has a girlfriend. Had. Had a girlfriend.

"On being approached—a joint approach by the Department and GIA—Catherine Copeland made the claim that she knew nothing of any false invoices or dummy payments, and said that the accounting assistant must have taken the opportunity to carry out the fraud while the Chief Accountant was off sick."

"But—" began Tom.

"We know," said David Pickles.

"I think we should be careful about prejudging the issue," said Archibald Urquhart. "The minister is most anxious to avoid negative and uninformed opinion developing about the whole—ah, unhappy situation." Tom stared at the junior minister, who ignored him and everyone else in the room to focus solely on the Director.

Ken picked up young Dick's farewell note. "It's a bit late to be thinking about that."

"Not at all," said Archibald Urquhart smoothly. "It is unfortunate that the news has already reached the press, but it is by no means too late to carry out a damage limitation exercise. It never is," he added, smiling faintly at his own joke.

Tom remembered George predicting that the Department would never touch the case, that Catherine Copeland would get the chance to repay some or most of the money she had stolen, that she would be transferred. All done and dusted forgotten.

His arms tightened around Mary and he found himself stroking her hair. She pushed herself back and looked anxiously into his face.

–I'm coming back with you tonight.

Tom automatically carried out a mental stocktake of his larder and then thought, to hell with it, they could buy something in for a change.

–I can't drive you back, he said. –Car's not fixed.

–I didn't say anything about being driven back, said Mary.

Tom didn't immediately take this in. His mind was still in the conference room in Audit House. –It was a bit weird after the junior minister guy left. Nobody said anything for ages.

Ken had got up. He strode to the window, hands clasped behind his back. He stood looking out of the window and everyone else looked everywhere except at each other.

"Mr Pickles, the junior minister would prefer that this matter is dealt with by GIA. As you have heard, he doesn't think anything would be gained by the Department pressing claims against Catherine Copeland."

Tom had become so used to using first names that it took him a moment to realise who Mr Pickles was.

"Yes, sir," said David Pickles.

"That being the case, I do not think there is any point in you personally having anything to do with the case. Is that understood, Mr Pickles?"

"Yes, sir."

"Mr Fulton, Mr Bradley—"

Tom started.

"—you will each prepare a report on the events at Milton Keynes. For me. Mr Fulton, I believe you have had experience of this kind of case before?"

George grunted affirmatively.

"Make sure your reports cross-reference satisfactorily and do not contradict each other etcetera etcetera. Give Mr Bradley whatever assistance he requires. I want these reports by Friday. Mr Pickles, you will ensure that cover is available for routine audit work." Ken fell silent.

–He stood there for ages, said Tom. –I didn't know what he was thinking about, but I think the others did. George told me afterwards, sort of.

In the conference room, Tom looked at David Pickles, who had pushed his chair back from the table and was inspecting the carpet as if some hidden audit truth lay there; at George, who had put his meaty hands on the table and was tracing a pattern invisible to all but his own eyes; at Vince Popplewell, who was carefully reading one of his own personal contact cards, turning it over, then turning it over again to reread in case the words on it had somehow changed; and at Ken, who continued to stand motionless, staring out of the window at the tops of trees bereft of leaves and the Thames beyond. He wondered what was going on. After what seemed like hours but was probably no more than a couple of minutes, Ken sighed and straightened his back still further. He turned around.

"Yes, Friday morning," he said. "I need to check my diary, but I believe I will be with Miss Carswell. Bring them to me there, please, Mr Fulton."

"Yes, sir," said George, in a tone of voice Tom had never heard him use before.

–So what was going on? asked Mary.

"So what was all that about?" Tom asked George afterwards, on their way back to Marsham Street.

"Ken has a thing about auditor independence quite right too," said George. "He didn't like Urquhart, didn't like the idea of—" more quotation marks in the air. This time it was Tom who had to dodge the flailing gold-tipped stick "—'damage limitation' did you get that?"

"I did notice that," acknowledged Tom.

"Julia Carswell you won't have met her, head of legal you work it out."

Tom thought about it. George didn't seem inclined to say any more. After a while he thought he understood what Ken's reference to the legal section implied. He replayed Ken's instructions through his mind, and after a longer while he thought he saw what they implied, too.

–He's not going to do what the junior minister guy wanted. He's going to get our legal people to look over the reports. He's going after Catherine Copeland himself.

–Good.

–But he didn't tell us that. He made sure David Pickles wouldn't be involved. He told us that we would be writing the reports specifically for him—he let us assume that he'll be passing them on to GIA.

Tom looked into Mary's eyes.

–He's protecting you.

–Yes, I think so.

–Good.

Tom's brain slowly caught up with the last few minutes. –What did you say?

–Good.

–Before that.

Mary coloured. –I expect Peter will let me use Jan's old room for one night, won't he? I—

Whatever she was going to say was lost as Tom bent forward and kissed her. His arms tightened again, and he put one of his hands into her long hair. She put her arms around him, her hands curling up over his shoulders. Neither of them saw the door open, Roger B pause in the doorway, purse his lips and raise his eyebrows, and carefully back out into the corridor, closing the door quietly behind him.

Despite Vince Popplewell's assertion, nothing appeared in the papers or on the television about the tragic events in Milton Keynes—not then, anyway. It made the news a few months later, when Catherine Copeland was charged. *Cabinet Minister's sister charged with fraud. Jamison's sister caught with hands in till.* There was no mention of young Richard Jefferson. Tom read the newspaper coverage, watched the news bulletins, remembered George's instructions. "Not your usual report young feller-me-Tom put in when we arrived who we spoke to what poor wet seaweed said what the monstrous CC said all the stuff not usually in a report." It had taken him two days to write, even with the dragon Margaret helping out with typing. After an hour or so George had stood up and said he couldn't abide working in the office he was off someplace else; and he went. He called in two or three times afterwards to compare notes with Tom, and then on Thursday to collate the two reports together. "Like my style better than yours," he remarked, but made sure Tom could see him winking at Margaret as he said it. Months later, when Tom couldn't understand why young Dick was so conspicuously absent from the news, George supplied the sad answer. "Because he isn't news young feller-me-Tom that's why."

Course work started in earnest. Tom and Mary were inseparable. They did coursework together, they went out in the evenings together, they even went to the snooker hall together. They sat on his bed in Peter's house, arms tight around each other. One day he screwed up his courage and murmured into her ear.

–There's something I want to tell you.

–Mmm?

He kissed her. Her eyes asked a question. He pulled her close and breathed into her ear.

–But I don't think I can, he said.

–Mmm.

–I love you, Mary.

Their mouths met. For the first time he probed cautiously with his tongue. Her lips parted willingly. Long seconds later she buried her head in his chest and mumbled almost inaudibly.

–What? he said. His heart was beating so wildly he could hardly hear anything. He could hardly think. –What?

–I want to tell you something too, Tom.

Her face was scarlet. He could feel her breathing in nervous gasps. He could feel the thunder of her heart, pressed so close to his own.

–But I don't think I can.

They sat on the end of his bed, his arms around her shoulders, one hand stroking her hair, her face pressed up against his chest. This was another moment he knew he would never forget, to put alongside the moment she turned towards him in her office on the twelfth floor, the moment he took her hand in a judo grip, the magical moment beneath the yellow lamppost outside her residential hall. He had a funny feeling there were going to be a lot more moments to remember in the days, months and years to come. Gradually his heartbeat slowed and he felt her relax in his arms.

–You prefer me to Red Sadler, then?

He felt her giggling.

His examination results had arrived the day after hers and rather than phone he had taken the opportunity to climb up the stairs to the twelfth floor. When he had opened the door to her office, it was to see her chatting with a dark-haired, red-shirted man in his early thirties. "I was instantly jealous," he told her afterwards. "I could tell," she said. The red-shirted man had turned, and Mary introduced them. "Tom, this is…"

"Red," said the red-shirted man.

"My boss," said Mary. "Red, this is Tom, my er who works down-stairs." Red Sadler had advanced, hand outstretched.

"Your er, eh? Pleased to meet you, Tom."

"He plays chess," Mary said.

"You play chess?" he asked Red Sadler. "I'll give you a game if you like."

Next day he told Margaret all about his challenge and the Drag-on hooted hysterically.

"What's so funny?"

"You'll find out," hooted Margaret.

Which he had. Red Sadler subsequently beat him three times within half an hour and it emerged during over-the-board conver-sation that he was ranked within the top fifty in Great Britain. Tom had confronted Mary about it later. "Why? Why would you do that to me? You knew, didn't you?" and she had batted her eyes, pushed her arms straight down and linked her fingers, and virtually stood on one abashed foot. "Well he was so unhappy about losing his last games in the European Championships, and I fancy him so much, so I thought if I could get you to come upstairs and mmmpgphh—" This last as Tom's patience snapped and he grabbed her and kissed her.

Downstairs he had remonstrated with Margaret—Why didn't you tell me? Why didn't you warn me?—and she had laughed so loudly for such a length of time that David Pickles emerged from his office and barked "What? What have you done to Margaret?" and when Margaret had recovered sufficiently to tell him, he guffawed even more loudly, so that someone irritably banged on the wall in the next office. It was at that moment, when Tom wasn't quite sure whether or not he was in a foul temper, that his phone rang. When he picked it up a female voice said, "Tom? Tom Bradley? You probably won't remember me."

The funny thing was, he did. "Sylvia?" he said cautiously. She had been one of the students taught by Beryl on the arcane arts of interviewing technique.

"Tom, it *is* you. I heard you worked for the Department."

Tom suddenly recalled Beryl telling him that Sylvia had got herself a job as a journalist. "How did you know?" he asked.

Sylvia evaded the question. "Is it any better than jobcentres, eh? Is there anything that isn't better than jobcentres, eh? Hey, what are you up to?"

"Taking examinations, mostly," said Tom. He didn't feel inclined to tell her about Mary. Unexpectedly, he found he didn't feel inclined to tell her anything. "How about you?"

"No more exams for me," said Sylvia. "Did you read about somebody or other got caught with their hands in the till? Somebody from the Department caught them out. It wasn't you, was it?" she joked. Except Tom knew she wasn't joking. He didn't want his name in the papers. *Junior Auditor Catches Cabinet Minister Sister.* He was evasive in his turn. "Me? I've only been in the job two minutes! Listen, got my boss here, got to go. Catch you later, okay?"

Mary had been upset when she heard about it. "Sylvia used you to try to get a story?"

"I think so."

"Well, that's not very nice," complained Mary.

Two weeks later they were driving beneath cold stars, the car hood down, their breaths frosting in the clear night air. Mary wore the same woolly hat she had worn in Aberdeen, thick gloves, and an enormously bulky coat that effectively wedged her into the narrow seat of the sports car.

–See, it's all right, he told her.

–Mad, she said.

–See the moon? See the stars? It's a wonderful night.

–I see them, Tom.

He squeezed her hand.

–Every night is wonderful with you, he said. –Every day.

He turned his head and found she was looking at him. Shadows shifted across her face. She smiled. –Watch the road, she said.

Abruptly he slowed the car, eased it beneath trees beside the country road, stopped and killed the engine. He leaned over and grasped her vast bulk into his arms. She strained towards him. Their lips met. Their tongues tangled.

–Mary?

–Yes?

–Will you marry me?

He had been agonising for weeks how he was going to ask this question. Should he kneel down? Should he buy a ring? Should he arrange a meal out somewhere, or go to a sports event and arrange for his proposal to be shown on a giant screen? How should he propose, anyway? What words should he use? She already knew that he loved her, so what purpose would be served in saying it all over again? On the other hand, she said she liked being told, and truth to tell so did he. *I love you* wasn't a phrase which became boring if repeated over time. Most agonising of all, how could he—Tom-Are-You-Overtaking-Bradley—possibly summon up the courage to ask a girl to share his life? His bed. His innermost life. His everything. And yet, despite all the agonising, here it was. It had happened and he had done it. The question had popped out without his having to think about it, in an open-topped-car under the frosty stars.

He realised that Mary was staring at him, quirking her eyebrows. He had been so lost in the wonder of the moment that he had failed to hear her reply.

–Er, what?

She grabbed at his head, pulled his mouth down to hers. Her own tongue quested.

–Fool, she whispered into his disbelieving ear.

He undid his seatbelt and leaned further over, almost eviscerating himself on the handbrake. He undid one of the buttons on her coat so that he could insert an arm and hold her more closely. Fleetingly she was reminded of Gregory Updike and the way in which he fumbled at the buttons on her dress. But this was completely different. In the first place, Tom was only fumbling at the outermost layer of several inches of warm clothing. And in the second place, she suddenly realised, she wasn't at all sure that she would have objected if it had been the final layer. This thought was so unexpected that she squirmed in the car seat and blushed brightly.

–Sorry, sorry, you're cold. Tom started to withdraw his arm but she grabbed at it clumsily to prevent him from moving away.

–It's all right.

–How does it feel to be the future Mrs Bradley?

–*Mrs* Bradley. Mrs *Brad*ley, she mused. She looked into his eyes. Above him, the sky twinkled with a myriad stars. She knew she would remember this moment for the rest of her life. –The world must be told, she said gravely. This struck them both as being so funny that they giggled uncontrollably and it was ten minutes before Tom was sufficiently recovered to strap himself back in and drive off again. He remembered how much the same thing had happened after that first kiss under the lamppost; how he had to wait ten minutes before he felt able to drive away. The difference was, this time his future wife was sitting in the car with him.

They rang their parents. When Tom informed his mother he was engaged she said, –That's splendid! To Mary? Tom confirmed that yes, it was Mary he was engaged to. –Splendid, said his mother. –Couldn't have made a better choice. Although it didn't occur to him at the time, Tom wondered afterwards whether *choice* was the best way of describing what had happened. It wasn't as if there was a steady stream of girlfriends passing through his life, and he had selected the most appropriate one for marriage. On the other hand, if there had been a steady stream of girlfriends, he was quite sure he would have picked Mary. Perhaps, he decided eventually, *fate* had made the choice for them.

Mary's mother said, –Good. We liked him. She passed the phone. –By liked him, she means that we all did. Your sister said he couldn't keep his eyes off you. Mary imagined her father nodding complacently at the success of his information network. *Couldn't keep his eyes off me, eh?* She wasn't able to keep her eyes off him, either. –Well done, girl, said her father, and she found her eyes swimming with tears.

Tom arranged to meet Beryl for lunch in Victoria Street, to break the news in person. She took him to a Vietnamese restaurant and he hated the food.

–Engaged? spluttered Beryl. –Who to? You don't know any girls. She's not *Chinese*, is she?

Tom grinned inanely at her. Beryl never let him forget that he once eyed up a Chinese girl as she undulated past their table in another restaurant in Victoria Street, and berated him for not finding what she called a nice British girl. Tom told her he had used a Chinese quote to start off a story: *I do not know whether I was then a man dreaming I was a butterfly, or whether I am now a butterfly dreaming I am a man.* It was almost thirty years before he discovered how badly he had mangled the pronunciation of the author's name.

–Well, come *on*. Out with it.

–She's not Chinese, Tom said. He continued to grin inanely at her, and she continued to stare back, eyes growing wider and wider until she clutched at her hair and screamed:

–Well, out with it! Who. Is. She?

Nobody in the restaurant so much as looked up. Tom had been thinking of an incident the previous week. He had arranged for Mary to have a lesson from Beech at the snooker club, and on the next morning as he escorted her from St James Park to Marsham Street he asked "How do you feel?" and she said "A bit stiff, I'm not used to"— her high, clear voice carrying to a pedestrian close behind—"having my limbs in those positions." The pedestrian had stiffened and almost stumbled with shock.

–…LISTENING?

–Eh? Oh.

–Congratulations, said Beryl heavily.

–Thank you, Tom said. –Look, you'll see for yourself in a minute.

–She's coming *here*? said Beryl. –Oh, my God. She got up, walked around her chair, sat down again. –Oh, God. She lit a cigarette with trembling fingers. Tom watched her with surprise.

–What are *you* so nervous about?

–It always makes me nervous, seeing the course of history change.

–Har de har.

–So *tell*. Where meet?

–Marsham Street.

–E&AD?

–Yes.

Beryl looked pleased with herself. –*Told* you it was a good idea, didn't I?

–Well, I believed you, didn't I?

–Age?

–Two years younger than me.

–Looks?

–Great.

Beryl sighed.

–Oh, all right. Long dark hair, grey eyes, slim figure, nice smile, nice legs actually, and when she walks…

–That's enough.

They paused. Tom sipped his tea. Beryl puffed at her cigarette.

–She smoke?

–Certainly not. Disgusting habit.

–Good at sports?

–No.

–Chess, snooker, bridge?

–No.

–So what have you got in common? No, no, you'd better not answer *that*.

Tom thought *No, better not.* Mary had moved in to Peter's madhouse and they slept cupped together in Tom's single bed—although slept might not be an apt description. Their hands explored their bodies—Tom nervous, even at that stage, of driving Mary away. They hugged and kissed and explored beneath the blankets, and slept tangled in each other's arms. Neither of them was used to trying to sleep with someone else in the bed. Neither of them gave up trying. "Tom," Mary said one night. "What?" Tom whispered over the sudden thundering of his heart. Her grey eyes looked up at him, perhaps not as steadily as usual, and she said, "If you want—" and Tom needed no more words to know what she was offering. She shifted, her long bare legs sliding against him. "Well?" she murmured, her own voice trembling. Afterwards, they clung to each other and talked of nothing as they drifted into sleep.

–…FROM?

–Eh?

91

–I said, said Beryl heavily, –where is she from?

–London, originally. Brought up in Derry.

–Met the parents?

–Yes.

–OK?

–Yes.

–Met your parents?

–Yes.

–OK?

–Yes.

Pause. Sip. Puff.

The door opened. Tom looked up, remembering the last time this had happened, when the Chinese girl had undulated in. This time it was Mary, wearing her long pale raincoat and practical shoes. Beryl turned around, simultaneously trying to grind out her cigarette. Mary smiled as Tom introduced them, and it was clear that she captured Beryl's heart.

–Sit down, my dear. Sit down.

–Well? Mary asked. –Have you asked?

–I haven't had the chance, Tom said. –I have been cross-examined.

–He told me *everything*, said Beryl. –Everything. What he didn't tell me in words, he told me in other ways. There *are* no secrets, she said impressively. –Ask me what?

–Are you coming to the wedding?

Beryl looked away, and for a moment Tom thought he saw a tell-tale watery glint in her eye.

That evening Mary finally got through to Christine to tell her the news. She said, –You remember you said it didn't matter what I did?

–Yes, said Christine tinnily.

–Well, you were right. I didn't do anything, and we've got engaged.

There was a long tinny silence. –You sure you didn't do anything? No, never mind. You got engaged?

–To be married, explained Mary redundantly.

–Woo-hoo! cried Christine. –What's he like? Is he tall or short? Is he bright or dumb—no don't answer that.

–He makes me laugh, Mary told her. She added, –And my brain turns to mush, and my legs wobble.

–Oh my God so it's really trooo-ooo luurve? carolled Christine. –Do you know how lucky you are?

Mary felt her eyes filling with tears again. Why did her eyes keep filling with tears when she was so happy? She knew she was lucky. –Be my bridesmaid? she asked.

Tom had always been able to slip, genie-like, into the bottle of some memories and live them again from the inside, as if he had left the present for a while. So, before the wedding, Tom the genie watched McEnroe and Borg slug it out under the summer's sun while Mary and Christine went hunting for a dress. He lay on the floor, head on a pilfered pillow, drinking Coke and eating a secret bar of chocolate which he thrust hastily out of sight when he heard the front door and Mary's high, excited voice but he needn't have bothered because her footsteps echoed by Christine's clattered immediately up the stairs and he knew without having to ask that they had been successful and he thought, both in the future and at the time that this, watching tennis on a hot summer's afternoon and hearing his fiancée happily come home, was a perfect day.

Long afterwards they could only remember two things about the wedding itself. "Cross words?" Tom would ask anybody who would listen. "We didn't have any. Well, almost, at the wedding." Mary would sigh and roll her eyes, although secretly she loved being part of the same sort of double act that her parents had subjected her to so many times. "Vanity thy name is Mary didn't want to wear her glasses so when we came to sing the hymns—"

"I thought I knew them by heart, but my brain had turned to—"

"—mush," supplied Tom. "I was supposed to sing so she could follow the words, only she elbowed me, right there in the nave—" he would laugh at his own joke, and Mary would say "—and he *stopped singing*. I ask you."

"How was I to know?" he complained.

"He wasn't singing loudly enough," Mary complained. "He sings like a tone-deaf sparrow."

And the other thing that they never forgot was how odd it was to have all their friends and relatives from different compartments of their lives all appear on the same day; to have friends from school meet for the first time friends from work; to have Mary's relatives cheek by jowl with Tom's; to see Mary's sisters Josephine and Catherine mind-bogglingly meet with the schoolteachers Jo and Catherine; to see their past represented by so many familiar faces, intermingling into a new tapestry that would be identified in the times to come not by *me* and *I* but by *we* and *us*.

Outside the sun set without fuss, clouds loomed from the west, and the bright-lit colourful noisy cheerful church hall was a bubble against encroaching darkness, against encroaching time. The genie waited for them in the sports car, aware of the moment that they slipped away—their coats on, their parents' goodbye, a hasty walk across the dark space beyond the church hall doors and Tom slipped into the car, into himself waiting patiently as Mary sat beside him, then both turning as the church door opened again spilling out bright light and noisy, laughing, waving guests. Tom always remembered the feel of the wheel beneath his hands, Christine stumbling but helped to her feet by an unrecognised in-law, the gate posts flashing white as the headlights passed over them and the blessed silence as they drove away, Mary's hand reaching out to press against his own.

They drove towards towering clouds. They got as far as Salisbury Plain before the storm broke, loosing a wind-lashed deluge. Lightning smashed dizzily around them. Tom remembered, as he wrestled the car through howling, horizontal rain, coming back home late, once, on the train—coming back to their new flat—and outside the station there was no light, just roaring rain and as he made a dash for it lightning forked and thundered, turning the whole world inside out in a terrific flash of negative-white. Then, he was drenched in an instant, blind and dizzy; now, he saw the headlights cutting through the cloudburst, showing the slick winding road and water rushing, flooding, on either side. He drove slowly while the windscreen wipers swept frantically at double speed, edged through the flashing, virulent, crashing storm until it diminished to mere heavy rain, and they came at last to the hotel. Then, from the moment they went into the ancient wood-panelled room and Mary came into the circle of his arms and they took off their dripping clothes, until the moment they woke entwined to puzzle over the slanting light cord, everything was perfect.

Next morning, they discovered that all the cars but Tom's had gone, and Tom had incurred his first parking ticket. Afterwards they couldn't remember if they laughed or cried. They held hands, and walked around the Cathedral. They made love, and dozed, and ate, and went to bed. For most of the week they shut out the external world, and concentrated on knitting themselves ever closer together. In those few delicious days he and Mary—inevitably, it seemed—became one.

–Come and look at this, Mary called. She was watching the news. A reporter, dressed in casual slacks and without a tie, stood in bright sunshine outside the Houses of Parliament. A black car was waved through security in the background. The reporter, an earnest dark-haired young man with a vaguely Irish accent, had to raise his voice over the sounds of traffic and Tom wondered, as he always did, if it was strictly necessary to have someone on location. Politics could be reported just as well from the newsroom, couldn't it? –As expected, there is no place for Caitlin Jamison. She cites family reasons for standing down but sources believe the Prime Minister feels that it would be difficult for her to continue while her sister is due in court next month, charged with fraud and attempting to pervert the course of justice.

–I suppose that's family reasons of a sort, said Tom.

–Looks like you'll get your day in court.

Tom stared at her, aghast.

–You'll be fine, she said.

Back in the office, Tom found himself mildly surprised that nothing appeared to have changed. His outlook on life had been turned completely upside down. His *life* had been turned completely upside down. How could the dragon Margaret sit at her desk as if nothing had changed? How could David Pickles stick his head out of his office and bark instructions as if circumstances were the same as a year ago? It made no sense.

On his first day back the door banged open in the middle of the morning. –Ah hello young-feller-me-Tom we have an appointment with the delectable Julia Carswell Wednesday at nine write it down.

–Morning, George.

–All went well wedding and so forth?

Tom acknowledged that, yes, all went well. He thanked George for his card.

–Good good. See you on Wednesday don't forget your report.

George turned to leave. Margaret sighed and held out her hand. George turned back again, fishing his travel claim out of a cavernous pocket, and beamed at her. –Priceless woman, he told her, then winked broadly at Tom as he swept out.

–So some things don't change, then.

–What? said Margaret.

Something that had changed was that he had moved with Mary out of Peter's madhouse into a small brightly painted flat in Catford. The previous owners had been West Indians who, it seemed, had liked to decorate everything garish yellow, virulent orange or glaring red, careless that the various shades didn't exactly blend together into a harmonious whole. It was an upstairs flat situated at the top of a hill and, because it was the first place they lived together, Tom and Mary loved it.

The head of legal services, Julia Carswell, really was delectable. She was in her early thirties and wore her thick, dark hair in a bob and her trim figure in a light grey suit. Her eyes were green, her features attractively regular, and when she smiled she somehow did it with her whole face and not just her cherry-red lips.

–I'd marry her in an instant, Tom told Mary. –Except she's scary.

She systematically went through Tom and George's reports, asking awkward questions and probing for weaknesses. George was unusually subdued. Tom found out later that he once tried to chat up Julia Carswell at a Christmas party before discovering that she wasn't actually at the party—she had gate-crashed it to ask a Director a technical legal question that had been bothering her.

"Did Richard Jefferson seem distressed when you sent away the tea?"

"Um," said George. He raised his eyebrows at Tom.

"Don't look at him," said Julia Carswell. "He won't be there. But you can be sure that he'll be asked the same question."

"Did you see Richard Jefferson obtain the final invoice from Catherine Copeland?"

"Did you check that it was Catherine Copeland's signature on the invoices?"

"Did you retain the original invoices?"

"Did you check that it was Catherine Copeland's signature on the cashed cheques?"

"Did you retain the cashed cheques?"

"Yes," grunted George triumphantly.

"One out of five isn't good, George."

"GIA did a lot of the legwork afterwards why ask us this stuff?"

"Because if they can discredit you, George, they discredit the case before it even gets under way. Are you getting this? Do you understand what I'm driving at, Mr Bradley?"

–Her eyes looked right through me, Tom told Mary, shivering theatrically.

–You just fancy her, pouted Mary. –Is the date set?

–What, with…

–Don't say it.

They were in the freshly decorated flat at the time, washing up after something that resembled spaghetti Bolognese, and Tom grabbed Mary to show her just who he fancied, and it wasn't Julia Carswell. In the event, the trial was put off, and put off again. Catherine Copeland claimed that she was too ill to stand trial, and her lawyers claimed that they had not had sight of all the alleged evidence against her. Tom shivered again when he realised that the alleged evidence included his own report. The story appeared in the news for a few weeks, and then dropped away and was forgotten.

–Is it ever going to happen? Tom asked David Pickles.

–Oh, it'll happen, said David Pickles. –But tangled webs. You'll see.

Tom brooded about this. David Pickles' tone of voice hinted that he knew more than he was telling, and that it was not all good. He tried to tell Mary about it, but discovered that Mary was brooding too.

–You remember Jennifer Huntley? she asked. How could he forget Jennifer Huntley, possibly the most attractive girl he had ever met—except for Mary, he acknowledged mentally and a little guiltily. –She's very ill, said Mary. An icy chill made Tom shiver; a vague, half-formed premonition. He grasped Mary's hand, resting on his chest as they lay curled together in darkness. –Anne found out the other day. Apparently… apparently… they might not have caught it in time, whispered Mary.

Anne frequently visited them, usually accompanied by her boyfriend Gregory Danvers, a six-foot rugby player and almost-qualified barrister who made Tom feel totally inadequate. Anne was one of the most selfish people Tom had ever met, but she was so totally unselfconscious about it that he could not help liking her anyway. She never did anything to deliberately hurt or upset anyone else, and would probably have been surprised if anyone told her that they had been. She suffered from severe asthma and Tom once had to drive her to the hospital because she had lost her inhaler, and the doctor on duty told her that if she did that again, she risked losing her life. Anne dismissed this as scaremongering, and promptly left her replacement inhaler at the hospital, and Tom had to drive back to fetch it.

–She's going downhill, Anne told them one night over something resembling chicken curry.

–You not eating won't help her, rumbled Gregory Danvers, who had put away as much curry as Mary and Tom combined. –It's good, Mary. Come on, pet, you've got to keep your strength up.

–I made it, remarked Tom. The scene with Jan in Peter's old house jumped into his mind.

–Come on, pet. Gregory Danvers spooned up a morsel of curry and held it encouragingly in front of Anne's mouth. He was so big and Anne was so small that he looked like a concerned father trying to get an errant child to eat. Tom half expected him to say *here comes the train, where's the tunnel?*

–It *is* good, admitted Anne, reluctantly chewing on the morsel.

–Is she still in hospital? asked Mary, whereupon Anne stopped chewing and Gregory Danvers glared at Mary disapprovingly.

Later, Mary warned Tom never to call her pet.

–Of course not, darling.

And then, when the ensuing fight had resulted in mutual exhaustion: –I wonder how they communicate—you know—in bed. Her face would only come up to his middle.

–There may be some advantages to that, said Mary gravely, and although neither of them quite knew what she meant, it struck them both as being so funny that they went into paroxysms of giggles.

In the event, and apparently to the surprise of the doctors at the hospital, Jennifer Huntley began to recover. A few months later Tom met her outside Audit House, although he did not immediately recognise her. She was smaller, thinner; her eyes looked permanently sunken, and her face permanently bruised; her long lustrous hair had been cropped and was only now beginning to grow back. Tom felt guilty that he no longer lusted after her. He wondered what it was about women, that they always made him feel guilty, even by becoming ill and getting better again. At least it meant he could talk to Jennifer without spouting nonsense and without his face growing scarlet. In a slightly hoarse voice that he had to strain to hear she congratulated him on getting married. He told her that she was looking much better and when she looked querulous because the last time they had met had been months before when she looked in the prime of female life, he explained that Anne had been giving them regular bulletins so they had been aware of how ill she had been. "Ah, Anne," Jennifer said and her face split into a weary smile that momentarily reflected her former beauty. "Will she ever forgive me?" At the time Tom had no idea what she meant by this cryptic remark, but he found out later when Anne complained that she had been telling everyone how ill Jennifer was, how unlikely it was that she was going to recover, and now here she was gallivanting around looking almost as good as new and didn't that make her, Anne, look such a fool.

–Anyway, said Anne, once she had nibbled enough curry to satisfy Gregory Danvers. –What about your Director then? She was looking at Tom as she said this.

–What, Ken? said Tom.

Anne looked surprised. –You call your Director Ken?

–It's is name innit? said Mary in a passable imitation of Peter's voice.

–What? Anne couldn't understand why they were falling about with laughter. –Include me in.

–Sorry. Sorry. He asked me to call him Ken, gasped Tom. –What about him?

–Well, he's resigned, hasn't he?

–Has he?

–The talk is, did he jump or was he pushed?

Tom suddenly didn't feel like laughing any more. His mind flashed back to that curious tableau in Audit House, the long moments dragging by as Ken looked out of the window and George and David Pickles and Popplewell sat silently around the big oval table thinking thoughts that at the time he, Tom, would not have understood. Now he understood. It occurred to him that he still didn't know Ken's surname and he had forgotten Popplewell's first name.

–Tom?

Anne and Mary were looking at him.

–Archibald Urquhart, he said.

–What? said Anne. –Include me in.

–He was pushed, said Tom. –Probably.

–You might not get your day in court after all, said Mary.

Rather to his own surprise, Tom hoped that he would. He rather hoped he would be able to help bang the nails in Catherine Copeland's figurative coffin. Absently he heard Mary telling Anne about Archibald Urquhart and his cold assessment of damage limitation. For the first time in what seemed like a long while, he thought about young Dick and his poignant epigraph. *Except for the tea money.* He thought about Julia Carswell, and Ken, and Archibald Urquhart and reflected that probably none of them ever gave young Dick a passing thought. And despite all the work focusing on Catherine Copeland and her manipulation of the accounts, even he had almost forgotten about Richard Jefferson and his bottle and a half of sleeping tablets.

> We come in
> Free of sin.
>
> We go out
> Full of doubt.
>
> In between
> We mark our slate
> And try, too late
> To wipe it clean.

"Oh, Tom," said Mary when she read it. "This is *good*."

Tom made a mental note to send the poem off somewhere, but he never did because examinations rose up and rolled over them like an academic tidal wave, and he forgot all about it. The exam results were supposed to come out before Christmas, but Christmas passed with no word. Mary went to lunch with Melanie Smith one day to seek out information. Melanie Smith was the Training Officer for the Department, who happened to be mutual friends with someone Mary knew at university.

"Catch her away from the office and she's very nice," Mary said.

"I'm sure," said Tom dubiously. The first time he had met Melanie Smith had been at a meeting of all the new students when she had made it clear—abso*lutely* clear—that anyone who failed their first foundation exams would be out. "O. U. T," spelled Melanie Smith, in case anyone had failed to understand what a fragile thread supported their existence in the Department. "In our experience, twenty per cent of intake fail at this stage. And so they are out. O. U. T. Out." Her gimlet gaze swept over the assembled, petrified students as if by arcane means she had already assessed the entire group and identified the unfortunate twenty per cent who were going to find themselves O.U.T. on the street.

–Really, insisted Mary. –She lets her hair down at a party. Tom tried to remember whether Melanie Smith had any hair.

–She treated me to lunch, Mary said as further evidence of Melanie Smith's humanitarian nature. –She knew fine well what I wanted, of course. She mentioned you.

Tom stared at her. He tried to imagine any circumstance in which he would like to be mentioned by monster Melanie, and could think of none. Perhaps he was on her list of people who had failed. Even if he had escaped that list, no doubt he topped another list of people who were bound to fail in the future. Almost certainly he had been marked down in Melanie Smith's black book full of the names of people who irritated the hell out of Melanie Smith and whose careers she would subsequently blight by secret subversive manipulation of their training records.

–She plays bridge, remarked Mary. –She mentioned that if you manage to get to the end of the course and qualify, you ought to join the Department's club.

Tom had known that there was a Department bridge club, of course, but never in his wildest dreams had he imagined that monster Melanie might be a member of it. He continued to stare at Mary.

–She said, acknowledged Mary, –that she wasn't allowed to tell us. She said she wasn't allowed to tell us we were on the pass list.

It took a moment for Tom to realise what Mary had said. Then he pretended that this was no more than he had expected all along. –Bridge club? Melanie Smith in the bridge club? I pity anyone who passes one of *her* forcing raises.

They had spent Christmas in Derry with Mary's parents, unaware that this would be their last visit to Ireland. Later that year Evelyn fell ill and Graham decided to move to Scotland to be closer to Evelyn's family, which consisted of an elderly aunt, a sister, and a bevy of nieces and nephews. Tom later remembered unexpected Christmas stockings; congregating in Evelyn and Graham's bedroom, surrounded by Mary and her two unmarried sisters Josephine and Catherine; thinking that not so long ago he had been terrified of even talking to a woman and now here he was, in his pyjamas, surrounded by three of them in theirs. Cardigan the cat leaped for his lap, misjudged the distance and slid down his legs with claws fully deployed. "We call him Cardigan," Josephine had explained earlier, "because he isn't a jumper." She said that many was the time the entire family had gathered beneath a bedroom window, where Cardigan was contemplating a leap to the next window, or to a neighbouring tree, shouting, "Don't do it, Cardy! Use the stairs!" "He always misjudges," Josephine told Tom. "Under or over. One of these days he's going to do himself a nasty injury." Tom remembered this as the sisters rushed about on Christmas morning, fetching warm water and bandages. "I thought you said he was going to do *himself* an injury," he complained. "He will," said Josephine. "You all right, Mary?" Mary had her hands clasped over her mouth and was shaking in a curious fashion. Catherine rushed off to make her a cup of hot, sweet tea and later Tom further complained that nobody thought to make him one.

Also later that year director Ken quietly finished working his notice and left the Department. He left with very little fanfare on a Friday and by a curious coincidence the trial of Catherine Copeland commenced on the following Monday. Tom sat for two days in the waiting room reading a battered copy of *Papillon* that a previous witness must have left behind, perhaps as a dire warning at the length of time trials could take. Then the trial was adjourned for three months because of a technicality to do with the inquest of young Dick Jefferson.

–You'd think, said Tom, –that the various long arms of the law would know what they were doing. Doesn't one arm know what the other arm is doing?

Mary didn't respond immediately. She had been rather quiet all evening. They had eaten something that resembled lasagne, cleared up, and were sitting side by side, with a crossword. Tom put his arm around Mary's shoulders. –What's up?

–I didn't want to tell you before.

That cold, half-formed premonition swept over Tom again. The muscles of his stomach clenched.

–The case is really delayed? asked Mary.

–Yes. What is it? What's the matter?

–I'm pregnant.

Their eyes connected. The crossword fell, forgotten, to the floor. He had never been able to hide his feelings from her, and now she saw a lack of understanding march across his face, followed first by dawning comprehension and shock, and then by undisguised happiness. A barely acknowledged apprehension of her own, that he would not be happy and would not see the impending arrival of a new baby in the same way as she did, slipped into oblivion as if ashamed that it had ever existed.

If they had listened closely perhaps they would have heard Tom the genie drift up the outside steps to the flat and pass through the front door which was newly painted a chocolate brown but which glinted orange in reflected streetlight. Outside in the dark hall the genie would hesitate. It had not, after all, been there for many years. But it would feel its way through ragged memories, past the darker blot which represented coats and scarves hanging silently on the wall, past the bedroom to the corner of the hall leading into the combined sitting room and dining room. There a low light threw shadows onto the ceiling and turned a set of porcelain horses into a stampede across a distant wall. The genie remembered that in the future, Tom bought Mary a porcelain horse every anniversary. Now they sat close together, wreathed in both darkness and light. Unseen and unheard, the genie would cross over to them, would slide into the memories of Tom as they became imprinted on time, and rekindle that moment when he lifted a hand to her cheek glistening with unashamed tears.

Their first son was born in Edinburgh, where they transferred to be closer to Evelyn and Graham—although, curiously, Evelyn seemed to pick up and feel much better once they had moved away from Derry. Tom always thought that not only curious but also exceedingly suspicious.

–She only wanted to move to get your dad away from Derry, he surmised.

–To get him to retire. Mary nodded and shook her head, and Tom eventually realised with chagrin that everyone else lready knew this, even Graham.

In Edinburgh Tom's new boss was Bob, who had flaming red hair, equivalent temper, spoke in a broad Scottish accent and insisted that he was Scottish despite his wife secretly telling Mary that he was actually born in Sidcup. Bob told Tom that if he was going to live in Scotland he would have to learn how to play golf, and Tom responded that he already knew. "Aye?" roared Sidcup Bob doubtfully in his mock Scottish accent that sounded more real than the real thing. "Then ye'll be wanting a game then, no? Bring your clubs in Wednesday afternoon and don't be telling me you can't make it, as I'm your boss."

Tom had spent the previous nine months fussing over Mary despite her telling him that she was absolutely fine and didn't need fussing over, except possibly on the occasion she slipped over and landed on her bottom in an icy car park. Tom *didn't* fuss over her when that happened. He laughed until tears crept out of the corners of his eyes and froze half way down his face. "You *bounced*," he told her. "You were like one of those toys you push over and they always come back upright." He saw her serious face and tried to compose himself. "Seriously," he said, as seriously as he could, "by the time I realised you were down there, you were back up again. Boingg, and there you were. Are. You know what I mean."

The day after their son John was born, he went shopping for supplies, trudging up to the top of their hill to the main road where a small group of shops clustered together as if for mutual protection so far from the centre of the city. Just beyond the shops was the doctor's surgery, and beyond that a combined infant's school and nursery. The main road turned right after that, but Tom knew that it passed a straggly string of houses before pushing on into countryside dominated by patchwork fields and grim, dark, obstinate evergreen woods.

–Two pounds of sausages, he told the butcher. –And another two pounds of mince. And...

–Here, the butcher interrupted. –This isn't your weekly order, is it?

–Yes, Tom told him.

–Because if it is, I wish you would place your order on Friday, otherwise... Well. You can see the queue.

Tom's blood boiled.

–Normally I would be only too pleased, he said icily. –Only as it happens, yesterday, Friday, as it happens I was in the hospital, I was up until five in the morning, as my son was being born.

What Tom didn't tell him was that, Friday morning, all the windows of their house were removed to make way for double glazing and all the workmen were tiptoeing about whispering *don't make a noise, don't make her jump, Christ, is she really due?* Tom told them yes, as they wrapped up warm because not only were the windows out, but two inches of snow lay over the Edinburgh roads.

Tom didn't tell him that when the time came, and the workmen started whispering *you made a noise, didn't you? Who did then?* he and Mary discovered they were not as ready as they thought, and the car refused to start and he had to ring for a taxi, which came slip-sliding down the hill as soon as it could when he told the operator why they needed one in a hurry.

Tom didn't tell him that they supported each other into the hospital, and Tom excitedly told the nurses that the time was *now*, and they took one look at Mary and boredly said, no, it obviously wasn't quite yet, and sauntered into a cubicle with her, only to come rushing out two minutes later shouting *bed! we need a bed!* and, as it turned out, they needed a chair as well because Tom became wobbly and faint, whereas Mary stayed calm and *breathed* and *pushed*, and produced John at five in the morning, the only time to Tom's future knowledge that he was ever up early.

–What? said the butcher, confused. –When? Last night? He offered Tom his meaty hand across the counter and the queue of customers burst into spontaneous applause.

What Tom didn't tell him was that on another night another storm rode the black skies, bellowing peals of thunder, strafing the cowering world with bolts of lightning, drowning it with torrents of sizzling rain. Their window burst open while they wrestled and groped and Mary rode him amidst sweat-slicked sheets; the curtains flapped wildly; a vase toppled from the sill, smashing unheard as the storm growled about the room and blood thundered in their ears, and Mary shrieked and arched, silhouetted against lightning flares, her long hair draping her shoulders, and Tom gasped and shuddered, almost passing out. Then, quickly and goosepimpled, he dashed to close window and curtain against the frigid wind, finding a long edge of bedclothes soaked by rain, while Mary snickered and asked *was anybody watching?* and *could anybody see?* as he leaned naked into the night.

Tom was certain that was the night that John was conceived, and entertained the notion that the storm was the same one that had unleashed its fury on them on their way to their honeymoon in Salisbury. "It went away for a while, and came back," he told Mary. "It's our storm."

–So, said Beryl when she and Ralph visited one wintry February, –what's it *like*, being married?

–Great, Tom said. –We do a lot of—

–Careful, warned Beryl.

–Housework, said Mary. –We do a lot of housework. And shopping.

–Ah, said Beryl thoughtfully. –And what's it like, being a *dad*?

–Well, Tom said. –Um, we don't do as much—

–Careful, warned Beryl.

–Going out as we used to, said Mary. –We don't go out as much as we used to.

–You didn't go out much anyway, accused Beryl.

–Well, Tom said, –um, now we go out even less. He thought for a moment. –We go out a negative amount now.

Beryl grimaced. –That's too *mathematical* for me. Why do you always go all mathematical when you talk to me?

–Okay. We have, um—

–no social life, said Mary.

–You've got *me*, said Beryl. –I'm here, aren't I? And *Ralph*, wherever he is.

Tom and Mary didn't reply.

Beryl said, –Are you making a point here? Never mind. She turned to Mary. –And you've given up working?

–Yes, Tom said.

–No, Mary said.

Tom clapped a hand to his forehead.

–I've given up going into the office, said Mary. –I don't think it would be right to say I've given up working. She glanced over to the corner where number one son was, blessedly and momentarily, sleeping.

–Quite right. Not, Tom muttered.

`Beryl looked politely from Mary to Tom and back again.

–He sleeps seven hours in twenty-four, explained Mary.

–Not always at night, Tom pointed out, –as you can see.

–It's a nightmare, said Mary. –A *waking* nightmare, she added, pleased with this clever turn of phrase.

–Do you *sing* to him? asked Beryl.

–All the time, said Mary.

–And?

–Pink Floyd puts him to sleep, Tom told her.

–Pink Floyd puts anyone to sleep, said Beryl.

Ralph shouldered in, having been smoking outside in the sub-zero back garden. His face, what could be seen of it beneath his black beard, looked red and chilled. He was rubbing his hands together and stamping his feet.

–So what's new? he said. –What's it like, being married?

–It's a waking nightmare, said Mary.

The door behind Ralph swung shut with a noisy thud which woke up number one son, who immediately started crying lustily for whatever it was he wanted.

Tom never forgot the times when, in the middle of the night, he would have to strap John into his pushchair and struggle around the narrow pavements with him. Eventually John would fall asleep, but he would be wide awake by then and have to sit downstairs for a while, drinking hot chocolate and working on his first children's book. By the time he became sleepy, John would wake up again and Tom would cradle him in his arms and pace round and round the living room to the muted strains of *Wish You Were Here* and *The Dark Side of the Moon.*

–What happened in court? asked Ralph.

–I got to finish *Papillon*, said Tom, remembering the long slow hours closeted in a waiting room while the legal people did whatever they did, and his surprise at discovering *Papillon* still sitting on a windowsill, looking much the same as it had a year or so earlier, if a little more well-thumbed.

Beryl and Ralph exchanged a glance with Mary and made little circular motions with their hands to indicate that Tom had clearly been driven mad by his experiences in court.

–Were you *cross-examined*? asked Beryl gently.

Tom admitted that he had been, but that it hadn't turned out quite as he had expected. Julia Carswell had led him through their carefully rehearsed script, detailing what happened in Milton Keynes. They had been through it so many times that Tom trotted out his answers without having to think. "And what did Richard Jefferson say when he brought in the missing invoice?" "He said he'd found it at last." Tom found that he had time to think about the audit, time to remember little irrelevant details: the drooping pot plants, the dreary weather, the perpetually surprised look on young Dick's face caused by the magnifying effect of his glasses. He found he had time to look around the court; at Julia Carswell standing in front of him, still looking delectable despite being severely dressed; at Catherine Copeland sitting in a chair beside a portly man who resembled Graham. With a shock Tom realised that this was

Catherine Copeland's lawyer, and he would be spitting Tom on the points of his razor-sharp cross-questioning any minute now. There were surprisingly few people dotted around the court, given that the very existence of the case had cost a senior Member of Parliament her job. Two press journalists sat in one corner pretending to take notes, but even Tom could see they were doodling.

"And when did you join the—ah—Exchequer and Audit Department?" inquired the portly man.

After a brief calculation, Tom told him.

"So this was—ah—three weeks before going on the audit to Milton Keynes?"

Tom agreed that it was.

"And you were previously employed in a—ah—in a jobcentre, am I right?"

Tom said that he was.

"So not actually connected with—ah—audit or indeed with—ah—accounting in any way? Would that be fair comment?"

Tom could see where the portly man was heading now.

"In short, you had no experience and no training," remarked the portly man. "We are basing this entire case—ah—this entire case," he emphasised, "on the words of a young man with no experience and no training."

Tom opened his mouth, but Julia Carswell gave her head a brief, almost imperceptible shake, so he closed it again. He discovered afterwards that she had made the point that George had been in charge of the audit, and that he had sought the views of his senior management, and that most of the actual evidence had been obtained by vastly experienced Government Internal Auditors. "Did I blow it?" Tom asked her before the verdict. "You did very well," Julia Carswell assured him. "They were clutching at straws. I told them that facts were facts, no matter who discovered them." Tom also later found out that George had lost his temper with the portly barrister and had been told by the judge to calm down. That explained why Julia Carswell's attractive face had creased in a faint frown, and her green eyes had taken on a slightly vacant look, and Tom realised afterwards that she was trying to calculate if *George* had blown it. George had left the Department not long after the Copeland case.

–Well, she got her comeuppance, said Beryl. –How many years was it?

–Three, said Tom. –D'you think George went because of… Oh, this is John.

Mary approached carrying John, who peered at Beryl and Ralph and then buried his face in Mary's shoulder.

–No, said Ralph.

–Do you think I don't know my own son?

–He left because a cousin invited him out to join his business. San Francisco. New York. Somewhere like that.

–Geography *not* Ralph's strong point, interposed Beryl.

–Popplewell left too, remarked Ralph. –Went to India for a holiday and came back with a horrible disease.

Tom remembered again sitting at the table in Audit House while Ken, with his back to them, looked out of the window and thought about the step he was about to take. Now he had resigned, George had left, and Popplewell was struck down by illness. He could not help but notice the similarity between the meeting at Audit House and Howard Carter forcing open the entrance to Tutankhamen's tomb.

–Is David Pickles all right?

Ralph raised an eyebrow and said yes, as far as he knew. –How're you getting on with Sidcup Bob? he inquired.

Tom said he was getting on fine.

–You just wait, said Ralph darkly.

–Don't wind him up, said Beryl.

–One day he'll have you by the throat, predicted Ralph. –Like this, up against a wall. Or throw a book at you. Or tear up your file and…

Ranting, Ralph sought out the kitchen.

–They're best mates, explained Beryl. –Bob has got a temper, mind. She tickled John to the accompaniment of tiny screams, poked Mary in her swollen stomach and asked when the next Bradley was due to appear.

When John was four, he came downstairs one morning, his hair sticking out in all directions and declared "I have had a helluva night," and couldn't understand Tom and Mary's subsequent hilarity. Adam, who by this time was almost two, laughed along with them, spraying baby food over a wide area. Tom remembered looking down at him on the night he was born, a tiny, bawling, wrinkled, red-skinned bundle. "He looks just like you," one of the nurses said affectionately and, Tom fervently hoped, dishonestly. The next day Tom went out shopping.

–Two pounds of sausages, he told the butcher. –And two pounds of mince. And a chicken.

–Here, this isn't your weekly shopping, is it? Because if it is—

–It is.

The butcher peered at him suspiciously. –It's you, isn't it?

–Have you got chipolatas? asked Tom.

–You've had another one, haven't you?

–I have, said Tom proudly. –Last night, midnight, another boy, I've got two now, he added, in case the butcher had trouble remembering. He didn't go into details. He didn't explain that he and Mary had been lying curled up in bed, both pretending to sleep, both listening anxiously for any sound coming from John's room. He didn't explain that they weren't used to John being quietly asleep and that for two years they had lain awake every night, wishing that he would go to sleep and not spend half the night calling out for them, or demanding to be pushed around the block in his pushchair or—worse—be driven around Edinburgh with Pink Floyd playing on the car's cassette player. "What's he doing? Why's he so quiet?" wondered Tom. He felt Mary shift uncomfortably.

"Tom?"

"What is it?"

"Could you… aahhh, fetch a towel," said Mary pragmatically, "and then see about getting me to—aahhhh—hospital." And, standing on the sanded floor of the butcher's shop, Tom didn't describe how on cue John woke up and started shouting and he leaped out of bed and danced about on the spot, uncertain what to do. "Towel," reminded Mary. "Yaaaarghhhh," reminded John. Tom fetched the towel, stuffed John into an outsize baby suit, grabbed Mary's overnight bag and made a dash for the car. Mary followed slowly, hobbling, swathed in several layers of dressing gowns and one of Tom's coats. "I must look like an elephant," she mumbled. "You look beautiful," Tom told her, and leaned across to the passenger seat to kiss her. He remembered a night long ago when he did exactly the same thing, under the bright stars, Mary swaddled up and almost as huge. He could tell from the look in her eyes that she was remembering the same thing. "I wonder if the seatbelt will reach right round…" he muttered and grinned as she swatted at him in the darkness.

The butcher offered his congratulations, the queue of customers murmured theirs, and Tom went home unable to stop yawning one second and grinning hugely the next.

When Adam was four, he looked especially puzzled one evening when Tom was reading out the night-time story. "What is it?" asked Tom. "Do hobbits have tails?" asked Adam. It was Tom's turn to look puzzled. Mary plastered her hands over her mouth and rocked silently in place, overcome with mirth. "Dragons have tails," John informed them. "Dragons can join my club." "Don't start that," warned Tom. Two evenings before, Adam had wailed inconsolably because John had made up an imaginary club and had not allowed Adam to join it. The fact that the club did not exist and there were no members of it didn't seem to matter. He wailed for over an hour, finally hiccupping himself to sleep, and now Tom glared at John before turning his attention back to the story. "Gandalf looked at Bilbo as if he suspected there was part of the tale he had left out," read Tom. Understanding dawned. "Tale, Adam, not tail." He laughed, Mary's giggles finally escaped, and young Lucy—who was just two—joined in, spraying baby-milk over everyone. John and Adam laughed too, their differences forgotten, and their puppy Gus danced around the entire group, barking happily.

Tom the genie, uneasily aware that time was passing quickly now, slipped through the front door and drifted up the stairs. He passed Lucy's room which Tom would later decorate with dozens of leftover scraps of children's wallpaper, an artistic effort which became widely admired by other parents, and hesitated at the door at the end of the corridor where homely yellow light spilled out into the darkness. Was it safe to go in? They were all laughing—it was a scene the genie engraved in Tom's memory—his entire family doubled up with laughter, Mary clutching hard at young Lucy who was herself giggling at the top of her tiny voice even though she had no idea of what was going on; John and Adam laughing helplessly, tears streaming down their cheeks; Gus bouncing, barking, wagging. Could he go in and join them, or would the puppy see the future ghost? Would his barks turn to growls, his fur bristle? Would the laughter dry up as Gus jumped forward and snapped at an invisible presence? This was what the genie feared, for there was so little laughter still to come.

He moved, unseen, undetected. He became Tom, doubled over in the bedside chair, laughing so hard that his stomach ached and his eyes watered, laughing so hard not just because Adam had exposed a fatal flaw in Tolkien's deft prose, but because they were all laughing. He had never been so happy in all his life.

When Lucy was born, he had been glad to see that she was a normal pink colour and her skin more or less fitted her body. She lay quietly in his arms, looking peacefully up at him.

"Isn't she beautiful?" remarked one of the nurses. "She looks just like your wife."

"Do you think so?" Tom asked resentfully.

That was Wednesday. At the weekend he wrapped Lucy in several layers of clothing, tucked her into her carrycot, and went out. Mary waited for them at home, feeling unaccountably anxious.

–This is the world, Tom told Lucy. –That's the sky up there, you won't often see that bright blue colour, so remember it well.

Lucy gurgled up at him. Tom was sure he had read somewhere that babies saw upside down to begin with. Did it look to Lucy as if he was standing on tiptoe, peering over the edge of her carrycot, instead of looming above it? His brain began to swim as he tried to imagine it.

Lucy waved tiny, clenched fists. A bus rumbled past. Tom hefted the carrycot from one hand to the other, wondering what it was about babies and children that they always gained weight whenever they were being carried.

The door to the butchers was propped open. Machinery hummed inside, keeping the produce cool, and one of the junior members of staff was using another, silvery machine to slice ham. Posters advertised Scottish Beef, Home-Made Haggis and various Money-Saving Packs. Tom joined a small queue and felt rather than heard somebody come in to stand behind him. Lucy had gone to sleep. Back at the house Mary lay down on the sofa and dozed, more tired than she remembered being after the births of John and Adam.

–Not quite enough, dear, said the butcher to an old lady at the front of the queue. She held out a shaking hand, and he picked out some change, his stubby fingers surprisingly delicate. The till rang. Other people came into the shop behind Tom.

–Let Mummy rest, Mary told the boys. –Daddy will be home in a minute. She closed her eyes and dreamed that Tom was looking down at her, a dark silhouette against a star-filled sky. No, he wasn't there. A falling star streaked across the heavens, growing smaller, diminishing with distance and she suddenly was convinced that it was Tom falling away, disappearing. She awoke with a start, heart pounding uncomfortably.

–Two pounds of sausages, began Tom.

–Wait a minute, interrupted the butcher. –Don't tell me. Two pounds of mince and a chicken.

–Any chipolatas? inquired Tom.

The butcher came around the counter, wiping his hands on his apron. –This is the new one, is it?

–This is Lucy, said Tom proudly. The butcher, two assistants and all the other customers gathered round. Lucy slept on peacefully, despite what sounded like an empty lorry rumbling and bouncing past outside. A woman wearing a red bonnet suddenly said –It was you with them boys, weren't it?

Tom acknowledged that it was.

–I was in here *both times*, she said impressively.

Afterwards, Tom complained to Mary that the other customers congratulated the old woman more fulsomely than they congratulated him. Mary nodded and smiled and clutched tightly at his arm. She couldn't say why she was so glad to see him striding back up the path, the carrycot swinging gently from his hand. She couldn't explain why she was standing anxiously at the door, opening it the moment his blurred shape darkened the frosted glass. Perhaps she was just naturally anxious to see new-born Lucy back home safely, but she didn't think so. It was Tom she was so glad to see, but she couldn't explain why she was so anxious, so she didn't say anything about it at all. She clutched at his arm and laughed a little weakly as he described

Lucy's first adventure in the outside world. If Tom noticed anything odd about her behaviour he put it down to the strain of producing Lucy, and made no mention of it.

When Lucy was old enough, he asked if she could remember anything about that day. Lucy shook her head, and Tom asked, "But you remember about the time in the car, don't you? Even though you were only three?" Lucy assured Tom that she remembered that, although of course at the time she hadn't really understood why Tom had nearly swerved off the road. They had been going home, just the two of them, after Tom had picked her up from her best friend Lynne's house. He asked Lucy if she had had a good time, and they discussed in some detail the games that had been played and what exactly had been consumed for tea. After a while the conversation paused and then Lucy's voice piped up from where she was strapped in her child seat in the back, "It's nice that we can talk like this, isn't it, Daddy?" and Tom had burst into laughter and all but swerved up onto the pavement, coincidentally outside the church hall where he had taken to playing bridge with Bram Jacoby, another senior in the office. Bram had the sort of memory that Tom wished he had.

"He remembers everything," Tom told Mary. "He can even remember all the plots of all the Biggles books he's ever read."

"Very good," Mary had acknowledged. "But who would want to?"

After several months, Mary found that she still felt tired. Without telling Tom she made an appointment with the doctor and arranged for Molly—their go-to baby-sitter ever since John had been born—to come around. It was a particularly bright and sunny day when she walked up to the main road and turned past the little row of shops that included the butchers. The doctor's surgery sat back from the road, behind its own private car park. She knew it well, having taken both the boys there for various inoculations or when they developed infections or managed to damage themselves—especially Adam, who had already managed to fall through two glass doors and impale himself on a stray cocktail stick and, the doctor told her, was clearly going to need a season ticket for the accident and emergency unit at the hospital. But this was the first time she could remember going there because she felt unwell. She looked a little uneasily around the waiting room, as if its cool, dark interior was more inimical now that she was there for her own reasons.

She waited, flipping the pages of a magazine without taking any of it in. A woman in the corner bounced a toddler on her knee. *She* looked tired, Mary thought. She wondered whether it was the toddler or the mum who was poorly. Or both. She wondered if her own tiredness was just the result of having two—three—children to look after. A man hobbled in on crutches, one of his legs in plaster. –Don't worry, ladies, he said cheerfully. –I'm perfectly safe.

–Just sit down, Mr Dunleavey, called one of the receptionists. –And behave yourself.

–If I sits down, the man responded, –one of yez will have to help me back up agyin, so you will. Mary saw the receptionist roll her eyes as Mr Dunleavey lowered himself awkwardly into a chair at the end of a row. The red digital numbering system on the wall clicked. It was her turn. She replaced the magazine in a rack; found her way down a short corridor. Her heart was thudding painfully and she wished Tom was there. She wished she hadn't made this appointment without him knowing.

Dr Hunter was a pleasant woman of indeterminate age. Her pale hair was tied back in a severe ponytail and her eyes were a startling blue. She ushered Mary into the chair by the table.

–And how are you?

Mary was reminded that Tom always thought it was funny how doctors asked how you were. She wondered what Tom was doing. Probably having a cup of tea and either discussing golf with Bob, or dissecting bridge hands with Bram.

–Mrs Bradley?

She started. –I'm sorry. I'm not… I'm just feeling tired.

–You look pale, remarked Dr Hunter. –Let me check you out. How's Baby Lucy?

–Fine. She's fine.

–You're breastfeeding her?

–Yes.

–And the boys?

–Fine.

While they were talking Dr Hunter scribbled notes, took Mary's pulse, felt underneath her ears and chin. –I'd better listen to your chest, okay? Could you go behind the curtains and take off your blouse please?

Mary sat on the edge of the plastic sheet covering the little bed behind the curtains, unbuttoned her cardigan and slipped out of her blouse. She shivered, although it was not really cold inside the doctor's office. After a few moments Dr Hunter followed her into the cubicle.

–Breathe deeply, she instructed. Mary breathed. Dr Hunter listened. –And again. And again. Lie down.

Mary lay down. Dr Hunter poked and prodded. Her eyebrows rose fractionally.

–How long have you been feeling tired?

–Only since Lucy. Well, a bit before, but what with the boys and…

–Yes, yes.

–What is it? asked Mary.

–You seem to have a little lump here, said Dr Hunter.

The blood drained from Mary's face and she started to breathe unevenly. Dr Hunter smiled. –I don't think it's anything to worry about, okay? You can get dressed now.

Mary mechanically picked up her blouse. Dr Hunter brushed aside the curtains, sat down at her desk, scribbled more notes.

–But we'd better get it checked out. I'll make an appointment for you.

Mary fastened the buttons on her cardigan, picked up her coat. She moved over to the doctor's desk, found that her knees were wobbly.

–Sit down, said Dr Hunter. –The appointment will be up at the hospital, probably take a few weeks to come through. I shouldn't worry too much about it—easy for me to say, I know. They'll take a biopsy and then call you back for the results, probably another few weeks later. Okay?

–So you think…?

–Probably nothing, said Dr Hunter firmly. –We women get all sorts of lumps and bumps and most of them mean absolutely nothing. Okay?

She looked searchingly at Mary's pale face. Mary summoned up the ghost of a smile.

–Here.

–What is it?

–Prescription for a tonic. I think you're tired because you've got three children under the age of six, okay?

Mary took a deep breath and willed her knees to pull themselves together. Pull themselves together? What sort of a joke would Tom make out of that?

–I'll be fine, she said, more to herself than to Dr Hunter.

Outside she was surprised to discover that the sun was still shining and the sky was a deep, cloudless blue. Traffic still roared past; shrieking youngsters thronged the primary school playground; a plane glinted in sunlight as it lifted into that mapless blue, leaving behind a vapour trail that slowly dissipated and thinned until it vanished altogether. Mary stood for a long time outside the entrance to the surgery, thinking that none of it seemed real. She felt that she should be tucked up in bed with Tom, his arm around her shoulders, while she dreamed this nightmare masquerading as a dream. Then she took a step forward, and another, and felt warm air shift against her skin. It *was* real. She *had* been to see the doctor. She *was* going to get an appointment to go to the hospital in a few weeks' time.

She made her way slowly back, past the shops, around the corner, down the hill. With otherworldly eyes she would have been able to see Tom the genie sitting disconsolately on the roof of their house watching her close the garden gate with exaggerated care before walking, head down, towards the front door where she disappeared from view beneath the eaves. The genie looked around at the neighbourhood painted in sunlight. It reflected that the past it recorded was strewn with thunderstorms, downpours and grey damp days and wished with all its time-travelling heart that the weather had not changed. It sat there, the sun warm on its shoulders, remembering the telephone call.

"Tom? I'm not feeling so good. Could you come home early?"

"Yes, I—"

"Could you come home *now*, Tom?"

Refusing to slip into the memory, it saw in its mind's eye Tom gabbling excuses to Sidcup Bob, jumping into his car, wishing he still had his sports car but in any case ignoring speed limits to turn into the hilly street mere minutes later, tyres screeching, Tom himself running up the path almost before the car engine grumbled into silence, the shock of the sound of its slammed door still reverberating through the treacly atmosphere. The genie closed its eyes and resisted, but the memory was too strong. It kept returning. It kept imposing itself on the here and now, the future Tom unable to resist its grisly enveloping grasp. Shrieking soundlessly, it was sucked from the sunlight, dragged down through the darkness of the attic into the rooms beneath, and into those still darker moments it did not want to rekindle.

–But the doctor said she thought it would be okay? said Tom wildly.

Mary, head buried in his chest, nodded.

–Then it will be. Won't it?

Mary pushed herself away, brushed a hand across her nose. Her eyes were red. Tom had never seen her in such a state before.

–Well, we'll find out soon enough, won't we? she said, her voice unsteady. That icy premonition clutched at Tom again. She didn't sound full of hope. Why did he think the look in his eyes mirrored the look in hers as they held each other tightly again? Why was it that he sensed some awful scales of fate shifting, balancing; good against bad; light against dark; happiness against grief? Unexpectedly, he heard Evelyn say in her usual clipped tones, "Broad shoulders… broad shoulders," the phrase bouncing down the corridors of time. And by broad shoulders, he thought, she meant that he would provide a rock for Mary to cling to in moments such as these.

–It'll be all right, he said, more firmly. –We're together, aren't we?

–Is Mummy all right?

It was John, appearing in the bedroom doorway.

–She's not feeling well, said Tom.

–But the doctor will make her better, won't he?

–I expect so, said Tom, forcing a smile.

Mary swept John off his feet and carried him back to his bed.

Later, as Tom slid into their own bed, and waited for Mary to settle Lucy down, he found himself thinking about Jennifer Huntley, about the uncharitable thought *thank God it's not Mary* that had flitted through his mind when he heard that she was ill. Illogically he felt a wave of guilt. Had he tempted fate? Was it his fault that Mary was going to have to take tests, and… He refused to think of possible consequences. He knew it wasn't his fault, but he couldn't stop feeling guilty. When Mary came in a few minutes later, she took off her nightdress before joining him, and they made love without any words, without any need for words, before drifting off to sleep in each other's arms, content that whatever the future held, they would be part of each other.

The next day, with sunlight streaming through the windows, two boys running around the house like minor demons, and a small baby demanding to be fed, their fears seemed irrational.

–It'll be weeks before an appointment, Mary said. –And then more weeks. Doesn't seem all that urgent, does it? She picked up Lucy and undid the top of her nightdress.

Tom, munching on cereal, conceded the point.

–I'll take the tonic. Sit down, John. Don't make so much noise, Adam.

–Rest when the boys are at nursery.

–That's not as easy as it sounds. No! Don't—

Adam poured milk onto the floor for Gus, who lapped it up enthusiastically.

–Rest, enunciated Tom. –When. The. Boys.

This was an old argument.

–I'll try, interrupted Mary. –You'd better go. Better not keep Bob waiting.

Tom nodded and shook his head. She was right. He had an appointment with Bob that morning and he had learned over the last few months that if there was anything absolutely guaranteed to set off Bob's fiery temper, then being late for a meeting was that thing. He pulled on his jacket and kissed Mary. Lucy gurgled happily at him without removing Mary's engorged nipple from her mouth.

–You okay then?

–I'll be fine.

Tom ruffled John's hair and trotted out to the car, reflecting that while Lucy was still a baby he really did represent the average family with two point four children. He wondered why Bob wanted to see him. He had a suspicion that it was connected with a phone call last week—somebody had called Bob and whatever they had said sent him into a towering rage. *Of course we cannae... Are ye suggesting...? It's policy, man, since when did the Department...?* His bellowing voice echoed around the office. Janice—Scotland's tamer version of Dragon Margaret—and Tom exchanged a glance. Although Bob was bellowing angrily, he seldom got to finish his sentences, which implied that whoever he was talking to had no qualms about interrupting him, which in turn implied that it was someone senior. *You whit? How can ye do a study on something already decided? All right, all right, it's a bluidy nonsense but... All right, I hear ye.* Both Tom and Janice had winced at the sound of a receiver crashing back into its cradle.

Tom started the car.

Earlier that same day Roger had unexpectedly called from London. *Roger?* thought Tom while making non-committal remarks to whoever it was. *Who's Roger?* "Thought you might like to know Margaret's retiring," said the voice. *Margaret?* thought Tom. *Oh, Margaret. Oh, that Roger.* "Is she?" he said and Roger explained, "Going off to live with her daughter, Brighton, Hove, something like that." Tom said that sounded nice, and agreed to contribute to her leaving present. "How's Mary?" Roger had asked. Yes, how was Mary? "Fine, fine," he had said, wondering if Roger could detect his uncertainty and worry.

He jerked back to the present and was moderately surprised to find that he had driven the entire way to the office without any memory of the journey. Inside, Bram was already seated in Bob's office, ostentatiously glancing at his watch.

–Sit down, sit down, rumbled Sidcup Bob then, ignoring his own command, jumped up to close the door. –How's Mary?

Tom suddenly realised that neither he nor Bram knew that Mary had been to the doctor. Bob sat back down.

–Um, Tom said. –Perhaps I could tell you, er, later.

–Don't tell me, anither one!

It took Tom a moment to realise what Bob was getting at.

–No, no. Nothing like that.

Bob frowned, then shook his head. He picked up a pencil, turned it round, and put it back down again as if to signify that the initial part of the meeting had finished and its most important part was about to begin. Tom and Bram exchanged a glance.

–Got a call frae bluidy HQ last week, said Bob peremptorily. –Thay's a new national study. 'Flavour' they call it. Bob sketched quotation marks in the air. Tom recalled George quoting something on the pavement outside Audit House, simultaneously almost decapitating him with his gold-tipped stick.

–… stupit idea but who listens tae a puir old Scottish cha, eh? Bob sighed heavily. –An this one—ye'll nae believe it—is a review of the latest policy oot of Downing Street. Can ye believe it? Since when did the Department review policy, eh? Bob glared at Bram and Tom, who shook their heads sorrowfully.

–What policy? asked Bram.

–I'm coming to tha'. Bob mumbled and grumbled as he sorted through a mass of papers. –Here. FMI. Financial Management Initiative. Personal brainwave of her at the top, so I'm told but don't ye go spreading that aroond.

He passed copies of papers to Tom and Bram.

–Just read up on the thing fer now, figure out whit it's fer, whit it's all aboot. Bob chuckled. –And if you figure it oot, you better tell me. I think the whole thing's nonsense, but whoever listens, eh? Nae body, that's who.

Tom and Bram nodded and shook their heads while looking at their sets of papers, most of which were headed up by the logo of the House of Commons.

–Find oot whit ye can, said Bob. –Contact in London is Derek Worth. Number's there somewhere.

–Derek Worth? said Tom.

–Ye ken him?

–Aye, said Tom. –I mean yes.

Bob glared at him balefully.

–We trained at the same time, said Tom hastily. –He's good at computers.

He remembered Mary taking Derek Worth to task about his back-up strategy.

–Right, muttered Bob. –Here. When yer know aboot the bluidy FMI, yer need tae know aboot the even muir bluidy flavour. He handed out more sheets of paper, this time headed up by the Department's logo. –Take a couple days. Then get back tae me. I'm gonnae meet up with someone in the Executive, get a list of folk fer you two tae interview. Whit nonsense, them telling us who tae interview. I tried to tell Gabby that, I mean policy, and then this list, I mean… Bob trailed grumpily into silence.

–But who listens to a puir old Scottish cha, eh? remarked Bram.

Bob glared at *him* balefully. –Jist get out, haven't ye got enough work tae do?

Bram grinned and jumped to his feet. Tom stayed where he was.

–Give me five minutes.

Bram shot him a curious look, then half-shrugged and left, closing the door behind him. While it was open Tom heard the chuffing of the Department kettle. He glanced automatically at his watch.

–Whit?

How was he supposed to say this? Unexpectedly he saw a vision of Marsham Street, saw himself standing there awkward and tongue-tied as Mary regarded him with her calm, grey eyes; felt ripples in the fabric of time.

–Fae goodness sake, Tom.

–Mary's got to go to hospital. For tests. She's got a lump in her breast.

Bob, his fiery hair sticking up in a way that reminded Tom of mad Peter the landlord, stared at him with astonishment which slowly changed into horror.

–Whit? he muttered, not asking a question.

–I might be a little… Tom sought for the right word, –distracted.

–When? asked Bob, meaning the appointments.

Tom shrugged. –Weeks yet. They take a biopsy, and then we get the results some more weeks after that. So the doctor says.

Bob passed a hand over his face. –Okay, okay. Thanks for telling me. Let me know what happens, won't you? Tell Mary I'm thinking of her.

Tom noted that his Scottish accent had all but disappeared.

At lunch Tom told Bram that he might not be able to play as much bridge over the next few weeks. –Mary's got to go for some tests. Should be okay. But—you know.

Bram nodded. –No problem, no problem. Let me know when she's feeling better. Tom nodded evasively. –Who's Derek Worth? asked Bram.

Derek, the archetypal, fussy, precise accountant, had qualified in London at the same time as Mary and Tom. When they visited him in his strange, pink flat in Fulham it was mainly because he wanted to see Derek's Amstrad word-processor. "Just think," he told Mary excitedly. "If we got one I'd be able to store all my stories and poems on disk. I wouldn't need all these files and bits of paper," he added, thinking that perhaps a tidier flat might swing the argument. "There's something funny about someone who lives in a pink flat," said Mary. But even she had to admit that Derek was able to cook something that really was spaghetti Bolognese, and even she was impressed with the neat boxes of floppy disks and the grey-and-green Amstrad with its equally neat rows of green text. "Look at this," said Derek, holding up one disk. Tom and Mary looked at it. "This," said Derek impressively, contains all my essays. Politics, economics, you name it, it's on here."

"What happens if you lose it?" remarked Mary, ever practical.

Derek rummaged in one of the neat boxes, paused, scratched his head worriedly, rummaged some more. The neat piles of disks spread out in an untidy sprawl. Tom and Mary watched with interest. Eventually Derek gave a cry of triumph and held up another disk, which looked identical to the first one. "I've got a copy," he said triumphantly.

"But," said Mary inexorably, "you keep them in the same place. What happens if you lose the box, or someone steals it, or your beautiful pink flat goes up in flames?" Derek stared at her with horror. "You lose both copies, that's what," she informed him.

When Tom finally bought an Amstrad the first thing he typed in was a poem he had written more than a decade before, when he was a teenager.

THANK YOU FOR YOUR GIFTS

'Tis Christmas Eve and twelve o'clock.
The blinds are drawn, the doors are locked.
The children's prayers, they have been said:
All wait for Christmas Day.

Then suddenly, where naught has been,
A pair of booted feet are seen.
Down the chimney comes a man
Carrying a sack.

His robes are red, his beard is white –
This is his long-awaited night,
And as he moves about the room
His sack begins to fill.

He leaves, and where presents have been
There are none left which can be seen.
A message, pinned upon the door, says:
'Thank you for your gifts.'

He had no way of knowing that at another time just before
Christmas, long in the future, he would edge with Mary into a grey
waiting room already almost full. A sad two-foot Christmas tree
surrounded by obviously false, wrapped parcels stood in one corner, ignored by everyone. The door swung closed. Hardly anybody
looked up to see who had come in, but a young woman with swept
back yellow-hair and bright eyes at one end of a row shifted up one
seat so that two were available together. She looked, Tom thought,
as if she belonged at the prow of a ship, heading out into the wind.
He sat down, murmuring his thanks, while Mary registered at reception. He looked at his watch. The yellow-haired woman noticed
his perplexed expression.
    –Nurse or doctor?
    –Oh, said Tom. –Doctor.

Mary had come in to see the nurse several weeks earlier. When the appointment came through Tom said he would take a half day and cancel his golf game, but Mary would hear none of it. Since her first reaction after her visit to Dr Hunter she had steadied down and if anything was in a calmer state of mind than Tom.

"The doctors aren't going to let anything happen to me," she told Tom.

"No, of course not."

Mary must have heard doubt in his voice, because she smiled and said "I'll be fine. You'll see."

Tom looked again at the hospital appointment card. "Even so—"

"No, you go. I'll be fine," Mary said. "It's not as if I'm going to get any results or anything. They'll take this biopsy thing and I'll be off."

"If you're sure," said Tom doubtfully.

"Let's not upset Bob," said Mary.

"So," Bob had asked. "Any news?"

The sun was shining. A light wind off the sea ruffled glinting rows in the rough. Bob had already driven, his ball a distant yellow spot on the fairway. He told Bob the words the doctor had used—just a precaution—but could not dispel a tremor of fear. He squared up and swung. In his mind's eye he saw Mary climbing into the taxi, turning to look back out of the window, smiling. "Shame," said Bob insincerely, as Tom's drive sliced out into the wind, out over the edge of the fairway, and disappeared into rocks lining the beach. But none of it was real, the sun, the sea, the game. Reality was Mary waiting in a hospital to be tested. There was no sea, just four painted walls and a sign saying If you have to wait for more than twenty minutes, please see the receptionist. And it was no game, despite the book held in Mary's trembling hands; Brother Cadfael unearthing the secrets of the past, but she took in none of it even though she read the words as the minutes ticked by. She looked up, thinking of Tom on the golf course and irrationally both felt that their eyes met across the miles. "Good Lord," said Bob. Tom's ball unexpectedly reappeared, bouncing up from the rocks. It seemed to move in slow motion, rising up into the unreal blue of the sky, sinking down into the grey rocks, again and again, before trickling out onto the equally unreal green of the close-cropped fairway. It finished scant feet behind Bob's. "Amazing," said Bob dourly. He didn't seem to notice the misty outlines of the hospital room, or Mary waiting in the sombre crowd. He strode forward off the tee and Tom followed, seagulls squawking above. Tom should have been pleased, but none of it was real. It wasn't important.

–Your appointment's for two-twenty, right? said the yellow-haired woman.

The sunny golf course faded and the walls of the hospital waiting room sprang into grim existence. With a shock, Tom found himself part of the sombre crowd. He nodded as Mary came to sit next to him.

–All our appointments are for two-twenty, said the yellow-haired woman. –It's how they do it.

–Ah, said Tom.

–There's three doctors, not just one. You might not get to see the same one two weeks running.

–Ah, said Tom again. –You've been before.

–Oh yes, said the yellow-haired woman. She looked at him appraisingly, as if trying to determine how much difficult information he could take in. –You're okay if they call you early, she said. –If they call you towards the end…

Tom shifted uncomfortably.

–It's… how they do it. The yellow-haired woman shrugged abruptly. –God knows why.

Tom realised that although her eyes were bright, it was mainly because they were glinting with fear. He got the impression that she was barely holding herself under control. –Thank you, he murmured.

He looked around the waiting room. Two women at the end of a row of seats at right angles to their own and who had obviously come in together were talking quietly to one another. It struck Tom that he had no difficulty in detecting which of them was the patient and which the accompanying friend. The small woman on the left had eyes as wide and bright as those of the yellow-haired woman: she rubbed at her mouth and was breathing heavily, whereas the older woman on the right was murmuring constantly, gently, and rested her hand on the small woman's knee. Unconsciously he reached for Mary's hand and held it tightly.

–You okay? he whispered.

Her eyes were calm. Her hand gripped his.

–What're you thinking? he whispered.

–I hope Molly's getting on all right.

Molly was baby-sitting the three children, something she had done a dozen times before.

–She's done it loads of times, whispered Tom.

Mary was really thinking about the first time they had held hands, in the National Gallery, so long ago it seemed. She remembered having to hunch forward as his inexpert fingers linked with hers, and the hurt look on his face when she eventually made him let go. She remembered how he had nervously taken her hand on the bus; how they had linked fingers after the adventure of the Great Aerial Robbery, a story which they never tired of reliving down the years, along with the story of the time Tom had accidentally driven the car down a set of steps instead of across a car park, much to the amazement of a group of people watching from a nearby restaurant window. "I sort of turned and smiled at them," Tom would say, "as I went down the steps bonk bonk bonk; and they all smiled back. One of them waved."

Mary shuddered, resisting, as the immediacy of the waiting room assailed her. It was a different room from the one where she had waited for the nurse. That room had been quite bright. Posters covered most of the walls, announcing *Drink and drive—don't do it* and *Let's Dismantle Domestic Abuse*, along with warnings not to park in the private streets around the back of the hospital and multicoloured self-portraits of children from a nearby primary school. This waiting room looked as if it had started out with the intention of being bright, but somewhere along the way the grey despair of its occupants had taken over. There were no posters, other than a functional listing of the oncology unit closing and opening times, and a board which could be adjusted to show which doctors were on call. Mary couldn't help but notice that although the plastic chairs looked new, the carpet was threadbare and shabby and the paint on the wall was beginning to peel.

She glanced at the far wall, at the pair of huge bay windows. At least the sun was shining outside. She thought the grey room would be unbearable if its dark, gloomy atmosphere was matched by dark, gloomy weather outside. The woman opposite lifted her eyes and looked at her for a moment. She looked tired.

–Mrs Bradley?

Tom shot to his feet. Mary looked at him, a little vaguely.

–That's us, he whispered. So it was. How wonderful. It was her turn to go and speak to the doctor, to find out if she was going to get the chance to see her children grow up. She reached up for Tom's hand and pulled herself out of her chair. The receptionist had told her that she was to see Dr Pravinder, and given her directions to his surgery. Or her surgery. She leaned a little on Tom as they navigated a short, curved corridor, and allowed her mind to dwell on the fascinating question of whether Dr Pravinder would be a man or a woman.

He was a man, a short round, brown man wearing round wire-framed glasses. He had a chubby round face and his fingers were round and stubby. He reminded Mary of a circular cartoon character from one of John's books, but she could not remember his name. She frowned.

–Sit down, sit down, Mrs—

Dr Pravinder glanced at the cover of a file he was holding in his stubby fingers.

–Bradley.

Tom and Mary sat down. Tom saw a stack of files to one side of Dr Pravinder's desk. Some of them were pink, some grey, and there was one particularly thick file with khaki-yellow covers. He wondered if the different colours meant anything of medical significance, or just represented supplies bought in at different times. He reached out for Mary's hand again. Her fingers interlinked with his.

–Yes, yes, yes, yes, said Dr Pravinder, turning the pages of Mary's file, which was pink. –Hmm, hmm, uh-huh. Referred by Dr?

He looked up.

–Hunter, said Mary.

Dr Pravinder made a scribbled note. –Yes. Came in, yes. Tests back, yes. Uh-huh. Yes, these look to be all right.

Both Mary and Tom looked at him blankly.

–Your tests, Mrs uh Bradley. They are being clear. But I had better check you over while you are here.

Mary looked at Tom, eyes swimming. Her fingers clenched his tightly, and then let go. Without needing to be told, she got up and went to the tiny bed behind the screen. Tom was glad that he didn't have to get up at that precise moment. His heart was pounding with exhilaration, but his legs felt as weak as water. As soon as Dr Pravinder disappeared behind the screen he took several deep breaths and knuckled at his eyes.

–Yes yes yes yes, I see what they have been thinking. Yes, I do see. Uh-huh. And this is all?

Mary murmured something.

–Check like this, and like this. You are right, nothing, only this. Uh-huh, well the tests are being clear. Okay?

Dr Pravinder reappeared and walked with a slightly rolling gait back to his desk. Tom saw Mary's legs swing down from the bed, and moments later she too reappeared, buttoning her cardigan.

–It's nothing, then? said Tom.

Dr Pravinder continued scribbling in the pink file for a few moments, but Tom gained the impression that he was thinking about how to phrase his answer.

–There's just the one anomaly, he said at last. –The tests are indicating it is benign. All we have to do is, we will have you back—Mrs Bradley—in a year. For a check-up, routine. He finished scribbling, closed the file, looked up over the edge of his spectacles. –We will be sending out an appointment, Mrs Bradley.

Tom and Mary suddenly realised that the current appointment was over. They got to their feet. Tom grabbed his jacket. Mary thanked Dr Pravinder. They couldn't get out of the surgery fast enough. Outside, in the small, curved corridor, Tom glanced around, although truth to tell he couldn't care who saw them, and kissed Mary, whose eyes were dancing. –Later, she promised. Holding hands, they edged back through the waiting room, the number of its occupants much reduced. Before they reached the exit Tom looked to see if the yellow-haired woman was still there. She was. Their eyes met, and Tom knew that she divined their good news, knew that their body language and happy faces would give it away. But she was still sitting there, waiting, frightened. She gave Tom a tremulous smile of congratulation, and he nodded once, reassuringly, before Mary dragged him out of the waiting room, out of the hospital, and out of the nightmare that had haunted them for the last few months.

Back home, they couldn't wait for the children to go to sleep that evening, after which they fell into bed and made love, laughing and giggling, moaning and sighing. –Love you, he murmured afterwards in the darkness. He thought she must already be asleep, but her arm briefly tightened about his chest. It came into his mind that the last time they had made love so passionately was after they had heard the news about Jennifer Huntley. It was Anne who had told them that. She had been visiting them at their London flat. Anne and her boyfriend. What was his name? He could see him sitting there, a giant of a man trying to spoon food into Anne's reluctant mouth. *Here comes the train, where's the tunnel?* –What was Anne's boyfriend's name? he asked. Mary propped herself up on one elbow, her breast brushing his chest. –Are you mad? she asked. –No, really, I was trying to remember, he said. –Anne's boyfriend? mused Mary. –He was that six-foot hunk who played rugby but had the brains of a lawyer. Tom grabbed her, rolled over so that he was on top. –Never mind his physical attributes, he said. –What was…? Oh, never mind. Mary wrapped her long legs around him again, and they made love far into the night.

Back in the office the next day, Tom made himself a cup of tea and went in, a little blearily, to see Bob.

Bob jumped up to shut the door. –Whit news?

–Tests were clear.

Bob sat back down and heaved a huge sigh. –Good, he said. –Bluidy good.

–Routine check-up in a year, said Tom.

–Good, good, said Bob, clearly not listening any more. –Tell her she ought tae look in.

Tom imagined John and Adam running amok in the office and suppressed a smile.

–Bram's aff, said Bob. –Hurt knee, ligaments, some bluidy thing.

Tom raised his eyebrows. He hadn't heard anything about this.

–He'll be aff fae a few weeks, said Bob agitatedly. He picked up a slim file and waved it at Tom. It was green, Tom noted, as if the brief sojourn in Dr Pravinder's office had ingrained a habit of noticing the colour of files. –Bluidy awfa timing. This just in.

It was at this moment that a hesitant knock sounded at the door and when it opened, the ghost of Dick Jefferson walked in. Tom shrieked and propelled himself upright, incidentally spilling lukewarm tea over his trousers. The ghost of Dick Jefferson gave him a puzzled look, as did Bob.

–Whit? asked Bob.

Tom realised that it wasn't the ghost of Dick Jefferson after all. The new arrival had the same red hair, the same rather unfocused gaze swimming behind glasses of the same style, and there was a certain similarity about his facial features. But he was a little older, and was wearing a sober suit that young Dick would not have been seen dead in. *Not seen dead in?* thought Tom wildly, wondering if his subconscious had deliberately served up this inappropriate phrase.

–Er, hot, er… He waved a hand in front of his face. –Tea too hot, burned myself.

Bob made an exasperated noise, somehow managing to do it with a Scottish accent. He transferred his glare to the new arrival.

–Er, said the new arrival. –I'm Bryan Boswell.

–Bryan Boswell? roared Bob, losing patience. The ghost of Dick Jefferson paled. *Can ghosts pale?* wondered Tom.

–The new trainee? squeaked Bryan Boswell.

–The new trainee? said Tom, surprised. He hadn't known the section was acquiring a new trainee.

–The new trainee, said Bob heavily, calming down. –Aye, right. He waved a hand dismissively. –Wait ootside. Janice'll make some tea fer ye.

Bryan Boswell, looking more than a little relieved to be dismissed, slid backwards out of the door, closing it behind him. Bob regarded the doorway thoughtfully. –I'll be having words with the Smith woman, he grunted.

Tom paused in the act of scrubbing tea stains with his handkerchief. The Smith woman? What was Bob going on about now? –Melanie Smith? he said.

–Aye, her.

–She plays bridge, said Tom inconsequentially.

–She keeps sending me red-haired trainees, growled Bob. –She knows it… whit?

Tom never did get to find out exactly what effect the posting of red-haired trainees had on Bob, because it all suddenly became too much for him. A snort turned into a snigger, which developed into first a hoot and then brays of hysterical laughter. He flopped back in his chair, threw his head back, and laughed until tears streamed down his face.

Afterwards he told Mary, –I think it was because, well, first there was all the tension of yesterday, and then we stayed up late…

–So we did, said Mary archly.

–and then there was the shock of seeing Dick Jefferson's ghost come in the door, not to mention spilling tea all over myself, followed by a sketch right out of Monty Python, and then on top of it all I find that Bob's been fighting Melanie Smith—Melanie Smith!—about red-haired trainees…

–I told you she wasn't so bad.

–Look at this floor, said Tom.

Bob had sent him home early, saying that he was far too wet and stressed out to do anything sensible. "We'll talk aboot this tomorrow," he told Tom, waving the green file again. "And what was that about?" asked Mary when she delightedly opened the door to him in the middle of the afternoon and discovered what had happened. "No idea," said Tom. They bundled up the boys and took them for a walk with Gus, then after dinner played with them until their bedtime. Lucy dozed off and the house was at peace. He put his arm around Mary and they both regarded what could be seen of the floor.

–The Hoover's getting withdrawal symptoms, said Mary gloomily.

Most of the floor space was covered with toys, books, colouring pencils, paints, Adam's army of toy soldiers and John's barricade of cardboard boxes.

–Every night, said Mary. –This.

–I made a cupboard, said Tom defensively.

–You try making them put things in a cupboard, said Mary.

Tom scratched his head thoughtfully. The glimmerings of an idea came to him. –All right, he said. –You're on.

> Once there were three children who lived in a
> house half way up Witch Street.

–Oh, Tom, said Mary.

–Just wait, said Tom. He shuffled the pages and looked importantly at John and Adam—and at Lucy, although she had gone to
sleep already. –You listening? he asked. –Yes, Daddy, they chorused.
And so The Toyman was born, the first of a number of spooky stories
written over the years as all their lives irrevocably changed.

> Well, I should think you can imagine how long
> it took the children to go to sleep that night. And
> the next day – much to their mother's surprise
> – they started to look after their toys and books.
> None of them ever saw the Toyman again, but I
> hope – I really *hope* – that you have not left out
> a spooky book, or a book of monsters, anywhere
> where your father can tread on it or spill something
> on it, or do anything to it which the green, glowing
> eyes of the Toyman might see.

Tom sent The Toyman away, along with all the other spooky
stories which the children insisted that he write every Halloween,
but they kept coming back.

"Why does no-one want my stories?" he complained.

"Keep trying," said Mary.

"At least they started putting things away," said Tom proudly.

"Um, yes," said Mary. *For at least two weeks.*

On the day after his bout of hysterics, Tom had barely arrived
back at work before Janice nodded dourly at the door to Bob's office.

–You want… she hesitated meaningfully, –more tea?

Tom sighed.

He found out later that as he went into Bob's office, Mary picked
up the phone at home. Her parents, it seemed, had decided to visit.

–How are you, m'dear? boomed Graham. He always used the
phone as if there was actually no need for it, and whoever he was

talking to would be able to hear him without its benefit. Mary moved the receiver fractionally further away.

–Fine, Dad, she said. She wondered if Graham would be able to detect the enormous relief she felt at being able to say that, and she felt additional relief that she and Tom had not told their parents about the hospital tests.

–Thought we'd come to visit, boomed Graham. –Your mother and me, he added, as if to assuage any possible doubt. –Boys okay?

–Everyone's okay, Mary told him, reflecting that her father always forgot to ask about Lucy.

–The weekend after next, boomed Graham. –What d'you think?

–I'm writing it down, said Mary.

Meanwhile, Tom carefully carried a cup of tea into Bob's office.

–Sit down, sit down, said Bob, jumping up to close the door.

–Sorry about yesterday, said Tom.

Bob waved a hand dismissively. He sat back down.

–Bram's still aff, he said.

–Well, you said he'd be aff—I mean off—for several weeks, said Tom.

–Yes, said Bob. –But thay's this. He tapped a pencil on the slim green file sitting squarely on his desk. –This is the list, he said gloomily.

–The list?

–Of people fer you and Bram to interview, explained Bob. –FMI, bluidy national flavour, ye nae doot recall?

In truth Tom had all but forgotten about the impending national study as weeks had drifted into months and the powers that be continued their deliberations on who exactly should be allowed to take part.

–Only, said Bob, –Bram's nae here, is he?

–Never he is, agreed Tom, and fended off Bob's suspicious glare with a bland look of his own.

Back home, Mary put down the phone, whereupon it trilled importantly at her again. She picked it up expecting it to be Graham.

–Yes?

–Mary?

–Oh, yes.

–I suppose Tom's not there, is he?

It was Tom's mother. She frequently appeared to forget that Tom was now old enough to go out to work, and would therefore not be in during the day.

–No, said Mary. –He's at work. Again, she could not resist adding.

–How are you?

–Fine, said Mary.

–And Lucy? Oh—and the boys?

–All fine.

–We were thinking of coming to visit. How about the weekend after next?

Mary hesitated.

Tom opened the slim green file and found at the top a letter addressed to the Director, Robert P Sommerville.

–See attached, said Bob.

The sheet of paper attached to the letter listed twenty or so names, together with job titles and contact telephone numbers. Nineteen of the names meant absolutely nothing to Tom, but the one at the top jumped out at him.

Archibald Urquhart, minister for business portfolio,
appointments through secretary only

–Whit? asked Bob shrewdly.

–Er, nothing, said Tom. –There's, what, twenty names here?

–Too many fer you, grunted Bob.

–How long have we got? asked Tom. –The whole thing was supposed to be finished a month ago, wasn't it?

–All the fieldwork, grunted Bob.

–Whatever.

–These top two, Urquhart and Toshner, see this? Bob pointed to a paragraph in the letter which explained that because of their extensive work commitments, Archibald Urquhart and Melvin Toshner were only able to meet representatives of the Department at the weekend—in fact, only on one weekend in the foreseeable future.

–Bastards are trying to get oot of it, said Bob.

–That's, what, the weekend after next? said Tom.

Afterwards, Tom was never able to decide if the plan came into his mind there and then. All he could say for certain was that he saw a vision of slim, dapper Archibald Urquhart sitting at the table in Marsham Street, studiously ignoring everyone except Tom's first Director, Ken; remembered Anne later saying "Did he jump or was he pushed?" and Archibald Urquhart himself talking smoothly of collateral damage or damage limitation or whatever the phrase was that he had used; and felt a sudden burning desire to interview the minister for business portfolio.

–That'll be nice, said Mary on the phone. She wondered what Tom would think of having both sets of parents at the house at the same time. Come to that, she wondered, where would they all sleep?

–I'll do it, said Tom.

–Time aff in lieu, said Bob, waving a hand. –Manager's discretion, aye.

Tom drove back that evening at peace with the world. As he parked the car in the driveway the front door opened and John hurtled out. Adam followed, his face smeared with chocolate. Mary appeared in the doorway, cradling Lucy.

–Luke's et my chocolate!

–He et mine, sprayed Adam.

–See I can open the front door by myself!

–Mummy said—

–Granny and Grandad are coming, shouted John, anxious to prevent Adam repeating whatever it was Mummy had said.

–And Nanna and Nandad, shouted Adam, not to be outdone. He put up his arms. –Carry me in.

–Yeuk, said Tom. –Keep that chocolate away from my suit.

He managed to fend Adam off, but Gus got in under his guard and jumped up excitedly, barking.

–At the same time! exclaimed John triumphantly.

–Boys! called Mary. She frowned as Tom and the boys came in through the front door. –What have they been saying? Gus, get in here.

–Something about Mum and Dad, and your mum and dad.

–Ah. I told them not to tell you.

–Coming at the same time.

–I told them to let you sit down first.

Mary giggled. Tom leaned forward and kissed her.

–I'm sure we'll cope, he said. –When's all this supposed to happen?

When Mary told him, he grinned briefly and said, –I mean, I'm sure you'll cope.

As the weekend approached, they planned sleeping arrangements and meals at home, while Tom planned his approach to the FMI flavour at work. Mary asked, without much hope in her voice, if somebody else could do the interviewing that Saturday, and Tom reminded her that Bram was unable to move, and added that the ghost of Dick Jefferson was not only far too new to undertake such a delicate interview but also that, in Tom's opinion, it was unlikely that he would ever be able to undertake such a delicate interview.

"He's stupid?" hazarded Mary. "No," said Tom thoughtfully. "I wouldn't say that. He's already got an accountancy qualification thing as well as a degree. No, he's not stupid, but he… doesn't come over too well."

Mary quirked her eyebrows quizzically. "Shy?" she hazarded.

"No," said Tom thoughtfully. "I wouldn't say he was shy. He's very, um, confident in his own abilities, and he's perfectly able to talk to people."

"Big-headed, then?" hazarded Mary. Tom considered.

"No," he said. "I wouldn't say that. I wouldn't call him big-headed."

They were sitting on the sofa. Mary banged her head against his shoulder and made a frustrated squeaking noise. "What would you say?" she cried. "Say something, out with it."

Tom looked at her solemnly and said, "Well, I've been thinking about it, and I think I know the answer."

"What? What?" squealed Mary.

"I don't think he's got a sense of humour," said Tom. "None at all. De nada. Zilch. Do you know how hard it is to talk to someone who hasn't got a sense of humour?"

Mary didn't, but on reflection she could see that it might be difficult. A long time ago her grandmother had told her that *a man that makes you laugh is worth a dozen that make you swoon,* and her mother had said *laughter. Good for you* in her usual clipped tones. She thought about the hundreds of times over the years that she and Tom had collapsed, laughing, into each other's arms. On reflection, she could see that anyone without a sense of humour might have difficulty in striking up a rapport with somebody else, never mind a relationship. "Poor man," she murmured. Tom gave her a surprised glance, then divined what she was thinking. He thought, as he had thought so many times, how lucky he was to have found her. Who else would have considered, not the effect that Bryan Boswell's lack of a sense of humour had on others, but rather the effect that it had on Bryan Boswell himself? He put an arm around Mary and hugged her gently.

As soon as his parents arrived that weekend, Tom jumped into his car. Both sets of parents said they were sorry to see him go, but everyone knew they were really only visiting to see the children. Nobody knew that by the time he got home, the second most amazing coincidence would have surfaced and even the children would be forgotten while they all marvelled about nothing else for the remainder of the weekend.

Tom parked his car in an almost empty car park and wondered if Archibald Urquhart really worked at the weekend. If he didn't, then he had been hoist by his own petard by suggesting that he did. Tom grinned to himself. He doubted that a minister, junior or otherwise, got time off in lieu.

A bored-looking security guard checked his Department identification, ticked him off a list, and directed him to a room on the third floor. His attention drifted back to a tiny black-and-white television.

–Mr Urquhart often in on a Saturday? asked Tom conversationally as he slipped his card back into his wallet.

–Couldn't say, gov. I ain't.

It was clear that the security guard did not hail from Edinburgh. The television made a tiny bleating roar and Tom deduced that it was showing a football match. He stepped past the reception desk and started up the stairs. Lift technology had no doubt improved since he had worked in Marsham Street, but he still shivered at the thought of empty space steadily increasing beneath his feet. The stairwell at

Marsham Street had been narrow, steep and claustrophobic. These stairs were broad, carpeted easing their way up through the middle of the building. Making a virtue of necessity, thought Tom. As he reached the first floor, he mentally rehearsed the questions he was going to ask Archibald Urquhart. He wondered if the minister would recognise him. He doubted it. He doubted if the minister for business portfolio recognised even the existence of anyone below Director level. He started up the next shallow flight of stairs. He had not told Mary the detail of this meeting—not exactly who it was with, or what he planned to do with the results. It was the first time he had kept anything from her—well, apart from lusting after the young Jennifer Huntley, which Mary probably knew all about anyway. He certainly hadn't told Mary about the call he made to Sylvia, who had learned with him about interviewing techniques as taught by Beryl, and who was now a journalist.

He pushed open the glass door to the third floor, located the room the security guard had described, knocked, and walked in. It flashed through his mind that he hadn't hesitated, unlike that time when he had been convened to the meeting caused by young Dick Jefferson and his plaintive suicide note. Perhaps he was more confident than that nervous new auditor; or perhaps he didn't care if he upset Archibald Urquhart.

He found himself facing what was obviously another reception desk, although there was no sign of any receptionist. No doubt sensibly at home, thought Tom, maybe even watching the football. A door to the right had a sign *A. Urquhart* on it. Tom hesitated, then knocked peremptorily and marched in.

"Tom?" Sylvia had asked in a surprised voice. "Is that really you?"

"Yes, it's really me," said Tom. "So you're still there, then."

"What, here?"

"At the *News*."

"Oh, yes. Sometimes I even get a byline. You still with the Department? At Marsham Street?"

"Yes. And no," said Tom. "I'm in Edinburgh now. Listen, I may have a story for you." He could almost hear Sylvia's interest quicken over four hundred miles of telephone wire. "Unnamed source. The *News* has learned. A leaked Departmental memo. Blah."

"Got it," said Sylvia. "What's the story?"

"Check out the links between Archibald Urquhart and Richard Jefferson—remember him?"

"*The* Archibald Urquhart?" muttered Sylvia. "Jefferson, Jefferson… oh, the Copeland thing. Urquhart was involved? I didn't know that."

"Check out the links between Archibald Urquhart and Ken…" It occurred to Tom that he still didn't know Ken's surname, or he had forgotten. "Ken-my-first-Director."

"Ken-your-first-Director," repeated Sylvia.

"Forgot his surname," admitted Tom. "Anyway, I'm interviewing Urquhart in a couple of weeks."

"Urquhart," said Sylvia admiringly, in a way that implied she fell for men who referred to ministers, of whatever rank, by their surnames only.

"Just so," said Tom. Four hundred miles away, Sylvia blinked and regarded the receiver in her hand, disconcerted by the unexpected bleakness of Tom's voice. She put it back to her ear in time to hear him say "… are ways and ways, as I am sure you know, of writing up reports."

The door squeaked as it opened, and Archibald Urquhart looked up. He looked exactly as Tom remembered, even down to the red bow tie. No glimmer of recognition crossed his face. The door squeaked again behind Tom as he stepped into the office. His feet sank into plush carpet.

Archibald Urquhart said, –And you are?

Tom resisted the temptation to answer Yes, although the question clearly demanded it. Catherine Copeland had asked the same question of George, and had regretted it. *Thank you, George.*

–You weren't expecting me?

Archibald Urquhart looked mildly disconcerted. –Ah, he said. –The auditor.

–Tom Bradley, said Tom. He sat down and extracted papers from his briefcase. His heart was pounding. –I'm based in Edinburgh but I'm here to gain evidence for the national flavour.

–The national flavour?

–Yes.

–Ah.

"The minister for business portfolio," Sylvia wrote ferociously, "did not at first remember the existence of the initiative."

–The FMI, said Tom.

–Ah yes. Archibald Urquhart nodded. –A central government initiative, though I was not part of the originating short-life working group…

"He distanced himself from the concepts behind the Initiative…"

–and of course I deal very little with actual financial reports.

"… and did not think that it was likely to affect the way in which he worked."

–On what basis, then, asked Tom, –do you make the day-to-day decisions which affect the business community?

"Couldn't have put it better myself," said Sylvia.

–Ah. Archibald Urquhart steepled his fingers. –I deal more with strategic thinking rather than the tactical.

–Look after the pounds, and the pennies look after themselves?

–Precisely, said Archibald Urquhart. –Couldn't have put it better myself.

"I swear, he made a note," said Tom. "I bet he's going to come out with that comment at one of his press conferences."

"Not after I've finished with him, he won't," said Sylvia. "Making smart comments will be the last thing on his mind."

Tom asked, "Did you check out those links?"

"I did," confirmed Sylvia. "Cold-hearted fish, isn't he? What a coincidence you got to interview him—you of all people."

"Coincidence," said Tom. "Let me tell you about coincidence."

While Tom extracted ambiguous comments from Archibald Urquhart, Mary made cups of tea. The kitchen was blessedly quiet and she reflected that grandparents had their uses. Despite the tonic prescription, she still felt tired and, at times, unaccountably depressed. It was a simple, infrequent pleasure to make cups of tea without John hurtling through the kitchen pretending to be an airship, or Lucy studiously emptying a cupboard of pans, or Adam trying to alter the wallpaper design. She opened a packet of biscuits.

–Let me help you, m'dear.

–Thanks, Dad. Here, take the biscuits.

Graham was excited. –Guess what! No, you'll never guess.

–What? Mary picked up the tray and prepared to rejoin the mayhem in the main room.

–Something strange! said Graham excitedly. –And by strange, I mean really strange. Here, give me that tray.

Mary gave him the tray and picked up the biscuits.

–Talk about coincidence, burbled Graham. –Come and listen to this.

In the main room all three children had vanished into a pile of cardboard boxes, confident that if nobody could see them, nobody would know they were there. Mary could hear Lucy giggling, and an old crisp box on the edge of the cardboard city slid surreptitiously along the ground.

–Chalky White, said Tom's mother, and Evelyn burst out laughing.

–I remember now, said Tom's father as Graham came back in with the tray. –We called him Bolshover. Every couple has its moments, remember that?

–Bolshover! That's it! cried Graham excitedly.

Unnoticed, the genie hovered just below the ceiling, watching what Mary later described to Tom. It watched the cardboard city shudder and reform, catching glimpses of childish shapes concealed inside. It recorded Mary offering biscuits, a slightly befuddled expression on her face. She said afterwards to Tom that everything had been perfectly normal when she went out to the kitchen, but when she came back all the children had disappeared and all the grandparents—so it seemed—had gone completely mad. The genie grinned sardonically. There were three coincidences remaining, but they would not come to light until unexpected new worlds had opened. For now, it watched the giggling cardboard and heard grandparents swapping names.

–D'you remember Fags Botton? I don't know, he was a couple of years ahead of me, his dad was a government minister…

Evelyn leaned towards Mary. –Your dad. Went to school at Alleyne's. Yes? Mary nodded. –Philip too.

Mary looked at her, astonished. Philip was Tom's father.

Graham leaned over. –Told you it was a coincidence, didn't I? You know your mum went to school at Honor Oak? Mary nodded. –Well, so did Joyce! Mary looked at him, searching for any indication that it was a joke, but Graham was grinning like a Cheshire cat, more excited than Mary had seen him in years.

John careered out from under a particularly battered box, grabbed the biscuits, and vanished back into the city. Mary barely noticed.

–You mean, Dad and Tom's dad both went to Alleyn's?

–Remember Bolshover? called Tom's father. He crossed his eyes, scratched at the top of his head, and squeaked in a falsetto voice, –I've got the power!

Graham roared with laughter.

–And you and Tom's mum went to the same school?

–Coincidence, said Evelyn. –Fate. Something.

Something was right, thought Mary. She remembered Tom rambling on about the first coincidence; remembered Jo and Catherine meeting with her sisters Josephine and Catherine at the wedding, although schoolgirl Elizabeth had long since disappeared into the past and her sister Elizabeth had long since moved away. Now here was this second coincidence, even more bizarre than the first. She shivered. It really did seem as if fate was personally involved in bringing her and Tom together.

–What about when the stage collapsed? exclaimed Joyce.

The genie flattened itself. It slid across the ceiling and angled itself down the wall, encompassing the door as Tom arrived back home. Tom stepped into the memory that he relived so many times in future years.

A mountain of cardboard shook and mumbled and made various noises, on the verge of collapsing all over the floor. A few moments later, that is exactly what it did, revealing three chocolate-smeared guilty children inside who all made a simultaneous dive for the last remaining box which Tom vaguely recalled used to contain hundreds of nappies and he and Mary had had terrible trouble heaving it into the back of the car a couple of years before. But at the moment when the door swung gently open and bumped against the wall, the cardboard city still stood; no children were visible; Mary was staring in wonderment at her mother, who had put a hand over her mouth and was pointing in a curious fashion at Tom's mother, who had put a hand over *her* mouth, and was pointing back. Tom's father was sitting over by the window, all his remaining hair standing stiffly upright, and Graham was sprawled in an armchair, roaring with laughter.

"That was normal enough," remarked Tom later. "Your dad often sprawls and roars with laughter. But as for the rest…"

The cardboard dam broke, flooding the floor with boxes. Lucy shrieked because there wasn't room in the nappy box for her, Adam screamed because the corner of a cardboard flap caught him in the eye, and John shouted that it was his box and he wasn't sharing it with anyone else. Graham was laughing so hard he didn't even notice, Evelyn and Joyce were so busy conducting an ancient Honor Oak initiation ceremony that neither of them bothered to notice, and Tom's father sat nodding happily to himself, in a world of his own. Mary caught Tom's eye.

"It was a madhouse," said Tom later.

"Yes, but you already knew your parents were mad," said Mary. "I didn't know mine were bonkers too. How did the interview go?"

The interview had gone extremely well, from Tom's point of view. He doubted that Archibald Urquhart would see it in the same light once the report had been written and had emerged into the public domain, and he was certain that Archibald Urquhart would not see it in the same light after Sylvia had got hold of the report and translated it into journalese.

The minister for business portfolio distanced himself from the Initiative, stating that he did not make business decisions based on financial information, but instead took a strategic view. It is interesting to note that Mr Urquhart is a non-executive Director of at least three firms which have recently benefited from government sponsorship.

When Tom read the article three months later, he reflected that he should have realised Sylvia would undertake research of her own.

–Did you know aboot this? roared Bob angrily.

Tom shrugged. –The report's published, he said. –Can't stop anyone from reading it.

–You know this woman? asked Bob.

–As it happens I do.

Bob glared at Tom. Tom stared steadily back, although his heart was pounding.

–Did ye tell her aboot the interview?

Tom pretended to think, then shrugged again. –I can't remember, he said. –Months ago. It wasn't a secret, was it? There was a list of people, wasn't there? Lots of people must've known about the list.

–Nae lots of people knew this reporter woman.

–Maybe. Maybe she has contacts.

–Are ye being clever with me, laddie? Because if ye are, ye need to think twice aboot it.

Tom steeled his resolve. –I did the report. I don't like Urquhart—never have, ever since the Copeland thing—but that's it. I did the report, that's it. I can't help who reads it, can I?

Bob continued to glare at him, as if he was acting as a human lie-detector. Then he sighed. –Aye, all right. I'll tell Peter. He'll tell his nibs. This is going tae the top. Ye ken that?

Tom nodded.

–Get oot.

Tom stood, went to the door.

–Pickles was on the phone, said Bob. Tom paused, hand on the doorknob, back to the room. He could almost hear Bob trying to decide whether to say what he said next. –He said Urquhart's a bastard.

Tom gave a small smile without turning around and went out into the main office. When he later related the conversation to Mary, she said what he knew she would say.

–You should've told me.

–I wasn't quite sure how Bob would take it, said Tom, trying to deflect her.

–You used Sylvia, didn't you? Well, never mind.

–He let me know that he approved even if he couldn't say so in so many... What?

He trailed off. Mary handed him a green appointment card.

–It's the same as before, said Mary. –Nurse first, doctor after. She reached up to touch Tom's cheek. –It's just a check-up, she said. –Remember, that's what the doctor said.

Tom nodded, gave a strained smile, and enfolded her in his arms.

–I'll be fine, she whispered, although truth to tell she had been feeling more and more tired. She put it down to the rigours of three children. That, and her loss of appetite.

–You'll be okay at the nurse's?

She nodded, bumping her chin on his chest.

–Just the doctor's, then?

She nodded again.

–Broad shoulders, Tom muttered to himself.

–What?

Tom pushed her to arm's length, met her eyes and smiled. –Just remember the coincidences.

It was their code for *we were meant to be*.

Mary gave a deep breath, pushed the appointment card under a pile of magazines, out of sight. She eyed Tom askance. –Do you think there are any others?

–How could there be? asked Tom. –What could be even weirder? He hesitated. –You didn't... you didn't cut out pictures of Hayley Mills when you were young, did you?

–I most certainly did not, said Mary indignantly.

–Well, that's all right then. I can't think of anything weirder than we both cut out pictures of Hayley Mills, can you?

–Coincidentally or otherwise, agreed Mary.

The appointments weren't until the next new year, and that Christmas Tom wrote Christmas Wishes, a story about a monster on top of a house which stole the wishes of a family as they sent them up a chimney. Mary sat with Lucy on her lap, the boys sprawled on either side of her. She watched Tom as he turned the pages, watched the way his lips moved, heard his calm voice with just the hint of a lisp. She hugged Lucy as the monster sent back its own wishes, taking

147

away all the love and happiness from the family. Mary blinked, tears unexpectedly swimming in her eyes. She remembered dreaming about a distant, falling star. *You can wish on a falling star*, thought Mary. *Can you wish on a falling star that you dreamed? What would I wish?* Tom chose that moment to look across at Mary and smile. *I'd wish for nothing to change. I'd wish I didn't have an appointment to keep.* –Dear Father Christmas, said Tom, finishing the story. –Please may I have, Love, Mum. Now Mary could not hold back the tears spilling from her eyes. –Oh, Tom. He stared at her anxiously. –It's beautiful, she sniffed. –Why don't you send it away?

Almost eighteen months to the day after their first visit, they edged back into the grey hospital room. Unsurprisingly, their appointment was for twenty past two. As Tom sat down he looked around for the yellow-haired woman, but there was no sign of her. He squeezed Mary's hand, and she smiled at him, although there was a shadow in her eyes. Only routine.

–Read your book.

–What?

–You brought it, you read it. It's okay.

She knew that he didn't feel right reading a book while she didn't, but he turned pages in a desultory fashion. Somebody was called. An older woman wearing a grey overcoat with a feather in its lapel clambered to her feet and disappeared in the direction of the consulting rooms. More pages. Afterwards he could never remember what the book had been, what its title was or what it had been about, but he remembered the grainy feel of the pages inside contrasting with the slick, cold feel of its cover. A woman wearing a bulky jacket and black boots was called, although Tom hadn't seen the woman with the feather emerge. Just two other women left in the waiting room and Tom's stomach clenched with apprehension. He hadn't told Mary about the conversation he'd had with the yellow-haired woman, but he remembered it clearly.

–Mrs Bradley?

A nurse with her hair tied up in a severe bun preceded them along the short corridor. Mary held his hand reassuringly, as if she could sense his growing trepidation.

–Mrs Bradley, announced the nurse, guiding them into the consulting room. She closed the door, but remained inside, standing discreetly to one side. For some reason this only heightened Tom's fear.

Dr Pravinder leafed through a file. It was a pink file. Had it been a pink file at the time of the first visit? Tom couldn't remember. Probably it didn't matter. What mattered was the time. Surreptitiously he reached out and felt Mary's hand creep into his own.

It was nearly four o'clock.

–Yes, hmm, remarked Dr Pravinder. –You were in here, what, a year ago. Yes, yes, I see.

He peered at Mary over the top of his round spectacles. –The results are not being as clear this time, Mrs Bradley.

Mary stared at him, then shook her head. Tom couldn't determine whether she was trying to refute his words, or if she just didn't understand the conversation and didn't know what to say.

–We must send you for more tests, said Dr Pravinder.

–What? said Mary.

Dr Pravinder put down the file. Tom saw that there was a red dot stuck on its top left corner.

–More tests, hmm? I am afraid there will be a few of these. So that we can work out the best form of treatment, Mrs Bradley.

–No, said Mary. –I mean… She turned to Tom.

–She means, what do you mean exactly by not clear?

–Ah. Dr Pravinder picked up the file and opened it again. You bastard, thought Tom, surprising himself. You know perfectly well what's in the file. A telephone rang somewhere outside. Stopped abruptly. –The, hmm, lump in your breast is not benign. It does contain—ah—cancerous cells.

Mary's lips moved soundlessly.

–And? said Tom. –That means what?

–What? asked Dr Pravinder.

You know exactly what I'm asking.

–What's going to happen? asked Mary in a voice so small and fragile that Tom grasped her hand still more tightly. –To me.

–We're going to do more tests, said Dr Pravinder with an air of exercising great patience. –So that we can work out—

–Not that, said Mary. –I mean, what's going to happen to me?

Dr Pravinder closed the file again and sighed. –All is not doom and despair, you know. There are being a lot of treatments now.

–What are the tests for? asked Tom suddenly.

–Yes, the tests are important. We need to find out the best way to treat your wife, Mr Bradley. That's what they're for.

–Yes, but no, said Tom. He tried to firm his grasp on the conversation. –What are the tests looking for?

–There is a lot we don't know, said Dr Pravinder.

–Such as? said Tom grimly.

Dr Pravinder sighed again, glancing at Mary. –It is important we discover whether it is an aggressive form… of the disease, and also how far it has reached.

–Reached?

–Spread, said Dr Pravinder.

–How far… whispered Mary, and fell silent.

–You said Mary was clear last time, said Tom. Unnoticed, the genie coalesced and slipped into his body as Dr Pravinder met his stare, an unreadable expression on his face. Was he sad? Sympathetic? Apologetic? Guilty? In the future, Tom replayed those moments again and again, trying to read meaning into the way Dr Pravinder looked, as he said the words that neither Tom nor Mary would ever forget: –Yes. You have, I am afraid, not been well served by the system.

You have not been well served by the system.

Time passed. Every night Mary lay in the circle of Tom's arms. Every night Tom said that he loved her. He came home early one day and found her weeping over books lying open on a table. He held her close, and over the top of her head could see that she had been researching her own illness, and time and again he could see the headline featuring five-year survival rates. He didn't know what to say, but tightened his arms protectively, and felt her do the same.

They told the children that Mummy wasn't well, and that the doctors would do everything they could to make her better but it might take a long time.

–But they will make her better, won't they? asked Adam.

–They will do everything they can, assured Tom, thinking that he was sidestepping the question just as Doctor Pravinder had tried to sidestep his own. Their life descended into a blur of tests, waiting for results, waiting for phone calls, more tests, going for scans and more scans. The disease had spread. Once Tom pulled what he thought was a light cord in a hospital toilet, and when he emerged a few seconds later it was to find two nurses waiting for him, together with an attendant with a wheelchair who insisted that he get in immediately. A doctor hurried into view. In the background Mary doubled up in a rare fit of laughter and the receptionist, eyes wide, clapped a hand across her mouth.

"How was I to know it was an emergency cord?" complained Tom later.

"They were trying to find a key to get in," said Mary. "Imagine if they'd—"

"I didn't even know toilets had emergency cords," complained Tom.

During the day he sat in the office, sometimes trying to read a file, mostly staring out of the window. Sidcup Bob said he could go home whenever he wanted to, and growled something incomprehensible every time he walked past and found Tom still sitting at his desk. Long afterwards he remembered seeing his own drawn reflection in the window and try as he might he could not remember the view beyond. He remembered thinking about Marsham Street, sitting opposite the Dragon and wishing time away so that he could shed the office shackles and go out to meet Mary; George's voice bellowing from behind the closed door of David Pickles' office; David Pickles' sharp bark, and Dragon Margaret refusing to tell him the telephone number of the new student on the twelfth floor. And now he wished that time would slow. Days sped by immersed in appointments with specialists, trips for chemotherapy, esoteric scans.

They went to see *Sleepless in Seattle*. The cinema was half full. Tom had no idea what the film was about, only that Mary wanted to see it. As the story unfolded a sense of horror gripped him and he clutched at her arm, wanting to drag her away from the screen.

–It's all right, she whispered in the darkness. –I want to see what happens.

He didn't want to see what would happen. He sat with his eyes closed and tried to conjure up bridge problems, or the plot of his latest story, but wasn't very successful. He could still hear what was going on. Hot tears leaked out from under his eyelids as onscreen Jonah made his call to a talk show.

Five years.

Not been well served by the system.

Hand in hand they sat in the grey hospital, waiting the long wait before Mary was called. The nurse who ushered them along the corridor swayed elegantly, her dark skin contrasting with her white uniform.

–Here.

It wasn't their usual room. It wasn't Doctor Pravinder who sat behind the desk and waved them into plastic chairs. The nurse stayed inside the consulting room and Tom felt a wave of fear that summoned the genie into being.

–It's, let me see, Mrs Bradley, yes?

Neither Tom nor Mary responded. The consultant who wasn't Doctor Pravinder didn't look much older than they were. He had a shock of black hair and wore a stethoscope around his neck.

–Let me see, Doctor Hunter referred you, right? I see, hmm, then the routine test, hmm, hmm, I see you've been going up to Glasgow for treatment, is that right, Mrs Bradley?

–Where's Doctor Pravinder? asked Mary. Tom glanced at her anxiously.

–I, uh—

–Only, said Mary, –I've been to so many hospitals that I've lost count, and nobody tells us anything, and every time—

–Mrs Brad—

–every time, Mary ploughed on, although the genie recorded that her voice was tiny and beginning to fracture, –we have to go through this, again and again, and now even here you, you're asking me to go over it all again. Why can't I see someone who knows my case? Why have I got to go through all this again?

For the first time in her life Mary burst into tears in a public place. She turned blindly and Tom pulled her into his arms.

–Some consistency would be good, he told the doctor who wasn't Doctor Pravinder over her shaking shoulder. The young consultant met his eyes and gave a slight nod, and Tom felt another wave of fear. Mary pulled away, wiping at her eyes.

–I'm sorry.

–Not at all, Mrs Bradley. Take your time.

–I'm all right now. It's just that… She trailed into silence.

–I understand, Mrs Bradley. Please, could you go behind the curtain? Nurse?

The nurse came forward to guide Mary to the bed behind the curtain. When they were out of sight the young consultant spoke in a low voice without meeting Tom's eyes and the genie tried to strain away, to avoid his words.

–Were you planning on having any more children, Mr Bradley?

–What?

–You have three, I understand?

–Yes.

–I would advise against making any plans for a fourth, said the consultant who was not Doctor Pravinder, gently.

The genie fluttered and struggled to escape. Tom could feel it; a wild heartbeat, blood thundering and coursing. He gripped the edges of his plastic chair so tightly that afterwards red indentations across his palms took an hour to fade away.

–I would advise against making long-term plans, murmured the young consultant and, before Tom could say anything, abruptly stood up and made his way behind the curtain.

Even as their lives descended into horror Mary gained strength from somewhere. She told him that whatever happened, would happen, but they would always be together. Tom never told her what the consultant who was not Doctor Pravinder had advised, but a few weeks later she was summoned to what they thought of as the emergency cord hospital for a suite of scans and tests which required an overnight stay.

–I'm so tired, Mary said.

The children were asleep. Tom and Mary lay together, in darkness.

–I go to the tests. I go to the scans. I have therapy.

Tom's arms tightened around her.

–It's not going to work, is it, Tom? I've lost everything, haven't I?

Tom tried to blink away tears. He wanted to say, you've still got me, haven't you? but it seemed trite. It wasn't enough. There were no answers.

–We need to get another dog, said Mary.

–What?

–The children will be at school. You'll be at work. How can we… how can we leave Gus on his own all day?

–But—

–What will happen, will happen, said Mary. She didn't have to say any more. She just held him fiercely in the darkness. The next day, a Friday, an ambulance arrived early to transport Mary and a number of other patients to the hospital. The other patients all looked grey and ill, and then Mary blotted them from view as she hauled herself into the back of the ambulance, grimacing with pain, and when she sat down Tom realised with a dull shock that she too looked grey, and gaunt, and ill. He phoned in sick and kept the children off school.

–Where are we going? trilled Lucy.

–You'll see.

–Is it a mystery? Can I wear my Sherlock Holmes hat?

–You can wear what you like, John.

–Can I wear my spiderman costume, then? asked Adam earnestly, and was upset when Tom told him that no, the spiderman outfit might not be suitable for where they were going.

–Where are we going? trilled Lucy, forgetting she had already asked.

"Where did you go?" asked his mother on the following day. "Oh, and we've decided to move up to be near you."

"You've what?"

"Your father and I," said his mother.

"I know you mean Dad and you," said Tom after a pause. "But you and Dad what?"

"What?"

"What have you decided?"

"To move up nearer to you," said his mother. "We've put this house on the market. We're looking for another one in your area. Don't worry your head about it. Where did you go yesterday?"

They went to a farm about three miles away, Tom manoeuvring their unwieldy white estate car carefully along single roads
that were scarcely more than tracks while the three children shouted
with excitement whenever they saw a tractor or a flock of sheep. They
tumbled out into a muddy farmyard and a tall thin woman came
out to meet them. As they introduced themselves Adam jumped
experimentally into a huge puddle. Tom grinned briefly at the thin
woman and was rewarded by a slight twitch of narrow lips.

–Boys will be boys, she said. –You phoned about the puppies?

–Puppies! Puppies! shrilled Lucy. She jumped up and down
excitedly, slipped and fell over in the mud. John, wearing a deerstalker
and gravely holding on to Tom's hand, said: –But we've already got
Gus.

–Gus? said the thin woman.

–Our dog, said Tom. –Short for Disgusting. My wife… my wife
thought of…

He trailed off. He was sure he could see Mary lying in a darkened ward, one corner of which was curtained off. The shape of the
farmyard twisted, closed in; the sky paradoxically became both whiter
and duller as it swooped down and spread overhead, becoming a
faded, white-washed ceiling. A row of beds lined a pastel wall. Tom
was sure he could see Mary's hair, dark on white sheets, and her pallid
face. Her eyes were shut and her breathing uneven.

"I thought I saw you," he said later, and described what he had
seen.

"Behind the curtain," Mary whispered. "A woman behind there,
screaming in pain, all night. All night."

"There was a curtain?"

"I thought I saw you too, Tom. You were looking down at me.
Sometimes I dream about a falling star." They were lying together
quietly, their new acquisition quivering somewhere under the bed.
"They took her out in the morning. Carried her out."

"For treatment?" hazarded Tom.

"I think they thought most of us were asleep, but how could
we be? She was covered up, Tom. It was awful. That pain, all that
pain, and then in the morning they covered her up and opened the
curtains and took her away."

Small snoring noises came from under the bed. Mary didn't have to say any more: Tom knew what she was asking, and he didn't have to reply because she knew his answer.

–Well, said the thin woman awkwardly.

Tom realised that half a dozen tiny black-and-white puppies had tottered out into the yard, and the children were amongst them. One puppy emerged from the press and scrambled through the mud until it reached Tom's feet, which it sniffed with interest before tugging furiously at his shoelaces. Tom bent, unexpectedly seeing his shadow bending beneath him, and scooped the little creature up.

–This has to be the one, he said. Lucy skipped over.

–Can I hold him, Daddy? Can I?

–It's a girl dog, said the thin woman. Tom started to reach into his pocket, but the thin woman said, –No charge. There was a curious expression on her face, a mixture of sympathy and sadness and humour.

Tom looked at her, puzzled.

–I know Mary, said the thin woman.

On the way home, there was a vigorous discussion over what to call the new puppy. Tom rejected Spidergirl and Superdog, Spot and Smally and eventually settled on Jess.

–The first book I ever read was called *Shadow the Sheepdog*, he told the children. –But Shadow is a boy's name, so we'll call her Jess. That was Shadow's mother.

–Jess! called Lucy. –Your name is Jess! The tiny puppy, curled up in a cardboard box on John's lap, did not seem very impressed. She opened her eyes briefly, yawned, showing tiny, white, pointed teeth, and went back to sleep. When they got back home Gus, easily six times her size, nuzzled her curiously, stepped forwards a pace, and urinated all over her. That necessitated her first bath and rubdown, after which she hid from Gus underneath Tom and Mary's bed, refusing to come out.

–Thank you, Tom.

–The lady said she knew you. Mrs Eaglesham?

–Oh, Linda. Really? I didn't know she'd had puppies.

–It wasn't—

–Tom.

–Sorry.

–But, Tom. I don't think… I'm sorry, but I don't think I can come on any more dog walks. I'm too tired, and it… hurts too much.

Suddenly there was no more time, and there was no hiding Mary's illness from the world. When she complained of the pain, she was whisked to another appointment and another scan. Jaundice, noted the consultants. Tom wondered what that meant, and the consultants said it meant she would need an operation. What for? asked Tom. To fit a stent, they told him. Yes, but no, said Tom. What was it for? The consultants explained that a stent helped the functions of the liver. No, said Tom. What was the operation for? Oh, he added dully, the liver. The liver, agreed the consultants. Does that mean that the disease has reached the liver? said Tom. We didn't say that. What are you saying? asked Tom. Has it or hasn't it? It might be related, said the consultants cautiously. We'll have her in for the operation and we'll try to clear out some of the… we'll try to clear her out a bit at the same time. We recommend you get your wife a wheelchair. You can order one through your GP, they added brightly, almost as if they were advertising.

Tom made sure the children went to school every day, and he sometimes went into the office and often didn't. Mary spent more and more time at the hospital and at night Tom would curl up alone, a ball of misery, unable to sleep. It took months for his parents to find a buyer for their house. By then Lucy had had her fifth birthday party and Mary was in a wheelchair.

–Is Mummy going to get better? asked John one evening.

–I don't know, said Tom. –She might not.

–Don't the doctors know?

–No. There's a lot doctors don't know.

–I'm going to be a doctor when I grow up. I'm going to find out what's wrong with Mummy and make her better.

That night Mary was home and they clung to each other. It seemed to Tom that their life together was accelerating, or it was in freefall; in any case, it was no longer theirs to control.

–They've let you out, he murmured.

–They can't keep me from you.

–I'm getting John's secondary school uniform on Saturday.

–I'm only out until Friday.

–I know.

–I was talking to a nurse today, Freda. She comes from Norway, somewhere like that. She's been at the hospital for years.

–Oh yes?

–She says we ought to sort out a few things. Go to the bank. I'd better write some letters.

Mary's voice hitched.

–Now don't—

–I've already made an appointment, she said. –Tomorrow.

The genie crept away, disappointed that the deal was still struck, the conversation unchanged, the following day cemented into its perception of time. It waited, unthinking, through the night hours. It watched as Tom helped Mary to dress while the children got themselves ready for school. It was released as Tom drove to the primary school and Mary dozed on the sofa, but found itself chained above the High Street, unable to flee the events of the day. The wind blew. The air was damp and muggy. The genie saw shoppers, taxi-drivers, two policemen in bright yellow jackets, queues at bus stops and ATM machines, and eventually, although it twisted this way and that in an attempt to avoid seeing it, an avenue opening between scurrying pedestrians as Tom pushed Mary's wheelchair towards the bank. Tom swivelled expertly, a miniature three-point turn, when he reached the entrance, and the genie was sucked downwards as the electric doors slid open—like something, Tom always thought, out of a Star Trek movie.

They were early. Mary smiled, but she was nervously twisting her wedding ring round and round on her thin fingers. The genie knew that, scant weeks in the future, she would give it to Tom to wear because it slipped off so regularly that she was frightened of losing it altogether. Tom was thinking of the grey hospital room and its fake Christmas presents. He was thinking that in many ways, this appointment was far worse, despite the bright weather and the bright, brisk, busy surroundings.

–Mrs Bradley?

A smartly dressed young woman sought them out and preceded them into a tiny room that featured glass on every side.

–What can I do for you today?

Mary explained, while Tom listened helplessly, that they held three accounts at the bank in joint names and that she wished to remove her name from all of them so that they were held by Tom only, and she understood that she had to sign a mandate to that effect.

The smartly dressed girl opened up a file, tapped on a keyboard and peered at a bulky monitor.

–I see. I see. Yes, this shouldn't be too much of a problem. May I ask why you have reached this decision?

The genie fluttered wildly.

–Why? asked Mary.

The smartly dressed girl was reaching behind her, taking forms out of a rack. Tom felt a surge of apprehension.

–For the forms, said the girl. –I need to put in a reason why you've made this request.

–For the forms, repeated Mary. Something in her voice made the smartly dressed girl look up, but she couldn't possibly see, as Tom saw and the genie recorded, that Mary's hands were trembling underneath the impersonal plastic table. –The reason, said Mary, – since you ask, is that—Tom saw her swallow; her eyes flicked in his direction momentarily—is that I don't have long to live.

Not been well served by the system.

–Oh.

The smartly dressed girl turned white and her eyes widened, and her hands, clutching a sheaf of forms, also started to tremble.

–Oh. Oh. I'm—

Tom's heart was beating frantically and at one point his eyesight actually blurred and fragmented and for an instant he wondered if the walls of the glass cubicle had shattered and starred. He reached out and gripped Mary's hand fiercely, and she squeezed back as hard as her thin fingers and wrist would allow. It was the first time either of them had heard the words spoken aloud. Mary felt a tremor in Tom's grasp but nevertheless felt his strength augment hers.

–So I'd like to fill in the forms, she said, emphasising *forms* with a tinge of contempt, –While I still can.

–Yes. Oh. Yes. Oh, stuttered the smartly dressed girl, but then to her credit she swiftly marked off a batch of forms and said, –Just sign here, Mrs Bradley. And here, Mr Bradley. And here, where I've marked—yes, I'll fill in the detail afterwards—thank you, Mrs Bradley, I think that's everything. If there's any problem I'll— She looked rather helplessly at Tom, who didn't reply but stood up and seized the handles of the wheelchair. The girl put a hand to her forehead and didn't get up.

–I'm sorry, said Mary, gently, and partly over her shoulder as Tom wheeled her towards the exit. –You've been very helpful. Thank you.

The smartly dressed girl looked up and the genie noted a complicated expression shade her eyes; sympathy, gratitude and guilt. –Have a good— she started to say, then stopped. Her eyes met Mary's while Tom wrestled open the glass door. Something passed between them and the smartly dressed girl half nodded and straightened in her chair. –Have a good day, Mrs Bradley, she said firmly, but still she did not see them out into the main body of the bank, or show them the way out to the street, where, astonishingly, the sun still shone.

The genie must have fled, for Tom remembered nothing of the journey home. He must have pushed the wheelchair back along the High Street to the awkward, gravelled car park by the river, helped Mary into the passenger seat, loaded up the wheelchair in the space usually occupied by Gus, and driven all the way home, perhaps reaching out to hold Mary's hand when it was safe to do so, or perhaps not; perhaps saying something to her over the thrumming of the engine, or perhaps not. The thick wind had cleared the sky to a uniform pale blue as they arrived back at the house, and he put his arm around Mary to help her inside, both of them unknowingly threaded by the genie as he back-heeled the front door shut and they went into the main room and collapsed, in each other's arms, on the sofa. Both of them were crying.

–I'm so sorry, Tom.
–It's not your fault.
–I shouldn't have said anything.
–Shhh. It doesn't have to be… like that.
She didn't reply. They clung to each other still more tightly.
–We've got an appointment next week, haven't we? Why would we be having appointments if… His voice trailed off.

–I'm tired of appointments, whispered Mary.

It was Tom's turn not to reply while he tried to find a way to avoid the future. The room started to darken as the fickle wind dragged clouds out of the west.

–Have you been to bridge lately?

–No.

–Have you been to golf lately?

–No.

–Have you even been to work lately?

–Not often.

–You can't—

–Yes I can. You are my life, Mary, you and the children. You know that.

She chose to take comfort from his answer, and rested her head against his chest, and closed her eyes.

–Anyway I speak to Mum and Dad and your mum and dad, and Molly when I see her at the school, oh and Derek Worth rang the other day…

–Hmm-mm, said Mary sleepily.

Derek Worth, who had once been appalled when Mary pointed out that his Amstrad backup disks were as much as risk as all his other disks, had rung up to enthuse about connecting his home computer to the internet. Tom was scarcely interested, scarcely paid any attention, but he was not to know that the internet would help to turn his life around long days in the future.

Mary dozed off and Tom closed his eyes. He had not been sleeping. He had lost his appetite. Outside, the wind died, leaving grey clouds overhead. His mind played tricks, transporting him back to another time when he could not eat. He walked again the grey London streets while Mary was with her family in Ireland. A wind tugged at him, whirling him away into shadows until he saw a small, guttering light apparently perched on absolutely nothing. It was a candle, its flame wavering sideways in the gusting wind, sitting alone in a darkness absolute except for its own wavering pool of radiance. Tom knew that the candle wasn't Mary; it represented both of them and their lives together, and the howling wind was time itself, threatening to blow them away. Well, he would stand with his back to the wind, shielding the fragile flame. But when he tried to move, he found that his limbs were frozen, or they were heavy, or they were tied. He did not know what it was, but an inner sense told him that by the time he strained to the side of the candle, the ferocious wind would already have scoured it away.

Mary dreamed of the falling star but this time she felt herself hurtling through space and she realised for the first time that the falling star was not Tom. It was her. And at the same time as the earth fell away, spiralled away in a vast dizzying loop, she felt herself rooted to its surface, watching the distant, dimming, falling star as if she was another person watching herself. She battled the confusion. She heard a tremendous pounding, and even in her dream she knew that she was lying with her head against Tom's chest, and she was hearing his heartbeat. Tom was holding her. Tom was watching over her. Then she understood.

They awoke at the same time, twined together on the sofa. Somehow they both felt as if they had attained some measure of peace. The genie reluctantly opened its eyes and gazed into Mary's as she kissed Tom gently and murmured, –I will always be a part of you.

Tom did not reply but, paradoxically, felt the candle of his dream burn more brightly.

–Don't be alone, whispered Mary. –I don't want to think of you being alone.

–What am I going to do? said Tom. –What can I do?

Mary smiled as memory stirred; the floor of their first house covered with toys, and the Hoover having withdrawal symptoms, and what did Tom do about it?

–Write a book, she whispered. –Write about us.

–I will, said Tom. –I promise.

–And get that internet thing.

–What?

–It can be my Christmas present to you. How do you get it, anyway?

–Er, I don't know, Tom admitted.

–Well get on to Derek and ask him. You never know. I expect you can meet all sorts of people on the internet.

–But—

Mary pressed a finger to his lips, shushing him, then took the finger away and kissed him instead.

–What shall I get you? asked Tom. –For Christmas? He refused to read the look in her eyes.

–Pictures, she said. –Photographs. What about my birthday?

–Oh yes.

–And Lucy's before that. We can take some pictures, Mary decided.

But the following week, during their appointment, round Doctor Pravinder announced that Mary needed another operation to check over and possibly replace her stent as it didn't seem to be working as effectively as it should be; the hospital would be sending out an appointment, he told them. Inevitably the date for the operation was Lucy's birthday, and although Tom spent what seemed like hours on the phone trying to get it changed, no other dates were available or offered. Molly came to help keep the party going. Tom took some photographs but even when he saw them later, he did not remember taking any of them. He did not remember the party at all, only that moment about half way through when the phone rang. As he walked towards the sepia-coloured wall out in the hallway where the phone was hanging, he saw his shadow forming, growing, coming to meet him, not knowing that it was the genie which had been waiting for him, and now came forward to cement his memories; only knowing that he felt a terrible sense of precognition as he reached out to take the receiver in his trembling hand.

–Hello?

–Hello? Is that Mr Bradley?

–Yes.

–Would you hang on a moment, please? I have Dr McKenny for you.

–What? Who—? But the phone had gone momentarily dead. Tom found himself clutching at the receiver so hard that its plastic casing creaked ominously.

–Hello?

–Hello.

–Is that Mr Bradley?

–Yes.

–My name's McKenny, I'm the surgeon who operated on your wife this afternoon.

–Oh yes? Tom leaned his forehead against the sepia wall, feeling infinitely tired. Lucy ran past, shrieking, pursued by Molly's daughter and another small girl in pigtails. Tom straightened, smiled and waved at them.

–Could you come in to the hospital, Mr Bradley?

–What—what's happened?

–Your wife is sleeping now, Mr Bradley. She won't wake until tomorrow morning. But there are one or two things we ought to discuss.

–My daughter's having her fifth birthday party right now.

–Ah.

A pause. Tom heard distant screaming and the thud of rapid footsteps above his head somewhere. His eyes traced the blurred shadow of the telephone cord. He couldn't think of anything to say. He was too tired to say anything.

–Could you come in later, Mr Bradley?

When he went in later, he didn't get to talk to Dr McKenny, because he had already gone home, but was instead directed into the consulting room of a matronly woman who had an unexpectedly piercing gaze. Tom was sure she introduced herself, but he instantly forgot her name. Even the genie forgot her name, although it was able to recall with terrible intensity the words that followed. "I am afraid," said the matronly woman, "that the disease has progressed further and quicker than we thought." Tom felt constrained to point out that the initial diagnosis had been clear, but he spoke dully. "It is a particularly aggressive form of the disease," said the matronly woman, ignoring him. "I am afraid." She lowered her eyes, tapped her fingers in a way which indicated that she was considering how best to frame her words. "We think there may now be benefits to your wife moving onto a pain-relieving regime, and transferring to the hospice." Tom looked at her numbly. "They're very good there, you know," said the matronly woman. "I need you to sign these forms. I've checked, and they have a space."

He didn't sign the forms immediately. He spoke to Mary first, leaning over her hospital bed, staring anxiously into her pain-filled, drugged eyes, telling her what the nurse had told him, but not everything; knowing that he did not have to tell her everything for her to understand. He expected her to let him make the decision, but she surprised him. She never failed to surprise him. "Take me there, Tom," she said, her voice dry and throaty after the impact of the latest operation. "I don't want there to be any shadows over the house."

She insisted on being driven to the hospice in their old white car and not in an ambulance. As Tom helped her out, her hand brushed against the car door and her wedding ring flew from her finger. Tom hunted high and low for it, and finally discovered it lodged in the tread of one of the car's tyres.

–Keep it for me, Mary said when he offered it to her. She turned it into a game. –Let's see, which finger does it fit?

It turned out to fit the smallest finger on his right hand and he wore it there until, in circumstances that he could not possibly imagine, it flew off again and was nearly lost. After that his mother bought him a gold chain and he wore it around his neck permanently.

–You sure?

Mary nodded, and shivered, drawing her coat around her shoulders, and Tom wheeled her into the hospice, a place which he always afterwards hated despite its cheerful decoration, airy rooms and constantly friendly, helpful staff. Mary was given a quiet room to herself and for days after her operation she lay quietly, trying to use what strength she had to recover. The nurses juggled with her medication, sometimes giving her too much so that she slept like a log, at other times not giving her enough so that she lay in pain, never complaining, but whispering to Tom that perhaps the dosage had dipped below what she needed. Tom hated the room. He hated the nurses. He managed to get Mary home for her birthday, where she laughed and cried as the family gathered to present her with a birthday cake, and she tried and failed to blow out the candles. The children clung to her, all of them knowing that Mummy was very ill and would soon be going away forever. When they visited at the hospice the three of them were subdued and quiet, standing around Mary's bed or in the armchair where she sometimes sat, telling her what they had done at school that day, or regaling her with tales of the dogs. Mary took it into her head that she wanted to see Gus and

Jess and Tom, with the helpful connivance of one of the nurses and a dog-loving receptionist, smuggled them in one afternoon. At first it didn't go well as both dogs sat shivering in the middle of the room, ill at ease and unwilling to go anywhere near Mary, but eventually Tom helped her out into the armchair and they came closer so that she could scratch behind their ears, and then a woman from across the corridor came in and wanted to do the same, and before Tom knew it word had flown up and down the wards that there were two dogs in the building, and he had to transfer Mary into her wheelchair and visit every last room so that everyone could meet Gus and Jess, who by now had perked up tremendously, partly because they were now the centre of attention, and partly because a large number of biscuits and sweets were unexpectedly on offer.

By this time Tom's parents had moved nearby and one of them— usually his father as his mother quickly found and joined a number of local bridge clubs—looked after the children while he spent his evenings with Mary. They talked about their friends, they remembered how they met, sometimes Tom would take her out in the wheelchair and they would parade around the nearby roads and Tom could not help remembering the times when, in the middle of the night, he would have to strap John into his pushchair and struggle around the narrow pavements with him, trying to get him to sleep. Mary's room had a television with a video recorder in it, and they sometimes watched films, although the only one Tom could ever recall afterwards was *The English Patient*, and what he remembered most about that was not so much the film itself, but sitting on the bed with his arm around Mary, watching her eyes fill with tears as the story unfolded, his mind going back to the time they saw *Sleepless in Seattle*. He hated *The English Patient*, and gave it away to a charity shop. One evening he arrived to find the curtains drawn around Mary's bed. "Nothing to worry about," a nurse reassured him. "She's just having a bad day, the poor dear, so we have increased her medication a little."

–Mary?

She didn't reply immediately, although her eyes opened and looked into his own.

–I've written the Christmas story, Tom said. –It's called Wings. You lie there quietly and I'll read it to you.

So Mary closed her eyes again, and Tom read her the story about the great white angel floating silently through snowflakes, and a tiny baby listening while her grandfather, somewhere out of sight, told a story about a journey through a terrible storm. Tom never knew if Mary heard the story, because he forgot to ask in the short time afterwards; there were so many other more important things to say.

–Did we pass? asked Mary, a little wildly, her eyes still closed. –Has Christine called about her dress?

Tom pushed her hair, no longer thick and lustrous, away from her forehead.

–Mary? My dear?

After a few moments her breathing slowed. Her eyes opened. She and Tom looked at each other for as very long time.

–I will miss you, Mary whispered.

As Tom bent to kiss her, her brow wrinkled.

–Mum? she asked. –Jo?

–They were here yesterday, said Tom.

–They were?

–They'll be back on Friday.

–Time is all muddled up, Tom. I thought I saw Anne last night.

Tom would remember this remark later.

–Time doesn't matter any more, Tom, does it?

–No, he told her.

–How are the children?

–They're fine. Dad's looking after them.

–You will look after them, won't you, Tom?

–Of course I will. They're looking forward to Christmas. We're all looking forward to getting you home for Christmas.

Mary didn't reply. She didn't have to. Her eyebrows twisted quizzically, sadly, and he read her answer in her eyes.

As it turned out, Evelyn and Josephine didn't come on Friday, or for the next couple of days. "The damned car," Evelyn told him. "Say sorry to Mary." Tom thought she sounded a little odd but put it down to being kept away from the hospital. Josephine came on the line. "Tuesday, we should be there on Tuesday. Tell Mary, will you?"

Tom said of course he would. "The car will be fixed by then, will it?"

"What?" asked Josephine. Muted discussion which Tom couldn't hear. "Oh yes, I see what you mean," said Josephine. "Yes, the car. Yes." Tom thought her voice sounded a little odd, too.

"Only," he said carefully, trying not to break his own composure, "you might not want to leave it much later than that."

"What?" asked Josephine again. "Oh, I—" But whatever she was about to say was lost as Tom, suddenly unable to continue the conversation, hung up.

–My dear?

It was Monday. On Sunday Tom brought the children in, to find Mary asleep, drugged, snoring gently, her swollen body bulking out the pristine sheets. Her face was drawn, yellow; her hair thin. "That's not Mummy," said Lucy, and Tom's heart stopped, but Adam went forward to take Mary's right hand and John walked around the bed and took her left, and Mary struggled awake. To his amazement Tom saw genuine happiness in her eyes. He saw her hands squeeze the boys', and then she reached out for Lucy, who clambered up onto the bed. "You've grown so big," whispered Mary. "And you, Adam." Everyone looked at John, who shifted from foot to foot. He had not been blessed with whatever gene gifted height. "Your uniform is splendid," whispered Mary. She coughed. Her eyes rolled. For a moment Tom saw her arms slacken their grip on Lucy. Then her eyes refocused and her arms tightened again. She leaned closer to Lucy and whispered in her ear. "All right?" Lucy was nodding. "And you've grown so... so heavy."

Mary's eyes caught Tom. He swept Lucy, giggling, up into the air, then sat at the end of the bed and held her on his lap. "Let me see your tie," whispered Mary. "Did your dad do that up for you?" John insisted that no, he had done it himself. "We looked in the mirror," he explained, and Tom further explained that he couldn't do up a tie unless he was facing away from it, as it were, so he had shown John how to do it as they stood, side by side, in front of the big mirror in the bedroom. "Not bad," said Mary, drawing John close. She tweaked his collar and straightened his tie, then pulled him still closer and whispered in his ear. John rubbed at his eyes and, Tom thought, glanced at him with a slightly guilty expression.

"How are the dogs?" asked Mary. Her voice caught, her eyes started to roll up again, and Tom saw her arms shaking violently.

"Good," said Tom.

"Good," breathed Mary. Adam reached out to hold her hand again, and she recovered sufficiently to turn her head and smile at him. Then her eyes closed. "Tired," she whispered. "I'm sorry, I'm so tired." Tom stood, carrying Lucy. "We'd better let Mummy rest," he said. "Let's see if we can creep out without waking her." He glanced back as the door swung shut, to see that Mary had slipped back down, was snoring gently, but he thought that perhaps her face was marginally more peaceful than it had been before.

Years later he asked Lucy and John what she had whispered that day, but they both refused to tell him. John clamped his mouth shut and obstinately remained silent, while Lucy's eyes filled with tears and a look of such reproach that Tom hastily changed the subject.

–My dear? Josephine's here.

–Mum's coming later, said Josephine, perching on the edge of the bed.

Mary's eyes struggled open; her breathing momentarily quickened.

–Later?

–Later, confirmed Josephine. –How are you feeling today?

–Is it the morning? asked Mary.

–Yes. Tuesday morning.

–Soon be Christmas, said Tom.

Mary's eyes closed again and her head drooped.

–Can I leave you while I pop home? said Tom. As he and Josephine had come in that morning, a nurse had asked if he would like to have a bed set up so that he could stay the night.

"Just get your stuff sometime," said the nurse brightly. "We'll sort it."

Josephine said, –Yes, don't worry about it.

Mary opened her eyes and looked up at Tom.

–Just to get my pyjamas and stuff, Tom reassured her. –The nurse says I can stay here tonight.

–That'll be—Mary coughed, grimaced.

–Go along now, ordered Josephine. –We girls need to talk.

Tom stood up. He had no idea how many times he would replay this scene in his mind later. He didn't know that the genie awaited him by the door, already in place, looking back over its shoulder. Tom slid into the memory, looked over his shoulder, saw Josephine sitting on the bed, her short legs not quite reaching the floor, saw Mary looking at him, saw her make a tremendous effort to lift her hand and wave. Her eyes connected with his, conveying a message that he didn't understand, not then. Her lips framed a word.

–Later.

The door swung closed behind him, shutting her from view. When he came back, everything had changed.

–Mr Bradley?

It was another nurse, not smiling as much as usual.

–Your wife has taken a… bit of a downturn, Mr Bradley. I thought you ought to know before, well, before—

Tom said nothing, but walked on quickly, his heart pounding. When he walked into the room it was to find Josephine standing, gently stroking Mary's forehead and Evelyn sitting in the only chair. A cot had been set up against the far wall. Mary was sleeping again, her breathing hoarse and uneven.

–She's not sleeping, said Josephine. –The doctor says she has slipped into a coma. The doctor says she— Josephine stopped. Evelyn turned sad, tired eyes to Tom. For long seconds the only sound to break the silence was Mary's ragged breathing.

–When she was born, said Evelyn, –a light bulb exploded, right above the bed, quite a shock it was, I can remember it now, and the nurse jumping in the air and then hunching over her, over Mary, to protect her from the glass. Sit down, Tom.

Tom sat on the end of the bed. He had never heard Evelyn speak such a long sentence before.

–We'll be going in a little while, said Josephine.

Tom said nothing, but looked from Mary's drawn face to Josephine.

–I think you'd better tell him, said Evelyn. –Mary can't hear you.

–We don't know that, said Josephine. –The doctor said— She stopped again.

–What did the doctor say? asked Tom.

–Her hearing, said Josephine slowly. –Her hearing might be the last thing to go. Nobody knows, it seems.

The door opened and a nurse came in carrying a tray on which sat three cups of tea and a plate of biscuits. They sat and ate and drank quietly, politely. Mary dragged in her breath, slowly released it, dragged it in again, sometimes it hitched and a few seconds of silence made everybody tense, but then she would release it again. Tom's hand trembled when he put down his cup. He didn't find out then why Josephine and Evelyn had to go, because the doctor summoned him outside, across the corridor, into a tiny room to talk to him, and by the time he got back they had left.

"I am afraid your wife has entered a terminal stage," the doctor told him gently. "We don't think it would be wise to try to waken her." Tom said nothing. "Because it would mean terrible pain for her. You do understand, Mr Bradley?" Tom asked if Mary would be able to hear him, and the doctor looked at him for a long while before saying cautiously that it was possible, but nobody knew for sure.

Back in her room, Tom took Mary's hand and began to talk. He reminded her of the day they met and the giant crane looming outside her window. You remember Beryl? said Tom, squeezing Mary's hand. You remember how John kept us awake night after night? Mary never answered, never stirred, and Tom couldn't tell if her breathing slowed or evened, or whether it would be a good thing if it did. You remember Adam and the Tolkien tale? You remember how I nearly broke your hand at the National Gallery? Was that our first date? He talked all afternoon, except for two short periods when nurses came in to check on Mary, and, he suspected, on him. He talked through the evening, never letting go of her hand, even though it never responded, never clenched or twitched but lay limp and as unmoving as Mary herself.

As the evening lengthened into night, a male nurse he had never seen before came in to gently wash Mary's face, clear the room and push the cot away from the wall. It was getting dark. Tom climbed into the cot and reached out awkwardly, trying to hold Mary's other hand. The children will be fine, he told her. Mum and Dad are looking after them and tomorrow they're going to the beach. Lucy says she's going to watch out for giraffes. It'll be freezing out there, just as well we're in here, in the warm. He fell silent. Mary's breathing rasped in, paused, rasped out. Somebody's shadow loomed and faded on the frosted window on the door, barely visible in the darkness. He closed his eyes. He remembered dreaming about a candle. Once he had dreamed he was falling off a cliff but that something saved him, and awoke to find Mary, laughing, hauling him from the edge of the bed, telling him that she had dreamed he had fallen from a hill or a building, she didn't know what, but she had woken in the nick of time to prevent him disappearing from view off the edge of the bed onto the floor. Over the years, whenever he had been worried or uncertain, he had dreamed of descending the stairs into the basement flat at his grandmother's old house, twisting and bending to navigate the awkward entrance, his breath misting in the cold air always emanating from below; he would dream that he descended slowly, carrying a candle, and knew that at the bottom he would have to turn into the room with the ghost, the woman who moved soap around the flat, and hid keys, and sometimes left faint footprints in layers of dust deeper into the flat. Once Tom woke terrified, the ghost looking down at him, its long hair obscuring his view, but before he could scream Mary leaned down to kiss him, and thunder growled outside, heavy in the charged atmosphere.

The genie thought it remembered the door opening.

–How is she?

–She's not good, the poor dear.

–Look, he's still holding her hand.

–He did it all day too.

–He'll have cramp in the morning.

–Do you think—?

Both question and its answer were cut off behind the door. Tom was never sure it really happened. The genie, still chained to Tom's dreams, imagined lifting away from the cot, drifting up through the ceiling into a star-spangled night sky, swooping gleefully over tree-tops and roof-tops, back to the house where the children slept uneasily, their dreams barely visible as they moved and murmured and their eyelids fluttered. Downstairs Mary was sleeping peacefully. Tom wondered about that, feeling that something wasn't quite right. He drifted lower, easing through the bedclothes rather than sliding beneath them. He smelled the well-remembered smell of Mary's hair, felt her curve back, pressing against him as he curved forwards, encircling her with his arms. Upstairs the floor creaked, as it often did regardless of whether one of the children had hopped or fallen out of bed, and the curtains over the window billowed slowly, soothingly as he closed his eyes and felt Mary's hand twitch against his own, and even as he hugged her reassuringly he slid asleep, joining her in her dreams.

Much later he awoke to find that she had turned. Her head was on his chest, her long legs tangled with his, her shoulder pressing against his arm. He winced and tried to move, but something prevented him. It wasn't Mary. She weighed nothing at all and even her hair spreading out above him in a black fan, hiding the light from his eyes, floated weightlessly so that not one strand touched his face. Panicked, he tried to twist away and instead his eyes flew open and he found sweat-soaked hospice sheets tangling him so tightly that he felt as if he was tied to the bed. Faint morning light seeped in around the edges of the curtains across the windows, and his right hand still held Mary's left. Her rough breathing was all he could hear in the morning quiet. As far as he could tell it was unchanged from the previous evening. His shoulder felt as if it was on fire.

Neither he nor the genie remembered much of that day. It was mired in horror, but still, he must have got up, must have got dressed, and probably one of the ever-smiling nurses brought him a breakfast of tea and toast. He didn't remember any of it. He didn't remember Evelyn arriving, but she must have done, because he did remember her standing quietly at the head of the bed, smiling sadly down at her daughter, occasionally bending down to wipe her forehead with a damp flannel, or brush away an imaginary strand of hair. He sat on the edge of the bed, trying and failing to prevent tears from running down his cheeks, and Josephine and Catherine must have arrived sometime, because his memory served up an image of them sitting close together on two chairs, holding hands, but he didn't remember their arrival either. Once Mary's mother looked up at him and said, "You know this is the last day, don't you?"

The hours must have passed and the day moved from morning into afternoon. Mary's breathing slowed, became uncertain. The afternoon advanced into evening, and still Evelyn stood at the head of the bed, and Tom held Mary's hand. Tom knew all this must have happened, but he retained no clear memory of it. What he did remember was finding himself standing a little way away from the bed, perhaps stretching. The door to the room was not quite shut and he could hear the sound of a television from somewhere outside. When he looked at Mary, her eyes opened and she appeared to stare at him across the distance between them. Tom swayed with shock. Her eyes were almost completely a virulent yellow. He remembered when he had seen her eyes for the first time, grey and clear and calm, as she had turned around to see him in the Marsham Street offices, and weirdly he could see himself standing awkwardly in the doorway, an inane grin on his face. He remembered his old sports car. "The world must be told," Mary said. What was happening? He closed his eyes and visions jumped into vivid clarity; Mary elbowing him in church; Mary watching him as he held John awkwardly, almost bouncing him from hand to hand as if he was too hot to touch; a thunderstorm; himself wheeling a pushchair out of the house, seen from an odd angle, as if it had been Mary watching him from an upstairs window and it was not his own memory at all; Gus jumping up at him and leaving muddy paw-prints all over a brand new suit. Faster and faster. A strange image of blue sky and a warm wind blowing against his face.

The sounds of Star Trek drifted from the distant television. When he opened his eyes, she had closed hers, and was gone.

MONIQUE

I watch clouds streaming, white on grey
And through the dusk a single star
Whose light has fallen long and far
Glinting low as night claims day.

In age-old starshine from above
I share millennia past with you.
You know that, lit by fires of love,
I would share our futures too.

1

Tom did not wait at the hospital: his Mary was no longer there, so what was the point? He drove home blinking furiously to keep his vision clear. To the end of his own days he would remember how Mary moved slightly, and her eyes opened, strange, and yellow, and fey. Tom willed her to see him as her life fled. Part of him fled with her, forever.

–Did she see me? he asked the doctors.

–She opened her eyes? they replied. –That's very unusual. Perhaps she did.

When he took the children upstairs to tell them what had happened, Lucy and Adam became still, seemed to contract into themselves, become smaller, while John growled and smashed his twelve-year-old fist into the plasterboard wall. They all cried. Even as they sobbed and hiccoughed together, Tom remembered talking to Mary about *afterwards*.

"There will be no afterwards," Tom whispered. "I will never be lucky enough to find someone like you."

"Perhaps." Her thin fingers tightened on his. "Cry for me. I would like to think that you will cry for me."

"Mary—"

"But don't be alone for the sake of it. I will understand. I do understand."

Much later, Tom walked out of the house, trod the icy streets to the top of a hill that overlooked hedged fields. They lay dark, apparently uninhabited. The sky above was black but littered with stars, all of them glinting as if rimed with earthly frost. Tom had not put on a coat. His breath plumed in the frigid, wintersnight air.

–Why? he asked the stars.

He stood under the twinkling void, not feeling the cold, not feeling anything, not finding any answers. When at last he turned, he slipped slightly and started to shiver. He felt that he was turning his back not just on the empty, silent fields but also on part of himself; that part that belonged to Mary, as she belonged to him. Two sides of one coin, he remembered people saying.

Back at the house his mother was still up, waiting quietly by the log fire. She didn't need to say anything. Together they sorted through the presents under the Christmas tree, removing all those labelled 'To Mary' or 'To Mummy'. Tom had bought Mary an expensive bottle of perfume. A few days later, with the blessing of the funeral director, he put it into Mary's coffin where she lay—he tried to tell himself—peacefully at last.

Before that came the phone calls.

–I'll ring round the family, his mother told him.

Beryl said:

–Oh *God* no, no. Oh, I am so *sorry*. I didn't *know*. Beryl was now living in a distant part of southern England. Tom had great difficulty in persuading her not to jump into her car and drive up to Scotland immediately. He just managed to tell her about the funeral arrangements and ask her to pass on the news to all their mutual friends in the Department before he had to hang up and burst into tears himself.

–Hello?

–Hello? Who's there? It was a man's voice.

–This is Tom Bradley. Is Anne there? My wife—

–Ah yes. You're on the list. I'm afraid—

–What list?

–Some rather bad news. I'm Anne's brother.

–Ah, muttered Tom. He had a horrible feeling he knew what Anne's brother was going to say.

–I'm afraid that Anne—a couple of weeks ago—she fell over and hit her head, and, well—

A silence. Tom closed his eyes, remembering self-centred, likeable Anne, his favourite of all Mary's friends. Something else. Mary had dreamed about Anne while she lay in the hospice. Tom shivered. He decided he didn't want to work out if the dates fitted.

–She never came round, said Anne's brother.

–Jesus, said Tom. –I'm sorry to hear that.

–She had been feeling dizzy, said Anne's brother. –We think she had forgotten her inhaler.

Tom remembered Anne leaving her inhaler behind at the hospital. When was that? He shook his head irritably.

–Sorry, he said. –I was ringing up with bad news too.

Silence. Tom imagined that Anne's brother was feeling the same sense of icy precognition that he had.

–My wife Mary was one of Anne's best friends. I was ringing up to tell her... to tell her— He couldn't say the words. It occurred to him he didn't even know Anne's brother's name.

–Same list, eh?

–Yes.

–I knew she was ill, Anne told me ages ago. I didn't know... I'm sorry.

A third silence. Eventually Tom said:

–I don't know all Mary's friends that Anne knew... if you see what I mean. Can you pass the word?

–Will do, said Anne's nameless brother.

They both hung up.

–I wanted to thank you, Tom said, when Josephine answered the phone. –You know, for being here, and—

–Don't be silly, remarked Josephine in her forthright way. –Of course we would be there. Except that, I wanted to say sorry for the last few days.

–What?

–The last few days, repeated Josephine. –We weren't there as much.

–You weren't?

–No.

Tom rummaged in his damaged memory.

–I don't—

–The thing is, interrupted Josephine. –The thing is, Dad passed away a few days before Mary.

Tom stopped thinking. He thought, if he stopped thinking, that this latest horror would somehow go away.

–We didn't tell Mary, said Josephine relentlessly. –And we didn't tell you. You had, you know, enough on your plate. That's why we made it up, about the car.

Enough on my plate, thought Tom. There was probably a name for using such a trite phrase in such circumstances. Rather than listen to Josephine's voice, he spent a few seconds idly wondering what that name might be. He couldn't think of it, if it existed.

–What? he said reluctantly. –I missed that.

–He had been ill, said Josephine. –He had to go into hospital. Mum was, you know, to and fro.

To and fro, thought Tom. From her daughter dying in one hospital to her husband dying in another. He closed his eyes again, imagining the anguish Evelyn had been going through.

–It's been a rotten Christmas, he said eventually.

–Yes, said Josephine, and fell silent. Tom imagined she was parsing his trite remark.

–Tell Evelyn… tell your mum… I'm most dreadfully sorry.

–I will, said Josephine.

–We… we… must come over sometime, said Tom desperately.

–Tom.

–Yes?

–We'll see you in two days. Josephine must have sensed his mental panic, his inability to think. She added, –At the funeral.

–Oh yes. Yes. Thank you.

–Have you been sleeping?

–Er…

–You need to get some sleep.

–Right, said Tom. –Bye for now. Bye, bye.

§

He remembered the funeral as if it were a series of still photographs. He could recall nothing of what happened in between each frame. The three children, side by side on the front pew of the church, looking serious and quiet, but dry-eyed, perhaps not fully understanding what was going on. People in the yard outside, shaking his hand. Condolences. So many of them. Lots of people he didn't know, lots of people that he did. Old friends from the Department, which he had left when Mary became so ill. New friends from the place where he now worked, the local authority; even two Directors had turned up to shake his hand.

"I didn't know Mary knew all these people," he whispered to his mother. She was captured in a frame, giving him a lopsided smile.

In the limousine following the hearse. He could see the coffin through the back window of the hearse, and piles of flowers. At one place, a small village somewhere, a tall man in brown clothing doffing his cap and bowing his head as they passed. In future years Tom often wondered who he was. The driver glancing at his watch and muttering into a microphone, after which the hearse and the following limousine gradually speeded up until they were both fairly hurtling along country roads. The remembrance service had been held in one place, but the burial service was to be held close to where Mary's family lived, forty miles away. Clearly the remembrance service had overrun, and now they were in danger of missing the allotted time for burial. Tom had to suppress inappropriate snickers as they swayed, faster and faster, through narrowing roads. Mary would have loved this. All he could recall of the burial service itself was the red rose he had brought along turning over and over as it fell into the open grave. He drove back with the children. How had he done that? There must have been prior travel arrangements that he had forgotten about. Or perhaps someone else drove his car from one service to the other. It didn't matter.

It didn't matter.

Afterwards, after the frenzy of arranging the funeral and the pain of Christmas, Tom had no desire to go out or mingle. He sorted out paperwork. He hoarded the last little pieces of craft that Mary's trembling hands had made at the hospice. He cried. He could not sleep, so took to staying up very late, working on all sorts of inessential projects. He surfed the internet—the connection was Mary's last present to him—and on impulse added his name to a singles chat list. All around the house he found unexpected reminders of Mary. At work well-intentioned condolences from colleagues would not let him forget. The road ahead looked bleak and lonely.

§

Apart from one instance, the children handled the situation far better than he did.

"Dad," Adam asked him once, after an item on the televised news. "Is that what Mum had?"

"Yes," Tom told him.

"And does it always kill you?"

"Nearly always, I'm afraid."

"And does it always take about five years, like it said on the television?"

"Yes," Tom answered, wondering where this was leading.

"So you knew about Mum five years ago."

"Yes, Adam, we knew."

Adam looked at him, his face creased in thought. He was ten years old.

"Thanks for not telling us then," he said.

Most days Lucy would walk to her primary school, half a mile away, while Tom took the boys to their secondary school, which was a stone's throw from where he worked. His mother was usually in the house by the time first Lucy, and then the boys, returned. One day in March Tom came back to find John and Adam unusually quiet, and his mother tight-lipped.

–Where's Lucy?

–Upstairs.

–Oh.

Tom divested himself of coat and shoes and prepared to start cooking. His mother put on her coat and shoes and prepared to set off home so she could start her own cooking.

–She's upset.

–Oh? Tom looked up sharply.

–She won't say why.

It was very unlike Lucy to be upset. After his mother had left, Tom trudged up the stairs and went into Lucy's room, where he found her curled in a small ball of misery on the bed. He heard stealthy footsteps as the boys crept up after him, eavesdropping. He sat on the bed and after a moment asked:

–What's up?

–N-nothing.

–Come here.

The ball of misery unreeled itself and scrambled onto his lap. They put their arms around each other.

–S-something, Tom whispered. –Tell me.

Lucy heaved a shaky sigh, hiccoughed, and whispered, –School.

–School's the matter?

Lucy nodded, her chin bumping his chest.

–Tell.

–Making Mummy cards, whispered Lucy. –Only I don't have a Mummy any more.

Tom tightened his arms around her as he tried to process this information. He glimpsed movement and looked up to see John come into the room.

–She means Mother's Day cards, he said.

Tom closed his eyes. He had contacted the school and told them about Mary; asked them to be careful with Lucy for a while. True, he hadn't specifically said Please don't ask a little girl who has just lost her mother to make Mother's Day cards, but how hard could it be to work that out?

The next day he rang the school in a temper. A woman from the general office answered and said that the headteacher, Mrs Richardson, wasn't in her office right now and could she help. Tom explained that he wanted to make a complaint, and he wanted to make it to Mrs Richardson. The office woman became condescending and inquired as to the nature of the complaint. Tom, blood beginning to boil, remarked that as soon as she became the headteacher, he would tell her all about his complaint. But in the meantime, as she wasn't a headteacher, he wouldn't. He trusted that he had explained this sufficiently clearly for her to grasp his intentions. The woman became frosty and repeated that Mrs Richardson wasn't in at the moment. Will she be in later that morning? Yes. Then, Tom said, he would await her call. Fine, said the condescending, frosty woman. Tom gave her his number and hung up.

Needless to say, nobody called back and so early in the afternoon he phoned again. A different woman answered. Tom explained that he wanted to speak to Mrs Richardson to make a complaint but before that he wanted to complain that nobody had called him back. Something in his voice warned this new woman that he was not in a very good mood and it might not be wise to provoke him any further. She apologised that nobody had called back. Fine, grunted Tom. Mrs Richardson was in her office now and she would put him through. Good, grunted Tom. There was a pause. Tom imagined that this new woman was warning Mrs Richardson that there was a disgruntled parent on the phone who sounded as though he could easily lose his temper.

If she did pass on a warning, it was ignored. Mrs Richardson was even more condescending than the first woman had been. The teacher, she explained, could scarcely build her daily activities around the needs of one child. And why not? inquired Tom. In any case, he said, making Mother's Day cards was scarcely an important educational topic, was it? He wondered if Mrs Richardson liked having *scarcely* quoted back at her. It is an important topic to the mothers, said Mrs Richardson icily. My daughter, Tom reminded her, lost her mother just before Christmas. I asked you to take some care. She's been in tears ever since yesterday morning. This was not entirely true, but Tom felt it strengthened the point he was trying to make. Nevertheless, said Mrs Richardson. She refused to accept that Tom had any point to make. Tom got the impression that she thought he was a typical parent burdening her with trivial parenting issues. She didn't say she was sorry. Tom boiled over and remarked that if her teachers' collective attitudes were the same as hers, in the sense that she didn't seem to care about upsetting her pupils, then God help all the poor children at the school. Mrs Richardson remarked acerbically that she supposed everyone was entitled to their opinion but that Tom didn't know what he was talking about and he was wrong. Oh, said Tom. Was Mrs Richardson suggesting that he didn't know when his daughter was upset, and that even if he did, he shouldn't expect the cause of the upset—the school—to take any responsibility for it?

The exchange of views went on for a short while longer before Tom theatrically declaimed that he gave up, and disconnected. He didn't give up. One of the Directors who had shaken his hand at Mary's funeral was the Director of Education, a man known to everyone by his surname, Thorley. Tom and Thorley played squash every week or so, and the next time they met up, Tom had no hesitation in telling Thorley all about the Mother's Day Card Incident, as he had started to think of it. Thorley nodded and grunted and didn't actually volunteer any comment. About a week later he received a letter from Mrs Richardson apologising for her attitude on the phone and for the insensitivity of Lucy's teacher in getting the class to make Mother's Day cards when Lucy had so recently lost her mother. Reading between the lines, Tom thought the teacher had probably come in for a right lambasting from the icy Mrs Richardson. He didn't have to read between the lines to know that Mrs Richardson had also been admonished, likely by Thorley in person.

But before all that happened, he opened his eyes to see Adam cautiously following John into the room. He didn't know what to say. How on earth could Lucy's teacher have been so thoughtless?

–Did you make one? asked John.

Lucy twisted around and nodded.

–Can we see it?

Lucy hesitated, then clambered off Tom's lap and ran across to her table. Her card was black, with one shining star in a corner. Inside she had carefully written, not 'To Mummy' but 'My Mummy'.

–Let me see, said Adam.

–It's just right, said John.

–But Mummy won't see it!

–We don't know that, said John.

Tom had the good sense to stay out of the discussion.

–If she was here, she would've liked it, wouldn't she?

Lucy considered.

–I want to do one, said Adam. –Come on, let's all do one.

Lucy clambered off Tom's lap and all three children ran through into the boys' room. They left Lucy's card behind. Tom picked it up and kept it for himself.

§

Gradually the world reasserted itself. The future still seemed black, but as the weeks and months passed at least the present was slowly turning grey. Tom's parents gave a hand with the impossible logistics of dealing with a full-time job, three young children and two dogs. They settled into a kind of routine and Tom moved through it as if in a dream, as if one day he would wake up and find everything had restored itself to the way it had been. To the way he wanted it to be.

It didn't, of course. The world was telling him that his life would never be the same again, and in small stages his exhausted, bewildered brain was beginning to accept it. But what the world did not tell him was that good things could still happen, as well as the bad. Perhaps he would not have believed it anyway. Certainly he had no inkling of what was to come when he received an unexpected reply to the forgotten advert he had posted on the internet almost two years ago.

2

When Tom switched on his computer in the morning it took several minutes to grumble into life and several more minutes for the dial-up connection to establish itself. More time passed while any emails he might have received plinked, one by one, into his Inbox. Meanwhile Tom had wandered off to make himself a cup of coffee. He wandered back into the study almost ten minutes later, not really expecting to find anything interesting on the screen.

> Hi there!
> Read my advert too, and if you're interested I'll write back to you. On one condition: will you feed me first thing in the morning, after you have fed your dogs etc? I too work with the government, in Malta. I'm curious to know more about you. I await your email. Bye for now.
> Monique

Tom forgot all about his coffee, sat down as if in a trance, and read this message all over again. Then he instructed the computer to find this Monique's advert. It took a while. First came a grudging search of—or so it seemed to Tom—the entire internet in order to track down the chat site. Then came a lengthy wait while a rudimentary search function tried to home in on Monique in the chat site database. It found several Monicas, Monikas and Monas before hesitantly displaying the profile of Monique, location Malta.

> Dear Monique, I've read your ad and I don't see how anybody in his right mind could not want to respond!

He meant every word of it. The picture on her internet advertisement showed a beautiful woman holding a vase of flowers with green stems and rather odd purple-brown blossoms; she was smiling, looking up towards the camera.

> I must work out how to send you a photo of me.
> I am going to work now: I am afraid it is boring
> audit work! But I do like to write stories and poems,
> so perhaps I can hold your attention…
> Tom

He didn't really know if this was the right sort of thing to say. Conversation by email was not something he knew much about. He assumed he would think of nothing else but Monique all day, but when he finally got to the office it was to find that a meeting had been called by the Finance Director.

–Stuff's happening, said the Director, a man younger than Tom by a good few years and who believed he was tuned in to the modern way of thinking. His name was Gilbert Haines but he insisted that everyone call him Bert. Well, that's is name, I s'pose, thought Tom, and had to suppress a grin. When was the last time he found himself grinning?

–I got the fifty thou from the top man, said Bert mysteriously. Tom thought for a moment he was boasting about his salary.

–It looks like we're going to be nesting with the Region, burbled Bert. –So we're going to have to tranche up the workload going forward.

Tom resisted the urge to root around in his ear with a finger in case he simply wasn't hearing properly.

–Audit, said Bert. Tom jumped. Bert had said something he understood.

–Cross-functional, joined up and customer centric, continued Bert. Damn, thought Tom. Bert had reverted to sounding like a business-speak dictionary. He tried to work out if the terms he had used had been in alphabetical order but discovered he had already forgotten them.

–There's been some blue sky about independence, said Bert. Tom thought he almost understood this. –Meantersay, can't have audit reporting on moi.

Moi? thought Tom bemusedly. Never mind the Region; were they going to merge with a French arrondissement? He felt obscurely pleased that he had remembered that word from somewhere. Rumours about the Council merging with the Region had been around for months, of course.

–… CX, said Bert.

Tom leaned sideways and whispered to Claire, the other senior auditor in the section, –What was that? I missed that last bit.

–Just the last bit? whispered Claire.

Tom snorted.

–We're moving to Chief Exec, whispered Claire.

–I'll be cascading over the next few, said Bert helpfully. –Keep you in the loop. Might be some downsizing. It's all in the weeds at the moment but I'll touch base again when I've got the storyboard. Any questions?

–Er, said someone in the front row. Tom thought it might have been Payroll Bill.

–Good, good! chirped Bert.

Fortunately Tom's immediate boss, Dan LeMarechal, knew what Bert had been talking about. Not because he understood Bert, he told them, but because he had been present at a briefing by the Chief Executive who, Dan explained succinctly, spoke English.

–The bottom line is, the Council is merging with the Region.

–But—said Claire.

–Indeed, said Dan, nodding. –The Region is about five times the size of the Council so it'll be more of a takeover.

–But—

–True, said Dan. –It's not going to happen overnight. Couple of years, at least. Think of the different computer systems.

They all dutifully thought about them. Tom suddenly thought of his own computer and the message he had found on it that morning. He glanced at the clock, wondering if there was a time difference between Scotland and Malta.

–And anyway, said Dan with an air of finality, –we are going to move to be under Chief Exec and we're going to be a damn sight more secure there. Let's get some damned good reports in and up our profile so much that nobody in their right minds would consider getting rid of any of us.

Tom thought rather gloomily that in his experience decisions about staffing and structures were seldom taken by anyone in their right mind.

> Dear Tom
> Audit! Don't talk to me about audit! They come for me every year. Yes please a photo. I see you have three children, so do I. They are all almost grown up but still need their mama. What sort of things do you write? Can I read some?
> Monique

Tom still could not really understand why such a stunning, intelligent and warm woman would want to chat to him, but he replied, and she replied, and messages pinged back and forth almost daily. The first time she did not reply on the day after his latest message, he panicked. Had he upset her? Had he infringed some arcane Maltese protocol that he had never heard of? Had somebody much more interesting contacted her? He sat and stared moodily at the screen, hoping that the computer would heave itself into life and grudgingly admit that yes, a byte or so of data had come in from somewhere and if he would wait a few minutes the slowly growing blue bar that indicated its existence would slowly, chunk by chunk, report on download progress until a message would magically appear in his Inbox.

It didn't happen, but the next morning Monique prosaically wrote to explain that she was out with her family until very late the night before. After that she occasionally missed responding, and once he did too, when his dial-up connection disappeared off the face of the Earth for two whole days.

They learned more about each other as the weeks passed. Tom heard about her three daughters, all much older than John, Adam and Lucy, and about her estranged husband. He told her about Mary. He sent stories and poems.

OLD WELL-REMEMBERED

It does not matter that outside a storm is blowing.
I well remember your wet nose by the fire,
Head on paws,
Eyes turned up above the firelight
To ask me – is it time to be going?

I never saw that corner of the mat before.
It seems so threadbare empty,
Unlike the cupboard
Filled by mementoes of a lifetime
Out of sight, but nothing more.

Worn collar gathering cobwebs; rusty chain;
Chewed playthings; moth-balled blanket.
Old well-remembered
It was for the best,
Now I'm the one to feel the pain.

When her reply came next morning, Tom read it and then jumped up out of his chair and walked around his tiny study with repressed excitement, bounced back down into his chair and read it again.

> For your poem now… No words can express
> but tears definitely do… simply beautiful and hope-
> fully that is the real you. Anyway no dog lover can
> be anything but loving… when you tenderly touch
> the dogs think a bit of me, cause like them I like
> to curl at your feet and feel your tender hands ca-
> ressing my head. Yes I love to be spoilt but most
> of all I love to be loved. I am daring to bare more
> than I intend but distance makes me feel safe. Take
> care, for later.

At last Tom allowed himself to believe and hope. For later! He took the message everywhere, reading and re-reading it, trying to convince himself that this could mean Monique might care a little for him. For later! *This is a love-letter*, he told himself, astonished and exhilarated. *Surely not*, he cautioned himself. *Just read the words*, he answered. *Just read the words.*

He replied, hitting the send button before he could change his mind:

> Let me write a couple of things before I lose my nerve. I love my dogs, and they are always pestering me to be stroked or patted, but I would much rather run my hands through your hair… I will admit that I already think of you during the day, not just when I read your emails…

He waited for twenty-four hours, worried that he had said too much, worried that he might not get a reply and if he did, anxious of what it might say. But soon her name popped up on the screen and he scrolled it greedily. She had sent another message for him to hold against his heart. *Don't be!* she called it.

> I assure you there's nothing to feel nervous about. I appreciate your honesty and your outspoken way of writing.

Suddenly there was too much going on and Tom's emotions stretched, tautened; sometimes he felt as if he was walking on air, and at other times he could scarcely face getting up in the morning. At night he would lie alone, desperately wishing that everything that had happened over the last five years would prove to be a dream. He would roll over, facing the centre of the bed, hoping to see Mary lying here as if nothing had happened. Or he hoped she would be lying there in spite of all that had happened; he wished with all his heart that she would find a way to visit him. But the bed remained empty and increasingly cold as the year wore on. Once he was sure he heard a footstep upstairs, and quickly swung out of bed and went up to check on the children, in case one of them was up or sleepwalking. But they were all sound asleep. He would have thought no more of it, but next morning Lucy asked who the woman in white was, who came into her room and leaned over her. Both the boys gawped at her. Tom made haste to tell her she must have been dreaming, although his heart was pounding and tears threatened. That evening he went into Lucy's bedroom while all three children were downstairs watching *The Three Amigos* for possibly the hundredth time. He closed his eyes and turned in a shuffling circle. He heard a click, and when he opened his eyes it was to find that somehow the light had been turned on, although there was nobody there. He told no-one of these events, and nothing further happened until many years in the future, after the children had all long since moved away.

During the day he could not help thinking about Monique and their burgeoning relationship. The two junior auditors in the office, Roberta and Barclay, noticed the change in Tom's demeanour.

"You're happy today," Barclay would remark. Barclay was an older man who was especially skilful at mining information out of printouts or, increasingly, onscreen data. He himself was never happy. He fully expected to be working until he was eighty, to pay off the debt his daughter had run up at a private school.

Tom would shrug.

"Desperate Dan told you something, has he?" This was Roberta, a spotty girl not long out of school but who was unexpectedly very good at interviewing people and keeping accurate notes. She was peering at him in what she fondly supposed was a shrewd fashion.

Tom would smile and give a small shake of his head.

"See," Barclay would say glumly, "the Region looms, and he smiles."

Director Bert held another briefing session in which he mentioned that the Region had reached out to him, that they were singing from the same hymn sheet, and that a number of ideas had been run up the flagpole. "We're a strategic fit," Bert assured them. "And don't worry. There's no I in team."

These remarks did nothing to assuage the worries of the staff, and Tom was not immune. It seemed likely that not all of them would make it into the brave new world.

§

He forgot to write a story that Halloween. As Christmas approached, the children pestered him to write one and eventually he shut himself in his study and tried to put his mind into gear. He wasn't sure how they were going to get through Christmas again. Afterwards he could recall no trauma, but neither did he remember any joy. They opened their presents solemnly; watched Christmas films; ate their Christmas meal and pulled their Christmas crackers. They all knew that they were all thinking about Mary, and Tom detected an occasional tear, quickly brushed away. The story he wrote was a gentle ghost story called *That* Year. Long in the future, when he gathered all his stories into a collection, he realised something about *That* Year. He wrote in his introduction:

> It's funny how the mind works. It wasn't intentional, but I noticed some time after writing the story that Dad was telling it to the three children. That was it. There was no Mum in the present of *That* Year.
> She just wasn't there.

§

The winter wore on. One day there was sufficient snow that the schools closed. Tom stayed off work and they all built snowmen and threw snowballs at each other, coming in briefly for hot soup in front of the roaring fire before going back out again to freeze. The dogs, who had not seen snow before, tried to eat it. Jess leaped up to catch snowballs in mid-air. Gus, an old dog now, clearly intended to urinate on all the snowmen. Tom tried to yank him back and out of the corner of his eye saw the children hurling snow at each other, laughing hysterically. For a moment the genie pushed him back in time, and he was wrestling with a different dog, in wetter weather, and Mary was bent over, laughing and laughing at the muddy children swarming around her feet. Their eyes met across the intervening years and Tom felt himself fly away, back to the present, where he tried not to let his treacherous memory spoil the family snow day.

That evening he lay in a hot bath, recovering, while Lucy was asleep and the boys played Might and Magic on the computer. He heard the phone ring and unexpectedly found himself thinking about Monique. *Wouldn't it be wonderful if that was her?* He had no idea where the thought came from. It was not something which had occurred to him before. John stuck his head around the door.

–Phone, Dad.

–Who is it? Almost certainly he could get whoever it was to ring back.

–A lady. Monick? I didn't hear properly.

Tom surged up, setting the bathroom awash and, wearing not a stitch, rushed out to grab at the phone. His heart was hammering. *It can't be,* he told himself, and *calm down.*

–Hello?

–Hello? That was the first time he heard her voice, her lovely rich voice and accent. –Is that Tom?

–Yes.

–This is Monique from Malta. Hello.

They said hello to each other all over again.

–Hang on. Let me ... I want to get to another phone. I was just thinking about you. What an amazing coincidence!

–What?

He found the cordless phone together with a piece of paper and pencil and went back into the bathroom, away from the boys.

–I was lying in the bath. No, really; and when the phone rang I thought 'wouldn't it be funny if that was Monique?' She was laughing. Tom was grinning all over his face. –I was thinking of ringing you. Can I have your number?

She told him. They spoke inconsequentially for a few minutes, neither of them too sure of what to say. When she hung up, the silence of the house was different—it was the silence of not hearing her voice. As reality returned Tom could hear the boys talking in the next room, unaware of how their staid old dad's world had just turned upside down.

His head was still reeling. But his heart was on fire.

§

They spoke often after that first tentative phone call. They spoke about Monique's mother, about their families, about the day-to-day incidents of their lives. She went into hospital for a few days: Tom rang her mobile and heard nothing but silence. He fretted and worried. Eventually he caught one of her daughters in at the apartment and discovered that she had been obliged to turn the mobile off.

Tom sent her flowers and cards, and felt a sense of loss when he could not hear her voice or read her messages. He knew that he was falling in love—falling in love with a woman he had never even met—but he was powerless to stop it. When she came out of hospital he plucked up courage and all but told her.

"Be careful," she said. "There are many miles between us." But she sounded pleased. Tom wrote:

> I have had a chance to think about our con-
> versation of last night. For once I think I managed
> to say some things right, but as usual there were
> some things I should have said. I thought about
> making a list of all the things that are right about
> you, but it would have taken too long. Let's just
> say you manage to make my heart sing and ache
> at the same time.

He began seriously to consider how they should meet. The travel agents told him that it was difficult to get to Malta except in the summer months, and even then flights were infrequent. Monique wrote to tell him that her mum was poorly; was going into hospital; was out again and recovering. Somehow they decided that he should visit.

–Out on the Tuesday, back on the Thursday, is that right sir? the travel agents asked. –Business trip?

Tom said no, it was the most expensive dinner date in the world, and they grinned and obviously did not believe him. Tom tucked away the tickets and the Maltese money. He wondered what on earth he was doing.

–I'm sorry, my love, he said to Mary. –Is this all right? Am I being stupid?

He had felt her looking at him as he got ready for bed. Silence filled the house. The only light came from a bedside lamp, and the room was hatched in shadow. Her face gazed placidly from the picture on the bedroom wall. Tom more than half expected to hear a distant answer, but none came.

–Is it too soon? Tom asked her. –I loved you so much. I love you so much. You know I would not do this if you were here.

He heard her voice: I will understand. I do understand. But it was in his mind. In the quiet reality of the dark night, there was no answer.

–I think I love Monique, he whispered. He stared into Mary's eyes, cunningly crafted from a photograph, and listened with all his heart. Still there was no answer. He felt tears again as he thought of Mary. Was this all he had left of her? Tears in the darkness and a picture on the wall?

No, he knew that was not the case. He had the children. He had her safely locked away in his heart. He had the knowledge of what it was like to love and be loved.

–I am going out to see her, my dear, he whispered through his tears. –But you will be with me.

3

The plane thrummed through the sky and the pilot told everyone something garbled about French mountains. Lost in his own thoughts, Tom ignored him. He was thinking that, unbelievably, this was only his second date. He had never met any girl before Mary, and he had married her within six months. His first date became his wife; his second lived thousands of miles away. It was perhaps not a common sequence of events.

Later he was to discover that as he soared over France, Barclay leaped up in the audit room and shouted:

"Game on!"

Dan emerged from his office with an enquiring look on his face.

"Look! Look!"

Dan looked at Barclay's computer screen.

"Lot of wiggly things in boxes," observed Dan. "Oh look, they all squiggle upwards, except this one that goes down a bit, and then down a bit more…"

"They're graphs," explained Barclay. "Tom asked me to keep them. They measure…" Barclay looked around to make sure nobody was listening—which there wasn't, as he and Dan were alone in the office, "…income," whispered Barclay. "At various locations."

"Ah."

"Going up, more or less, in all these places," said Barclay, manoeuvring his cursor across the screen. "But going down in this one. It's… let me check… the sports centre."

"Ah," repeated Dan. He too looked around the office. "Why are you the only one here?"

"Well, Roberta's on that course and you persuaded Claire—"

"To go to the Audit Committee," interrupted Dan. "So I did. Ha. Just call me Tom Sawyer."

Barclay glanced at his watch.

"Tom will be, uh, up in the air somewhere by now, I should think."

"So he is," mused Dan. "Where was he going, exactly? And why?"

Barclay straightened in his chair.

"Barclay Dodds, BD2245813M, Audit Junior class I. Sir."

"All right, all right." Dan flapped his hands at the computer screen. "Keep your damned secrets. Examine the squiggle. Amounts. Dates. Names. Reasons. Predictions." He paused, then added triumphantly, "Stuff."

–Excuse me?

The man sitting in the seat next to Tom asked to borrow a pen. He appeared to be completing a crossword in a foreign language, presumably Maltese. Tom tried to concentrate on his book, but his eyes kept pulling away, to the sea and mysterious lands beneath. More, his *mind* kept pulling away. He wondered where they were. He wondered what Monique was doing; if she had yet left work; whether she was nervous.

Most of all, he wondered how they would feel when they met for the first time. He replayed conversations from over the last few days.

"I'm worried, Tom."

"So am I."

"There are so many miles between us."

"What are you worried about?"

"You know," she said.

"Yes." Tom thought about it for a moment. "I am worried that when we meet we won't hit it off, and you—you are worried that we will."

He could hear the intake of her breath. "Yes," she said in a small voice. "You already understand me too well."

When we meet. When we meet. While Tom daydreamed and Barclay dived happily into streams of data and Monique drove round and round the airport car park, searching for a space, the plane tilted downwards and that moment of meeting moved much closer. Warning bells sounded and flashing lights told everyone to fasten safety belts. The captain muttered something about landing and remarked that it was hot but showery. The plane shuddered and tilted more steeply. Tom's heart thundered.

What he assumed was Malta loomed below. He had time to glimpse houses, rectangular patches of brown vegetation, more houses. Then the ground was mere feet away and he held his breath as they landed. The engines roared, slowing the plane. Tom looked out at the warm sunshine and found it impossible to believe that he had taken this giant, impulsive step to Malta. Monique must be waiting scant yards away. His heart pounded again.

§

He had no baggage to collect—he was only going to be there two days, after all—and he had to wait only a few minutes at immigration. He found himself at the top of a flight of steps, descending into a throng of people. He looked down at them, and it seemed that everyone looked up at him. After a few seconds, he caught sight of someone at the back of the crowd, keeping pace with him as he went down the steps. When he reached the bottom, he headed straight towards her.

It was Monique.

She was wearing a white dress and she was leaning forwards a little as she walked, almost as if she was re-creating her pose from her photograph on the dating site. Her hair was long and dark, and her eyes were sparkling. Tom's thoughts were a muddle as he tried not to stare at her. *I will understand. I do understand.* Monique was smiling, a little nervously, and he drank in the sight of her. His first thought was—she is beautiful. What would a beautiful woman like this see in someone like him? She had written in one email *A great big hug coming your way*. His thoughts pulled him this way and that but eventually he got hold of them and focused on the present. He wanted to take her in his arms there and then, but lacked the courage. Perhaps she did too, which was probably just as well. Tom's knees would have given way altogether if she had made a move towards hugging him.

What was she thinking?

Tom's heart was pounding again, with excitement and trepidation. He suddenly realised that he was feeling as he had done so many years ago, when he had first met Mary. *Don't be stupid,* he told himself. *You have only just met*. But that wasn't strictly true. They had exchanged so many messages, spoken so many words over the telephone. And now here he was, standing in front of her. All that had happened before counted for nothing. Now was all that mattered. What happened between them *now* was all-important.

–Hello, they said together, and laughed.

Monique touched his arm and guided him out of the airport to the car park.

–It's been crazy here. Temperatures in the forties.

–This is warm enough for me.

–And the storms have been terrific. It's cooler now…

They found her little red car and climbed in. She chattered on, about the flight, about the car park, about the weather, and it dawned on Tom that she was nervous. It came as a surprise that anyone would be nervous of him.

She was still chattering, touching him on his arm, on his knee. Did that mean anything? Or was it just the Maltese way? Tom felt what was almost an electric jolt each time her hand brushed him.

They were driving through a continuous array of potholes. The car lurched and bumped. The sun disappeared, and he leaned forward, trying to look up at the sky. A few drops of rain hit the windscreen.

–Uh-oh, said Monique. She turned to grin at Tom, and his heart somersaulted.

–Thought I'd left this behind, he said as it started to rain more heavily.

–This is what it's been doing. It's ridiculous! She glared at the rain, at its sheer effrontery. Then she sighed. –I'll drop you off at the hotel, come back and get you when you've had a chance to shower and change. All right?

Tom clutched at the dashboard as she turned into a stream of traffic without, as far as he could tell, checking that there was a space for them. Having just arrived, he didn't want to leave her side so soon. He looked across at her. She sensed it and glanced across to meet his eyes.

–Won't take me long to change.

–I'm going to take you out to dinner, she said, smiling.

–I'm in your hands, Tom told her gravely.

§

The hotel was all but invisible behind sheets of bucketing rain. They hopped and skipped through pools of water into the reception area. Tom didn't bother unpacking. He found his change of clothes and got back downstairs as quickly as possible, where Monique was sitting quietly at a table with an enormous cup of tea. Before joining her Tom looked out of the windows at the front of the hotel: it was then that they had the first piece of luck that blessed that perfect holiday.

It was still pouring with rain. The streets and pavement were swimming with water. The air was thick with heavy raindrops falling vertically from a grey sky.

–Welcome to Malta, said the young receptionist at the desk wryly.

In the future the genie had no problem in slipping Tom whole-heartedly into the memory of the rain bouncing off the streets, the windows, the doors. Malta housed many memories. Perhaps the first was the airport and the whirling, confused, exhilarating experience of their first meeting. But this was the second: being forced to sit in for a while, out of the rain, drinking tea and talking to each other. There was no mad rush to get things done. Tom sat beside Monique, and looked into her eyes, and she looked into his. Neither of them remembered what they talked about. It didn't matter.

It didn't matter.

While they sat there quietly, with the rain barring their way to the outside world, their hearts began to beat together. Tom later wrote:

Now I see.

The gloomy evening
Is a magic twilight
And the slanting rain outside,
Our shield.

When the rain eased, they hopped and skipped back through the puddles to the car, and she drove through busy streets towards her apartment.

–Lola will be there. She's got a fever and is feeling rotten, but she won't be lying down even though I told her to get some sleep. She is a terrible patient.

I wonder where she gets that from?

She told Tom where they were, pointed out places, but he had no skill at remembering that kind of thing. Neither did the genie. When he tried to slip back into that memory, back into that time, he heard no words but only saw glinting flashes as a watery sun returned and Monique as she turned from time to time to smile at him. Her driving was a revelation. She appeared to turn corners whenever she wanted to, regardless of what other traffic was about or where it was going. And wherever they turned, the car bumped and bounced through potholes. When he commented on them, she launched into a tirade against the government and the way in which the roads had been allowed to deteriorate. Tom watched her as she spoke animatedly, drove, looked around, found time to smile at him. He looked at her lips and dark eyes and let Malta wash over him.

They reached her apartment building, and she parked so close to a wall that Tom had to clamber out of the driver's seat. She giggled, and he grinned uncontrollably. The apartment itself was large and spacious, but there was no sign of Lola—perhaps she had after all succumbed to advice and was lying down. While Monique went to look for her Tom wandered around looking at pictures, glancing out of the window, trying to identify photographs. The television was on but mute.

–That's Lola, said Monique proudly from behind him. –That's her winning photograph at her last competition. I've put the kettle on.

The photograph was of a beautiful young girl and was in glossy, magazine front-cover format.

–Is she okay?

–She's not asleep. But she should be. Here she comes.

Tom turned as Monique went behind the counter into the kitchen area, and saw Lola coming out of what was presumably one of the bedrooms. They smiled at each other and said hello. She certainly did not look well.

–You should be in bed! declared Monique irritably, and followed up with a flood of Maltese. Lola, who had sat down at the other end of the table, was obviously arguing back, although because she too spoke in Maltese Tom could only conjecture what she was saying.

–Ha! said Monique, dismissively.

Tom sat down holding a cup of tea and for the first time felt a touch of tiredness as the day's travelling started to catch up with him.

The early part of the evening passed in a blur. Another daughter, Zoe, came home and she, Lola and Monique engaged in a three-way simultaneous conversation which baffled Tom, even though much of it was in English. They moved to the sofa and talked, and watched the news. The girls moved away.

–Time to go, said Monique.

As they left, the third daughter, Lily, arrived. The door closed behind her. Tom wondered what the other two would be saying to her.

–Never mind Lola entering beauty contests, he remarked as they went back down to the car, –what about Lily!

–It is a different look. Not the sort of good looking that magazines want.

–Ah, said Tom. He wanted to say that Monique was more beautiful than any of her daughters, but his courage failed him again.

Considerately, Monique moved the car out from by the wall so that he could board through the passenger door.

§

A kind of magic was abroad that night. They drove through quieter streets away from the built-up area towards what Monique called Medina. She told Tom its history, which of course he promptly forgot, except that she told him she went to school there. They parked, and she showed him an area where she used to play games. They walked through narrow streets.

They came to a wonderful restaurant full of candles and space. By now Tom felt as if he was in a dream. It was the ultimate romantic setting, and he had been taken there by a beautiful woman who had already captured his heart. In those moments with Monique in ancient Medina, he felt himself beginning to heal. The pain and horror of the last years and months finally began to slip away; at the same time he became sure that he had fallen hopelessly in love.

They talked a little, and sometimes there was peaceful silence between them. Tom had the feeling that this was the first time she was making a conscious effort to weigh him up, to consider seriously what she thought of him. But he felt curiously at ease. Despite the fact that simply being out with a woman was a new experience for him—never mind the astonishing location and circumstances—he felt no sense of pressure or worry. They talked, or they did not talk. Time passed, and Tom found out that as well as loving Monique, he liked her too.

§

They left eventually, out into the cool but dry night, and made their way back towards the car. Monique kept bumping into Tom so that it was awkward to walk normally.

"Did you really not understand?" she asked later.

Tom thought she tripped, and put an arm around her.

"No."

It was momentarily easier to walk, but then he released her and she started bumping into him again.

"Fool."

At last he realised what she wanted, and put his arm around her again.

–This what you wanted?

She did not answer. They walked slowly back to the car and the feel of her pressing against his side was almost more than Tom could bear.

By now it was late, and she drove him back towards his hotel. The car radio played music, and she showed Tom various places lit up against the night. At last, but too soon, they turned into a road that Tom recognised and found a place to stop outside the hotel, too close to a hydrant or post. Tom looked at her and raised his eyebrows, and she smiled.

–Thank you, he said, meaning the meal and the evening. –It was beautiful.

She did not answer, but looked steadily at him. His heart was pounding. He knew what he wanted to do, but—oh, it was so difficult. Then he took his courage in both hands, leaned forward, and briefly kissed her mouth. It was awkward: he did not know if he was going too far, and the last thing he wanted to do was upset her.

–You are only the second woman I have ever kissed.

Tom cursed himself for a fool. He leaned forward again, and Monique slid across her seat towards and somehow under him. Their lips met. Tom could see lights reflected in her eyes. Then, astonishingly and wonderfully, he felt her mouth open and her tongue slide against his. She moaned softly. Tom put his hand to her face and tasted her mouth and tongue, and wished that time would stop.

But it did not. When they moved apart, she sat up straight and he could see indecision in her eyes.

–Won't you come in, for a little while? He knew how it sounded, but he truly wanted just to be with her, and perhaps kiss again. –You can trust me, he whispered.

–I know. She gave a quick half-smile. –But could I trust myself? No, I must get back to Lola.

Tom knew that now was the wrong time to try to get any closer. –All right. He kissed her cheek. –Till tomorrow, then.

–Yes. Nine. Okay?

–Oh, I'll be there, said Tom.

He opened the door as far as he could and squeezed out. If nothing else, he was going to remember this trip for the variety of ways he was obliged to get in and out of cars. Monique drove away, and he waved.

§

He replayed their kisses over and over in his mind. *Could I trust myself?* she had said. He remembered the feel of her tongue, the sound of her moans as their mouths met. He rolled over and clasped his pillow.

It took him a long time to get to sleep that night.

4

At nine o'clock the next morning he was sitting in the reception area, pretending to read a magazine. In reality he was watching the traffic outside the window. He glanced at the clock behind the reception desk and discovered it was one minute past nine. The sun was shining. He had eaten breakfast, showered, walked around his room waiting for nine o'clock to come into existence. The door to the lobby swung open, and his heart lurched, but it was a young girl coming in, clattering in, with a tall young man close behind. He was imploring her about something. Tom checked the clock. Two minutes past nine. He wondered what was happening back at home. All the children should be in school by now, the boys taking the school bus while he was away. His mother was probably tidying up and cleaning around, tut-tutting at the state of the house. At the office Barclay would already be poring over printouts; Claire and Roberta were probably getting coffee somewhere, and Dan wouldn't have arrived yet. In this he was wrong, because the audit section was chasing hotfoot after missing cash and all of them had arrived early, keen to get going and produce the damned report Dan wanted and needed to persuade Bert that all of them were invaluable employees, not to be dispensed with. But Tom didn't discover any of this until he returned to Scotland thirty hours later.

The young woman marched up to the reception counter and declaimed something in a shrill, angry voice, in Maltese, of course. The receptionist poured a look of scorn over the tall young man, who abruptly ceased importuning and instead shouted at the receptionist. Naturally it was also in Maltese, but Tom reckoned it was along the lines of 'What business is it of yours?' The receptionist shrugged and produced a key and slapped it on the counter. The young woman grabbed it and flounced off, up the nearby stairs. The tall young man looked lost for a moment, then turned and strode out of the hotel at speed. Tom couldn't tell if he was embarrassed or angry, or both.

Five past nine.

Every time a red car went past his hopes rose and his pulse raced, but in the end he need not have bothered to watch. He failed to spot Monique's car. The door opened and she walked in before he had any idea she was anywhere nearby.

She looked gorgeous. She was wearing dark slacks and jumper against the unusually inclement Maltese weather, but dark glasses against the morning sun. Her hair glinted. She moved with an elegance and assurance that seemed part of her nature. Tom stood up hurriedly to greet her.

–How's Lola?

–Still at home. She's better, but still running a temperature.

Outside it was bright and humid. They got into the car.

–What's the plan?

–I'm going to show you some of Malta. The Golden Sands first.

–Golden Sands?

–You'll see.

She started the car and swung out into the traffic—so far as Tom could see, without bothering to check if there was a space available. Probably there wasn't. She turned on the radio and Tom settled back.

§

Ever afterwards it was easy to slip back into that little red car, see the sun flashing signals between trees or sometimes taller buildings as they jolted past, listen to the radio shrilling love songs. Tom felt at peace, felt as if these moments were going to last forever, even though he knew he had a flight to catch the next day. It didn't matter.

It didn't matter. For the first time in years, he felt himself loosening instead of tautening; he was letting the atmosphere wash over him instead of battling against it all the time.

Monique waved her arms to show him all sorts of places, none of which he remembered. Nor did the genie. It possessed the ability to push him back into a different reality and into different times, but reality was inside the little red car, not on the streets outside. Reality was watching Monique driving, waving her hands, touching him sometimes. He did remember that at one point they drove through a small place and she said, "That's where my parents live." By the time she said it they were already past. Tom twisted around to look behind and gained the impression of a shopfront on a corner.

At another place they were able to see a ferry out to sea, rocking violently.

–I was going to take you to Gozo for a meal.

Tom watched the ferry listing and staggering its way through heavy seas.

–Okay going out before a meal, Tom said. –Not so good on the way back. He looked up at the sky, where white clouds chased grey in a streaming race. –See any shapes? The children always see dragons.

–Do you make a wish?

–Yes, murmured Tom. He saw her smile, and knew she could read his thoughts. They bumped and lurched down a slope and she pulled to a stop. Down below was a sandy yellow beach, and at one end stood an elegant hotel.

They got out of the car. On an impulse Tom held Monique's hand and was gratified that she made no move to pull away. The sun shone, although the wind was not warm.

–I remember when I first met Mary, he said suddenly. –I had never held hands with anyone before and I was doing it like… like… He shifted his grip and Monique giggled as she found herself walking hunched forwards awkwardly. He changed back and gave her hand a squeeze. –We used to walk around a museum near where we went to college. It was ages before she had the courage to tell me I was doing it wrong.

He fell silent. It was the first time, he thought, that he had spoken of Mary and their life together without wanting to cry. Instead he felt an aching sadness and sense of loss, but also an unexpected realisation that he had those memories to keep, which was surely better than having no such memories at all. Monique walked quietly by his side. He wondered if she had divined his thoughts. A couple who had been at the end of the beach, by the rocks, passed them on their way back towards the hotel. They walked the last few yards and stood, hand in hand, looking out over the sea. Tom felt peaceful, and a little more confident of himself.

–In one of your messages, or over the phone, you told me you were going to give me a hug at the airport. A great big hug, you said. What happened to that?

–*You* told *me* you were going to give me a hug at the airport, she said indignantly. –What happened to *that*?

They smiled at each other. Tom put an arm around her shoulders, and she hugged him.

–You're cold.

Tom tightened his arms around her.

–Not now, he whispered.

They stood for long moments while the sea rolled in and the wind stirred the sand. Tom wondered if he should kiss Monique, if she wanted him to. The genie intervened, pushing him back many years, to a time when he kissed Mary in the rain. He remembered her lips warm through the icy rainwater, and wondered if Monique's would feel the same in the chilly wind. Then the moment passed and she sighed. She moved away, but her hand sought his. Had she been remembering, too? Perhaps her own genie had tugged her away, to a time when she had been happy on the Golden Sands.

"Let's get a cup of tea," she said.

§

They wandered back towards a café situated past the car, higher up the slopes. They were the only customers. While they sat there quietly, Monique steepled her fingers and looked at Tom. He guessed that she was still weighing him up. He was not surprised. Their lives had collided so unexpectedly that it took a lot of getting used to. The tea was insipid and he was reminded of the horrible cup of tea and curled-up, stale sandwich he and Mary shared at Marsham Street— the best lunch, he had thought at the time, he had ever had. Well, this was the best morning elevenses. He wondered if there was a Maltese word for elevenses, but decided not to enquire.

Monique went outside while Tom paid for the teas with unfamiliar currency. He found her sitting on a low wall, looking out over the sea. He stood close and gently ran his fingers through her hair, as he had imagined doing so many times, before resting his hands on her shoulders.

–You remembered, she murmured.

–And so did you, he countered.

She leaned back against him momentarily, then stood. Behind her cloud-shadows raced across the beach. They climbed back into the car, and had lunch in a nearby village. Then she took him to Buskett Forest.

§

They avoided a party of schoolchildren and made their way along quiet paths, through dappled sunlight. At first they held hands, but then she leaned against him. Tom put his arm around her shoulders again, and she held him around his waist. They walked slowly. Tom admired the forest and told her about the walks in Scotland, by the river, along the beach.

They passed a tiny stream, climbed crumbling steps to another path. He tightened his arm around her and she pressed even closer.

–Are you glad I came?

–Yes.

They walked further, slowly.

–Are you glad you came?

–Oh yes.

–You must be tired.

–A little.

Suddenly she stopped and swung him around to face her. Before he quite knew what was happening, she had her arms around him and her lips were on his. They had kissed in the car, but this was different. This time her full length was pressing against him. Tom pulled away, nervous of his arousal, but she pushed her hips back again. He got the message. He wrapped his arms around her and lost himself in her kiss. Their mouths opened and her tongue teased his. Then she finally stepped back and Tom found himself with his hands on her shoulders, heart pounding, looking with astonishment into her smiling face.

–Does that give you energy? she said.

–I'll say, he whispered.

–I tell you, I'm high-octane fuel! Her arm came around his waist again and they walked, hips bumping, further into the forest.

–This is beautiful, Tom told her. She half turned, negotiating a narrow part of the path, and he could not stop himself from sliding his hands around her shoulders to pull her close. But she did not resist and they kissed again and again, lips and tongues tangling, arms straining close. And when they parted it was only to hold each other close again as they walked slowly, slowly, through the sun and shade.

–We're acting like a pair of teenagers, Tom told her. –You're making me feel young again. He used his left hand to hold hers, pressing it against his side.

–Alby, she said, softly.

–What's that?

–Qalbi, she said again, spelling it. –It means heart. She looked at Tom, then away. –It's what you are, I think. My qalbi.

Tom did not reply. He contented himself with squeezing her shoulder as they walked even more slowly through what seemed to him an enchanted dream. They came to a low stone wall, and she sat down on it with a sigh.

–Tired?

–No, I just don't want this to stop, she said. She lay back on the stones; put her hand over her eyes. –Too bright, she murmured.

Tom leaned close. –This is one way I can block out the sun, he told her. She opened her eyes and smiled as he bent to kiss her again. He stroked her cheek and tasted her lips and the corners of her mouth. Then the heat of the sun was cut off as if by a switch, and the shadows deepened. As Tom turned to look up, disaster struck. A branch of the bushes by the wall caught Mary's wedding ring, tugged it from his finger, and it tumbled out of sight.

The sun flooded back as the cloud passed and they knelt together to peer over the edge. They could see the ring trapped by leaves scant inches below. Monique cupped her hands underneath, in case Tom dislodged it and it fell further, and he groped gently with his fingers. In a few seconds he had retrieved it.

–That was close. Tom's voice was a little shaky. He *was* shaken, at how close he had come to losing his precious memento of Mary.

More clouds swept away the sun.

–Looks like another shower, said Monique.

–Take me somewhere where we can be alone for a while, Tom asked, surprising himself. –Please?

She looked at him for a moment and then—he was not sure it was deliberate—she nodded slightly. Holding hands now, and anxious to avoid the coming rain, they hurried back to her car.

§

They drove through a blinding downpour that overflowed the potholes and turned the windows into running streams of water. For once, Monique did not turn the radio on, and they spoke little.

–Where are we going?

–To the cliffs. There's a place we can park there.

The rain eased a little, but it still drummed on the car roof. A wind had sprung up from somewhere and the world stayed grey. Monique stared straight ahead, a tiny frown on her face. Tom wondered what she was thinking.

It did not seem long before she drove off the potholed surface of the road onto the equally potholed gravel of a car park. The gravelled area extended down behind a cluster of bushes, but she turned off and pulled up into a small secluded area. Tom could vaguely see other cars on the other side of the bushes, lower down, almost invisible behind branches and rain. Even that view was fast disappearing; Monique had turned off the engine and the car windows started to steam up. Tom unbuckled his seatbelt and turned towards her. He wanted nothing more than to gather her in his arms and kiss her, but for the moment she stayed still, making no move towards him.

–This is the cliffs, she said.

Tom raised an eyebrow and tried to peer through the windscreen, which by now was virtually opaque.

–If you go to the other side, you can see out over the sea.

–The other side?

–Of the bushes.

She was breathing rapidly. There was something almost desperate in her tone. Tom realised that she was nervous, perhaps suspecting that they were teetering on the edge of their own precipice.

–Ah. Not the weather for sightseeing.

Monique unbuckled her belt too. She glanced at the window, which by now was a solid grey colour, with only rainwater sliding down the outside of the glass visible. Then her eyes met Tom's, and they both knew that this was the moment. Tom leaned close while she slid over towards him. He wrapped his left arm around her body, put his right hand behind her neck, and kissed her. They strained against each other.

The rain drummed, and eased, and drummed again. The car rocked in the rising wind. Outside an older man wearing a bright raincoat walked past, alternately dragging and being dragged by a large, waterlogged dog. He glanced at the small red car and frowned. These teenagers. A man and a woman battled past not long afterwards, he helping her fight against the wind. They paused in the lee of the bushes. He looked at the car, taking in its steamed windows and its intermittent rocking that didn't always correspond with the gusts of wind. He caught his partner's eye and pointed with his chin. They exchanged a look, and smiled at each other, before venturing out again, around the fringe of bushes into the horizontal downpour.

Monique was moaning softly. Tom touched her breast and she seized his hand and pushed it under her coat, guiding him past her clothing. Later, much later, he remembered Mary dressed in goodness knows how many layers of clothing when he drove her out in his open-topped car and proposed to her. Now, in the hot, wet atmosphere of the red car perched high above the windswept Mediterranean, he could think of nothing but Monique's mouth and her body and her moans. The sky rumbled and groaned, but neither of them heard it; or if they did, they thought it was the other.

They pulled away from each other, panting. A strange, coy look passed across Monique's face. –I wish, she said, that I was wearing a skirt. For a second the implications of what she was saying escaped Tom. Then his heart skipped several beats and his throat went dry. He started fumbling with her clothing. The storm increased in violence, hurling sheets of water against the windscreen and across the top of the car. They could not see, encased in their own warm darkness, but other cars turned on their lights and started to nose away from the cliffs, back towards the road. A bang of thunder sounded close overhead, and a distant flare of lightning turned the inside of the car into an eerie half-light. Inside the car they were entangled with each other and Tom saw the look in Monique's eyes.

–I don't know if I should say this, he whispered, –but I want you. I didn't feel I could say it before, but I can now. I want you desperately.

A look of amusement crossed her face. –Why shouldn't you say it?

Another flash of lightning, closer, painted her face in stark black and white.

–Come back to the hotel? Tom pleaded. –Please come and make love with me.

She sat up straight, fastening her trousers and blouse. Without answering, she tidied her hair, started the engine, and then sat waiting for the gloomy surroundings to emerge from behind the clearing windows.

Tom looked outside for what seemed the first time in hours, to see that the grey of the storm—which, despite the thunder and lightning, was beginning to fade—had turned into dusk.

Monique abruptly put the car into gear and reversed.

–Where are we going?

–To the hotel.

Her words hit Tom like a bolt of electricity, as if one of the flashes of lightning had somehow penetrated the car and smashed into him. He felt a surge of both love and lust, and clenched his fists tightly in case she saw his hands trembling.

§

As they set off she picked up her mobile phone and spoke incomprehensibly into it.

–I've got to pick up Zoe, she said. –I'll drop you off first and do that, and then come back. Okay?

Of course it was okay. Tom didn't have to tell her that.

–I'm really nervous, he blurted.

–So am I.

–I have never done anything like this before.

–Nor have I.

Saying these few words eased the tension a little. She chuckled, then gave Tom a sideways look. –Do you know what I don't like? she asked.

Tom shook his head.

–The hotel, she said. –I just don't like the idea of going back to a hotel room.

Tom reached out to touch her hand, hoping that she would not change her mind.

–What room did you say? Two hundred and one, is that right?

–That's right.

It was dark now. All the other cars had their headlights on. Tom sat in silence for a while as they drove into town, into streets that he was beginning to recognise. She pulled up outside the hotel and turned to look at him. He could see that she was as nervous as he was, and his heart went out to her. He leaned forward and kissed her quickly on the cheek and then, without saying anything, got out of the car. She immediately drove off, into the traffic. He felt an illogical pang of separation, even though he knew she was coming back soon.

He walked slowly into the hotel and climbed the stairs to his room, unaware that the third strange coincidence was fast approaching.

§

He remembered every moment of the hour that followed. Every tiny movement that each of them made. As he had hoped, she came straight into his arms. In between kisses he tried to give her the chance to change her mind. Her answer was to kick off her shoes and fling herself down on the bed. They undressed slowly, savouring every moment, and melted into each other.

–Oh my God, Tom whispered, –you're so beautiful.

–You drive me wild, she whispered.

–That's the idea, Tom gasped.

She pushed him over onto his back and knelt on knees and hands above him, looking down into his eyes. She was smiling with open happiness and enjoyment, and even then Tom marvelled at how lucky he was, to be making love with this wonderful woman. He pretended to try to push her over onto her back and when she resisted, he pretended that the effort was too much for him. Her smile widened.

Afterwards, they both realised that they had somehow left their inhibitions locked outside of the hotel room. They kissed as they made love.

–Qalbi, she whispered as Tom shuddered and gasped. –Ohh, qalbi…

Eventually they were drained. They lay clasping each other, both of them slick with sweat. Tom stroked back her hair and looked at her face. She stretched like a cat, comfortable and utterly unashamed at her nakedness. Tom felt his heart completely full and at peace. The desire for sex receded temporarily behind the curtain of satiation, but his feelings for Monique were burning as strongly as ever—more strongly than ever.

He knew without a shadow of a doubt that he loved her past all reason and, as they lay there in the hotel room with the night pressing in at the window, he knew that she loved him too.

§

They lay, talking quietly, she on her back and Tom curled up by her side. They worked out that her excuse that she was at a German lesson would just about hold water as far as timing was concerned. It was a powerful time because they were *there*, talking, closer than ever after making love. It did not occur to Tom to roll over from her as if communication should cease as soon as sex did. It did not occur to either of them to get up straight away to shower, put on their clothes, and leave. Both of them wanted to prolong the moment. Tom would have lain with her all night, holding her, but of course that could not be.

He traced the scars on her breast and stomach while she told him about them. They argued over whose scars were the most interesting.

–Look, you have one on your knee.

–It was an axe.

–Ooh.

–I was just holding it—you know, just… holding it and someone called and as I turned, my knee…

–Ooh! Don't say it!

That someone had been Mary, calling him in for a cup of hot chocolate one cold winter's day.

–*You've* got one on *your* knee. Almost in the same place.

He let his hand stroke down her thigh and down to her knee. She wriggled.

–I fell over.

–Heh. Boring.

–On a roof. I was jumping from one roof onto another roof and I… fell over.

–What were you doing on a roof?

–I don't remember. I think it was a chasing game. More interesting than walking into your own axe, yes?

Tom pretended to sulk. He rolled onto his back and then made to get up.

–Where you going?

–Turn on the light. See you better.

–Don't.

He lay back slowly. Both of them stared up at the light.

–I'm afraid of light bulbs.

–What?

–I suppose I should be afraid of them when they are on, not when they are off.

–What?

Monique turned towards him.

–When I was a baby. In fact when I was born. Mum told me. Apparently a light bulb exploded as I was being born. Above me. I'm not explaining this very—Tom? What's the matter?

Tom was staring at her in shock. He heard Evelyn speaking in sentences on Mary's last day. *When she was born, a light bulb exploded, right above the bed, quite a shock it was.*

He burst into bewildered tears. Monique grabbed at him and hugged him while he stuttered out what she had just said, and what Evelyn had said, and neither of them said anything for a long while after that, lost in wonder at the mysteries of the world.

Eventually, Monique said:

–How weird.

–What do you mean, afraid of a light bulb if it's on? Oh, I see.

215

–I've always been afraid of them.

–I'm afraid of lifts.

She looked at him.

–Well, you know. They might fall down. And girls.

–Girls might fall down?

–No, I was afraid of girls.

Monique wriggled again, this time suggestively.

–I haven't seen much evidence of that, she remarked. –In fact what I have seen is—

But Tom never did discover exactly what it was she had seen, because he rolled over on top of her at that point, kissed her thoroughly, and proceeded to demonstrate that he was no longer as afraid of girls as he used to be.

§

Too soon it was time to go. They showered and dressed in an atmosphere of familiarity that felt as if it had been born of years. He kissed her cheek before they opened the door onto the outside world.

The genie recorded little of that evening. Lola and Zoe arguing about if it was possible to catch cold germs from bedclothes. Monique preparing food, occasionally meeting his eyes to share their secret. Sitting on the sofa to watch television afterwards, Tom longing to hold her hand, but knowing that was not appropriate. Monique refusing to let him help with the clearing up. He reflected that if she came to Scotland, he would give her a complete rest and the holiday of a lifetime.

It seemed little enough after what she had given him.

Later, when she dropped him off at the hotel, she insisted on going straight back.

–They would worry.

Already Tom knew her well enough not to try to change her mind. He leaned forward to kiss her goodnight.

–Thank you for a lovely evening. In fact, thank you for a wonderful day. This has been one of the best days of my life.

–It has been beautiful, hasn't it?

–Maybe one day I will write it all down.

Write a book, write a book...

–That would be nice.

Orange lights danced on a distant bridge or shore.

–I'll be here first thing in the morning, she promised. –I'll come up with you then.

They kissed once more, then Tom slipped quickly out of the car.

§

Nothing looked out of place. The bed was smooth; the towels were folded; no clothes were scattered on the floor. It was impossible to tell that anything out of the ordinary had happened there that evening. Tom closed the curtains and got himself ready for bed.

It took him even longer to get to sleep than it had the previous night.

5

He waited in the reception foyer again, and jumped up quickly when she arrived. If she had looked gorgeous yesterday, this time she looked stunning. She was wearing a black skirt, and jacket and blouse instead of an outdoors coat.

–Wow.

She said nothing, but smiled. Tom gained the impression that she wanted to get upstairs as quickly as possible, but whether this was because she wanted to avoid prying eyes or because she wanted to be alone with him, he did not know. They reached the room and she immediately kicked off her shoes and stretched herself out on the bed. Tom lay down beside her, stroked her hair and looked into her eyes. Just the thought of what they were going to do together set his blood boiling and his heart pounding.

–Do you—do you want me this morning? he murmured. This was not how he had meant to ask her if she was sure, but that is how the words came out. –You have ten seconds to change your mind, he whispered. He counted down to six before he could resist no longer and put his lips to hers. Her hand snaked up behind the back of his head and held him close, while she tried to hook her feet under his again, just as she had the previous day, in an effort to slide herself under him.

As they kissed he hurriedly undid the buttons of her blouse, and was confronted by complicated underwear.

–Sheesh. D'you always wear this? She sat up and started wriggling out of it. –Or is it special for me?

–This is my usual, she told him.

Again they explored each other, pressing close, each trying to squeeze into the other.

–This is a British hug. I—mmph—What was that?

–A Maltese kiss.

–I didn't quite catch it. I need more—

They drove each other to extremes of excitement. She insisted that even in their most intimate moments they should look into each other's eyes. It was like nothing Tom had ever experienced before, and he was not sure that she had either. Afterwards, they climbed down together from the high summit. Their breathing slowed, although Tom's heart at least was pounding at a terrific rate. She moved off him, and stretched out by his side.

Tom leaned over her, cradled her head in his hands, and found that he still wanted to kiss her. Their lips pressed together gently. While his eyes explored hers he tried to understand his feelings, and discovered no difference from the day before. It was crystal clear to him, as he lay there with the fires of sex dampened, that he loved Monique. He wanted her—all of her. He wanted her love, her body, her life, her problems and her happiness. Selfishly, he wanted everything, right down to the smallest scrap. He wanted every bit of her.

In return, she could have him and everything he had.

–I love you, she whispered suddenly. From pounding frantically, Tom's heart stopped. The world whirled about him.

She was crying quietly. He swept up some tears with a finger and licked their saltiness. –What are these for?

She didn't answer, but her eyes gleamed with tears.

–Because of what might have been?

She nodded and tried to turn her head, but Tom held her tight. He had seen too many tears in his life to think that shedding them made anyone less beautiful. Especially Monique.

She cried quietly, and Tom held her. His love. His heart.

His qalbi.

§

After a while, she stopped sobbing and they lay quietly, talking or not talking, kissing gently. The clock had started ticking. Soon they would have to shower and dress. Tom would have to check out of the hotel, and they would make their way to the airport and he would have to fly away. *Away.* He took a shaky breath, trying to keep in control of himself. It was not yet time for his own tears.

–Wouldn't it be great if I missed the plane?

–Wouldn't it? she whispered.

–You will have to come over, Tom told her.

She bit her lip, and did not reply.

–I suppose we'd better go, sighed Tom.

They showered, towelled down together. Monique went into the bedroom to put on her clothes, starting with the complex underwear. Tom watched, finding it almost as arousing to watch her put it on as it had been to see her take it off. She caught his eye and smiled.

–You're reading my mind again.

–Yerpff. She was applying lipstick. –It's not so difficult.

It was Tom's turn to smile. They both knew that they wanted his visit to go on and on. They dreamed that it might be so, but they both knew it was a dream.

Outside, the sun had decided to shine.

–Typical. Tom indicated the blue sky. Monique was unlocking her car and did not answer. He sensed that she was thinking about his imminent departure: sadness clouded his own heart at the thought. They got into the little red car, which Tom knew he would remember for the rest of his days, and they drove a short way along the front, where she managed to find another parking space. They dashed into a toyshop where she bought some trifles for the children, and on impulse Tom added a small, heart-shaped Malta key-ring, for himself.

–This will remind me, he told her.

–You will need reminding?

It was his turn not to reply. Both of them knew that neither of them would ever forget the events of the last two days. Neither of them would ever need reminders. But afterwards Tom took the key-ring with him everywhere, and thought of Monique every time he fingered its smooth curves.

He unashamedly let his hand rest on her thigh as they took their last drive, enjoying the feel of her movements. The little radio blurted old love songs. He loved her so much, but he could feel the moments slipping away.

–This whole trip has been perfect, apart from—

–Apart from? Apart from what?

–The parking.

Monique laughed her rich, throaty laugh, which was what Tom wanted most to hear. It seemed to be taking forever to get to the airport. He wished it really would take forever. He looked at Monique, stroked her thigh, felt the warmth of the sun through the windows. He wanted to remember everything. He instructed the genie to make no mistakes.

–What sticks in your mind? he asked her. –What will you remember best?

She chuckled and looked at him sideways.

–You have to ask?

Tom felt absurdly pleased.

–But otherwise, she added thoughtfully, –it has to be the Forest. No?

–Yes.

–I wish we could do it all over again, she said, so quietly that Tom could hardly hear her over the radio.

–You feel different than when you drove here to meet me?

–And how! Then, I was thinking, what am I doing? Driving here to pick up a man I have never met. I must be crazy! She swung the car around a corner, into the airport car park. Somebody was reversing out of a space and she parked there; turned the engine off. The car was suddenly still and silent. Tom didn't want to move.

–Kiss me, she said. –You won't be able to in the airport. I know too many people there.

He leaned forward and pressed his lips to hers, smudging her lipstick. It was the last time he kissed her. They stared at each other for long moments, Tom fighting back tears. Then he grabbed his single suitcase, and they made their way into the terminal.

§

After checking in, Tom bought two cups of tea with the last of his Maltese money. They sat at a small table. He touched her hand. She would have been mortified to know it, but her lipstick was still slightly smudged.

–You must try to come over, Tom said. He had already said it a hundred times.

–I will try, she told him. –I have a lot to think about. You have given me a lot to think about.

–Good.

She looked down at the table, then back up at Tom. He marvelled, as he had done since the day they met, so long ago, two days ago, at her beauty and elegance. –I didn't think this could happen, she said. –I didn't think this was going to happen to me again. Now everything is complicated.

–Good, Tom said again. –Was I what the doctor ordered, then?

She grinned and chuckled. He shivered with delight.

–You look more… er, relaxed, he told her.

–I wonder why!

–Yes, Tom said. There were so many things that they were not saying.

–This is like *Casablanca*, he joked, trying to lighten the mood.

–I love you, she whispered.

Tom blinked fiercely.

–I love you too, Monique.

§

There was no need to say more and suddenly there was no time. Tom's flight was called, and they both stood, as if delaying the moment would only prolong the pain. They moved out into the concourse. Tom wanted to hold her quickly and kiss her one last time, but she flashed him a warning glance and waved and said "Hi!" to somebody walking in the opposite direction.

They waved with false cheeriness. She spoke to her acquaintance and Tom went up the escalator towards Departures. At the top he stood and looked back down into the concourse. He saw Monique break free from her conversation and hurry towards the exit. Tom willed her to look back, but she did not. He stood and watched until she was hidden behind concrete and glass, while his heart broke anew. Perhaps it was fitting. This was where he had first seen her as she had skirted the waiting crowd, keeping pace with him as he descended the steps. At last he turned and, almost reeling from the force of emotions he had never felt before, made his way towards the departure gate. He was the last passenger to board the plane.

§

The aeroplane turned from the terminal lights and lumbered into the night. Darkness streamed past the windows. Tom closed his eyes tightly, trying to shut out what was happening, seeking his own, safe darkness. He heard the engines whine and felt the aircraft turn sharply before juddering to a halt. In his mind he saw the runway ahead, small winking lights indicating the safe route into unseen distance. But it was an illusion. The runway did not stretch ahead, only *away*. It was a means of flying *away*, of leaving life behind.

There was no waiting, of course. Within seconds acceleration pushed him back against the seat, holding his body fast but releasing his tears. He felt them leak beneath his eyelids and trickle sadly down his cheeks. He was not ashamed of them. Why should he be? He was leaving a part of himself behind, in circumstances which just weeks ago would have seemed utterly impossible. This trip was taking him *away* from the most amazing experience of his life. Only months ago he had been sure that he would never find love again, and now…

The aeroplane levelled. His ears popped. He refused to open his eyes: there would be time enough later for reality. He wondered if she was watching the lights of the plane lift into the night sky. Or did she too have her eyes tight closed, remembering? Was she crying for him?

In his heart, he knew that she was.

IVY

If you can find
The words between these lines;
Instinct, insight created
As we twine

If you can hold
Me from the jaws of time;
Your arms enfold me; know
Within the walls of mine

All I have not told,
Whispered, written, stated:
I will be content.
It must be so.

1

–What's the matter with him? He's grinning like a loon. Why's he doing that?

Roberta gave Barclay a disbelieving look. –You really don't know?

–Loon, said Tom. –Could be derived from lunatic. But there's a bird called a loon that makes a loud cry like crazy laughter.

He demonstrated.

Dan emerged from his office, wondering what all the noise was about. He looked suspiciously at his staff, who all looked innocently back.

–Ready to execute? he barked.

By which he meant, were they ready to carry out the investigation they had planned for that day?

–Aye, sir, said Tom, although truth to tell he had trouble focusing on anything going on at the office. He was trying to make his proposal to Monique as logical, convincing and appealing as possible. It was taking him days. He worked on it at home, as soon as the children had gone to bed, and he brought it into the office on a memory stick and worked on it at lunchtime. And teatime. And whenever nobody was watching, basically. From far in the future he leaned over his own shoulder and watched as he typed, and deleted, and saved; then copied a few sentences forward to a second draft, and did the same all over again, and again, until finally he sat back with a sense of satisfaction and proceeded to write out the whole thing by hand, as he felt that a printed proposal would look rather business-like and unromantic, the exact opposite of what he intended.

–Where's that… whatsername… Claire?

–You assigned her to Committee duty, sir.

–Ah yes, said Dan. –She'll enjoy that.

Tom doubted it. He doubted that anyone in their right mind would ever actually enjoy a Committee meeting, but somehow Dan had persuaded Claire that it would be fun.

"Just call me Tom Sawyer," said Dan.

It occurred to Tom that even Mark Twain might have had difficulty proposing to a woman three thousand miles away, who he had met only once, who had a family of her own and knew that he had one too. Still, he did his best. It took six sheets of paper to write it all out. From in the future, Tom saw that a synopsis would read:

> Dear Monique
> I love you very much and I think you love me.
> Will you marry me? If you feel you cannot come
> to Scotland, I am perfectly prepared to gather up
> my children and come to live in Malta.
> Much love, Tom

"Receipts," crowed Barclay. "Not the same as bankings."

He had emerged, beaming, from oceans of data.

"What?" said Roberta.

"Tickets," said Dan. "Tickets out, cash in, some of. Receipts where?"

"Bankings in," crowed Barclay. "Reconciliations *out of step*," he added mysteriously.

"What?"

"Teeming and lading," frothed Barclay.

"What?"

"Look it up," said Dan hastily.

Almost the entire human race, with the exception of Barclay, failed to understand the machinations of teeming and lading.

Dan said, –You, with me. Tom, you take Barclay to... which one was it?

–Blantyre, burbled Barclay.

Dan surveyed Barclay bouncing excitedly in his chair. –You drive, he ordered Tom.

On the way to Blantyre—one of the municipal golf courses in the district—Tom pulled over and posted his proposal to Monique. Then, armed with their audit passes, he and Barclay accosted as many players as they could, checking that they had a ticket or receipt to validate their presence on the course.

–Strike me pink, said one of the players. –It's you.

Tom reflected that this was correct, if not especially meaningful. He didn't recognise the player who had accused him of being himself, but when he saw the man's photograph on his season ticket—a younger version of *himself*—his memory served up an image of a shop queue and blue sky outside.

–Oh, he said. Tried to summon up a smile.

–Two pounds of sausages, grinned the man.

–Any chipolatas? responded Tom. His voice was dull; the butcher's grin faltered and he glanced at Barclay.

–Let me see that ticket, said Barclay, and led him a short way away. Tom knew exactly what he was doing, and why, and what he was saying. Good old Barclay.

–It was fine, mumbled Barclay when he came back, meaning the ticket.

–Thanks, said Tom, meaning Barclay's tactful talk to the butcher. They moved on, looking for more data to add to their burgeoning enquiry.

Tom could not help but remember poor Dick Jefferson: *I didn't do any of it, except for the tea money.* That investigation, even wrapped and smothered in politics and lies, was much more straightforward and simultaneously much more brutal. He much preferred strolling around a golf course with Barclay on an unseasonably warm day, chatting about the many layers of minor fraud they were inexorably uncovering, driven by his insistence that records would be kept and Barclay's skill at interrogating them. He doubted that all that much would happen once they had gathered together all the mounting evidence. They would identify somebody who was at the right place at the wrong time. That somebody would probably lose their job. Tom doubted that anything would appear in the local papers, never mind the national news, and it was even more unlikely that anyone was about to lose their life over it.

In the final report, Tom emphasised that it was Barclay's skill at data mining that underpinned the whole investigation. It seemed the least he could do, given that the amalgamation with Region was looming, and Barclay's position was probably most at risk. He was not to know that he would leave before Barclay.

My dear Tom
Thank you for your proposal. I have thought
very hard and have decided that I must stay with

my children, and I will have to go back to my husband to do that. You have made life so different for me, my qalbi.

    All my love
    Monique

It hurt. Oh, how it hurt, even though this was a future-self precis of five pages and even though he had suspected this would be her answer. But in at least one way it did not matter. His life had turned around, and he was not going to return to the dark days. The new spring in his step was there to stay. *You have made life so different for me.*

A woman in the Philippines sent him an email; she must have got his email address from the dating site which, Tom had ascertained, had ceased to exist. The woman had set up her own dating site and suggested that, for a mere $50, he could join it and make all his dreams come true. Those were the days. Everything was new. Tom emailed back, asking with tongue in cheek what guarantees came with the $50, and rather to his surprise she wrote back to say she would take personal charge of 'his case'.

Did he ever pay the $50? Not even the genie could remember that.

They communicated on new-fashioned ICQ, and she told him a long story about how she had been rescued by her husband, apparently an ex-marine, from one place in the Philippines and taken to another part of the Philippines, where she was living, illegally and on her sister's passport, a different and happy life. Tom theorised that about a quarter of the story was true.

<How about this one?>
<She looks nice.>
<Carla Castillo. Her name.>
<She lives in the Philippines?>
<Yes.>
My word, thought Tom, that's a long way away. I think.

The woman in the photograph was brown, was smiling a radiant white smile, and looked exceedingly happy. If she was exceedingly happy, Tom thought, why was she advertising on the website? He wondered exactly where the Philippines was. Or were. Carla wrote:

> Hi, nakatira ako sa isang magandang nayon.
> maganda ba ako? Mangyaring sumulat at sabihin
> sa akin. Naghahanap ako ng lalaking tapat at tapat.

<Does she speak English?>
<No. Is that important?>
For goodness sake, thought Tom.
<How about this one?>
Tom squinted at the screen. There was a photo—it was a very small photo—of a woman wearing colourful clothes, standing on a beach somewhere. Grey cliffs beyond blue sea angled away behind her, shrinking and turning a hazy purple-green before disappearing altogether in the distance.
<She looks nice.>
<Zhang Lan. Her name.>
<She lives in China?>
<Yes.>

My word, thought Tom, that's even further away. Probably. He recalled his geography teacher pointing at a giant map of the world and asking, "Bradley. Where's China?" And he hadn't known. He still wasn't entirely sure. "Geography's not my strong point," he told Philippines Woman. Not all that far in the future he said to the children, "Okay, you've all been abroad before. You know how it feels to be in a different country. But in China, you will feel as if you are in a different *world*." All three of them, all very serious, came to him one day to ask him not to get married again. He had not known what to say. After his Malta trip they came to him again, saying that they had changed their minds. He never found out why. Perhaps they preferred the new, improved post-Malta Dad to the old, constantly angry and miserable pre-Malta Dad.

> Hello Tom,
> How are u? I'm Ivy from China. I have read
> your profile and would like to make a friend with

u. I have a profile named 'orchid32' on the site. If
u are interested, write to me soon.
    Sincerely,
    Ivy

Well. Philippines Woman must have passed on his details to this
Ivy. He checked out her profile, and learned that she was Special and
Sweet: A romantic and traditional Chinese girl, easy going, optimistic, confident. Well. That ticked a lot of boxes, and she looked very
nice in her picture. It wasn't the same picture as the one Philippines
Woman had shown him. Was it the same person? Was Ivy another
name for Zhang Lan, or was he about to be deluged by messages from
hundreds of Chinese women? He read that Ivy was looking for A
idealist lifemate, who is honest, optimistic, open-minded, matured,
especially both responsible for career and family. Well, he decided
that he ticked a lot of those boxes for her, although he wasn't sure
about being matured. It felt like he was being compared to a block
of cheese. He found himself grinning. He had experienced his first
Ivyism.

    Dear Ivy
    Hello, thanks for your message. It was a nice
    surprise! I don't know anybody in China and I
    would love to talk to you – and then who knows
    what might happen?

Tom couldn't quite believe that he was exchanging messages
with a woman from China. He had grown up in a world where China was impossibly far away; impossible to properly understand; a
culture impossibly old and utterly different from that of the Western
world. He didn't know how long it would take to get there, or even
if visitors were allowed into the country. Yet here he was, swapping
emails with Ivy almost every day. You are Zhang Lan? he asked, and
was relieved to discover that she was. From the future Tom became
his own genie and summarised their conversation.

You look lovely – I am amazed that all the local men are not beating a path to your door!

I'm very pleased with your answers, since I can feel your frankness and seriously attitude to life from your letter. I was told some of people like to play game on net, I dislike it. Time is pasting so fast.

Let me assure you I am not playing games! I think long-distance romance on the net can work, in fact I know it can work.

I do agree that. A good beginning is a half of success, right? Will u share one of your poems with me?

I think you are a special lady. I hope that we are beginning a romance. Now I shall have a sleepless night wondering what you are going to reply.
Life is a single drumbeat
And you and I are echoes.
A thousand pities
We do not rebound together.

This is a concise poem with only two sentences, without any beautiful words, but I had to say I was deeply touched when I was reading it... well... have no idea what to say... Thanks God, let we two speak our mind totally, it's wonderful that we two are holding a sweety feeling now... Life is getting better and better.

Future Tom sighed. It took them weeks and months, but he supposed they had to dance the dance. Once he went on a holiday with the children—little more than a week—but both he and Ivy treated the separation with terrible, earnest nervousness. *I am going to miss you. I hope nobody knocks on your door while I am gone.* The first thing Tom did when he got back was to turn on his computer, wait an age for everything to load up, and send Ivy a message. She wrote back to say her heart was filled with happiness now that he was back. *I have been missing your letter, poem… When I write here, my heart is beating fast, as you know, I'm shy girl.* They both knew that their unexpected romance was becoming deeper and more serious with every day that passed, with every message they exchanged. But it was one simple phrase that told Tom he was falling for this optimistic, tiny woman in distant China. He asked for her ICQ number and they arranged a time for an online chat. At the appointed time he logged in, but there was no sign of her. Minutes passed. His heart, which had been pounding excitedly, filled with dread and sank to some unfathomable place. Surely, he thought, she must have meant what she was saying in all those emails? What was the point otherwise? Where was she?

The screen flickered.

His heart promptly jumped back into life as a connection made itself known. Orchid32 was online.

<I'm coming, dear.>

Well, thought both present and future Tom, never mind all the hundreds of email words; never mind their synopses. *I'm coming, dear* summed it all up, didn't it?

§

There was no going back after that. Tom started to figure out how he was going to get to China.

–You're what? asked his mother. What happened to Malta?

–Still there, as far as I know, said Tom cautiously. His mother gave him a frosty look.

–This woman from China… what's her name?… Lang Zany?… She's lovely too, I suppose?

–Er, that's why I've got to go to China, to find out.

His mother sighed. –Why can't you find a nice, normal British girl?

Tom started. Someone had said… someone… It was Beryl, he remembered. In a restaurant somewhere. Somewhen. And it was a Chinese girl who had walked in. Wheels within wheels, Tom thought.

–Your father may not be able to take you to the airport. He's in hospital. A trapped nerve thing.

–You didn't tell me.

–You've got enough on your plate. Tom started again. Somebody had said that to him recently, but he couldn't remember who. A shiver ran down his back. –You can take me there tomorrow night. Save me a taxi.

–Trapped nerve where?

–I don't know, Tom. That's why he's gone to hospital, to find out. Tom scowled.

–Somewhere near where he sits. They'll probably tell us tomorrow. You can tell him all about Zany.

–Her English name is Ivy.

His mother sighed again. –Well. Hospital tomorrow night, remember.

And China in five days' time, thought Tom happily.

§

Adam said that he used to think people walked upside down in China. John said no, that was Australia and Adam wasn't too sure if he was being serious. Monique wished him luck. In the days before his trip to Malta she had been as excited as a schoolgirl and he had been curiously calm. Perhaps his emotions hadn't been working properly at that time. They were working now, though.

His father was a bit dopey. Apparently various doctors had poked around and it was painful, so they had given him an injection.

–Tom's going to China to meet a woman, said his mother.

–Sure that's far enough away? asked his father after some thought. He closed his eyes for a few moments, then opened them again and said, –Everything is made in China.

His mother snorted, but his father turned his head towards Tom and winked, and Tom thought that perhaps he wasn't quite as dopey as he appeared to be.

At the office, Dan barked, "China? Have you lost your mind, Bradley?"

"Almost certainly, sir."

"Be sure to finish that damned report before you go swanning off."

"Yes, sir."

Late in the night, Lucy crept into his room. Her face was wet with tears.

–You are coming back, aren't you, Daddy? She suddenly seemed eight years old all over again. Her mother was gone and now here was her father disappearing off to somewhere far away.

–Oh, said Tom. –You don't think I'll be missing your school sports day, do you?

She curled into his side, like she used to. Tom stared up into the darkness. Mary with her quiet gaze was over there on the wall, hidden in the night. Monique with her zest for life was way over there, hidden by the miles between them. Ivy was still further away, on the other side of the world. He knew where China was, now. He'd looked it up. He wasn't worried, he told himself. He was looking forward to it. He was excited about it. He was going to fly for the best part of twenty-four hours to meet Zhang Lan, who no doubt wanted to make sure he was sufficiently matured. He already knew he would never forget that email.

§

The flight was interminable and Dan intoned *Have you lost your mind? Have you lost your mind?* in time with the engines as they thrummed. Tom wished he could get Dan's voice out of his mind, but not at the expense of the engines failing. In Hong Kong airport he was shocked to see armed police standing impassively in what were presumably strategic locations. It was the first time he had seen armed police in person, as it were; he was sure they existed in the UK but he had never seen any.

It was nothing like arriving at Malta airport. It was far bigger, with far more people milling about, most of them Chinese. People were hurrying in all directions, some pushing or pulling luggage, some with only a briefcase or overnight bag; many approached each other and fell, shouting excitedly and incomprehensibly, into each other's arms. The noise was tremendous. Somehow Ivy homed in on him because, suddenly, she was standing in front of him. He felt a welcome burst of joy as he saw her smiling face. He remembered meeting Monique in Malta and did not make the same mistake twice. He put down his bag and held his arms wide. She came to him willingly. She was small enough that when he hugged her, her feet left the ground and flailed wildly.

–A British hug, he said, putting her down again.

–We have to catch the train, she said breathlessly, but he could see in her eyes that she was pleased.

On the way to the station, they held hands. Tom Are-You-Overtaking-Bradley holding hands with a Chinese woman, in China, thought Tom. Nobody would have believed it, least of all his geography teacher whose name, he suddenly and ludicrously remembered, had been Mr Walkman, long before the days when that would have caused much electronic amusement.

In Malta, in her little red car, Monique had chattered about the weather, her children, the state of the roads, the government, all the while reaching out to touch his arm, or leg, or shoulder. In the train, Ivy sat silently, her two hands clasping one of his. She was turned away from him, looking out of the window at the passing Chinese landscape. Her fingers tightened on his, and he wondered if she was watching his reflection in the window rather than the sun-beaten terrain. He wondered if he ought to be watching the views out of the train window—it was his first visit to China, after all—but he was quite happy to watch Ivy as she watched whatever she was watching. He knew that she was thinking about him, just as he was thinking about her. But it was not as if they had just met, at a bar, or a party, or at work. After months of exchanging emails and conversing laboriously on ICQ, they already knew each other very well. So he sat with his hand in hers, and felt at peace.

She lived on the fourth floor. Most of the doors they passed on their way up irregular steps were wide open, probably in an effort to dissipate the heat, and Tom caught glimpses of Chinese life inside. Her flat was tiny and full of unsafe cabling.

–See the window?

The pane of a small window was cracked and broken, showing a patch of sky outside.

–On that last night, while we were chatting, a big storm. I was worried for your flight.

–Thank goodness, murmured Tom. Suddenly brave, he hugged her again and kissed her. Ivy beamed happily.

–Look! She unveiled Peking Duck, lovingly cooked on a minuscule stove. Tom was not fond of duck but she had clearly spent so much time and effort on this surprise that he could scarcely say so. After dinner she insisted that they curl together on a hard sofa to watch *You've Got Mail*, a message Tom received and hoped he understood. Later, when it was time for bed, he looked doubtfully at the sofa, but she pulled at his arm and led him to her bedroom.

Still later, as he drifted towards sleep with Ivy curled in his arms, tears leaked from his eyes—

Ivy stirred. –Zen me la? What is it?

–Nothing, my dear, whispered Tom.

—but because he was in this place, at this time, with this woman, he was not crying because he was unhappy.

They flew from Shenzhen to Beijing to try to sort out Ivy's visa, but someone there told them they needed to go to Guangzhou, inconveniently at the other end of China. So they took the long flight to Guangzhou, only to find that they lacked all manner of supporting documents, most of them to be provided by Tom back in Scotland. They stayed in a hotel that forbade unmarried couples to share a room, and Tom had to follow Ivy at a distance, across the reception area, up the stairs, and past the stern and suspicious woman doing chaperone duty at the end of the hotel corridor.

–Quick! Quick! Ivy bundled him through the door excitedly. It was room 201. Tom had no idea why he remembered the number and it wasn't until many years later that he realised that he had missed yet another coincidence. At the time, he doubted that the chaperone would suspect that he, a tall Westerner, was in any way connected to the tiny Chinese woman who had preceded him down the corridor, but Ivy grabbed his bag and slid it under the bed, pushed him to the window and pulled the curtains across, cutting off his view of the room.

–What—?

–Shhh.

Someone tapped on the door. Tom heard Ivy's footsteps and the door opening. A female voice said something, although because it was spoken in Chinese, Tom didn't have a clue what it was. It sounded like it might be a question. He hoped it wasn't an accusation. Ivy said something in response. Tom held his breath, wondering for an awful moment if his feet were visible at the bottom of the curtains, like something out of a Pink Panther film. Then the door closed and Ivy was giggling like a lunatic. Tom peered out.

–What did she say?

–She say, Nì hao ma, xiaojie?

–Right.

–And I say, Shide, xiexie. Yiqie douhao.

–Ivy.

She looked at him innocently.

–What did she want?

–She want to know if there is great big Englishman in here who wants to do terrible things to me, like—

But she never finished, because Tom grabbed her and proved, emphatically, that there was. Afterwards, as they coiled together in what was already becoming a familiar position, he said, –Really, what did the woman say?

–Mmm. Ivy was almost asleep. Tom was to discover that she could go to sleep in the blink of an eye, any time, anywhere. He squeezed her.

–The woman.

–Oh, she just ask me if I am all right.

–Okay.

–And I say, yes, everything is fine. Her arm was across his chest, one leg over both of his. She snuggled even closer. –And it is, she said, sleepily.

And it was. They gave up on the visa hunt, at least until Tom got back to Scotland. They returned to Shenzhen and spent the last days of Tom's holiday there. The genie must have stayed in the tiny flat, because in the future Tom couldn't remember much about the nearby streets, or where they went to eat, or indeed if they went anywhere to eat. He only remembered the flat with its big bed covered in a traditional cream and purple design, the hard couch and the shower cleverly designed so that all the water ran slightly downhill, down to a corner and hence out of sight. The hob. No oven, of course, no radiators and no bath. A big fan that whirred constantly, trying to keep the flat in general and the bedroom in particular from getting too warm.

–It gets cold in Scotland, he told Ivy.

–I was born in Heilongjiang, boasted Ivy, knowing full well he would have no idea where that was or why it was significant. –Minus twenty there, she boasted, and shivered theatrically. Years later she admitted her family had moved from there when she was a baby.

"You… you… liar," spluttered Tom.

"Too late now," said Ivy smugly.

As soon as he was back, Tom threw himself into what seemed the interminable task of filling out forms and writing letters, to arrange for Ivy to visit. His father was still in hospital.

–Still?

–Well, actually he came out and went back in again. They're still doing checks.

Tom did his best to suppress a stirring of unease.

–Well, out with it, said his mother. –What's she like?

–Small, said Tom. –Beautiful. Happy. Very–er–lovable.

–Er, sighed his mother.

–She's coming over. Soon as I can get the paperwork sorted. Probably in about a year, added Tom dismally.

–What?

–To check you out, said Tom. –And Dad. And the children. And, well, the whole of the West, really.

His mother's eyes widened. She looked baffled, panic-stricken and pleased all at the same time. –Well. We've got to go and collect your father Wednesday morning. You can tell him all about it then. You can get the morning off?

As it turned out, he couldn't. He and Dan were summoned to see the Chief Executive about what they called the Blantyre Thing. He rang his mother afterwards.

–Sorry. It was important.

–More important than getting your father out of hospital?

Tom winced.

"Give me the gist," instructed the Chief Executive, a pint-sized woman whose name was Caroline Midler. She liked to be called CM and was not much bigger, Tom thought, than Ivy. But much less agreeable. She was as hard as a small rock. Dan and Tom sat down gingerly. Finance Director Bert was also present, eyeing them grimly.

"Tom, the gist," said Dan.

"Right. We've been monitoring income codes and we noticed some income downturns. Barclay checked them out."

"Barclay?"

"One of my staff."

"Good with data analysis," said Tom. "What he found... well, it's all in the report."

"Give me the gist," repeated CM.

Tom went through the long list of minor frauds they had uncovered. In all they totalled over thirty thousand pounds over a period of three years. His mind wasn't really on the report at all.

His mother said, –They didn't let him out yet. The doctor says they want to do more tests. He's dopey again.

–Is he all right?

–I don't know, Tom. They haven't told us anything. I don't think they know themselves.

"But this woman... what's her name?... Grace something... She's been with us for how long?"

It's all in the report, thought Tom.

"Twelve years, CM," said Director Bert. "One of the best—"

"Fraudsters," barked Dan. "Good frauds usually perpetuated by staff who know the ropes," he barked. "In my audit experience," he added.

Good for you, Dan.

"Thank you," said CM, looking directly at Tom. "A most succinct report, both physical and verbal. Could you leave us now, please?"

Tom left, not especially worried about Dan, who was a canny fighter, but more concerned about his father. He went home early.

My dear dear

I got it! Visa. Got ticket! Arrive Glasgow airport 29th at 10.30. I could'nt wait until tell you! ICQ tomorrow? Better later, I'm going to Wuhan.

Your Ivy xx88xx

My Dear

Well done! Only a week away! I can hardly wait :-) How about 12? I will be at lunch, but late for you. I will wait for you then.

Love, Tom xx

It was all so confusing. On the one hand he was still struggling to get over the loss of Mary—and, he knew, not coping with it very well. He doubted that he ever would. On the other hand he was still feeling the electric boost he'd got from Malta; he was still walking on Mediterranean air. On the third hand Ivy was on the verge of coming to Scotland, and Chinese air was also cushioning his footsteps, although on the fourth hand those very footsteps were taking him up a hospital corridor to see his father, feeling the genie wriggle and writhe, trying to escape. That was a lot of hands pushing and pulling and turning his brain to mush.

He paused a moment, leaning on the wall.

–Tom? You all right?

His mother.

–Tired. Been overdoing it.

–Just around this corner.

Tom followed his mother into a small room illuminated only by the light coming from monitors. The curtains were drawn. His father was fast asleep.

–They think it might not be a trapped nerve.

There were two plastic chairs by the side of the bed. They sat down and Tom made a half-hearted querying noise.

–But they still don't know. Apparently they will know tomorrow. Some tests… you know. Coming in.

Tom knew only too well. He reached blindly and grasped his mother's thin hand. She grasped back. Tom couldn't remember the last time he had held hands with her. Probably not since he was a child. His father breathed stertorously but did not awake.

–When did you say your Ivy was coming?

My Ivy, thought Tom. –Next week.

–Ah, said his mother. –Good.

They loosed hands but continued to sit quietly. After half an hour, a nurse looked in. He's had painkillers, she explained. He won't wake up until the middle of the night. Come back tomorrow, she advised them. All right?

Tom's mother nodded wearily and Tom helped her to her feet.

–I'll pick you up in the… oh, after lunch.

He had almost forgotten he had an online date with Ivy at twelve o'clock. He dashed to work after dropping off children at various places, then dashed home, wishing he could break the rules and install ICQ on his office computer.

\<you late\>

\<back home from work. Sorry. You tired?\>

\<No\>

\<What are you doing?\>

\<ICQ with far away Englishman\>

\<Thank goodness\>

\<I am in Wuhan, mum & dad. They say hello\>

\<Hello back\>

Tom had some bad news for Ivy but he wasn't sure how to tell her. He hesitated, then typed a few words, then erased them, then typed again, more slowly.

\<What you doing there?\> she asked.

"The twenty-ninth," barked Dan. "Main buildings. Union reps. HR worker bees. Us. The— You all right?"

Tom had gone pale.

"Yes, I mean no, I mean, the twenty-ninth?"

\<I've got to go to a disciplinary hearing\>

\<A what? I check\>

Ivy had bought an electronic English–Chinese dictionary. Tom imagined he could hear her tapping away at its minuscule keys.

\<what have you done?\>

\<what?\>

<to have to go to distplinry thing>

Tom explained it wasn't about him. He was an auditor, remember? He explained to Dan why he needed to be off on the twenty-ninth.

"This woman—"

"Ivy," said Tom.

"Yes, her," barked Dan. "Is she mad?"

Tom thought about it. Ivy was thinking about giving up her job, selling her flat, leaving her family behind—leaving her entire culture behind—all to come across to Scotland to live with a man who already had three children.

"She's completely bonkers," agreed Tom.

"Good," said Dan with vast satisfaction.

<but the date of it. 29th>

<oh oh oh>

"But the date?" said Tom.

"Wait," said Dan. "See what I can do."

<wait. I check>

Check what? thought Tom. He listened to Dan's side of conversations as he rang up Ross, secretary to Head of HR—"She said it would be difficult, lot of people coming, blah"—and Director Bert—"No idea what he said, something about parallel tracks and diaries on the same scale."—and finally CM herself—"She said no."

"Oh."

"I really need you there, Tom."

Perhaps he could find someone to go up to Glasgow to meet Ivy. Goodness only knew who. And it would be such a cruel anti-climax that both he and Ivy would feel miserable about it. It would be the worst possible start to her visit. He could already feel misery coming on to add to the general mushiness of his thought processes.

<I can come the nexting day>

Tom stared at this message, feeling the mush thin slightly.

<30th?>

<Evening, 8.30. Is all right?>

<Yes yes yes. Clever you>

<This is China>

Even over ICQ Tom could detect Ivy's smug tone. Everything, she maintained, was more efficient in China.

There was mixed news from the hospital. His father had perked up, mainly, he grumbled, because they had stopped poking about. A nurse said he could go home. But no doctor came to see them; no results had come in. Tom drove his parents home and rang the office to say he wouldn't be back in.

–Am I awake? said his father.

–I'll make a cup of tea, said his mother. She was of the generation that believed the world could not turn without a cup of tea. Tom and his father listened to her happily rattling away in the kitchen.

–Mum says you have a trapped nerve.

–Seems so.

–But they haven't found it?

–Tricky blighters, apparently. Did you go?

–What?

–Maybe I dreamed it.

Tom realised he hadn't spoken to his father since he came back from China.

–No, you didn't. Yes, I did.

They stared at each other. Tom's mother returned bearing a tray with tea and biscuits.

–Well?

–Well what? asked Tom's mother.

–He wants to know about China.

–You really went to China?

–Everything's made in China, said Tom.

They all took their tea and Tom handed round the biscuits.

–He met a woman called Zany.

–That's not a Chinese name.

–That's not her name. Her name's Ivy.

–That's not a Chinese name either.

–That's her English name. Her Chinese name is Zhang Lan.

–She's coming here next week, said Tom's mother.

Tom's father sighed and leaned back, shifting uncomfortably. He looked a great deal better than he had the last time Tom had seen him, breathing heavily and awkwardly in a drugged sleep, but he still looked tired. And older.

–Tell me about this Ivy, he said.

§

<Only five days> Tom wrote but Ivy said no, it was only four. They wrestled with international timezone maths. And then suddenly it was only three days and then only two. Ivy wished him luck at his distpinry hearing and hoped he would not be locked up for too long.

<what happen?> she asked afterwards.

The woman, whose name was Grace McKinley, was according to her file thirty-seven and had, as Director Bert had said, been an employee for about twelve years. She wasn't a small woman. She was nervous, and kept tucking stray strands of her hair behind her ear.

<when you got to leave?>

<Hour. Brother drive me to airport>

CM sat opposite Grace McKinley, flanked by Director Bert and Director [Human Resources]. Tom couldn't remember the woman's name. "What's her name?" he whispered to Dan. "Grace McKinley," whispered Dan. "No, the HR Director." Dan looked at him incredulously.

<The CX read out bits from my report> typed Tom proudly.

<guilty bits?>

Tom wasn't sure what Ivy meant by that, so he ignored it.

"Jessica Freidman-Barker," whispered Dan. No wonder Tom couldn't remember it. Barclay was sitting on the other side of Dan, the three of them rather out of the way, off to the side of the main action. Two grim women sat close to Grace McKinley, presumably union representatives or some other sort of support.

Barclay leaned over. "This is a good bit," he whispered as CM launched into a description of an analysis of downturns against staff rosters.

<She started crying.>

"She's crying."

Tom didn't think this would much impress CM.

<oh oh. You feel sorry?>

<Not really.>

243

CM turned over the report and waited for the snivelling to stop. Conversation ensued between the union reps and the directors, which Tom didn't listen to. He was busy hoping everything would get wrapped up quickly enough for him to get back home and onto ICQ before Ivy left for Scotland.

<She said her boyfriend made her do it.>

<oh oh>

"Make a note," whispered Dan to Barclay. "Sangster, Jamie. Falling out of. Thieves."

"Got it."

<what happen?>

What happened was that CM wound up the meeting, to which the audit team had contributed nothing. Ivy could have come on her original flying date, thought Tom. They could have had an extra day together. As soon as they got back to the office Barclay parameterised Jamie Sangster and dived back into the oceans of data he had collected.

<Another meeting, later. Don't miss your plane.>

<8888888888>

These were Ivy kisses. He sent back his own, and suddenly there were no days left to wait, only one, long, never-ending night. The children were nearly as excited as he was. Lucy wanted to know what Chinese people ate; Adam had decided he was going to learn Chinese; John thought that Ivy might know Kung Fu and he practised what he fondly believed were martial moves, apparently determined to do battle with her when she arrived. Even the dogs caught the mood and trotted amiably about the house instead of settling down. Tom had to take them out for a bonus walk before they did. When he managed to get to bed he lay for a long time, wondering what Mary would have thought of his meeting up with someone all the way from China, and inviting her into his life. He imagined the two of them meeting, Mary with her calm smile and Ivy with her excited, bubbling, optimistic outlook on life. He saw their eyes meet and knew, without quite knowing how he knew, that they would have approved of each other.

When he finally did sleep, the genie slithered down the dark wall and slipped into the present. It discovered that Tom's sleeping mind was scrolling through images and events of the past in a berserk, terrible muddle. He was sitting in Peter's battered green van; they were driving up a mountain so steep Tom expected the front of the van to rear up and tip back over their heads. Both he and Peter leaned forwards to prevent this happening. He turned and saw Monique in the back seat although, as far as the genie could remember, there was no back seat in Peter's van. Monique smiled sadly; her face creased and tears leaked from her eyes. For goodness sake, Tom thought, I even make her cry in a dream. She leaned forwards too and whispered *not even the tea money, not even the tea money*. Peter shrieked and pounded on the steering wheel. Those idiots! he shrieked in Chinese, although Tom understood him perfectly. Look, look! Tom looked. A host of cars was coming towards them, barrelling down the mountain, which by now was almost vertical. Flaming idiots! On the wrong side! shrieked Peter. Chinese? wondered Tom. Don't worry about it, the genie advised the lucid part of his brain; this is all a dream, remember. Tom turned again and found Mary sitting placidly in Monique's place. Her eyebrows quirked up, perhaps in response to Peter's tirade, perhaps reacting to something else not even in the dream. Then she too leaned forwards and whispered *write a book…*

… write a book…

Tom's eyes snapped open, although he was scarcely awake. I haven't forgotten, he said in his mind. It's just been so hard.

> She turned towards me, unbuttoning her car-
> digan, and her eyes met mine.

Unbuttoning of jumper, said Mary from somewhere in the darkness. Six letters. What kind of book starts like that? Tom smiled and turned over, and his arm drifted into the cold, empty half of the bed. But it won't be like that for long, the genie told him gently as he fell back into sleep.

–Be careful how you drive, his mother said, as if he planned to drive wildly and erratically up the motorway. Well, maybe he would. He was certainly keen to get to the airport.

The motorway traffic wasn't especially heavy and the weather was calm and mild. Tom wasn't feeling calm. He was finding it hard to take in the idea that Ivy was actually flying all the way to Scotland. That very moment. A plane up in the sky somewhere, perhaps—Tom activated his basic geography skills—flying over France. Was that the right direction? She was up there in the sky somewhere, anyway, flying closer and closer as he drove closer and closer to some indeterminate point in the airport where their paths would meet.

He was going too fast.

Because the flight wasn't due to land until 8.30, he had gone into the office as usual. Barclay was already there, tapping away on his computer. Tom thought he was actually humming to himself.

"I thought you were going up to the airport?"

"This evening."

Dan emerged from his office.

"Director Bert warning," he said. "Be—what are you doing here, Bradley? Why aren't you collecting your madwoman?"

"This evening, sir."

Roberta came in, carrying a green file. Bradley grabbed it.

"This should do it," burbled Bradley. "Got him dead to rights."

"Good, good, Keep it going. Director Bert coming. Region update. Half an hour. Look busy. Do stuff."

"What are you doing here?" asked Roberta, as if Tom was an intruder in his own office.

Earlier, he practically had to tie up the children and forcefully carry them to the car, to get them off to school. He turned on his computer before taking the dogs out for their morning walk in the vague hope that Ivy might have sent him a message somehow. She hadn't, but Monique had.

> Good luck, babe. Bring her out to Malta. Be
> thinking of you
> xxx

When Director Bert arrived he said, "Audit," which was a good start, because everyone in the room knew what audit was. Tom noticed that Claire wasn't there and guessed she had been assigned Committee duty again. "In the green," said Director Bert mysteriously. "ASA." He nodded seriously, looking around the room. "Three of the

246

Region close to daisies. One's their chief of." He made a trigger finger and pointed it at Dan. "You the man."

Dan made a strangled noise.

Director Bert appeared to catch sight of Tom, who had been sitting in full view throughout the entire update.

"Hey. You've been grapevined."

Tom also made a strangled noise, perhaps appropriately given what had apparently happened to him. Director Bert pointed at him with the forefinger of one hand, and gave a thumb's up with the other. Then he left.

Tom jolted back to the present and momentarily panicked, thinking that he'd missed his exit. But no, he hadn't, although it was coming up fast. He turned off the motorway and started navigating a backstreet route to the airport. He stole a glance at his watch. Eight o'clock. Just enough time to get there and get lost in the maze of car parks, find the right terminal and await Ivy's arrival.

"What Director Bert means," Dan had said that morning, "is that—Bradley, are you listening?"

"Yes, sir," lied Tom. What he was actually thinking was that Ivy should be only half way across the world by now, instead of completely across it. He was trying to work out where 'half way' might be, without much success.

The plane turned out to be delayed by an hour, but he wasn't too bothered. What was an hour after all their days and months of planning? It was nothing, that's what it was. He wandered around the airport, found a payphone, and called his mother to warn her he was going to be back even later than he expected. She told him all the children were in bed and steadfastly refusing to go to sleep.

–Although I think Lucy's gone. Take care on your drive back, dear. We'll be fine.

He got himself a cup of coffee and sat down in the waiting area with a book. In the future he tried to remember what it was, and decided it was *The Sunset Warrior*, a paperback he had grabbed randomly from his bookshelves as he went out to his car. So Ronin fought battles and spoke archaic words, and Tom failed to read most of them, instead imagining Ivy as she flew ever closer. He imagined she was sitting in a window seat, looking out at bits of Europe underneath the plane, wondering where she was and what on earth she was doing. Perhaps he shouldn't have had that cup of coffee. Now he was all wound up.

The monitor dangling in front of his row of seats proclaimed that the flight was going to be ten minutes earlier than an hour late. That was fifty minutes late, calculated Tom, and it was now forty-five minutes since the time the plane should have landed. That meant… Tom closed up *The Sunset Warrior*, giving up any pretence of reading, and stared hopefully at the monitor. All its numbers and locations and times churned about, the way they did whenever the topmost arrival disappeared off the list and the bottom-most arrival was added. Was bottom-most a word?

Landed.

Tom gripped his book fiercely and swallowed, suddenly nervous. He could visualise Ivy waiting for the *Ping!* and the disappearance of the seatbelt sign on the mini-monitor in front of her; he was sure she would wait, even though every other plane passenger in existence ignored it. Everyone else would be getting up, opening luggage compartments, shrugging on coats, leaning awkwardly under the luggage compartments to eye up the endless tarmac of the airport sliding by outside. He was fairly sure Ivy would still be sitting, waiting patiently while all this illegal activity went on about her, gripping her own book or in-flight magazine as tightly as he was gripping *The Sunset Warrior*, probably feeling as nervous as he was.

Or not. When she finally emerged from the Arrivals hall she came straight into his arms as if it was the most natural thing in the world. She was carrying a small suitcase and pulling on another one that was nearly as big as she was.

–Welcome to Scotland, Tom said, and kissed her.

–It's too far away, complained Ivy.

–What, Scotland?

–I don't want come too often, she said.

Tom thought about it. Did she mean, she didn't want to come to Scotland often? Or did she mean that once she was in Scotland she didn't want to have to come again? He looked sideways at her but wasn't brave enough to ask for clarification.

On the way back to the house he took her—or so he thought—to a romantic spot over a local river in the countryside outside the town. She clung to him and he put an arm around her affectionately. Years later she told him she had been terrified, thinking he was going to throw her into the river. Which was why she had clung to him so tightly. Tom stared at her in astonishment.

"Why on earth would I want to do a thing like that?"

"Hah. You don't know," said Ivy darkly and uninformatively.

"I know I don't know," said Tom. "I mean, I just said… never mind. And I thought things were going so well."

"And then the Gus," said Ivy.

True, thought Tom. His mother had opened the door to welcome them when they got home, a bright rectangle in the darkness. And silhouetted against the light was a huge dog shape, barking deeply and loudly and, to Ivy, terrifyingly.

"I think he going to eat me."

"What, drowned and then eaten? Both?"

Tom's mother already had her coat on. She gave Ivy a brief hug and told Tom he must bring her around tomorrow. The children had all failed in their efforts to stay awake, she said.

Despite fears of being drowned or eaten, Ivy excitedly unpacked a brightly coloured cloth ball which she hung carefully over the bedpost on her side of the bed.

–Xìuqíu, she told him. –Important.

–Right, said Tom.

–Tell you later, she told him.

–Right, later, said Tom. –What shall we do now?

This was something of a rhetorical question, as he leaned towards her across the bed, and she met him half way.

§

In the morning there came a tremendous battering on the door.

–Dad! shrieked Lucy.

–Mmph.

–Dad!

Tom peeled open his eyes, stared at his bedside clock and leaped out of bed.

–Coming, he shouted as quietly as he could, although he couldn't help noticing that Ivy hadn't so much as twitched at all the commotion. Outside in the hall all three children stood waiting, dressed in their school uniforms and carrying an assortment of school bags.

Tom put a finger to his lips. –She's still asleep.

Three disappointed faces.

–She'll be here when you come back from school. Now, breakfast—

–We had it, said Lucy proudly.

–And lunch boxes—

–We done them, said Adam proudly. Tom decided that now would not be a good time for a grammar lesson.

–And—uh—uniforms and shoes…

John silently opened the front door.

Ivy discovered, while he was out, that the dogs were harmless. Gus trotted after her as she explored the rooms, while Jess made a beeline for the kitchen and sat there waiting hopefully. Ivy found the children's rooms and Tom's study, and his collection of books. One room was a bathroom, with an actual bath in it. In the kitchen she discovered not only Jess but also what she recognised from various films as a toaster. She hunted around, found some sliced bread, and excitedly put it in, marvelling at how the inside of the machine turned a fiery red and the smell of toast permeated the air. The dogs sat side by side and looked at her expectantly.

–Bu, said Ivy and then, in case the dogs didn't understand Chinese, –No. Might not be good for dog.

Tom was aghast to find her happily spreading jam and then butter on pieces of toast.

–I'm sorry I miss them, said Ivy.

–So were they.

–I was a bit asleep. But I will be ready for later.

Which she had to be. John came in, flung his bag to one side, and assumed a kung fu posture. Ivy did the same. Tom put his hand over his eyes and backed away, into his study. He heard shrill cries that reminded him of Bruce Lee, then unmistakeable sounds of violence ending with a dull thud and then a whole lot of giggling. He ventured back out into the hall. John was flat on his back with Ivy pinning him down and tickling him remorselessly. Tickle fu, thought Tom. It appeared to be very effective.

As they scrambled to their feet, still giggling, Adam came down the stairs, a serious expression on his face and his lips moving soundlessly. He took a deep breath.

–Nǐ hǎo ma? he enquired.

–Wǒ hén hǎo, Ivy responded. –Nǐ hǎo ma?

Adam glanced across at Tom, who shrugged, and then back at Ivy with a slightly despairing look.

–Means, she said, –I am fine. She smiled.

Adam's lips were moving again. He was frowning with concentration.

–Wǒ hěn hǎo, he said. Ivy's eyebrows shot up. She clapped her hands and jumped up and down.

–Dad! shrieked Lucy from upstairs.

–She's in her room, Adam informed them before disappearing into the kitchen.

–That clever boy, said Ivy.

–Dad!

–He wants to learn Chinese, Tom told her. –What is it? he shouted.

–Is Ivy there?

–Yes! shrieked Ivy.

–Come up here! shrieked Lucy.

Tom put his hand over his ears and joined John and Adam in the kitchen. He checked that the meal in the oven was cooking satisfactorily and remonstrated with the boys who were not only eating biscuits but also feeding them to the dogs. Tom clearly had not hidden the packet well enough. He would have to conjure up another hiding place, and the children would no doubt find that too. He thought he'd better go upstairs to see what was happening.

What was happening was that Lucy was standing on her head, her feet resting against the wall by the window, and Ivy was standing on *her* head, her feet resting on the wall close to the door.

–We're having a competition, explained Lucy, not without difficulty.

251

Tom shook his head, covered his eyes again, and backed out, nearly falling down the stairs.

–Good day? he asked later, when Ivy had him trapped by one arm and one leg, in bed in their accustomed places. The children had finally gone to bed after much negotiation and bribery. At dinner, Adam had asked Ivy if she happened to know if they walked upside down in Australia. Ivy said yes, they did that a lot, but—she leaned forwards conspiratorially—"They don't do it when anyone's watching."

Good one, thought Tom.

–You were a big hit with the children.

–They're lovely.

–And with the dogs.

–Huh.

–And with my mum and dad.

–They're lovely.

–Huh. Tom remembered his mother opening the door, his father struggling to get to his feet to welcome them. He'd glanced at his mother, but she had avoided his eyes.

"Made in China!" exclaimed his father, which ought to have been in poor taste but somehow wasn't. Beaming broadly, he opened his arms to give Ivy a hug. Tom's mother gave her one too, and then Ivy stole their hearts by putting her palms together and bowing slightly.

"Like in a film?" John asked later.

"Exactly like that," Tom said.

As they left, Tom's mother whispered, "She's lovely," and Tom could not help but remember her saying—what was it she said, the first time they met Mary? We like your girlfriend, bring her again. Something like that. We like your girlfriend. She's lovely.

–And?

Tom was almost asleep. What did she mean, and?

–Yes, he said. –Er, no. What?

–That, said Ivy. –With the children, the two dogs, the parents. Tom thought about it.

–And nobody else? asked Ivy. –Not a big hit with?

–Absolutely not, murmured Tom. Ivy kicked his shin, which woke him up. –You really know kung fu?

–Just a tiny, she said. –I learn a bit after school, because of the party and… him.

–Who?

–You don't need know his name.

–Right, right.

–At the end of schooling party, big hall, lots of people—Ivy wrestled with the duvet, freed her arms and made a sweeping gesture to indicate how big everything had been, a gesture that Tom could just about make out in the darkness—and he got me into a corner and tried to kiss me and undo my… undo my…

–Right. Tom felt the hairs on the back of his head prickle.

–And I escape! Ivy's legs flailed about, kicking him all over again as she relived the story. –And he chase me! And I stop, and… Well. Ivy's voice radiated satisfaction.

–You turned and held out your hand, whispered Tom. –And caught him under the chin, on his neck, just… there. He touched Ivy's neck gently. –And he came to a halt and his feet went from under him and he fell onto the ground, all unconscious.

Ivy heaved herself up onto one elbow and looked down at him. He looked up at her. Long moments passed.

–Magic, she whispered.

She lay back down again and assumed her coiled position. She heard his heart beating fast and waited, holding him gently. After a while, he told her how he knew, and they both lay in a web of wonder—Tom for the second time, after the bizarre coincidence of Monique's exploding light bulb—and drifted off to sleep together.

§

They all crammed into the car the following morning and set off to visit Josephine and Catherine, who lived about an hour's drive away. –Mary's sisters, explained Tom to Ivy. –You'll like them.

In the very back, Gus went to sleep and Jess barked at all moving cars until she ran out of energy and went to sleep too. From the middle back the children pointed out landmarks, the wizard's tower, the witch's cottage, and the other witch's cottage. The row of distant trees that looked like a huge undulating caterpillar and the two big, rounded hills that looked like—

–John, warned Tom.

–Buttocks, said John obstinately.

Ivy tapped at her electronic dictionary and pealed with laughter.

–They've got two dogs too, said Tom. –It will be chaos. It always is.

It was chaos. The four dogs played with each other. Lucy and Adam played with the dogs. John pretended he was too old for such games and stayed with the adults until Josephine asked him if he was strong enough to bring down a few more chairs from upstairs.

Good one, thought Tom.

–This is Ivy, he said.

Josephine hugged her, and then Catherine, and then Ivy put her palms together and bowed slightly. Tom knew this wasn't a trick.

–Am I hit? she whispered, much later.

–Oh yes, whispered Tom.

The children, exhausted, had gone to bed without any negotiations for a change. The dogs collapsed into baskets and forgot to ask for a walk. Tom and Ivy slipped into bed and made love and coiled together afterwards.

–One and one, said Ivy contentedly.

They had known each other for such a short time, but already they knew how each other's minds worked.

–Makes one, said Tom.

Ivy squeaked in Chinese and her arm tightened across his chest. Tom knew he had guessed right when he felt wetness on his chest and felt her trembling, crying quietly. Tom hugged her back and pretended he hadn't noticed.

The genie, which knew more than Tom, slithered down the bedroom wall and into the present. This was a night it did not want to escape or forget. It discovered that Tom's mind was still mush, still muddled, but much calmer. Unexpectedly it shared a vision of armed policemen in Hong Kong; then glimpsed Monique kneeling beside him to retrieve Mary's ring; and then Mary herself from what seemed like the distant past: *I will always be part of you...* He was almost asleep.

–Tom?

Tom jumped. What was Ivy doing? She was never awake in the middle of the night.

He made a puzzled and surprised grunt.

Not only was Ivy awake, but she was sitting up and turning on her bedside light. She leaned over him, her black hair framing her face and tickling his. She stayed, unmoving, for so long that Tom began to wonder if she had managed to doze off in that position. It wouldn't have surprised him.

–I have made a deciding.

–Ah.

Ivy turned away, fumbled at the bedpost, and turned back again. She was holding the coloured ball—the name of which Tom could never remember—on a red string. She paused again, looking down at it, then at Tom.

Then she gave it to him.

Tom wriggled more upright and took the red string gingerly. He wasn't sure what was happening, but he was beginning to suspect. His heart pounded.

–Yes, said Ivy.

–Oh! You mean—Tom swallowed—yes?

–Yes, said Ivy. –I do mean. She was suddenly looking very small and very nervous. He hung the coloured ball on his own bedpost and gathered her into his arms. He clasped her so hard his arms hurt, but she didn't seem to mind. Unnoticed by either of them, the genie shadowed away into the future to await Tom in a place he would not want to be.

–Xiùqíu? his mother asked him.

–It means we're engaged, Tom told her.

–Engaged? squeaked his mother. –You proposed to her?

–Well—Tom paused. Of course he had proposed to her, otherwise she wouldn't have said Yes, would she? She wouldn't have had anything to say Yes to. But just at that moment, he couldn't remember exactly when he had proposed. He frowned. Had he proposed to her? Or was she saying Yes to convince him that he had proposed, when he hadn't really? Years later he braced Ivy with the question.

"I can't remember when I proposed," he said, scribbling furiously in a notebook. Ivy leaned over him and tried to decipher his handwriting.

"What?" she said.

"What?" he said.

"Proposed what?"

"To you."

Ivy started jumping up and down, clapping her hands.

"Is it part three? Is it my part? Is it?"

"Yes," said Tom. "But I can't remember when I proposed to you. Can you?"

Ivy paused in her jumping for joy, and frowned.

"No. Not that."

They threw themselves into preparations. These included a practice service, during which they discovered that Ivy had trouble saying 'will'. She tried again and again over the following days. –I wie-el. No. I wi-iyl. No. I wee… No. She looked at Tom out of the corner of her eye. –Is easier to say I won't, she said, and Tom was obscurely happy that she felt secure enough to tease him.

Forms. A problem about Ivy's visa materialised and she had to go back to China for an obscure bureaucratic reason neither of them really understood. Tom felt awful while she was away. He felt a tightness in his chest and a perpetual headache.

His memory flew back to the time, so long ago it seemed now, when Mary's parents whisked Mary back to Ireland for Christmas. He had felt the same anguish then, but she had fallen into his arms on her return and it all vanished into a euphoric haze as if it had never been. So it was with Ivy.

He went to collect her from Glasgow Airport and waited anxiously at the arrivals barrier. After a while he became certain that everyone else on the plane had disembarked and found their way into the concourse, and he was beginning to fret that perhaps there was still something wrong with Ivy's passport and she was even now being interrogated by stern-faced uniformed airport security police, probably strapped to a chair and with a bright light being shone into her eyes. Then she appeared, trotting through the gateway, looking around expectantly. The tightness, the headache, the worry all vanished as if they had never been. He grabbed her and hugged her, not caring if other passengers thought this an unseemly display of emotion.

More forms. Complications over whether Ivy should sign the marriage certificate as Ivy or Zhang Lan, but Tom didn't care. He proudly led her back up the aisle, past his parents, his friends, his colleagues and Bailin, the one Chinese friend who happened to be in the UK at that time; led her out of the church's giant oak doors to stand on the shallow steps outside, to face a barrage of flashing camera lights.

On their honeymoon a few weeks later, they walked hand in hand along a stony beach.

–We'll be a team, Tom said. –Something will happen, some cultural difference will jump up to bite us…

They crunched a bit further. Ivy said nothing.

–You know I would never do anything to upset you. Not deliberately. So if I do, it will be an accident, right?

Ivy nodded, staring out to sea. Tom wasn't sure she was listening.

–We'll be a team, right?

Ivy didn't answer, but bumped her head twice on his shoulder. They walked a little further, more pebbles crunching. Then she squeezed his hand and bumped her head once more.

They walked on contentedly, Tom thinking that it really was all a form of magic that he had experienced before but had thought he would never experience again. He didn't tell Ivy about the coincidence Monique shared with Mary, but he turned it over and over in his mind, and compared it with the coincidence Ivy shared with Mary. He was beginning to wonder if they were really coincidences. Magic. Some kind of fate. He didn't really care. He walked hand in hand with Ivy along the beach, and slept with her every night; they ate their meals in the hotel rather than wander too far and eyed up an older couple who appeared to be doing the same thing but who failed to speak to each other for the whole of any of their meals but got up and left every evening without having said a word to each other.

–We'll never be that, said Ivy.

And they never were.

§

When they returned, the genie awaited them in the form of his mother and a phone call. Tom's father was in hospital again, she said. She added that Tom needed to understand that, this time, he would not be coming out.

–Not a trapped nerve, then?

–No, she said.

Tom saw him twice more. The first time he took Ivy, and his father perked up at the sight of her. He was grey, hollowed out. His eyes were sunk into his face and reminded Tom uncomfortably and horribly of Mary as she lay, uncomplaining, in her hospice bed. His father didn't complain either. He said:

–Everything made in China. His voice was a breathless whisper. Tom could see the effort he was making. –Even my daughter-in-law.

Ivy sat on the edge of the bed and held his hands. Tom told them about their honeymoon. It was hard to say how much his father was taking in: his eyes were flickering and closing and Tom knew he was on painkillers. He had seen it before.

After a minute his eyes opened fully and re-registered the fact that Ivy was there.

–See all these machines?

Ivy nodded. It was hard to miss them, screens with various graphical displays, tubes and wires in an apparent tangle but most of them ending up in or on Tom's father. There was a subdued sound of machinery, and the occasional apologetic beep.

–Where do they come from, eh?

He gasped. Ivy got up and peered at the machines, sometimes crouching so that she could see underneath, sometimes peering around at the back, careful not to touch anything. She sat down again and took his hands.

–You are right, she said, sounding amazed. –All made in China.

Tom's father smiled and his eyes closed. Tom thought he had gone to sleep, but again his eyes snapped open and this time he stared fiercely at Tom.

–A treasure there, he whispered. –Keep her close.

And then he was asleep.

As they tiptoed out a nurse carrying an inevitable clipboard backed her way in. –Oh, she said, turning. –You must be Mr Bradley's son?

Tom nodded. The nurse switched her gaze to Ivy. –Oh, so you are… oh, that explains it.

–Explains what? asked Tom.

–Mr Bradley yesterday. He asked me to check all the equipment. Where did it all come from, he asked me. He said he expected it all came from China.

–Ah.

–I think he was disappointed, said the nurse. She had gone to the foot of the bed where another clipboard awaited her.

–Disappointed?

–I mean, none of it is. The nurse made a vague gesture at the screens and dials and tubes and wires. –We source mainly from the EU. Are you planning to visit tomorrow?

–Right. Right. Er… yes.

–Then—the nurse paused writing whatever she was writing, —come early. Her eyes met Tom's, and he nodded slowly.

Ivy started sniffling and crying before they reached their car, and wailed loudly as soon as they were in it. Tom's mind was bouncing about, unsettled, not knowing whether to think about what was happening or try to evade it for a little longer. He tried to put an arm around Ivy but was thwarted by the gearstick and handbrake. Ivy's wails increased in volume.

–Ivy. Dear… He pulled at her ineffectually and found himself wanting to say It'll be all right, but stopped himself because it obviously wasn't going to be any such thing.

–He know! wailed Ivy.

What? thought Tom. –What?

–He know I tell a lie! He know I'm liar!

Tom gaped at her. He hadn't really taken in this aspect of their visit.

–He said you are a treasure.

Ivy hiccoughed and tried to wipe at her eyes. Tom fished in his pocket and found a handkerchief for her. She was quietening down—

not, thought Tom, because she was any less upset, but because she was finding it hard to breathe and wail at the same time.

–He said I must keep you.

Ivy wiped her entire face, which appeared to have been washed in tears.

–You his son, she said, rather obscurely.

–Well, yes, said Tom. –What I mean is—what he means is—Ivy, look at me.

Ivy looked at him. Her bottom lip was trembling.

–He knows *why* you lied to him.

Ivy's eyes turned inward as she considered this.

–Yes? asked Tom.

–Shì, said Ivy. –Maybe. She let Tom pull her closer. He gave her a hug and kissed her forehead, which was all he could reach, and which he was amazed to find tasted of salty tears.

–All right, then?

On the way home she started to cry again, snuffling into Tom's soggy handkerchief, this time because she knew as well as Tom exactly what message the nurse had conveyed. She didn't go with him to the hospital on the following day, ostensibly because they could find no childminder to help out; Molly was away with her own family and Tom's mother, of course, was with his father. She was sitting quietly by the side of his bed when Tom arrived.

–Oh, Tom.

–Mum.

Tom stood by her side, hand on her shoulder. His father was unconscious, a plastic mask strapped over his face. The equipment he was hooked up to was still humming and buzzing but to Tom it sounded as if it was just going through the motions.

–You shouldn't have come.

His father exhaled and it was only at that moment that Tom realised that was the first he had heard him breathe since he had come into the room.

–Of course I—

His father inhaled, a long, painfully drawn-out throaty sound.

–No. It doesn't do him any good now, does it? He doesn't know you are here.

–But—

–He won't ever know you are here, his mother said, with a touch of her usual authority. –And he wouldn't want you to be here while… She swallowed and fell silent.

Exhale. Tom suddenly thought that his father, had he been awake, would have cursed all this damned breathing. He remembered how Mary's breathing became slower and slower, more and more uncertain, and how he on the one hand willed her to take one more breath, even if it was her last, and on the other hand he wished it would stop, because she was in so much pain. How guilty he felt.

Inhale.

Funny how the mind worked. He could almost hear the strains of Star Trek.

–And it's not doing you any good, either, Tom. Is it?

Tom came back to the present.

–Go home, said his mother gently. –Be with Ivy and the children.

–I—

–Go home, she insisted. –I'll ring you when—

Exhale.

–when.

She swallowed again.

–I'll come to pick you up.

–You will not. I'll get a taxi.

–To our house.

His mother nodded as if conceding a point. She touched his hand resting on her shoulder, then waved him away. On the drive back it struck him that staying there might not have done him or his father any good, but what about his mother?

She called him a few minutes after midnight.

§

At the funeral Tom was surprised to see Dan and Barclay, and absolutely astonished to see Director Bert, who came across and briskly shook his hand.

–Comms, he said.

261

Everyone shook his hand or gave him a perfunctory hug and said they were dreadfully sorry and he should call them if they could help in any way. They all knew they couldn't help in any way, and they all knew that Tom knew they couldn't help in any way, but the proprieties had to be observed. Afterwards Tom couldn't remember who had been there, apart from his uncle and his mother, and Josephine and Catherine, and Director Bert and by association Dan and Barclay. He was exhausted.

–We need to get away, he said to Ivy.

If it occurred to Ivy that they had not long got back from their honeymoon, she made no mention of it.

–I'll see it, she said.

–See to it?

–Yes, that. My parents want to meet the children.

–But—began Tom, then paused. After all, why not? They all needed to get away, and they couldn't get away much further than China. Plus, as Ivy said with one of her sudden devastating bursts of logic, the children were growing fast and it might be the last occasion they got to go on a family holiday together. In this she was almost right. It turned out to be… Tom was fond of saying afterwards, one of his favourite words… their antepenultimate family holiday.

–Okay, Tom told the children. –You all know how it feels different to be in a different country. But in China, you will feel as if you are in a different *world*.

None of them believed him, not then, but they all came back with memories full of Chinese wonder. The genie went with them, although it need not have bothered, as Tom kept a diary of events. Adam charming Ivy's relatives with his rudimentary but burgeoning knowledge of Mandarin. Lucy, super fit as she was undertaking both gymnastics and badminton back home, running up and down steps at twice the pace of anyone else. Tom fainting from heat exposure on the Great Wall of China. John almost getting shoved off the heights of Huangshan mountain by enthusiastic sedan carriers.

–You didn't have a hat? asked Barclay incredulously. –On the Great Wall of China? In the middle of summer? Barclay knew everything.

–China is full of steps, said Tom sullenly. –And they all go up.

–Like Edinburgh? said Roberta brightly.

Tom also took Ivy and the children for a holiday in Malta.

"To see your another woman," said Ivy.

"*Other* woman. What?" he added innocently as Ivy glared at him.

Tom had to admit that Malta was a bit smaller than China so it didn't offer quite the same range of locations to visit and activities to try. Still, they went swimming in lots of places and saw a million churches. Monique drove them—not in her little red car, but in a bigger vehicle that kept breaking down. She took Tom's arm when they were all walking along a beach and Ivy was trying and failing to run faster than Lucy and said, 'She's lovely.' On the same day, or maybe it was the next day, Ivy took his other arm and said, "You have good flavour in womans." Tom laboriously worked this out, but wisely said nothing. More than once Ivy and Monique linked arms and wandered off on their own, usually in the direction of a shopping arcade and it did Tom's heart good to see them together.

Before the Chinese holiday, Tom and Dan had their day in court. The powers that be—mainly CM, Tom presumed, advised by inhouse lawyers—had decided to prosecute Grace McKinley and Jamie Sangster for their raft of mini-frauds. It was all very low key. Tom couldn't help remembering when the Department's wildly attractive Head of Legal—what was her name?—took him through a set of questions at the trial of—what was *her* name?—and told him afterwards that he'd done well, unlike George. This time it was nothing like that: there was no high drama. Tom recited figures, which the defending lawyer tried and failed to rebuff, and answered yes or no to almost all the questions, and was quietly satisfied when the lawyer asked him how long he'd been an auditor and Tom told him.

During the holiday Claire left the audit section to become—to Dan's chagrin and astonishment—a Committee clerk. "It's great," she apparently enthused. "They argue, you know." Her voice hushed. "They *call each other names*." She nodded wisely at Dan, Barclay and Roberta, who told Tom all this by doing a wonderful impression of Claire after she had gone. "But I have to redact all that," said Roberta in a complacent voice. "Just call me Tom Sawyer," said Dan mournfully.

A year after the holiday, or maybe it was the year after that, Tom and Ivy came to a momentous decision. The genie listened, and remembered, and didn't know whether to strain away or envelop those moments in time. It was both their best and their worst decision in all their married life.

2

Baby killer.

Ivy's face, creased at odd angles, her eyes wide and fearful. Her body foreshortened, descending into whiteness. Her lips moving soundlessly.

Baby killer.

Tom pulled away; tried to pull away. Opened his own eyes to find himself surrounded by the night; gasping; soaked in sweat. The cold half of the bed horribly familiar, as were the tears on his face.

He didn't understand. He wanted to remember how it had been; the sun shining every day, every single day. Everyone happy. The children happy in their lives growing up through school and beyond. His mother somehow reduced and growing frail but happy to sit in the house and teach Ivy the mysterious formations of English. John apparently happy to be relocated to the attic as a result of the requirement for an extra room. The expanding Ivy was happy. She proved to be much better than Tom at understanding the emotional needs of the family; perhaps at understanding his own emotional needs. You have the EQ of a dead sparrow, she informed him, proudly showing off a new phrase no doubt taught her by Tom's mother. Even Tom was happy, despite sometimes waking in the night terrified that the scales would have to balance. He was happy that Ivy was happy. She kept up with technological changes and he could hear her laughing as she talked with friends and relatives in China and all over the world, and wondered if she was laughing in Chinese. He said to Beryl, on the phone: "That wonderful time with Mary and then… and then Malta, and…. and now with Ivy, I just think… you know. Balance." "Absolute *crap*," Beryl told him authoritatively, but that didn't stop Tom waking sometimes, terrified of he knew not what. And now that he did know he awoke panting, gasping, his heart pounding rapidly in his ears.

The genie tried to tug Tom towards the day it began.

No, he wanted to think about the eternal summer. Other summers. Running about in a field near the bus stop to primary school. McEnroe and Borg slugging it out under Wimbledon's summer sun. Something tugged at his memory as his eyes closed and he drifted back towards sleep. Yes. Thanks God, let we two speak our mind totally… Life is getting better and better. Oh, my beautiful Ivy, thought Tom.

Baby killer. Her pleading eyes. Her trembling fingers. The silence in the cubicle; all sounds sucked away into other people's dreams.

Wearily, his eyes fluttered open again. Same unbroken darkness. Dawn probably a couple of hours away. He remembered now—not that he wanted to—the tall Indian doctor wearing a silver name badge glancing at the scrap of paper, nodding.

"We might have to take your wife and son to a different hospital," he had said.

Baby killer.

We'll be a team, right?

"Another hospital?"

Dr Aslan nodded. Tom looked down at Ivy's scrawled note, remembered the imploring look in her eyes. *Baby killer.*

"The nurses…" Understanding dawned. "The nurses aren't talking about Ivy, are they?"

"No." Dr Aslan said something about purple that Tom didn't follow.

"They didn't say—this." The crumpled scrap of paper.

"No."

Dr Aslan must have read his fear and confusion.

"They'll sort her out," he said.

Tom didn't immediately take this in. He only knew that his wife and new-born baby were going to be taken away somewhere, to a different hospital. His wife. Taken away. Again. Then the implication of Dr Aslan's words dawned on him.

"They'll—"

"Oh yes. They just need to find the right medication. Take a few weeks, I expect."

"The right medication," repeated Tom. He was finding it hard to think. On the one hand he had just become a father. On the other hand his wife was... what? Slipping away?

Baby killer.

We'll be a team.

"Should be this afternoon," said Dr Aslan. He made a deprecating gesture. "We need the bed, you see." He added, "The baby will stay with his mother. But they will check."

"Check?"

Dr Aslan glanced at the curtains surrounding Ivy's cubicle, Tom suspected to avoid his gaze.

"In case Mrs Bradley has... ah, any ill intentions towards the baby."

Tom stared at him.

"I am not thinking she does," said Dr Aslan hastily. "But they will want to make sure, yes?" He didn't give Tom the chance to answer. "This afternoon, all right?" he repeated. "We'll let you know. You keep her company, Mr Bradley, all right?"

Tom obediently went back behind the curtain, and everything had changed.

> Postpartum psychosis, or puerperal psychosis, is a rare but serious and potentially life-threatening mental health issue. It's one of the most extreme postnatal issues and yet it's rarely spoken about. It takes the form of severe depression or mania or both. It's rare, affecting between one and two women per 1,000 births.

Ivy no longer saw curtains, or the ward she was in, or the room. Or Tom. Or Xiao Xiao. Her eyes seemed focused on a different reality. Every now and then she shook her head briefly, as if disagreeing with everything she had thought about in the thirty seconds or so since she had last shaken it. Or perhaps it was a denial of reality in favour of her own distorted perceptions. Over the days, weeks and even years, Tom came to know that shake of the head far too well. But that first time, when everything was desperately and horribly new, he came to hate it. It came to represent everything about her illness—her refusal to take her medicine; her refusal to believe that there was anything wrong with her; her belief that he, Tom, was trying to kill her and had locked her up so that she could not contact any of her friends or relatives. The new hospital turned out to be what was in modern politically correct parlance a mental health facility. On the advice of her consultant he went to see her every day.

"So that, as she gets better, you are seen as part of the solution, not part of the problem. You see?"

Tom did see. He did his best.

–Ivy, I didn't bring you here.

A shake of the head.

–I'm not a doctor. I can't bring you here, or anywhere else, for that matter. Ivy, I love you and I want to see you better.

No answer, just a shake of the head.

"We'll sort her out," said the consultant.

Tom felt a slight lifting of his spirits. The consultant sounded so sure of himself.

"Although I wish we could get her to take her medication," added the consultant.

Tom's spirits plummeted again. "It's a Chinese thing," he said.

–Ivy, even if you don't listen to me, will you listen to the doctor and take your medicine?

A shake of the head. Tom wasn't even sure that it was a response to what he was saying. He suspected that she didn't hear him at all, refused to accept his existence, and he was unconsciously timing his own remarks to fill in the gaps between each shake of her head. Every day he would get Lucy ready for school and then drive to the hospital. He vaguely remembered that Ivy's nurse had bright blonde hair, pale blue eyes and an endless supply of patience.

–Xiao Xiao?

–Is doing fine.

–Ivy?

–Still refuses to take her tablets.

–It's a Chinese thing, said Tom dully.

–And she won't sleep.

–Oh. Oh.

–In case, you know, one of us creeps in on her at night.

–Yes, said Tom. –Of course.

–But, said the nurse enthusiastically, –she had some breakfast this morning. Toast.

Tom remembered Ivy experimenting in the kitchen. It seemed like a long time ago. It seemed like a different Ivy.

–Jam and then butter, marvelled the nurse. –She says she wants Chinese food.

–Oh. Tom brightened. –She's communicating? That's good, isn't it?

–Of course it is, said the nurse, even more enthusiastically. –You go to see her now. We'll have her right as rain, as soon as she starts taking her medication.

But Ivy was still sitting on the side of her bed, fully dressed, even down to her shoes, and still shaking her head at her own enigmatic thought processes. She ignored Tom completely. He spoke to her for a while, telling her small stories of events at home, of phone calls from the boys and their get-well wishes, of how Xiao Xiao's room was waiting for him. He often held Xiao Xiao at these times, marvelling at his tiny, puckered face, his chubby, kicking legs and his waving, uncoordinated fists. But Ivy either did not notice or did not care.

Over the next few days he brought stir-fried rice and vegetables. The nurses took it from him and passed him the empty container on each following day. Progress, thought Tom.

–Oh, she's not been eating it, confessed the blonde nurse eventually. –We have. We thought, you know, that she would start to eat it, but she hasn't.

–You've been eating my stir fries?

–We're sorry, Mr Bradley.

Tom checked that Xiao Xiao was asleep, sat down beside Ivy on the bed and sighed. He didn't know what to say. He didn't know what to do. He was running out of energy and hope. Even if Ivy came out of this dreadful condition, would she still be the same Ivy? Would she still love him and want to stay in Scotland? The doctors said she would, and he supposed the doctors knew about this sort of thing, but he was beginning to have doubts.

–I know what you doing.

Tom jumped. He actually looked around the room to see who had spoken, although he knew that it must have been Ivy. He reached out to hold her hand, but she shifted away.

–I heard it on the news.

Tom wasn't sure where this was leading, but it didn't sound promising. Except that she was looking at him and speaking to him, something she had not done for weeks.

–What did you hear on the news, dear?

–You know.

–No, I don't know. Won't you tell me?

A shake of the head as she turned away. Tom wasn't sure if it was in response to his words.

–Won't you tell me? he said again. –I'm here every day; I brought you Chinese food. Is there anything else you want?

No response.

–It's me, Ivy, your husband. One and one makes one, remember? Headshake.

–We'll be a team, remember?

No response. After a few seconds, another headshake. She retreated into her own world and Tom wasn't sure that her few words, which sounded like accusations, represented any improvement.

–Did she speak to you? asked the nurse brightly as he left.

–Sort of.

–Oh?

–She said she knew what I was doing.

–Oh. And what was that?

–I have no idea, said Tom. –She wouldn't say.

The nurse reached out and touched him on the shoulder.

–Don't worry. Doctor will sort her out and she'll be home before you know it. She just needs to—

–take her medication. Yes, said Tom heavily.

–Yes, said the nurse. She had lost some of her cheerfulness and Tom felt obscurely guilty.

–Tomorrow? she said.

–Tomorrow, he said.

§

Tom rang the hospital every evening. He learned to ask for staff nurse Edith or Brian, and they came to expect his calls. How is Xiao Xiao? Absolutely fine—oh, and could you bring in more nappies? And Ivy? Just the same, sitting fully dressed on the edge of her bed. Edith said, I think she's ready to leave, poor dear. Has she taken her medicine? Not yet. Has she asked for him? No, sorry. Has she asked for anything? No.

Tom went to bed late, but couldn't sleep. The cold, empty half of the bed was horribly familiar.

"Can I see her?" pleaded Lucy daily.

"No, not now," said Tom. And in an attempt to alleviate the gloom: "Not yet."

Adam and John, both at university, kept in touch. Adam came back some weekends, ostensibly to visit friends still in the local area but really, he admitted later, "To make sure you were all right, Dad."

He wasn't all right. His fingers pressed the pattern of numbers that called the hospital by rote, by muscle memory. Night after night. Drive to the hospital in the morning. Phone at night.

Is Xiao Xiao okay?

He's absolutely fine. Can you remember to bring in powdered milk?

Okay. How's Ivy?

Same. She had some toast and some vegetables.

Okay. Has she asked for me?

No, Mr B. I'm sorry.

He drove the car by rote too and not even the fleeting excitement of trying to find somewhere to park in the inadequate hospital car parks could bring him to life. He knew that when he got to the ward, it would be to find Ivy sitting on the edge of her bed, dressed ready to leave, with her hands neatly crossed on her lap, shaking her head every thirty seconds, refusing to recognise his existence. He could not eat, lost a lot of weight, couldn't sleep. He knew he wasn't managing the situation at all well.

One morning a doctor wanted to talk to him. Afterwards Tom couldn't remember much about him, except that he wore a stethoscope around his neck like a necklace, as doctors always did in television soaps but did not often—in Tom's experience—in real life.

–We may have to consider giving your wife an injection if she continues to refuse her tablets.

–Okay.

–Has she had a bad experience with tablets, do you know?

–Don't think so, said Tom. –It's a Chinese thing.

The doctor nodded. –Yes. We see that sometimes. I need you to sign this form to authorise us to give your wife an injection.

–Why, is it dangerous?

–No, said the doctor. –But she probably won't like it. It's a last resort. Maybe next week, if nothing changes.

Tom signed the form. He felt like saying they could give her the injection right now if it would drag Ivy out of her condition and start to get their lives back on an even keel. Instead, he said, –Will she be all right?

–Oh yes. The doctor sounded confident. –Her condition is rare, but we've dealt with it before. It's just her reluctance to take tablets that's complicating matters.

–Okay. When she finally comes out of it… Tom hesitated, not sure how to ask the question in his mind, but the doctor had obviously been there before.

–She'll be fine, he said. –A bit… fragile, for a little while. And she'll have to continue to take her medication and come here for review now and then. But she'll be fine, Mr Bradley. Think of it as a broken leg. She doesn't want a splint, which is causing a delay. But once the leg is mended, it'll be as good as new. Okay?

For the first time in what seemed like a long while Tom felt a stirring of hope. The room in which they were sitting had large glass windows set in the wall, and as he stood to leave he caught sight of a nurse he hadn't met before walking past, a female nurse with long, dark hair and a brown-yellow complexion. She was Chinese. An idea jumped into his head.

–Doctor, he said, turning.

–Yes?

–I've thought of something that might help.

§

Next morning Lucy woke up feeling ill. Worse than a cold, she told Tom, but not as bad as flu. Whatever it was, she took a day off school and Tom had to stay at home to look after her. He fretted all day, wondering what was going on at the hospital, and made his evening phone call a little earlier than usual.

–Mr Bradley? It was Brian, sounding disgruntled.

–Yes. How's Xiao Xiao?

–He's just fine.

Brian fell silent. Tom immediately worried that there was something he was not saying.

–Good, okay. And you don't need anything? Food, nappies, clothes?

–No, nothing, said Brian.

–Right. Okay. And Ivy? How's Ivy?

–She's improved a little, said Brian. –Look, Mr Bradley—

–Improved? interrupted Tom. –What's happened?

–The thing is—

Brian didn't get to say what the thing was. The phone made curious buffeting noises and other noises that seemed to indicate that it was being put down and picked up and generally wrestled with. Tom could make out voices in the background, though not what they were saying.

–Mr B? That you?

–Edith?

–Sorry about that. Brian's about as much use as a lump of cold custard. It was the end of his shift.

–Yes, but—

–Mrs B started taking her medication this morning. And also this evening.

–Oh.

For goodness sake, thought Tom. He'd been waiting and hoping and praying for Ivy to take her tablets for weeks and weeks, and now that it had happened all he could say was Oh. Edith didn't seem to notice.

–Su went in to chat, and Mrs B started talking back… It was all Greek to me, Edith confided.

Nice one, thought Tom. He found he was trembling and grasping the phone so hard that its plastic covering creaked. –What does it all mean, exactly?

–She'll get a good night's sleep, said Edith.

So will I, thought Tom suddenly.

–And tomorrow… What?

–I didn't say anything, said Tom. But Edith was no longer talking to him.

–Yes, yes, of course. Yes, he's on now. Here.

–Mr Bradley?

Tom reflected that this was the third time someone had asked him if he was himself. He wondered if he was going to talk to everyone on the hospital staff this evening. He recognised the voice as belonging to the stethoscoped doctor.

–Your idea worked, said the doctor. –Nurse Su Wei spoke to your wife in… Chinese—

–Mandarin.

—and that broke down the barrier. I have no doubt she will continue to take her tablets, now that she's started.

–Thank God, muttered Tom.

–But she will not be acting normally yet. Please be aware that she will still say things that make no sense, that are based in her illness. But she will gradually pull out of it now.

–How—

The doctor anticipated his question. He seemed to be good at doing that. –Another two or three weeks, I should think. We need to get her stabilised. Maybe a couple of day passes to see how things go. You didn't come in today?

–No, my daughter was poorly. I'll be there tomorrow.

–You'll notice a difference, promised the doctor.

Lucy wanted to immediately jump in the car and drive to the hospital, but Tom said it was far too late and anyway she would infect everyone in the hospital with whatever she had got, which wouldn't go down too well. Later, he told her. This was a promise he almost came to regret: when Lucy did eventually get to see Ivy in hospital, she nearly undid, with one ill-considered remark, all the good work the doctors had contrived. He did sleep better that night. And he did

see a difference in Ivy the next day, although she was still far from
the Ivy he knew. Staff nurse Edith was on duty, and greeted him with
a wide smile. Nurse Su Wei appeared from somewhere and said she
would join him for a few minutes, if he didn't object.

For once, Ivy was dressed in night clothes and a loose gown.
When he entered, she looked up in alarm and backed away slightly.
His heart thudded with unexpected horror as he saw the fear and
loathing in her eyes. He tried to look past it, seeking the Ivy on the
other side; the doctor had said he was not to be surprised at her
behaviour. She was a long way from being healed.

–Hello, dear.

Ivy didn't respond, but looked quickly at nurse Su Wei, and
then back to Tom.

–I hear you are a bit better today, said Tom.

Ivy shook her head. Tom hated the sight of it, but noted that
she was doing it far less frequently.

–How are you feeling? He sat down slowly in the one chair.

–You, said Ivy. She looked from nurse Su Wei to Tom, back and
forth, as if she was making a comparison between them. –Tried to
kill me.

–What?

–With food, said Ivy. Her eyes blazed.

Tom blinked, taken aback. –You mean… the rice and vegetables?
I thought… you know. Better than toast. He didn't know what to say.

–Dú yào, Ivy said.

–Poison, said nurse Su Wei.

–What? said Tom.

Nurse Su Wei said something in Mandarin. Ivy looked at her.
Tom was in shock. Ivy thought he had tried to poison her? Nurse Su
Wei spoke again and Tom wondered if she was repeating whatever
she had said the first time. An expression of doubt crossed Ivy's face.

–The nurse all eat your stir fry?

–Nurses, said Tom automatically. –Yes. For nearly a week. I
didn't know.

The penny dropped.

–Yes! The nurses ate it all and look— he held out both his hands
towards nurse Su Wei —they have all survived.

Ivy shook her head, but Tom noted that it was only the second time she had done so since he had gone into her room. She turned away again: Tom and nurse Su Wei shared a look. Tom mouthed thank you and she nodded gravely.

–You.

Ivy's expression had changed again, become cunning.

–Yes, dear?

–My parents.

–Yes, Maggie has been telling them—

Maggie, one of Ivy's Chinese friends, had been acting as a Scotland–China go-between.

–No. The look in Ivy's eyes was suddenly savage and Tom was hard pressed not to shuffle both himself and his chair backwards. –I hear it on the news. You stopped them.

–I stopped them what? On the news? Tom didn't know what to say again.

–They said, you stop them coming into this country. Stop them coming to see me.

–I did not, he said. –I… er… how would I do a thing like that?

Nurse Su Wei, speaking in English, said, –We had a young man in here who also heard the news on the television. Both Tom and Ivy stared at her. –He heard that in six months the entire population of Scotland was to be transported to another country so that the land could be used for war exercises.

She shrugged.

–That was over a year ago. Zhang Lan, you can't always believe what you hear on the television.

Nice one, thought Tom. A movement caught his eye and he got up quickly. Xiao Xiao was stirring, perhaps awakened by all the voices in the room. Tom picked him up and then, moving more slowly, crossed over to Ivy and held him out. She took him and held him close, looking at Tom suspiciously but, he thought, he hoped, a little less fearfully.

–I'll leave you to it, said nurse Su Wei. –Are you all right with that, Mrs Bradley? Wǒ jiāo géi nǐ mén xíng ma?

Ivy hesitated. –Xíng. Yes. She gave Tom a sideways look. He sat down on the bed, almost but not quite next to her, as nurse Su left.

–She seems nice, he said.

Ivy didn't reply, but neither did she shake her head.

–Everyone's been asking after you, said Tom.

Still no response, but Tom thought she was listening. He told her about Lucy being poorly, about Maggie acting as a go-between, about Adam's frequent visits. He told her how he managed the cooking and washing but not the ironing, how he had been driving up every day and phoning every night. He told her everything he had been telling her for the last few weeks.

–You are not at work, she said.

–No. They have given me some leave.

Xiao Xiao, who had gone to sleep, woke up again and started to suck his thumb.

–He's hungry.

–The nurses will see to it, whispered Ivy.

Tom reached out, hesitated, and gently touched her shoulder. She shivered but didn't shy away.

–I'm so pleased you are coming back, my dear.

Ivy bent her head over Xiao Xiao. Tom cleared his throat.

–So, shall I bring in vegetable stir fry tomorrow?

After a long moment, she raised her head and for the first time some of the pinched, drawn features of her face smoothed out and she looked more like the Ivy he knew.

She whispered, –Yes please, and—he was not certain, but he thought he glimpsed a tear in the corner of her eye.

§

The doctors determined that Ivy was well enough to be allowed out into the ward's enclosed garden. Tom brought coats and they wandered around the flower beds and the tiny, sculptured water feature—not, Tom thought, that a water feature was really required, as the skies were grey and overcast and occasionally dribbled icy droplets as a harbinger of heavier rain to come. Half way around the garden Tom paused and held out his hand. After what were for him agonizing seconds, Ivy took it and they walked slowly, shoulder to shoulder, back to the ward.

Some days Ivy showed improvement. On other days the head-shake returned and she demanded that he eat some of the stir fry before she did. Xiao Xiao was happy enough in his giant cot. The evening phone calls gradually became more optimistic.

"She's taking her medication, Mr B, like clockwork. She wants some Chinese magazines."

"I—"

"Someone called Maggie? Is going to deliver some to you." A touch of pride entered Edith's voice. "Mrs B phoned her today."

"Wow." Tom couldn't help smiling as he put down the receiver. Ivy was slowly returning to the real world.

§

Two or three days later Tom arrived and waited for Ivy in her room. He piled a new batch of magazines on her bedside cabinet, peered out of the door, sighed when he saw no sign of her, and sat down in the chair. She was probably talking to a nurse or walking in the garden. After half an hour he got up and sauntered over to reception.

–Hello, do you happen to know where Ivy—Mrs Bradley—is?

The nurse on reception was a thin woman whose eyes were so close together that she seemed to be perpetually frowning. Her name badge read Helen.

–Isn't she with you?

–No, I've been waiting a while.

Nurse Helen leaned back through a doorway leading into a staff room.

–Jim. You seen Mrs Bradley?

–No. What's up?

Nurse Helen turned back to Tom.

–She in the garden?

–I haven't looked.

–Jim, check the garden, will you? Pauline, check the ward—don't forget the food prep area.

Tom wondered if the food prep area was the same as the kitchen. He watched with mild amazement as a short man with a beard and an even shorter, stout woman barrelled out of the staff room and sped

277

off in different directions. Yet another nurse, a thickset bald man, stopped the staff room door from closing and leaned against the jamb.

–You've not seen her this morning? asked nurse Helen.

–No. I've been waiting half an hour or so.

–Mrs Bradley, is it? asked the thickset man. He looked over his shoulder. –You seen Mrs Bradley?

Nurse Su Wei appeared.

–I gave her her medication. I think she went to breakfast.

The bearded man returned, out of breath. He shook his head. All looked up as the rotund nurse also returned. She also shook her head.

–Oh no, moaned nurse Helen. –She's got out, hasn't she?

–If anyone was going to get out, said the thickset nurse, –it would be Mrs Bradley.

There was a murmur of agreement around the group. Tom felt an unexpected spurt of pride. This was his wife they were talking about.

–Gerard, said nurse Helen. –Stay here. Alert Staff. The rest of you—come on!

The nurses surged away from the reception area. Tom imagined them spilling out of the building, jumping into cars or onto bikes or just running, white coats flapping, along the pavements of the roads fronting the hospital.

Nobody told Tom what to do so he stayed where he was.

–Don't worry, mate, said the bearded nurse who had remained behind. Curiously, Tom didn't feel especially worried.

–This happen often?

–Couple of times a year.

–How can she... er... escape?

A shrug. –Probably slipped out as someone was coming in. Visitors don't have much of a clue.

Tom thought about it. True enough, sometimes when he had buzzed to come in, somebody else had made their way out. He generally didn't have any idea of who they were.

–The system's broken, grumbled the nurse. –Staff shortages. He was punching buttons savagely on a phone, listening, then punching them again. –Tech out of date... Tom tuned him out and wondered where Ivy had got to. He found out twenty minutes later when nurse

Helen and the thickset male nurse returned with Ivy trotting happily between them. Tom could not help smiling at the sight of her. She had been found walking briskly along the pavement about a mile away, searching for a supermarket. More of the staff returned, notified through some mysterious grapevine that the escapee had been recaptured.

–Apple juice, said nurse Helen grimly.

–Oh! exclaimed nurse Su Wei. –There wasn't any at breakfast. We'd run out.

Ivy beamed and Tom realised that her face had lost that strange, closed-in look of the last few weeks.

–Sorry, sorry, I only trying to help.

–She was going to get apple juice for *everyone*, said the thickset nurse.

Oh, Ivy, thought Tom.

–Oh, Mrs Bradley, said nurse Helen, as if she could read his mind. –What are we going to do with you?

§

Lucy insisted on cooking a batch of stir fry vegetables and rice and going with Tom to the hospital one Saturday morning.

–Be careful what you say, warned Tom.

–Of course I will, Dad. I'll just tell her about, you know, school and badminton and stuff.

She and Ivy fell into each other's arms and Tom couldn't help but notice that Lucy was the taller of the two by a couple of inches.

–You look great, enthused Lucy. –Here, I made this.

Ivy took the plastic container a little gingerly and glanced at Tom over Lucy's shoulder. Tom made a wry face.

–Thank you, dear. How's school?

Lucy sat in the chair and Tom was in the process of moving to the foot of the bed when someone rapped on the window inset into the door. It was one of the doctors, who crooked a finger; Tom pantomimed a 'Me?' and the doctor nodded.

–Right, muttered Tom. –I'll just be a minute. He retraced his steps to join the doctor in the corridor outside the room. Tom didn't recall seeing this doctor before and surreptitiously glanced at his name badge, which, it turned out, was mostly obscured by a fold in his white coat. Alrighty then, thought Tom. Dr Ar it would have to be.

–Glad I caught you, said Dr Ar. –We had a review meeting and agreed that it's time your wife had a twenty-four-hour pass. Despite the Great Escape, he added dryly. –We thought Monday, if that's all right with you?

Tom's heart jumped. –Yes, of course! Great, thanks.

–Three things, said Dr Ar. –One, take a note of the ward's phone number in case you need it.

Tom forbore from saying that the number was engraved in both his brain and his fingers.

–Two, you must make sure Mrs Bradley takes her medication. That's vital. It has a cumulative effect and if you break the sequence…

–I get it, said Tom.

–Okay. Three—what on earth is going on in there?

It took a moment for Tom to take in this change of direction. Then he whirled to look through the window into Ivy's room. Lucy was still sitting in the chair and Tom could see enough of her face to see that she was worried and puzzled. Ivy had shifted to the far end of the bed. She had hunched over. To Tom's horror, she gave the headshake he had come to hate.

He rushed back in, Dr Ar following.

–What—?

–Is it true? Ivy looked up and Tom tried to decipher her expression. It resembled the pinched look of her illness, but—not quite. Tom realised that she was fighting it.

–Is what true?

–Dad—

–What did you say?

–I just made a joke.

A joke? Tom rubbed a hand over his eyes. Ivy seldom understood British jokes even when she was well.

–What did you say? he repeated.

–I said I hoped Ivy would get better soon because… because… Lucy started to gabble. –Because you were thinking of letting out her room.

Dr Ar said, –I assume Mrs Bradley didn't take this as a joke?

–A joke? Ivy was looking at Tom.

–A joke, confirmed Tom. Over his shoulder: –Ivy has a knack of taking things literally. It's a Chinese thing.

–Really, I was just joking, said Lucy desperately. –I mean—

Ivy transferred her gaze to her.

–I mean, you don't even have a room. I mean, you know what I mean. You share Dad's room.

–Lucy.

–Sorry, Dad.

–Is true, said Ivy unexpectedly. –I don't have a own room. So you couldn't… couldn't…

–Let it out, supplied Tom.

–Yes, that. Ivy sat up straighter.

–No, of course not, said Tom. –I wouldn't anyway, even if I could. Which I couldn't, he added hastily.

–So is everything all right here? inquired Dr Ar.

Tom looked at Ivy and raised his eyebrows. Much later, she told him that this was the moment when everything started to click into place, when she realised that Tom was not trying to control her, never mind kill her. He was asking her if everything was all right. It was her decision. She suddenly beamed and jumped up and buried her head in his shoulder. Dr Ar turned to go, then paused.

–Three—make sure you get back on time. By nine thirty.

He left, closing the door quietly. Ivy extricated herself from Tom's embrace and looked up at him.

–Twenty-four-hour pass, said Tom. –Monday.

Ivy gave a little shriek, jumped up, and started to pack her bag.

–It's on Monday, said Tom. –Today's Saturday.

–But I want me out, said Ivy disconsolately.

Tom sat down next to her on the bed and put an arm around her. When she had just started taking her medication and he had done the same thing, she had been as skittish as… Tom's mind couldn't think of the conclusion to this description. She had been on the verge of leaping away, putting as much space between the two of them as she could in the tiny room. Now, she leaned against him and sobbed. It was a normal sob, Tom thought. Lucy sat on the other side of her and also put an arm around her.

–We all want you out, she said.

Tom told the boys that visiting restrictions had been lifted, and they went to the hospital one evening.

–How did she seem to you? asked Tom, when they gathered for a meal afterwards.

–Not bad, said John. –She was—

He and Adam exchanged a glance.

–Fragile? asked Tom, borrowing a word from the doctor's vocabulary.

–Yes.

–And cross, added Adam. –About, you know, she is still in.

–Your sister almost ensured she would stay in for much longer, Tom remarked.

–Dad, muttered Lucy.

–What did you do?, said Adam.

–Nothing.

–What do you mean, nothing? How can it be nothing if Dad says—

–I told a joke, said Lucy, mainly to cut off what was beginning to look like one of Adam's drawn-out logical arguments.

–Can't have been very funny, said John.

Tom, forking up lasagne, smiled contentedly. He enjoyed hearing his children pretend to get worked up over an argument. They never really argued. He remembered saying to Monique. "They know what's important, because of… because…" and Monique, who at that moment had her arm about his waist and was bumping her hip against his as they strolled through Buskett Forest, said simply, "Yes. I understand."

–Ha ha, said Adam.

–When is she coming out, anyway? asked John.

Tom shook his head. –Not certain. Not long, though. Maybe a forty-eight-hour pass, and then they have this big review thing. Tom ruminated. –They don't have it every week. But it won't be long.

And it wasn't. When the day arrived, Tom drove to the hospital and arrived an hour early. Even so, Ivy was packed and ready to go, perched on the edge of her bed looking rather like a sprinter in the blocks. The nurses smiled. Tom felt vaguely guilty that he and Ivy were desperate to leave the place where she had received so much care and he nodded and smiled at all the staff, and shook all their hands, not something he normally liked to do, and clapped one woman on the arm and grinned at her only to find she was a patient and not a member of staff. She gave a half-hearted scream and wandered off into the internal garden, looking fearfully over her shoulder.

–Not to worry, said nurse Su. –That's Irene. She'll be fine. Here. She handed Tom an enormous paper bag. –Tablets.

Tom nodded. He'd become familiar with them over the last few weeks.

–Sign here.

Tom signed.

–Thank you, Mr Bradley. You can go now.

Tom glanced at his watch.

–Ten o'clock, the doctor said.

–Yes, he always says that, said nurse Su. –He knew you would turn up an hour early. You always do. She frowned. –If you see what I mean.

–Thank you so much, said Tom.

–Bú kè qì.

Ivy was at his side, tugging him into her room to collect bags and suitcase.

–What did she say? whispered Tom.

–Don't forget Xiao Xiao, said Ivy.

Tom was puzzled. Why would nurse Su say that? Wait. She didn't say Xiao Xiao's name, did she? Oh. He realised he had picked up what appeared to be half a ton of baby clothes and other baby accoutrements Xiao Xiao had accumulated in the first six weeks of his life, and Ivy had picked up her suitcase and bags of extra clothes and Chinese magazines, and neither of them had picked up Xiao Xiao.

–We'll leave him here, said Tom.

They pushed together and rearranged suitcases and bags; Tom ended up carrying almost everything but at least Ivy had an arm free. She scooped up Xiao Xiao and they staggered off towards the exit.

–Goodbye! Goodbye! cried the nurses. –Hope not to see you soon!

It was drizzling outside and the sky was overcast. Grey. Every-thing was damp and grey. But Tom could see that Ivy was so happy to be outside the ward with no requirement to be back in twenty-four or forty-eight hours that it could have been blowing a hurricane or a blizzard and she would not have cared. He stuffed all the luggage into the boot while she strapped Xiao Xiao's carrier into the back seat, and they both collapsed into the front seats. The rain grew heavier, trickling down all the windows, but neither of them noticed. They leaned over the central console and shared a long kiss.

–Mm.

–It's my pleasure.

–Mm?

–What she said. Nurse Su Wei.

On the way back Xiao Xiao gurgled and hiccoughed and Tom remembered infant Lucy, also strapped into the back seat, remarking how good it was they were able to talk. Ivy dozed off. The rain wors-ened, and then slackened, and by the time they got home a watery sun was trying to find its way through the clouds. Everything seemed so very normal. Lucy rushed out and clasped Ivy in a hug, and then immediately dived into the car to fetch Xiao Xiao. Both the dogs made a terrible fuss; Jess jumped up but could only reach to a few inches above Ivy's knees, which she nibbled, but Gus was able to rear up onto his hind legs and plant them on Ivy's shoulders. Which he promptly did, and gave her face a thorough lick.

–I've lit the fire, said Lucy. –And made—

They were all in the house by now, depositing bags, suitcases, dogs and Xiao Xiao into various places.

–Yes? inquired Tom

–It's meant to be a… sort of… casserole.

–Sort of! cried Ivy. –My favourite!

–Dad? Lucy was frowning as she concentrated on her lines.

–Yes? inquired Tom again.

–Er, is it okay if I have a sleepover at Louise's tonight?

–I thought you were revising.

–She, er, wants me to help her with maths.

–Right, right. Both Tom and Lucy, without moving their heads, tried to look surreptitiously at Ivy, to see how she was taking this. Ivy didn't seem to be paying any attention. She appeared to unwrapping Xiao Xiao from a large number of blankets and then rewrapping him in identical new blankets. But you could never tell with Ivy.

–Help with maths, hm, that's different, said Tom. He winked at Lucy. –All right then. I suppose… I suppose… He had forgotten his own lines.

–Thanks, Dad.

–Stay for lunch, Tom remembered. –Casserole.

–Sort of, said Ivy.

Aha, thought Tom.

–No, said Lucy decisively. –I made it for you.

While Tom was out, ferrying Lucy across the town, Ivy wandered about the house, touching tabletops, furniture, the wardrobes in their bedroom. She felt very alone. Then she went into the lounge, where Lucy's fire was burning, and discovered that she was not on her own after all. She sat on the floor as close as she could to the fire, enjoying its warmth, and leaned back against an armchair. Jess curled up in her lap and Gus stretched out by her side, leaning against her, practically pushing her into the flames. She sighed and felt peace wash over her. When Tom came back not much later he found the three of them there, fast asleep. He wished he had his camera to hand. The genie, remembering from the future, wished that mobile phones had been available back then. Still, the image of them curled together, sleeping, engraved itself in his memory. Then Gus woke up and heaved himself to his feet to greet him; so of course Jess woke up and did the same; and so of course Ivy woke up and opened her sleepy eyes. She had been rehearsing for this moment, as she knew Tom and Lucy must have rehearsed for theirs.

–I want, she said, –sort of casserole food, a nice hottie bath, then my nice warm bed and sleep.

Tom thought about it. They both smiled.

–I think I can manage three of those, he said, –but possibly not the fourth.

The genie retreated, smeared into time, as their lives slowly got back on track. The boys returned occasionally, wanting vast amounts of food to eat and even more vast quantities of washing washed. Xiao Xiao became a toddler. Lucy slogged through exams and dragged

Tom all over the country to badminton competitions, which as far as he could tell were always held in halls with sub-zero temperatures even at the height of summer. He was happy enough. He even started writing again.

She turned towards him, and her eyes met his.

Better. Third person was better. It would probably be too painful to write in first person anyway. No unbuttoning of cardigan, my dear. But… too generic. It could be the start of a hundred different books. Delete.

Still, he wrote many pages of Mary's book—not in the right form; that evaded him—but he made a start. He watched Ivy grow back to become herself, watching her confidence grow. He didn't see the danger this posed and nor did the genie, so even when they revisited the days and weeks when she was deceiving him, there was nothing to see. Neither of them noticed.

–How are you? everyone asked Ivy, especially those who knew the nature of her illness.

–Fine, fine! she would say, beaming happily.

"And that didn't ring any alarm bells?" the Forbes woman asked Tom in the future, after his accident.

"No," said Tom.

–Better! beamed Ivy.

"And still no alarm bells? Nobody warned you?"

"No. And no."

"What happened?" asked the Forbes woman.

§

Tom wandered upstairs, looking for Ivy, and discovered her standing by the wardrobe, her two silver suitcases packed. His heart thudded in alarm as she faced him across the room. Her eyes seemed slightly out of focus and she shook her head.

–It's been very nice of you, she said. –Thank you so much. But it's time for me to go.

–What? Where?

–You've been so kind, said Ivy.

–Well. You are my wife. Tom already knew what was happening but was trying desperately to not believe it, to make it not happen. But Ivy gave that short headshake, then looked at him calmly.

–Maggie's coming. I'll be leaving in a little while.

A little while. So there was still some time. Tom put out his hands, palms down. –Wait. Wait. He turned and stumbled downstairs, to the phone. The number was hardwired into his memory despite the many months during which it had not been needed.

–Hello, it's Tom Bradley. Is Edith or Brian there?

–Who?

–The staff nurse on duty.

–That's me, Mr Bradley. My name is Gina. How can I help you?

A few frantic minutes later Tom discovered that Gina was unable to help.

–I'm sorry, Mr Bradley. We can only help if your wife has been allocated a bed here, or is an outpatient of this ward.

–But—

Tom stopped. They were about to go around in circles and he didn't have time for that.

–You need the mental health team in your area, said Gina. – It's… let me see. She gave Tom a number and he wrote it down. –Good luck, she said.

It was Sunday. When Tom called the mental health team an automatic message informed him it was closed, and suggested he call another number. He did so, and found himself talking to a frustratingly unhelpful woman. She wanted to know Ivy's phone number, address, full name, date of birth—

–Can she come to the phone?

–No! I keep telling you, she has a serious mental illness and she needs help from the mental health team.

Pause.

–She can't come to the phone?

–No!

Pause.

–Is she conscious?

–Yes, of course she is.

–Is her body clammy?

–What?

–Does she seem to have a fever? Has she been vomiting at all?

–No! Listen—she has a mental health problem, not a physical problem. I—

–I've arranged for a GP to attend you, said the woman, sounding aggrieved. –Please ensure that Mrs Bradley is kept warm and her airways—

Uncharacteristically, Tom slammed down the receiver.

§

Over the years Ivy developed a habit of becoming ill at a weekend, and Tom constantly found himself struggling through the same medical labyrinth. The ward couldn't help because Ivy had no connection with them any more. They always wished him luck. The number for the mental health team—sometimes two numbers; Tom couldn't keep up with the bureaucratic changes—invariably told him that the office was closed, that it would re-open at nine on Monday morning, and in the meantime, please call this other number. The other number was invariably answered by someone who immediately launched into a series of irrelevant questions clearly read from a crib sheet.

On one occasion Tom despaired. Ivy had admitted that she had stopped taking her medication again, and had been having strange thoughts again. Tom rushed upstairs to get a tablet for her and rushed back down again clutching one encased in silver foil, but by the time he returned she had re-entered her own reality. He knew instantly there was no chance of her taking it. Her face was pinched, drawn, closed-in. She was kneeling on the floor, her hands jerkily swiping from side to side, sweeping away something only she could see. She was muttering in Chinese and the headshake had come back.

I'm sorry, Mr Bradley. Try the mental health team. Good luck.

We are closed and cannot take your call right now.

Is she conscious? Can she come to the phone? Is her skin clammy at all?

It was enough, thought Tom, to drive you mad.

In desperation he dialled 999, and a scant hour later had a house full of mostly unwelcome guests. Afterwards, he thought it must have looked like a Pythonesque black comedy sketch. Ivy was still on her knees, still sweeping away what only she could see. The headshake had returned full force and tears streaked her cheeks. An ambulance had turned up. One paramedic stood in the doorway; another stayed outside the house, in the ambulance, trying to contact the mental health team because, they explained, they hadn't been trained for this type of emergency and were forbidden from trying to help in case Ivy became violent.

"Does it look like she's going to be violent?" asked Tom, but the paramedic in the house just shook his head, although his eyes were sympathetic.

A policeman turned up. He stood in the hallway and occasionally peered in at Tom, who was kneeling beside Ivy, trying to comfort her. A GP appeared—not, Tom was glad to see, the arrogant individual who had arrived on the occasion when Ivy packed to leave. This doctor strode in confidently, took one look at Ivy and admitted that he, too, had not been trained for such an emergency. Tom was not sure why he stayed. Perhaps he was learning on the job. Strangest of all, a fire engine arrived, fortunately without a siren blaring, although its blue hazard lights intermittently lit up the area outside the house for what seemed like miles. Tom deduced that he had not phrased his 999 call accurately enough. Three firemen clumped through the house, looking for evidence of any fire, nodded politely at everyone, and clumped away again. The policeman was the last to leave, as he had a form that needed filling in. He kept scratching his head and apologising for taking up Tom's time: the form didn't seem to cater for this particular type of emergency callout. Everyone else faded away when a member of the mental health team arrived, a woman Tom had met before by the name of Brenda. She coaxed Ivy into the ambulance conveniently parked outside and suggested that Tom visit her at the hospital—sorry, she said—she meant the mental health facility—next morning.

"It is next morning," said Tom.

"True."

"Did I do the right thing, calling 999?"

"Oh yes," said Brenda. "She's in a bit of a state, isn't she?"

He closed the front door at last, checked up on Xiao Xiao, and collapsed fully dressed onto his bed. He expected that he would lie awake, worrying, but instead he slipped into sleep and dreamed about a drag race between an ambulance, a fire engine, a police car and a doctor dressed in white on a pedal cycle.

§

The doctor summoned by the frustratingly unhelpful woman was the best-dressed doctor Tom had ever seen. His shoes gleamed. His coat looked as if it had been ironed. His tiny goatee beard was trimmed to a nicety and his round spectacles glinted as if they had been polished. He looked like a film director's idea of a Victorian—or possibly Austrian—doctor. None of these thoughts occurred to Tom as he opened the door and led the way upstairs, but they did later. This was the doctor who produced a phrase almost as memorable as the one spoken by Mary's consultant so many years ago.

You have not been well served by the system.

Tom re-entered the bedroom, where Ivy was still standing by her two suitcases.

–This is Ivy. My wife.

–Hello, so nice of you to come, said Ivy.

The doctor placed his own bag on the floor. He had come only a short way into the room.

–My name is Doctor Barnsfield. I've come in response to a call made by Mr Bradley. He said that you are ill and need help.

–Ivy is mentally ill, said Tom. –She has a serious condition called—

–I'm leaving! interrupted Ivy. She beamed at Dr Barnsfield.

—called puerperal psychosis, said Tom, ploughing on desperately. –Look, here's her medication.

Dr Barnsfield barely glanced at the boxes of tablets.

–You're leaving? he asked.

–Maggie coming to pick me up.

–Maggie?

–My friend.

–And do you feel ill in any way?

–What about Xiao Xiao? interposed Tom.

–Oh, we collect him later, said Ivy.

–Xiao Xiao? Dr Barnsfield mouthed the words awkwardly.

–Our son. He's three.

–Ah.

–Tom has been so kind, said Ivy, –but it's time for me to go.

Dr Barnsfield frowned. –You are feeling well? he asked again.

–I feeling fine.

–No headaches?

–No.

Tom was beginning to tremble. He wasn't sure what caused it. Fear, or anger, or dread anticipation. Maybe all three.

–You don't understand, he said, more loudly than he intended.
–Ivy has a serious mental condition. She has stopped taking her medication and will get worse. A lot worse. And she's planning to leave.

–Yes. Dr Barnsfield pursed his lips. –I have to say Mrs Bradley seems perfectly well to me.

–Have you even read her notes? demanded Tom.

–Oh, no, said Dr Barnsfield. –I've come in from a different district altogether. This sounded like a cue for Tom to thank him for the effort of turning up, but Tom was in no mood to say any such thing.
–I'm sorry, said Dr Barnsfield, about to say the words that would forever glue him into Tom's memory. –But I do not think there is a medical problem here. This looks to me like a domestic dispute.

Tom gaped at him, at a loss for words.

–I'm perfectly fine! trilled Ivy.

–A domestic dispute? said Tom in a wondering voice. –You think I'd call in a doctor for a domestic dispute?

–You'd be surprised what people do, said Dr Barnsfield. –Especially when they are stressed out, which you must be if your wife is planning to leave you.

–But—

–No, I think I must leave it to you, Mr Bradley—and Mrs Bradley, of course—to sort out this unfortunate situation.

He picked up his bag and turned to leave.

–Doctor.

Dr Barnsfield paused, but did not turn back.

–When Ivy is sectioned again, and I assure you she will be, I shall be reporting this conversation to her consultant.

Dr Barnsfield's thin shoulders stiffened beneath his immaculate coat and he gave an almost imperceptible nod. In that moment Tom gained a sudden understanding of the true position: the doctor was simply out of his depth and didn't like to admit it. Tom was about to ask if he at least knew a number to call when the front door bell clamoured.

–Maggie! exclaimed Ivy. She picked up her suitcases and hustled out of the room, following Dr Barnsfield down the stairs. Xiao Xiao woke up at all the commotion and started to cry. Tom went to settle him down. From the toddler's room he could hear the front door close, a babble of voices, more than one car door slam shut and more than one car engine start up, move off and fade away.

It took a while for Xiao Xiao to go to sleep. When Tom was finally able to tuck him in and go downstairs, he knew what he would find.

Ivy had gone.

3

Tom sat quietly in the darkened room. A television fixed to the wall flickered and bleated, but he ignored it. He was remembering how he used to catch a school bus to primary school. There was a field by the side of the bus stop and everyone played there, running, screaming, delaying the bus when it finally arrived so that the conductor usually had to disembark and round them all up, like a farmer corralling unruly sheep. It was always sunny, he remembered.

The nurse had turned down the lights, which was all very well, but now he couldn't read the newspaper. True, he had dozed off while he was reading it earlier, but still. He had put it down briefly while he thought back on the times he had appeared in a newspaper, and the next thing he knew the room was in semi-darkness. He turned his head, a little awkwardly. Yes, the curtains were drawn. The afternoon must have worn away into evening while he slept.

The entry he most treasured was an unexpected front-page headline: *Love on the Net brings joy to a family again*. He never did find out who reported the story to the newspaper. Years later he found out that it had run in several syndicated newspapers and its footprint was even planted across a portion of the internet.

His eyes must have closed again, because something banged outside and they flew back open. The television was still wittering and it was darker. Tom looked around slowly. What had he been thinking about? The school bus. Primary school. His grandfather took him to his first day at secondary school. On a steam train.

Clear voices from the past. "Oh, Dad!" the children always said every time he reminded them he went to school on a steam train. He never told them that it was marvellous in retrospect but less so at the time. His body jerked as his old schoolfriend pushed him backwards off the station platform after the Valentine's card incident. What was his name? His brain fumbled for a moment and then triumphantly produced the answer. Syd. The bastard. He relived flying through the air, fortunately landing on the cinders, and remembered that he had relived it all before, but could not bring to mind when. He felt a tug at his memory.

–No.

Thinking about the children inevitably reminded him of Mary and the genie tried to drag him towards things he didn't want to remember.

–No, he said, more forcibly.

Outside, in the corridor, two nurses peered through the glass set in the door.

–What's he doing? said the woman, who was short and wore her dark hair in a close-cut bob. The tall man behind her shrugged.

–Dunno.

–He took his meds?

–Yeah.

They watched as Tom jerked and both of them heard him say No.

–I better settle him down.

–Cup of tea.

–Something stronger.

–I wish. Mrs B will be here soon.

–That'll do it.

They exchanged a look. Tom seemed to quieten. The nurses thought he might have dozed off again, but his hand clutched convulsively at the newspaper.

–Right, said the dark-haired woman. She pushed open the door, wondering what Tom was thinking about.

§

He was crying silently. Tears ran down his face, queued at the point of his chin, and took turns to drip onto the newspaper. He had wrestled the genie to a standstill, but it hurt terribly and he didn't think he would be able to do it for much longer. The television flared suddenly, a white light…

… and another. And another. They were standing on the church steps, facing the crowd. All their cameras—because they didn't have mobile phones then—flashed, separately catching the moment. Tom wondered if it was really that dark or if people had forgotten or didn't know how to adjust their various photographic devices. From the future he scanned the crowd. Somewhere in there was whoever it was that sent a photograph and sentimental article to the local newspaper. He saw no obvious suspects and in any case the crowd flickered, morphed, faded into sepia shades. It was a different crowd, from twenty years before, and Mary was by his side.

–Mr Bradley?

It was that damned nurse, the one who had turned down the lights. Probably. The one whose name he didn't remember.

–Are you all right?

Tom wiped at his eyes. –No. It's the damned genie. I'm fighting it.

–Yes, yes, soothed the nurse, setting down a cup of tea and bending to gather up the newspaper from the floor where it had fallen. The damned genie, she thought. What was that about?

–It wants me to remember, said Tom, so quietly she almost did not catch the words.

–Yes, I understand. The nurse was wrapping a blanket around Tom's knees by now, but she stopped abruptly. Tom was left with both legs lifted from the ground; for some reason this put pressure on the back of his neck so, while with one hand he braced himself on the arm of the chair, he raised the other one and put it behind himself for support. It was damned uncomfortable and probably looked ridiculous. He wasn't used, he thought, to having his limbs in this position. Remember that, my dear? He would have laughed, but it would almost certainly hurt, so he didn't. He made a faint moaning noise instead.

The nurse started and noticed Tom's discomfort.

–Sorry, Mr B.

She had suddenly realised that she did understand, almost, what Tom meant. There were things in her own life that she did not wish to remember. Remember.

–I nearly forgot, she said, resuming her knee-wrapping, to Tom's relief. –Someone phoned for you this afternoon.

–Oh? Tom noticed that the television had been silenced. The nurse must have done it. –Where's the remote? he asked irritably.

The nurse placed it on his lap.

–Only I might want to hear the news.

–That'll do you good, said the nurse, meaning the opposite.

–Who? asked Tom.

–What?

–Phoned.

–Oh. He refused to say. He said he was ex-BD22—um, some long number. I've got it written down some—You all right, Mr Bradley?

Tom was shuddering. The nurse leaned forwards, a little anxiously. She thought he was maybe crying again, but found to her surprise that the opposite was true.

For the first time in quite a while, Tom was laughing. He remembered Barclay sitting opposite him, more or less invisible behind his monitor, making excited noises as numbers flickered and changed and turned into meaningful results. He remembered how proud Dan had been at persuading Claire to attend Committee meetings.

"Just call me Tom Sawyer," he used to boast.

–Your wife is coming, said the dark-haired nurse.

–Do you know what a loon is? asked Tom, a little spitefully. He resented having his genie-free memories interrupted. The nurse, who was turning up the lights, didn't know. She checked it on Google later that day and remarked, "Well, that explains a lot," meaning, as far as her confused colleagues could tell, that it did no such thing.

Footsteps approaching. He tried to remember what he had been thinking about.

–Tom Sawyer.

–Yes, dear?

Who was that? Who was creeping up from behind? He couldn't turn around to check and he started to tremble, partly from fear and partly from anger, but the footsteps didn't stay skulking behind. They came around, in front, their owner momentarily passing between him and the lights, casting him into shadow. He remembered blocking out the sun… leaning forwards… blocking out the sun… He couldn't quite remember when.

–I'm here, dear. How are you feeling today?

§

He knew what was confusing him. It was time. He would remember when he uttered the fateful overtaking words, or further back, to the noisy bus taking him to primary school. And then Mary would be turning towards him, unbuttoning her shapeless cardigan, a query in her calm eyes. Ivy was sitting next to him on the fast train, one of his hands in hers, watching the scenery fly past. Monique pressed against him in her little red car, bumped her hips against his as they walked in moonlight, lay back in daylight and complained that it was too bright. The genie tried to intervene, to take charge, to pull and push him where it wanted him to go and he did not. He resisted.

–No, no.

"It's all right," said the nurse. "Your wife is coming."

–What?

"SD22 something. He wished you well."

Good old Barclay.

§

He noticed that Ivy was sitting in another chair.

–Yes?

–Tom Sawyer, she said.

Tom was bewildered. Why was she saying that? This was clearly another Ivyism he was going to have to unravel. There had been so many of them over the years.

–You said Tom Sawyer, said Ivy.

Oh. It was him, was it? Tom wondered why he would say such a thing. Oh, wait. He had been thinking about Barclay, and that had reminded him of Dan. Oh, yes.

–I'd like to watch it. It must be on DVD. Can you bring it in?

–I expect so, dear. How are you feeling?

–The nurse keeps stealing the remote.

–Oh no.

–And Barclay rang.

–That's nice. What did he say?

–Well, I don't know. I was asleep.

–That's a pity. I expect he'll ring again.

–Yes.

Tom thought for a few moments. Ivy reached out and took his hand.

–Is there anything else you want?

It had been a few years since Ivy had been in hospital—sorry, Tom apologised to himself, a mental something something hospital. The fact that Ivy was in a ward again had become—not exactly normal, but almost routine. She stopped taking her tablets. Psychosis struck. Into the politically correct establishment, where nurses and doctors tried to persuade her to take tablets again. Eventual success. Slow improvement. Home passes, and the subdued joy of final release.

"I won't do that again," promised Ivy.

Tom pointed out that she had said this before.

"But the consultant, he say it will get worse every time. And maybe one day I will not come back."

Tom acknowledged that the consultant had said that.

Ivy shivered. "I won't do it again," she promised.

And she hadn't. For a long time the genie had nothing to record. Tom imagined it curled in a corner, or stretched in the attic, dozing. Xiao Xiao became old enough to go to primary school. The genie remembered that, because Xiao Xiao standing proudly in his new school uniform, having his photo taken by Ivy who was even more proud, reminded Tom of the time John had stood in his first uniform, at the foot of Mary's bed in the hospice. Tears unexpectedly pricked from his closed eyes and he opened them, and sniffed loudly.

Where was he? More damned time had passed, and Ivy had left while the genie tricked him away from the present. Footsteps from behind him again. The tall young male nurse appeared. He always appeared about this time in the late evening. He helped Tom to his feet, despite Tom resisting any help, and steadied him with a hand supporting an elbow as Tom tottered off towards his room despite Tom muttering, –Unhand me. I can make it on my own. At one point he forgot whether he should turn left or right and the nurse sniggered. When they got to his room, Tom ordered the nurse to sit down and not interfere while he slowly undressed, got into his pyjamas, shuffled into the bathroom and then a few minutes later back out again. Then he would wave his hand dismissively and wonder if he would dream that night. He had stopped dreaming, it seemed; or he had forgotten anything that he might have dreamed. It made him rather sad.

§

The dark-haired nurse and another nurse the approximate size and shape of a barrel helped him out of bed. They removed his pyjamas, sponged him down rather perfunctorily, and helped him to get dressed.

–I can do this.

–Not quickly, you can't.

–Have you no decency?

–None whatever.

That was the dark-haired nurse; the other was tying his shoelaces.

–Where am I going?

–Home.

Tom began to feel alarmed.

–How am I getting there?

–Oh, Mrs Bradley will be here shortly.

The barrel-shaped nurse stood up, a little out of breath. Tom eyed her.

–Prepare two beds, he said.

–What?

–If Ivy is driving.

The dark-haired nurse, who had disappeared somewhere, came in pushing a wheelchair. Tom transferred his glare to her.

–I'm not getting in that.

–Yes, you are.

–No, I'm not.

–Do we have to go through this argument every time?

Tom, disconcerted: –What d'you mean, every time? I've never been in a wheelchair.

The dark-haired nurse, sighing: –Well, *that's* true enough.

The door creaked open and Ivy's smiling face appeared. Tom's heart jumped happily.

–They want to put me in a wheelchair.

–Hello, dear.

–And… and you are driving me home?

–Mrs Bradley has been coming here, and back, every day you were here, admonished dark-haired nurse. –Sometimes twice.

–Then the odds are shortening.

Ivy took his left arm and dark-haired nurse his right, with every indication that they had done this several times before. He must remember to ask them how many times before, Tom thought, and then wondered if there was any point. He'd only forget the answer. Perhaps he had asked before. They tottered out of the room and along a corridor. Barrel-shaped nurse hefted Tom's overnight bag and followed behind. They crossed a glass-covered lobby and pushed open the doors. Outside the weather was grey and a damp wind tried to find its way into clothing. On the other side of a narrow road was a sea of cars.

–I had to park a way way, said Ivy brightly.

–Way away, said Tom.

–You wait here, said Ivy.

She headed off into the sea of cars. Barrel-shaped nurse took her place at Tom's right side. His first reaction was to wave her off, but truth to tell he welcomed the support. He was feeling a little wobbly.

They waited.

–Er, said Tom. –Thanks.

–For what? asked dark-haired nurse.

–You know. Looking after me.

–We get paid for it.

–Yes. But still.

Dark-haired nurse grinned.

–I found out some things. Like what a loon is. I looked it up.

–You did?

–I read Tom Sawyer, said barrel-shaped nurse unexpectedly.

Tom and the dark-haired nurse both turned to regard her.

–You did?

–What was it like?

Barrel-shaped nurse tilted a hand this way and that. –It was kind of fun. More than I—

She broke off. The top of a red car was hurtling towards them through the car park. All winced as the car failed to stop at a pedestrian crossing, narrowly missing an old woman pushing an even older woman in a wheelchair. As the car approached they could see Ivy smiling happily behind the wheel. She came to a stop half on and half off the pavement.

–Oh, said the dark-haired nurse. Her eyes met Tom's as she helped him into the passenger seat.

–You'll be fine, she whispered.

–Ready, ready, ready! chirped Ivy.

The nurses stood well back.

§

Tom became aware that he was lying in darkness, surrounded by darkness, gazing up at darkness. He knew where he was but he was not sure when. Was that Mary beside him, or was she on the wall, staring, forever calm, from her painting? Was Ivy still on the other side of the world? No. She was lying on his outstretched arm, nuzzled against him, her own arm flung across his chest. How was it, he thought, that this petite Chinese woman had given up her own life and traversed the globe to be with him and his family? He hugged her and, half asleep, she hugged back, muttering in Mandarin. It might or might not have been nonsense.

"We'll be a team," whispered Tom. "Something will happen, some cultural difference will jump up to bite us…"

"Mm–nn–mnn."

"What?"

"One and one makes—"

"One," said Tom. He squeezed her again. "You know I would never do anything to upset you. Not deliberately. So if I do, it will be an accident, right? We'll be a team, right?"

–What?

The darkness shifted, became heavier, more real. Tom understood that he had left the past and re-entered the uncertain, confused present.

–I can't remember things.

–I know, dear.

–Am I going or have I just arrived? Home.

–This morning, said Ivy.

–Oh, said Tom. –Good.

They lay comfortably together. Tom marvelled, all over again, that Ivy had chosen to stay with him. That sense of wonder was something that hadn't changed over the years. It was a constant whatever date his mind chose to serve up.

–I don't remember why I have to go to hospital, he said. He frowned. How long had he been in, anyway? Days? Weeks?

–How long?

–Two days.

Not so bad, he thought.

–I keep forgetting to ask the nurse. Silly me.

Nurse. Nurses. Hospital. Not the one, he told himself, where Ivy, white-faced and sweating, had passed him that scrawled note in her trembling hand.

–She's yours, said Ivy, a little indistinctly.

Tom blinked.

–Who, the nurse?

–Your another woman, said Ivy. –Like Monique.

They both smiled in the darkness. Ivy tried again.

–Sheezyurs. Zures.

Oh, thought Tom. –Seizures?

Ivy nodded, bumping her head against him. For goodness sake, thought Tom. Seizures. No wonder he couldn't remember things and when he did it was all muddled up. His brain was scrambled.

301

–You fell off—

But Tom didn't hear her finish. His memory flared into technicolour life, vivid in the darkness—of the room, of his brain; he could not tell which—like a screen in a cinema. The high walls of the house, looming, the gutter just out of reach, his feet tangling, the sky swinging into view as he leaned backwards over the void. Like before. He thought it now, as he had time to think of it then. Like before, when Syd sent him flying out over the train tracks. Syd's laughing face—and the others—spiralling out of view to be replaced by the sky. He had been lucky then to avoid the rails but he had not been so lucky off the ladder, plummeting down onto the plastic silver-green coal bunker and, worse, crashing his head against a window sill en route. He jerked and gave a muffled shout as the darkness abruptly returned, obliterating the sky.

Ivy switched on the light and the prosaic outlines of their bedroom walls and furniture sprang into view. He was trembling, pressing himself back into his pillow. Ivy hoisted herself up onto one elbow and leaned over him.

–You all right?

–Just… remembered it, Tom gasped.

–I was holding the bottom, but you fell off the top, said Ivy with her unassailable brand of logic.

–Banged my head.

–You certain did, agreed Ivy.

–Certainly, said Tom. As if the act of remembering the fall opened neural floodgates, Tom recalled waking in hospital, unbearable pain in his back and neck, impaired vision slowly normalising. He was incarcerated for many weeks. People came to see him. John and his family visited and, as far as Tom could ascertain, wrecked the entire hospital. Lucy and Adam were too far away. Dan sneaked in, looking over his shoulder as if he was ashamed of visiting. He had brought grapes.

"Someone got me these," he whispered. "I don't like them so you might as well have them. When you getting out?"

He didn't wait for an answer, but sneaked back out again. Barclay visited. He beamed excitedly and told Tom that Roberta had got married and left, and that Claire had… What had Barclay said about

302

Claire? Tom couldn't remember. But he did remember that, of all his visitors, Barclay was the only one who didn't make commiserating noises and ask how he was feeling. At some point he must have got home, because he had done the reverse journey, back to the hospital, more than once, to see his consultant.

You have not been well served by the system.

No, no. He cursed the genie away. When was it he realised the genie was no longer his friend? His consultant dumbed down, saying that he had squashed part of his brain, that it wasn't possible to unsquash it, and the damage might affect his memory. Well, he was right about that. Had that been Aslan? No. He remembered now—not that he wanted to. He membered the tall Indian doctor glancing at the scrap of paper, nodding.

Baby killer.

–Time for your medication.

Tom struggled to sit upright. Ivy pulled open a bedside table drawer to the accompaniment of much rustling of boxes and chinking of bottles.

–Jesus. It's like a chemist's.

–Mine are in here too.

Ivy passed him a green tablet and a glass of water. He swallowed it and grimaced.

–What's it for, anyway?

–Fix your brain, silly.

Tom seriously doubted it, but did not press Ivy on the point. Her views on medicine—a complicated mix of Chinese herbs and Western psychotic drugs—were fixed, immutable and largely nonsense. She took her own medication mechanically, closed the drawer and switched off the light. Tom settled down onto the pillow and they automatically coiled together. The cinema screen did not return: the darkness was softer, unthreatening.

–One of your clever children rang today.

–Huh. Which one?

–Guess.

It was a game they played. John, Adam and Lucy were all married and had moved away. Lucy lived in New Zealand, Adam in the United States and John, beset by five children, had settled down in

Devon, about as far away as it was possible to be and still be in the same country. Near where Beryl used to live, Tom suddenly realised. His memory made an entirely reasonable but lateral jump to the time he had taken Ivy to London for a long weekend. They had walked, hand in hand, in autumnal sunlight, all around the centre of the city. Ivy gasped with wonder and excitement and simultaneously remarked on how small London was. Then he had caught sight of a Vietnamese restaurant and stopped in shock.

"Congratulations," said Beryl. "He told me *everything*. There *are* no secrets."

He blinked back tears as his mind's eye transported him into the restaurant and he saw again Mary push open the door, her long dark hair contrasting against her fawn-coloured raincoat. For a moment he tried to make contact with his younger self. Tom, calling Tom, can you hear me?

"What? You don't like Vietnamese food," said Ivy doubtfully.

Tom walked to the window and peered inside, but he couldn't really remember what the layout had been all those years ago, so he couldn't really tell if it had changed. He did remember the Chinese girl. And now here he was, a Chinese woman hanging on his arm, looking anxiously up into his face. He shivered. Wheels within wheels.

–Well?

Ivy tapped him on the head, well away from the damaged area. Although, Tom thought, knowing Ivy, that could have been entirely by chance.

–Are you in there?

Right. Yes. He was still in there but he couldn't remember what they had been talking about. He used his backtracking trick. He had been thinking about the restaurant because… Ah yes, Beryl. And he had been thinking about Beryl because? That was harder, but he finally got it. Devon. Oh yes, near John. That was it; they were playing the guessing game.

–Hmm, he said, as if he had been giving the problem due consideration and not wandering around in the past. He didn't think Ivy was fooled, but he had his pride.

–Does it have long hair?

–Not allowed.

He could only use a question once. He must have used this one before.

–I can't remember what I've asked before.

–I can, don't be worry.

–Worried.

–Yes, that.

–Can I trust you?

–My memory is better than yours now, said Ivy smugly.

Tom grunted and she sniggered, snuggling closer. He tried to think of a question so weird he wouldn't have asked it before.

–Did it think hobbits had tails?

–Not allowed.

–Really? You're kidding.

–That was Adam. You asked that last time.

Tom grumbled. Who would have thought his damaged brain was so predictable?

–Does it play badminton?

–They all play badminton, dear.

–You know what I mean.

–Well. Alrighty then!

Tom winced. He regretted ever watching that Jim Carrey film with her. Whatever it was called.

–No, it doesn't.

So that eliminated Lucy, who played to national standard until she went to university and turned herself into a lawyer. He was getting tired, but he knew Ivy loved the game.

–Does it have children?

–Not allowed.

–Does it not have children?

Ivy was silent. He could practically hear her brain whirring, trying to decide if this was a legitimate question. He hoped it was. His own brain was running out of steam.

–Mm, mm.

She was still thinking. That was a good sign. Adam would have loved the question, bordering on a sort of quantum paradox. Is the cat in the box? Is it not in the box? Adam had learned all sorts of arcane mathematics and computer skills before emigrating to the United States.

–I'm getting tired.

–All right. No.

–No?

Ivy remained obstinately silent. Laboriously he worked it out. Does it not have children? No. Therefore must have children.

–John!

Bump of head on chest.

–What did he say?

–Wanted to know how you were. I said you were coming home today. And you did, said Ivy triumphantly, as if she had personally arranged his escape from hospital. Maybe she had, thought Tom. She'd done it herself once, after all.

–He says he's tired.

–He's always tired. Heh. Wheels within wheels.

Tom was remembering that John as a baby slept... what was it?... seven hours in twenty-four, and Mary saying, "It's a waking nightmare."

–They are all well, said Ivy. –He said the twins got loose in the library.

Tom winced.

After a minute, Ivy said, –Remember John on Huangshan Mountain?

Tom thought about it. It felt like a long time since he had deliberately tried to remember something. He used to joke that he couldn't remember when he last forgot anything. Now he couldn't remember when he last remembered something. He concentrated. The cinema opened up, flickering, unthreatening, showing in faded colour. The world was shrouded in mist. He saw their transparent cable car climbing through low cloud, tall peaks rearing on either side. Ivy was frightened of heights and unashamedly clutched at Tom, her eyes tight shut. He was hard pressed not to clutch back. Everyone got out of the cable car and started up steps climbing still higher, twisting around gigantic boulders, always upwards, disappearing into the mist. Those too tired to go any further could make use of a sedan carrier, consisting of two men, two bamboo poles, and a seat suspended in between. Tom watched, astonished and terrified, as he saw how they were swung out over the depths whenever the carriers had to edge around a tight corner. Everyone would press back against the wall as the carriers, shouting in Mandarin, barged past. At one point John stood gazing vacantly into space as they approached, bamboo poles jutting out like spears. "Look out! They'll knock you off!" cried Ivy. "Knock you off! Knock you off!" called the carriers cheerfully. John returned to the present and moved out of the way. "Knock you off!" shouted the carriers, rounding a corner and vanishing from sight. For all Tom knew, they chanted the same words to this day, their origins lost in Huangshan legend.

–Knock you off, he whispered, but Ivy had gone to sleep while he was reliving the mountain, and was snoring gently. He put his cheek against the top of her head and closed his eyes.

§

He awoke again to darkness, Ivy lying on his arm. After much discussion his consultant had told him that he might not dream any more, only remember and relive events.

"Brain damage takes weird and unpredictable forms," explained the consultant.

"Unpredictable?"

"This memory… uh, muddlement is—" The consultant paused. It was clear he was choosing his words carefully. "Uncommon, but not exactly rare. Sometimes it heals itself, or at least improves. Sometimes it doesn't." The consultant shrugged. "The truth is, we can't tell. We don't know."

Tom nudged Ivy and she stirred.

–When—? he began, and stopped. He had been going to ask when it was, whether it was now or an earlier time. But to Ivy it would always be the present, and at no time in the past, snuggled up in bed, had he ever asked *when* it was. Had he? Surely not. Maybe after the accident, he thought. But if he had, he didn't remember doing it. For goodness sake, even Einstein couldn't work this out. He turned towards Ivy, linking his left hand with his right, holding her closer, and decided it didn't matter.

It didn't matter.

Sometimes he remembered a dream, an odd experience during which he felt as if he was outside himself, peering into the workings of his own brain. He remembered what he thought of as the Exam Dream—knowing that he had an exam coming up but he had done no work at all for it and had no chance of passing it. In the dream, the exam was two weeks away, and he was wondering if he could condense two years' study into fourteen days, knowing all the time that there was no possibility of doing so; and then he started to wonder how he was going to explain his dismal failure. He would wake up, trembling and sweating, and feel a surge of relief that his examination days were over.

He had replaced that dream with a memory of their frantic efforts to sort out Ivy's passport and visa—emails, letters, invitations, birth certificates, proof of financial viability, proof of nationality... An endless list. And then, at some random time, someone somewhere stamped Ivy's passport, and she liquidated her Chinese assets and bought a one-way plane ticket to Scotland.

§

–How has he been?

It was the dark-haired nurse. Tom didn't open his eyes but instead surveyed the kaleidoscope patterns on the inside of his lids. As far as he could tell he was at home.

–All right. We watched a film and now he's sleeping, said Ivy.

Hah, thought Tom. Sleeping, was he? But they had watched a film, he remembered that now. On getting him back home, Ivy had proudly given him a present, wrapped in left-over Christmas paper, and it turned out to be a DVD of *The Adventures of Tom Sawyer*. They both enjoyed it.

–Taking his meds?

–Yes.

–Eating okay?

–Yes.

–And how has he been? persisted the nurse. Ivy must have expressed puzzlement, because she continued,

–Sleepy? Happy? Cross? Confused?

–Oh.

During the pause Tom wondered what the nurse was doing at his house. Checking up on him, he supposed. She'd probably done it before but he'd forgotten, he supposed.

–All right, said Ivy cautiously. –He remembers…

–What?

–Things.

Tom could hear hesitation in her voice. He opened his eyes and was rewarded with the sight of his bedroom ceiling, swathed in gloom. It felt as if it was late afternoon. Neither Ivy nor the nurse were visible. They must have paused at the door, in the hallway.

–Yes. That's helpful, said the nurse, meaning the opposite. Everyone knew that Tom remembered things but not always in the right order.

–But, said Ivy. –He can't… he doesn't… There's this thing.

She didn't know how to explain, but the nurse surprised both of them.

–The genie.

–Yes, that!

–We might have to discuss that with Mrs Forbes.

The damned genie, thought Tom. It had teased him with golden memories—Borg and McEnroe slugging it out under the summer's sun; holding Monique on the Golden Sands—but soon enough focused on things he had no wish to remember—Mary, walking in a daze back from the doctor's surgery. *You have not been well served by the system.* Not for the first time, he wondered when the genie had stopped being his friend. As he thought the question, Tom finally knew the answer. It was when it had oozed and slithered across the ceiling above the curtained cubicle, above Dr Aslan, falling ecstatically, shuddering, into his being, into his psyche.

–Tom says it takes him places he doesn't want to go, said Ivy.

Who's Mrs Forbes? thought Tom.

Baby killer.

The damned genie had hardwired the memory of that terrible conversation with Dr Aslan into his brain and forced him to relive it again and again.

Dr Aslan had said: "You keep her company, Mr Bradley, all right?" but everything had changed.

–Mr Bradley?

Someone else was saying his name. Tom opened his eyes and wasn't surprised to see the dark-haired nurse leaning above him, the gloomy ceiling of his bedroom above her. He surmised that only a minute or two had passed.

–I wasn't asleep. I heard you two talking about me.

She nodded and turned away. Tom heard rummaging noises and knew she was getting her portable blood pressure machine organised.

–You're mine, he added.

The nurse swung back into view. She knew him well enough that she was smiling.

–And what would Mrs Bradley think of that?

–It was her idea, said Tom. He shifted his gaze and saw Ivy standing a little further away. Her eyes were twinkling, not like—Tom shuddered—not like that other time. Not like that at all.

§

Heavy darkness, Ivy curled against him. He remembered driving home for their first day-pass, both of them as excited as teenagers on a date. Xiao Xiao gurgled from his baby seat behind them. At home, they transferred him into a pram and went for a walk along the seafront. They made themselves lunch and Ivy examined all the congratulations cards and explored Xiao Xiao's new room. She pronounced herself satisfied. She took her tablets without any complaint and told Lucy, when she came home, that they had decided to let out her room. Tom asked if she wanted to watch some television in the evening, but she shook her head. She wasn't ready to face that yet.

In bed, she lay stiffly by his side for long minutes. Tom knew that she still had trouble sleeping, and that sleeplessness could prove a trigger for her illness. It was the only time—that he could remember—that he actually wished he could hear her snoring. He wondered what was going through her mind.

"I'm sorry."

"About what?"

"What I said. About you. Not trusting you. You were the baddie. I thought you were the baddie."

Tom reached out for her, and she came into his arms, snuggling into their usual position. Tom realised that she had been unsure that he would welcome her. He hugged her.

"It wasn't your fault," he said. "The doctor told me, it was like you had a broken leg, and we just had to get it fixed. Not your fault," he repeated.

Ivy's arm tightened across his chest. She murmured something incomprehensible but he didn't ask her about it because he could feel her falling into sleep. He shifted to be even closer to her, and tears leaked from beneath his eyelids. He opened his eyes and lifted a hand to wipe them, and found himself not in the bed with Ivy but in a chair. There was a television on the wall, turned down so that he couldn't make out whatever it was saying. The lights were also turned down low. His tears ran down his face and gathered at the point of his chin before dropping down onto something on his lap. He flexed his fingers. It was a newspaper.

"Mr Bradley? Are you all right?"

"No. It's the damned genie. I'm fighting it."

"Yes, yes."

"It wants me to remember."

"Yes, I understand. Oh. I nearly forgot. Someone phoned for you this afternoon."

"Oh? Where's the remote? Only I might want to hear the news."

"That'll do you good."

"Who?"

"What?"

"Phoned."

"Oh. He refused to say. He said he was ex-BD22—um, some long number. I've got it written down some—You all right, Mr Bradley?"

Yes, he was fine. Good old Barclay. But when he closed his eyes again, the genie sneaked in through the temporary sentimental breach in his defences, and took control. It replayed Ivy standing, bags packed, in the bedroom. I'm absolutely fine, she told that perfectly turned out doctor. *This looks to me like a domestic dispute.* Maggie's coming to collect me, said Ivy. Which Maggie did, leaving him alone with baby Xiao Xiao.

But, she wasn't gone for long.

§

–And why was that, Tom?

A woman was sitting, companionably enough, in an armchair placed at about forty-five degrees to his own. Tom wondered who she was. She reminded him of someone. She was wearing a smart dress that came down below her knees—which were demurely crossed—and a black thing draped around her shoulders that looked to Tom to be half way between a scarf and a cardigan. Her blonde hair was aggressively swept back, so that she resembled a figurine at the prow of a ship, forever facing into the wind. She was taking notes.

–Tom?

He felt he should know who she was.

–Er, yes?

–Why was that? asked the woman.

Why was what? wondered Tom. What had they been talking about? He should definitely know who she was, he decided, if only because they were in his house, in his lounge, sitting in front of his log fire.

–You were telling me about the time your wife stopped taking her medication and left with her friend.

Oh yes. So he was.

–Is Ivy here?

–She's gone to get some milk. To make some tea.

–Right. Tom nodded. Now that he thought about it, he did remember Ivy, wearing a coat, leaning in through the opened door to give a brief wave. Right, he thought. He could bluff his way through until she came back.

–Er. I got a call from Maggie not long after, a few hours after they left, begging me to take her back. She was worse than she expected, she said.

–I see. So she brought Mrs Bradley back.

–No. I had to go to collect her. She wouldn't get back into Maggie's car. Tom's brow creased. –I don't remember how we got her into our car, but anyway we did.

Tom heard the gate outside the house squeak as it opened. Footsteps.

–It was on the way back—on the motorway—that Ivy tried to get out of the car. We were doing sixty or seventy, for goodness sake.

The blonde woman made a moue, as if she was considering whether to be retrospectively alarmed.

–And not a police car in sight, added Tom. –Do thirty-five in a thirty limit and a SWAT team turns up. Have your mentally ill wife try to exit your car on a motorway, never a single policeman to be seen.

The front door banged.

–But why would she? asked the windswept woman.

–Why would she what? asked Tom, playing for time.

–She got into the car okay, so why did she decide to get out?

–Oh. Well. The road signs at the start of the journey didn't show our hometown on them, so she thought I was taking her somewhere else.

–Ah. The woman nodded. The door opened. Ivy looked in.

–You tried to get out of the car on the motorway, Tom accused her.

–Your driving, said Ivy placidly. –I'm back. She retreated into the hallway.

–That's what she always says, muttered Tom. –Excuse me. He heaved himself to his feet and stretched his legs. –Won't be a minute.

In the kitchen Ivy had already laid out three mugs and a bowl of sugar. The kettle was burbling.

–Who's the woman? inquired Tom.

–That's Mrs Forbes.

–Is she a doctor?

–No, she's higher than a doctor, said Ivy. –That's why she's a Mrs and not a Dr. Maggie explained it to me. She was here last week two time, too.

–Two times?

–Two times.

Ivy didn't ask Tom if he remembered those visits, because he clearly didn't.

–She's a... higher up from a doctor.

–A consultant?

–Yes, that. She say her name. It was—

Ivy made a face.

–Yes?

–Enspraith.

–Right.

Ivy tried again, naming Mrs Forbes All Spice and then, remark-ably, Elephant. Tom stared at her, a grave expression on his face.

–Mrs Elephant Forbes, he said.

–Spith, said Ivy.

–Mrs Spith Forbes?

They both started to giggle. Eventually Ivy elbowed Tom and told him to bring in the milk. She picked up the tray and returned to the lounge.

–This is very nice, said Mrs Forbes.

Tom poked at the fire. Ivy poured out tea, an intense expression on her face. She glanced up at Mrs Forbes several times. It was clear that she had something on her mind. At least, it was clear to Tom, and he suspected that Mrs Forbes didn't miss much. He put the poker back in its place and accepted his tea.

–Mrs Forbes?

–Yes, Mrs Bradley?

–Please, call me Ivy.

Tom held his breath. Would this gambit work? But no; Mrs Forbes merely nodded and took an experimental sip of tea. Tom didn't notice that Ivy failed to follow up with a question, but after-wards he thought Mrs Forbes probably did.

–Mrs Forbes?

–Yes, Ivy?

–I am so sorry but… your name… is hard for me to say.

–Forbes? said Mrs Forbes. Tom saw that she was smiling slightly. Ivy cast him a despairing glance, and he squared his shoulders.

–It's my fault.

Mrs Forbes sipped more tea and raised her eyebrows at him from over the edge of her mug.

–I, er, forgot your name, so Ivy… In fact, he went on desperate-ly, as if admitting further failure would make things better, –I even forgot you were here before.

–My—

–I mean, babbled Tom, –I don't even remember why you are here. Sorry. Sorry.

Mrs Forbes waited to see if Tom had finished and, when it appeared that he had, she said,

–My name is Elspeth.

Enspraith, thought Tom. Close.

–And I'm here to explore the problem of your memory. Maybe help to sort it out.

–Your squishment.

Tom transferred his gaze to Ivy, who was tapping the side of her head.

–Squishedness, he said.

Mrs Forbes leaned forwards and put her mug on the table.

–Squishiddity, she said.

Tom grinned. His nervousness and embarrassment faded. At least this Elspeth Forbes, whoever she was exactly, had a sense of humour.

–You were telling me about—

Ivy jumped to her feet.

–Yes, sorry, Ivy. I forgot. We'll call you when we've finished.

Ivy gathered up the mugs onto the tray and shouldered herself out of the door. Her footsteps clicked off towards the kitchen.

–She doesn't like to be reminded of her… episodes, said Elspeth Forbes.

–No. Yes. She doesn't like to be reminded of anything much from the past, said Tom. –I don't know if that's a Chinese thing or an Ivy thing. Or both.

Elspeth Forbes glanced at her notebook.

–What happened when you got her home, that time? she asked.

§

What happened was that two members of the mental health team came around, a man and a woman who Tom forever after thought of as Mr Right and Miss Left. Miraculously, while Ivy was away with Maggie, he had managed to make contact with the mental health team based in Maggie's area, and they had managed to make contact with the local team on his behalf. Ivy, still carrying her suitcases, marched upstairs to the bedroom, her head shaking furiously. After only ten or fifteen minutes the front door bell rang and she appeared at the top of the stairs, face shining.

"Maggie?"

"I don't think so, dear. I'll go and see."

When she saw who it was, and understood that they wanted to take her away to hospital again, Ivy gripped the banisters, planted her feet, and refused to move.

"Come on, dear. You know you have to go. I can't look after you when you're like this."

Tom put an arm around her and tried to help her downstairs, but it was like trying to shift a lump of rock.

"Come on, Ivy. You don't want to be sectioned all over again."

Ivy wasn't listening.

"Have you got her?" called the male nurse.

Tom nodded.

The male nurse climbed the stairs and took hold of Ivy's right ankle.

"Come on, Mrs Bradley," he urged. "Hold tight," he warned Tom, and pulled. Ivy resisted, but he succeeded in yanking her foot forward, over the edge of the stair, so to keep balance she had to descend one step. The female nurse sidled up the stairs alongside her colleague and took hold of Ivy's left ankle. "All together now," she panted. Tom eased Ivy forward a little, and her left foot joined the right. The male nurse took up the strain. "Yes!" he panted. "Well done, Mrs Bradley."

Ivy flung her head back and stared at Tom accusingly. Tears were streaming down her face. Her hair was wild. Suddenly she gave a shriek and launched herself forwards, into space. Tom tightened his grip on her with one arm, and grabbed at the banister with the other. The male nurse lurched up and performed a kind of body check, halting Ivy in mid-flight. Her resistance dwindled.

"That's it," gasped the female nurse, scrambling backwards down the stairs. They half lifted, half guided Ivy out of the front door, where a car was waiting. Tom dashed back upstairs, grabbed her two suitcases, and thrust them into the car as well. Ivy kept her head averted from him the whole time.

§

The room was quiet. Tom hooked a log from the basket and tossed it onto the fire, where it started to burn with a blue flame.

–Salt, he said. –Or there's a ghost. Take your pick.

Elspeth Forbes finished writing. She closed her notebook and laid her pen on top of it. There was a sense of finality in the action.

–After that, it was just waiting again, said Tom.

–How long?

Tom shrugged. –Three weeks, four. Something like that. Refusing to take medication. Refusing to see me. Thinking that I was trying to kill her—this time by throwing her down the stairs. Sleeplessness. Both of us, I guess. Then one day taking a tablet. Gradual improvement. Day passes. Twenty-four-hour passes. Home again.

–But why? asked Elspeth Forbes. –Why did she stop taking her tablets in the first place?

Tom roused himself. His lips tightened.

–That was Sheila. One of her so-called best friends.

–Oh?

–Advised Ivy that she didn't really need tablets. She was just feeling down, missing China, blah.

–For Pete's sake, said Elspeth Forbes. She opened her notebook and scribbled in it.

–Sheila not her real name, said Tom. –Ivy's friend. Can't pronounce her Chinese name.

–Is she a doctor?

–No.

–Does she live nearby?

–No. She lives in the States.

Elspeth Forbes was puzzled. –So she must have visited, then? To be able to… advise Ivy?

–No, said Tom. –She hadn't visited before, and she most certainly hasn't been invited since.

–I'm not surprised, murmured Elspeth Forbes.

–It's a Chinese thing, said Tom. –I've noticed it a few times. Prone to give advice even though they don't know what they are talking about. Ivy believed her, and started to palm her tablets. I didn't catch on.

317

No doubt the advice was well-intentioned, thought Tom, but it was ill-advised and irresponsible. Perhaps it hadn't even been particularly well-intentioned. Perhaps it had just been Sheila's way of showing that she knew it all and could advise Ivy on anything, even her illness. Whatever, it had certainly led to one of the worst days he could remember, on a par with the day when he had to force the bathroom door open to prevent her from trying to bring up her medication. Or the day he had fallen from the sky, cracking his head open and breaking his memory on the kitchen window sill.

–How many times? asked Elspeth Forbes.

Tom caught her eye and raised an interrogative eyebrow.

–Ivy sectioned.

Tom calculated. First time. Sheila. Once the consultant suggested trying to stop medication. 999 and the firemen. Two or three times she stopped by herself.

Part of the illness, a consultant told him. Watch out for it. Tom felt like saying, he did watch out for it, but he refrained from doing so. Ivy was just so good at palming the medicine. It usually took six weeks before the inevitable effects showed themselves.

–About seven, hazarded Tom.

–And you can remember them all? asked Elspeth Forbes. –Even the first one?

–Especially the first one, said Tom. He thought, thanks to the damned genie.

–Did you report that GP? The one who said it looked like you were having… what was it?

–A domestic dispute.

–Did he really say that?

–He said that, said Tom.

–For Pete's—, said Elspeth Forbes, interrupting herself. –Sorry. Did you report him?

–Yes.

–What happened?

Tom shrugged. –Don't know. Don't really care.

–You remember when you first met Ivy?

Tom immediately thought of the hustle and bustle of the airport, Ivy's beaming face appearing in front of him, the feel of her against him as he lifted her up in a hug.

–Yes.

–Where was that?

–Hong Kong airport.

–And your first wife?

Tom tried to hold back sudden tears.

–Yes.

–And where was that?

–Marsham Street. Twelfth floor.

Elspeth Forbes was nodding slowly, as if she had been making tricky calculations and the answers were becoming clear. Perhaps she had, and perhaps they were, thought Tom.

–It's time we called Ivy back in, she said.

§

–I'm going to tell you some things that might surprise you.

Tom and Ivy, sitting side by side on the sofa, looked at Elspeth Forbes curiously and a little anxiously. Tom's right hand found Ivy's left. Elspeth Forbes seemed in no hurry to begin. She tapped her pen on her closed notebook and appeared to be marshalling her thoughts. Tom suddenly realised who she reminded him of. That woman—left behind, possibly the last to be seen by the doctor, which was possibly the worst harbinger of bad news—he catching her eye as he left with Mary, clutching her hand jubilantly at what at the time they had thought was good news. He remembered the dull waiting room, the straggly Christmas tree hiding in a corner. He remembered trying to give the woman a reassuring smile. Now, his hand clutched at Ivy's, and she clutched back.

–Here's the thing, said Elspeth Forbes. –Mr Bradley. Tom. We've been talking, on and off, for a couple of weeks. You've told me lots of things. A lot of things about your life. School. Your first wife, her struggles with illness. Children. Trips to Malta and China. How you met Ivy; her struggles with illness. The thing is, Elspeth Forbes repeated, –you remember it all very well. In my opinion you have a very good memory.

319

Tom gaped at her.

–But—

–Wait. Let me finish. No, let me ask something. What's the first thing you remember?

As it happened Tom knew the answer to this, as it had cropped up in conversations before. He vividly remembered being in a push-chair, being pushed across a road towards a house he could describe in some detail. He could even picture the grass verge outside the wall of the front garden.

"Goodness me," his mother had said. "We moved from there when you were two."

–Exactly, said Elspeth Forbes. –Not many people have any memories from before the age of two.

–But—

–Wait. Something else before we get into it. You've told me, and Ivy has told me, and your nurse has told me, about the genie.

Tom wondered which nurse. He guessed it was the dark-haired bob-cut one who came to take his blood pressure and who sponged him down so ruthlessly. Except she had moved to another job not long ago. He noticed that Elspeth Forbes had said something and was watching him expectantly.

–What? Sorry.

–I said, there is no such thing as the genie.

The words struck Tom like a hammer blow and for a moment he actually felt as though the breath had been knocked from his body. He wanted to protest. The genie had always—well, not always, but for a long time—been there to guide his thoughts and memories. But as Elspeth Forbes spoke the words, he knew they were right. Some deep part of him immediately knew they were inescapable truth. Still, he wanted to argue. He didn't want to accept it without a fight.

–No, he said. –Or rather, yes. There is. It takes me to places where I don't want to go.

–Really? asked Elspeth Forbes.

But why didn't he want to accept it without a fight? It had been a long time since he had considered the genie to be his friend.

–You used to enjoy the genie's memories, didn't you?

He did. His brain skittered through a partial inventory. Borg and McEnroe. Tug of war with an enormous dog in the falling rain. The thunderstorm, Mary arching her back, her hair falling in a wave. The Golden Sands. *I'm coming, dear.*

There were others. He didn't need to check. He knew there were lots of others.

–What went wrong? murmured Elspeth Forbes.

Tom saw again the genie as it slithered across the ceiling above Dr Aslan's elevated, angular head. His brow creased. Did he really see it?

The fire spat and crackled. Its flames danced and faint shadows cavorted on the walls, even under the electric light. There were no blue flames. Did that mean there were no ghosts present?

–You are the genie, Tom, said Elspeth Forbes quietly.

Tom stared into the fire; Elspeth Forbes sat with her legs still demurely crossed; Ivy—Tom glanced at Ivy. Her expression was both troubled and puzzled. The three of them sat quietly, while Tom pondered the demise of the genie.

§

"Leaving?"

The dark-haired nurse nodded.

"Promotion."

"Congratulations," said Tom morosely.

The dark-haired nurse was unpacking her bag.

"See, this is Rosemary. She'll be coming out to see you now."

Tom regarded Rosemary doubtfully. It looked to him as if she was barely old enough to be out of school.

"Not that she'll be here as often. You're a lot better now." The dark-haired nurse caught his expression. "Oh, here, she's a better nurse than I am. Don't worry, Mr B."

"She's not the one getting promoted," objected Tom.

"You'll be fine. Here." She passed the blood pressure machine to nurse Rosemary, who untangled it with a professional air and strapped it around Tom's arm. "See," said the dark-haired nurse, "sometimes he needs reassurance."

Nurse Rosemary said, "You'll be fine. Good numbers. Good numbers."

"But underneath it all," said Tom, "underneath that hard nurse exterior, does she have that soft interior, like you do?"

The dark-haired nurse grinned.

Nurse Rosemary peered at Tom uncertainly. "Is he always like this?"

"Sometimes he's worse," said the dark-haired nurse.

"You'll be fine," said Tom, and all three of them burst out laughing.

§

–Mary.

Elspeth Forbes had stood up and was smoothing down her skirt. Ivy was already standing.

–We thought you gone to sleep.

–I was thinking.

Elspeth Forbes hesitated, then sat down again.

–I suppose, she said to Ivy, –that you never met Mary?

–No, agreed Ivy.

–Yes, you did.

–And Monique?

–Not that Mary.

Tom held out his arm and mimed wrapping something around it.

–Oh, that Mary, said Ivy.

–What? said Elspeth Forbes.

–You said you didn't want to remember her name. His nurse, Ivy added to Elspeth Forbes.

–I can remember it now.

It was true. Tom could remember the name. It triggered an immense sadness, but not so much pain. He felt curiously light-headed.

–You didn't want to remember her name because…?

–Of her name, said Ivy obscurely.

There was a pause while Elspeth Forbes digested this.

–What about Monique? Have you met her?

–Oh yes. She's Tom's another woman. Ivy sounded positively proud.

–Other, said Tom.

–Yes, that, agreed Ivy. –She's ever so nice.

–She's been here. We've been there, said Tom. He became animated. –You know, you can get here quicker from Malta than from London.

–Works too hard, said Ivy.

Elspeth Forbes was silent for so long that Tom opened his eyes—at which point he realised he had closed them—to make sure she was still there. It was Ivy who finally spoke.

–But he gets muddled.

Elspeth Forbes nodded. –Yes. That's the squishment. Think about it. What is it you most often get muddled up about? What do you forget?

They thought about it. Ivy looked at Tom and her expression was still puzzled. Elspeth Forbes didn't offer to help.

–If I may say so, she said slowly, –I think you have been lucky. You, Tom. Well, you both.

–Right. Right, said Tom. He found Elspeth Forbes unnerving. She had already turned his world upside down once. Now what?

–You were lucky to meet your first wife.

True, thought Tom.

–Your children are happy and healthy.

Elspeth Forbes was bending back fingers on her hand as she counted off Tom's blessings.

–You were lucky to meet your friend in Malta. And then to cap it all you were lucky enough to find Ivy.

Ivy's face ceased being puzzled and beamed instead. Her hand squeezed his.

–And Xiao Xiao, she said.

–Yes, that, said Tom, smiling in spite of himself.

–Would you rather have these memories or not have them? asked Elspeth Forbes softly. Tom knew she was mostly asking about Mary. It was a question he had asked himself over the years, and the answer had never changed. He didn't reply. He didn't have to. He knew that Elspeth Forbes knew the answer, and Ivy too.

–Oh, he said. –Of course. It's only recent memories that get muddled up. I can remember—past stuff—fine.

–Yes, said Elspeth Forbes. She noticed that Ivy was still looking uncertain. –Think of a record. You know, a record? Going round and round?

–Before my timing, said Ivy with dignity.

–She knows, contradicted Tom.

–It's like there are scratches on the edge. So the needle jumps about and the music is confused to start off with. But the further back you go, the closer to the centre of the record, the smoother it gets.

Tom nodded slowly. That sounded right. He felt a sudden overwhelming sense of relief, almost exhilaration. He felt energy and purpose returning. Maybe things weren't as bad as he'd thought. Maybe a lot of things. Why had nobody told him these things before? His heart shifted as he met Ivy's beaming gaze and felt her hand, warm and comforting, in his.

§

Later, Ivy flung her arm across his chest and nestled her chin into the groove beneath his shoulder that he was sure she must have created over the years. Tom frequently remarked that he was just a piece of furniture to her.

–You feeling better.

Her voice was muffled by bedclothes and Tom himself. It wasn't a question.

Tom said, –She was quite something, that Mrs Spith.

–Quite the something, agreed Ivy.

Tom thought back over the conversation. No genie. He felt he had successfully banished the genie, and did not regret its loss. He felt he could now direct his own thoughts, subject only to squishment. Ivy's arm began to relax as she drifted into sleep, but he continued to stare up into darkness. Better to have those memories than not to have them. Yes. Better to remember how he met Mary, and how they lived and loved together, than to brood on the terrible way in which he lost her. Better to remember the heady excitement of his one-night dinner date in Malta than to brood about how Monique had finally returned to her husband. Better to think about how he

324

had met Ivy and how she had enlivened all their lives than to brood on her illness. It was as if Elspeth Forbes had shone a light into corners of his brain that he hadn't known existed. She had shown him new routes, new paths. Why, he thought again, had nobody told him these things before? He felt that his memory dreams would be kinder now. No doubt he would find out soon enough. Ivy snored and dribbled on his chest. He tightened his arm around her; sleepily, she tightened hers around him.

–Heh.

–Mm.

–One and one makes—

Pause. Tom wondered if she had gone to sleep.

–One, she murmured.

–Yes, said Tom. –And I just thought of something else.

–Mm?

–Three into one, said Tom. He knew that Ivy would be unable to resist thinking about it. After a few moments he felt her shift.

–Thrinto un? she said indistinctly, having burrowed a little further down into the bed.

–Does go, whispered Tom.

§

Most days they would go for a walk.

–Barclay's still in there, Tom reflected. They were walking, hand in hand, past the great grey Council building.

–So would you be, said Ivy, –if it wasn't for squishment.

True, thought Tom.

–No squishment for Barclay, though, said Ivy.

Tom squinted at her. Did she mean that he was lucky to be out of the Buildings despite squishment, or that Barclay was well situated inside, free of squishment? As usual, he found it impossible to tell what she was thinking. A woman passed them going the other way: one of her dogs was on a lead while the other roamed free. Gus and Jess were long gone, but he still remembered walking them along the beach in all weathers. The woman walking her dogs reminded him of the peppermint lady, who had also been walking two dogs. She had approached and asked Tom if she might give Jess and Gus a peppermint each. Of course, he had said. Jess, being Jess, had crunched and gulped down hers in less time than it takes to tell about it, but Gus, being Gus, had snootily refused. He always was wary of strangers, Tom remembered. The woman proffered. Gus refused. A little perplexed, the woman passed the peppermint to Tom, who thanked her and popped it into his mouth. Whereupon the woman had looked even more perplexed. She had expected him to relay the peppermint to Gus, not eat it himself. He told this story nearly every Christmas, along with the tale of driving his car down stone steps adjoining a hotel car park.

"The punchline, Dad."

"I don't even like peppermints," Tom admitted. "I was only being polite."

–He might not be if it wasn't for you, said Ivy.

Tom frowned. As Elspeth Forbes and nurse Mary had predicted, he was a lot better, but sometimes he still found it difficult to keep track of conversations. Especially conversations with Ivy. He made a non-committal sound, hoping that she would say something that would remind him what they had been talking about, but she remained silent. She had muffled the lower half of her face with her scarf, citing sand blowing into her eyes and mouth. Tom had protested that there was no wind and, because they had not crossed the road, no sand either. But still, Ivy had muttered darkly. Maybe at lower levels, Tom had conceded, and received an elbow in the kidneys by way of reply.

They moved out of the shadow of County Buildings and that jump-started his memory. Barclay. The golf course fraud. Dan leaping to his feet, excitedly mustering his troops. Barclay diving into rivers of data. Tom had written the final report in such a way that everyone—but especially Director Bert—knew that Barclay had underpinned the whole fraud investigation with his data mining. And now Barclay was still there, but he wasn't. Because of a stupid, failed attempt to clear a gutter.

–I was probably going to leave anyway.

He was rewarded by Ivy's puzzled expression. He could almost see her thought processes churning through lateral logic, trying to

326

figure out why he had said what he had said. –Let's go this way, he added.

They turned down one of the town's few remaining cobbled streets.

–I used to come this way. Back when, you know. Come home for lunch.

He had already been clock-watching by then, winding down to early retirement. At lunchtime he would go home and usually found the house full of other mothers and their offspring. Nearly all the mums had foreign, if not Asian, origin. They spoke together in English, with varying degrees of success, but addressed their children in their own languages.

Tom poked a thumb in the air.

–Chinese.

A finger followed the thumb.

–English—or Scottish, I suppose.

More fingers.

–Japanese. Russian.

He let go Ivy's hand to continue counting.

–Korea, Thailand, Hong Kong. Have I missed any?

–Dalisay. Daisy.

–Oh yes, Philippines. Now I've lost count.

–Lots, said Ivy comfortably, latching onto his hand again. –You said, the tower of babble.

–Yes, that, agreed Tom.

–You all right?

–A bit tired, admitted Tom.

–Giddy?

–No.

One of the many doctors had warned Tom that he might sometimes feel giddy and he should guard against falling down at an inopportune moment. Right, Tom had thought. Fall down only at opportune moments.

–Splintered? asked Ivy. –Chipped? She smirked. She had come downstairs one morning, stretching and yawning, and announced, "I'm cracked." Tom had raised his eyebrows and remarked that he couldn't possibly argue with that. After the inevitable subsequent violence had subsided, discussion revealed that Ivy had meant to say that she was shattered. The conversation had passed into family lore, and associated terminology had been enthusiastically adopted by everyone.

–Now you're the one who's cracked! Ivy said delightedly.

True, thought Tom.

They got home and set about lighting the fire and making hot chocolate. They sat companionably, side by side, on the sofa. Tom put an arm around Ivy's shoulders and she leaned back against him. The armchair opposite was empty, but Tom momentarily imagined Elspeth Forbes sitting there.

–Mrs Spith was right, he said. –I'm remembering things better. I'm not remembering—he hesitated—all over the place. Not so… fragmented.

–No genie? asked Ivy.

–No genie.

–But you remember what tomorrow is?

Tom did remember, and Ivy knew that he did.

–No. What?

–You've forgotten! she cried, dismayed.

–Oh no! What have I not remembered?

He hugged her; she pushed back against him. They both sipped hot chocolate, mentally rehearsing their lines.

–We did an awful lot of paperwork, said Tom.

–A lot, agreed Ivy.

They watched the fire gradually take hold, spitting half-heartedly on kindling.

–I went here, and back, and there, and back, said Ivy.

–True, agreed Tom. –And expensive. Be a shame to waste it.

They both clasped mugs and stared at the fire.

–You got another man? inquired Tom.

–No. You got another woman? Apart from… you know.

–No, said Tom regretfully.

They both sighed.

–Keep going, then? suggested Ivy.

–Might as well.

–Another year?

–I suppose so, said Tom. He pulled his arm from around her shoulders, groped down by the side of the sofa, and produced a small package.

–Happy anniversary.

–But it's tomorrow.

–Close enough.

Ivy excitedly tore at the wrapping paper, although she knew perfectly well what lay inside.

–Oh! She sounded surprised and delighted. –It's a stature!

–Statue.

It was a figurine of a couple sitting side by side on a bench; the man had his arm around the woman's shoulders. It was hard to determine their age, but they were not young. Tom had long since given up trying to convince Ivy that figurines were not big enough to be called statues. He watched as she examined this new one closely, turning it this way and that, and then stood to arrange it on the shelf alongside all the others. Tom could not help noticing that there were more figurines than horses in the display. How had that happened? He found it hard to believe that so much time had passed. Ivy sat back down, he put his arm around her again, and they surveyed the latest addition together.

–It's smaller than last year's, complained Ivy.

–They're sitting down.

–And they look older.

–We are older.

–I've put it in the perfect.

–So you have, agreed Tom.

They both glanced at the fire as it settled with a hissing rattle.

–I didn't get you anything, admitted Ivy.

–You never do.

–But—Ivy turned to look up at him, eyes wide and beseeching—this is from both of us.

Tom grinned. He made his face look resigned.

–From both of us, he said.

Ivy beamed.

–One and one—

–Make one, she said.

Tom leaned forwards and kissed her.

§

The first time he fell over was unpleasant but not a disaster. It was, Tom thought afterwards, an opportune moment to fall over. Ivy was in the kitchen preparing vast amounts of food because John, his wife Caroline and family had decided to pay one of their increasingly infrequent visits. Tom thought of them as invasions. When the doorbell rang he jumped up and the world immediately whirled in a great loop. His legs refused to support him. Got up too quickly, he thought as he fell. His knees landed on the seat of Mrs Spith's armchair. He expected the world to stop revolving at that point, but it didn't. He flapped his arms ineffectually, failed to grasp anything, and toppled forward. His progress was arrested by his forehead making contact with the back of the armchair. At which point the door opened and John came in.

–Hi, Dad. Hey, you all right there?

John's eldest son hurtled in, saw what Tom was doing, and leaped onto the sofa to imitate him. The twins toddled in behind and immediately started to rearrange the books on Tom's bookshelves. Even from his compromised position Tom was intrigued to note that they were able to reach up to a height of three shelves instead of the two they had reorganised last time.

–The twins have grown, he remarked.

Ivy shouldered past John and helped him back away from the armchair. He swayed on his feet for a moment, but then the world steadied.

–I, er.

–You falled over?

–No, no. I tripped.

–Hello, Tom, you look great! enthused Caroline, barging in past everyone. –What do you two think you are doing?

–Is the same thing, grumbled Ivy.

–Leave those books alone. John, do something!

–I'm being Grandpa.

–Turn around, Tom. Sit down, Tom.

The twins shuffled past the books and homed in on the stereo and TV equipment. Tom had put an old metal fireguard in the way and the twins pressed up against it, their chubby fingers reaching through at the knobs and buttons tantalisingly just out of reach. It looked to Tom like a miniature zombie apocalypse.

–Nainai! shrieked John's oldest, noticing Ivy. He hurtled back across the room and leaped into her arms from a distance of about six feet. Ivy staggered, pirouetted, and collapsed onto the sofa. She was giggling. The TV unexpectedly sprang into life.

–Don't touch that! shrieked Caroline. John swooped, picked up the twin who was microscopically larger than his brother and flung him over his shoulder. The twin gurgled happily. His brother started to scream, annoyed at being left behind. Tom noticed that the TV was showing the weather forecast. It looked as if the afternoon was going to be dry, if a little cloudy. The forecaster had a fixed, glassy smile on her face and Tom fancied she could probably see what was happening on the other side of the screen.

–When we're settled, we could go out for a walk, he suggested.

Nobody heard him.

§

Monique agreed to visit, for what turned out to be the penultimate time. Tom and Ivy punched the air and high-fived. They had been trying to persuade her to visit for many years. The previous time had been pre-Xiao Xiao, when the older children still lived in the house. When Tom had gone to meet her at the airport he had been disconcerted to find that he was nervous, as if he had travelled back in time and was meeting her for the first time in Malta. When she appeared through the arrivals gate, looking around anxiously, their eyes met and Tom's heart thundered as he realised instantly that the connection between them was still there. He remembered her parting comment at Malta airport and the way she had walked away without a backwards glance. Heh, he thought as she approached. Payback time.

"There are dozens and dozens of people who know me in the airport," he lied. She quirked an eyebrow. "But I don't give a damn."

He enfolded her in his arms and kissed her.

"Welcome to Scotland."

"What would Ivy think?" she gasped.

"Who knows?" said Tom as he picked up her bags. "The workings of Ivy's mind are extremely mysterious."

It had been a week or so before Christmas and Tom had walked with Monique, unashamedly hand in hand, up the High Street where she exclaimed in delight at all the brand shops that apparently didn't exist in Malta. He had held on to a stepladder while she wobbled up it to plant a cross on the top of the Christmas tree.

–Why would you remember that? asked Ivy.

–I, uh—

–Wait. You were hold the ladder? She was climb up in front of you?

–Er.

–I don't want to know, said Ivy.

But that was all years ago. Now the three older children had moved away, Xiao Xiao had taken their place, but Monique hadn't returned for another visit.

–Why she not come here?

–I don't know, said Tom fretfully. –Maybe it's because I'm asking. You write.

–Okay, said Ivy. She promptly wrote a long email inviting Monique to take a holiday with them because Tom had told her (Ivy) what she (Monique) meant to him and *life is short, we are not young any more.* To Tom's simultaneous joy and annoyance, this brought an immediate response.

How about January?

–For goodness sake, grumbled Tom. –All those years I asked her, and then you ask her once.

This time Ivy went to collect her from the railway station. It was very late. Tom's job was to keep the log fire burning. The clock ticked inexorably past the time Tom estimated they should arrive home. *Where are you?* he messaged. *Is she here yet?* Ivy replied *I'm at.* Tom stared at his phone screen, but nothing more appeared. I'm at? he wondered. What was that about? What was Ivy up to now?

More time passed. Tom became disgruntled, then a little worried. He tended the fire and tried to read a book, although he soon gave that up when he realised he'd read the same page two or three times. The clock ticked. The fire crackled tiredly. At long last he heard the front door open and a quiet confusion of voices. He felt a thrill of excitement but resisted jumping to his feet. This would be a very inopportune moment to topple over. Instead, he stood up carefully and straightened just as Ivy and Monique came into the room.

–What? he yelled—quietly, so as not to wake up Xiao Xiao. He thought Monique looked as she always did, although her hair was streaked with—silver, he decided. Not white.

–We stopped off.

–For coffee, added Monique. Her eyes met his and he felt a thrill even in the middle of his tantrum. He steeled himself.

–Couldn't you—? he yelled, waving his phone.

–No battery, said Ivy.

–Coffee at midnight? yelled Tom.

–I'll make you a hot chocolate, said Ivy in a placatory tone. Monique edged past her, crossed the room and put her hands on Tom's chest.

–Aren't you pleased to see me? she asked.

–Well, hmm. Tom looked down at her. He'd forgotten she was even shorter than Ivy. –Hmm. Close your eyes, Ivy.

Ivy closed her eyes. Tom gathered Monique in his arms and kissed her thoroughly.

–Welcome to Scotland, he whispered.

–I was peek, said Ivy.

–Now you're in trouble, said Monique.

–How do I get divorcing paperworks? asked Ivy.

–Tell you tomorrow.

–It is tomorrow, said Monique.

–You look tired, said Ivy.

Monique sighed and nodded. –Been a long day, she admitted.

–Alrighty then! said Ivy. Tom winced. –Let's get you to bed.

–What about my hot chocolate?

–You, snorted Ivy. She tossed her head.

–I kept the fire going, wheedled Tom.

Ivy scowled and said, –I'll see to Monique. Then I might. Or not.

–Goodnight, Tom, whispered Monique.

–Goodnight, my dear, whispered Tom.

Ivy rolled her eyes and held the door open.

§

Over the next few days they sat by the fire or went for walks along the beach, in various combinations. Sometimes all three of them went. Sometimes Ivy and Monique, arm in arm, marched up as far as the harbour, talking non-stop, mainly about life in general and Tom in particular. When they returned they would gravitate to the fire or a radiator and refuse to move until Tom made them both a hot drink.

–You talk about me?

Ivy, curled against him in bed, bumped her head on his chest.

–That's nice.

–We *complain* about you.

–You? What have you got to complain about?

–You know, said Ivy darkly.

Tom pondered.

–What has Monique got to complain about? I haven't seen her for years and years.

–Exactly, said Ivy, even more darkly.

–I'm so glad you two get on, said Tom.

–She's lovely, said Ivy. She hoisted herself up on one elbow and looked down at him. Her long hair tickled his chest and face.

–You've got good taste, she said. There was an air of expectancy in her voice. There was an air of stating the premise to an argument to which she already knew the conclusion.

–Thank you, said Tom.

–She is a great choice, said Ivy.

Tom unexpectedly heard his mother.

"Splendid. Couldn't have made a better choice."

But that was about Mary. He remembered thinking that *choice* wasn't quite the right word. He turned his head. He smelled a scent; the sweet fragrance of a talcum powder or perfume that Mary used to use. He didn't know its name, but he recognised it. The scent was very strong, but Ivy did not seem to notice it. Tom wondered whether,

334

if they were to light the fire in their bedroom, the flames would turn blue. Was the fragrance just his imagination, or did it signify some form of approval? For goodness sake, now there were tears in his eyes. He was as bad as Monique.

–And then you choose me, said Ivy triumphantly, and slid back down under the bedclothes, leaving Tom alone to breathe in the dying fragrance. He never told her about it, or Monique.

Sometimes Monique could not be prised away from the fire, and Ivy and Tom would venture out for their regular walk, circling the Buildings and returning via the cobbled street.

–I think she's enjoying herself.

–Yes. But a bit cold at night, she says.

–Well, we could always—

–Tom.

–find an extra blanket, I was going to say.

They paused to allow a pair of joggers wearing bright orange kit to overtake them.

–She likes your cooking, said Tom.

–Does she? Ivy beamed.

–She especially liked that chicken curry the other night.

It was Ivy's turn to ponder. After a while, she said,

–You made that.

–I did? So I did. Well, fancy that.

Sometimes, when Ivy was busy cooking an umpteenth meal for Xiao Xiao, or was on an interminable WeChat conversation with her family in China, Tom took Monique for a walk, showing her hidden nooks and crannies and cobbled streets, most of which emptied out onto the seafront. He pointed to windows in County Buildings and told her in a portentous voice that Internal Audit still worked there, to this very day. They held hands. Tom was inordinately proud that he could take walks with two different but beautiful women, on alternate days, and hold their hands. At one place they stopped and looked out over the sea, which was grey and undisturbed all the way to the slightly curved horizon.

–It's peaceful, said Monique.

After a moment she loosed his hand, put her arm around his waist, and pressed close. Well, that's romantic, Tom thought.

–And cold, she said. –Can we go back now?

–I'm just a radiator to you, complained Tom.

They reversed their route along the seafront, pausing to let two joggers in bright yellow kit overtake them. Tom wondered if they were the same two who had overtaken him and Ivy. Perhaps, he thought, the two joggers spent all their time running up and down the seafront, overtaking people.

–Does that mean you think I'm hot? he asked.

–Maybe. Maybe not.

The two joggers disappeared around a bend, clearly heading for the local sports centre. Tom felt an irrational desire to turn off the main promenade before they returned.

–I'm a radiator to you, he said, –and furniture to Ivy. Am I a man, or a…a…

–Thing, said Monique.

–Yes, that.

–Ivy's lovely, said Monique. –You're lucky to have found her.

–I know, said Tom. He remembered Elspeth Forbes saying much the same thing. –I'm so glad you two get on.

Genie-free, he conjured up three pictures: Mary turning towards him in her Marsham Street office, unbuttoning her shapeless cardigan; Monique in Malta airport, edging along the crowd awaiting arrivals, keeping pace with him as he descended the stairs; Ivy appearing in front of him in Hong Kong airport, beaming happily as she came into the circle of his arms. Monique said something about it being impossible not to get on with Ivy, but he missed it, lost in a triplicate vision of the past.

–Did you like my story? he asked. –About my visit?

–Of course I did.

They crossed the road, angling away from the sea. The wind dropped.

–Do you ever… think about that time? I— Tom fell silent. Monique didn't answer. He looked at her out of the corner of his eye and saw that she was staring straight ahead. He couldn't decipher her expression. But she made no move to unlink her hand from his. He said,

–When I think back to then, I feel sad. And happy. I feel both sad and happy.

He sneaked another look at her and saw that there were tears trickling down her cheeks.

–So do I, she whispered.

For goodness sake, thought Tom. More tears. Although he was obscurely pleased to see them. He fumbled around in his pockets and found a handkerchief.

–Here.

–You're making a habit of this, said Monique, stopping in the street to wipe at her eyes.

–Well, you're making a habit of bursting into tears, grumbled Tom. –Remember the last time in—

–I remember.

Monique offered Tom the wet handkerchief and he pantomimed that she should keep it. They both smiled, Tom ruefully, Monique tearfully. They started up the final stretch towards the house.

–You told me you were going to write a book, said Monique. –You said that Mary asked you to. I want to read that.

–I'll send you a copy, promised Tom. –Although, er, it's not finished yet.

§

He opened the door, and saw a young woman turning towards him. No. Way too vague. *He didn't know, when he pushed open the door, that his life was about to change.* Well, an improvement, but still generic. Tom cursed. He had written a lot of the book, but much of it was not joined up. He had a lot of notes. He had the story he wrote for Monique, although that would have to be repurposed. Why couldn't he figure out how to start? Why weren't the lines he thought of working? He needed to think about this before he made more false starts.

On an impulse he checked out the start of one of his Halloween stories: *'Look!' cried Jenny. 'There's the old lady and dog who aren't really there!'* He'd thought of that first line before he had any idea where the story was going. Now it was the other way around. He knew where Mary's book was going—in fact he'd already written much of it—but he couldn't figure out the best starting line. Something wasn't

337

right. *He could not have known that when he started work in Marsham Street...* For goodness sake. No. Awful. Wait. What did he just think? *He didn't know... that his life was about to change.* Well—that was it. The reader didn't know either. Meeting Mary was a turning point in his life, but how was anyone supposed to know that if they didn't know what his life had been like before meeting her? How could a turning point even be a turning point if you didn't know what it was turning from and to? He imagined a curve on a graph, gradually descending, as his unhappy life had been before meeting Mary, then levelling off during those amazing times when they met, and then turning steeply upwards as they tackled a happy life together. Mary could still turn towards him, unbuttoning her cardigan, but not on the first page. Hmm. He needed to describe that gradual descent first. Hmm. How about

> When he found out there was another student
> on the twelfth floor...?

Hmm. Too long. He deleted a few words.

> There was a new student on the twelfth floor.

Tom stared at this for a while. It had a certain something, but it still wasn't quite right. Not *immediate* enough. He vaguely remembered—
–Is it time for bed, dear?
Ivy looked hopefully around the edge of his study door.
–Um.
Tom gazed at her a little blankly.
–Tom! Are you all right?
–Um. Yes. Fine. I was just thinking.
Whatever he had been about to remember slipped away.
–You, said Ivy, shaking her head. –Always thinking. Come on, you got to take your medi.
–You got to take yours.
–Your brain, snorted Ivy. –It's always working.

338

–Whereas yours, began Tom, but stopped as Ivy advanced into the room and adopted a threatening kung fu posture. Later, as they curled up together in bed, he admitted to himself that she was right. He *was* always thinking. He was supposed to be going to sleep, but here he was still writing in his head. He sighed. Ivy snored and dribbled on his chest. He wondered what she was dreaming.

Logic. Never mind the actual words; start with the structure. He needed to find a way to start in Marsham Street with the reader already knowing how he got there and indeed who he was. Phrased like that, the answer was obvious. Young Tom would have to be in Marsham Street either thinking about or talking about his past. But—

Ivy's eyes snapped open.

–Jiǎo zi! she said. –Yum!

Tom rubbed her back gently.

–Yes, dear. In the morning.

Ivy's eyelids came down like shutters and her head dropped back to its accustomed place. So that's what she'd been dreaming about, thought Tom. No wonder she'd been dribbling. He closed his eyes, tiredness creeping up at last. The answer to the first line problem eluded him, but he knew it would come. Part of his brain would probably keep working at it even while he was asleep. No doubt Ivy would disapprove. Jiǎo zi, eh? That virtually exhausted his skimpy knowledge of Mandarin. But he didn't much like dumplings, and Ivy disapproved of that, too. The three children had eaten enormous quantities of them during their visit to China. Ivy's mother had spent hours making them, and he had said no, sorry, he didn't like them much. He couldn't really remember what he ate while he was in China. He did remember the heat. He'd succumbed to heatstroke for the first time in his life, under a merciless forty-degree sun on the Great Wall. He had suddenly felt dizzy and nauseous, leaned back against part of the wall so thoughtfully built for him so many thousands of years ago, and slid down into the patch of shade it offered. His limbs splayed out like those of a flattened spider. But, he had thought dizzily, not so many of them. It was, oh, more than forty degrees, he told Barclay and everyone else in the office afterwards, and I didn't have a hat or anything, and I almost passed out. Barclay and everyone shook their heads, partly with sympathy but mostly, Tom suspected, in amazement that anyone could be so stupid. They wanted to know what the Great Wall was like. Lots of steps, Tom told them. All of them going up. China, Tom told them, was full of steps, all of them going up. There were steps up to the fourth-floor flat where they were staying in Beijing. There were steps up to Ivy's tiny flat in Shenzhen, also on the fourth floor. There were steps crawling forever up the sides of Huangshan Mountain. But the steps Tom remembered least fondly were those at a site known as the Seven Waterfalls. They wound up ahead of them into hazy distance. Lucy, who at the time was super fit from doing gymnastics, would run up a handful of steps, wonder where everyone else had got to, and skip back down again. She must have navigated double the number of steps as anyone else in the family. To the left were the waterfalls, each cascading over what was essentially another, giant step cut into the rocky landscape. People climbed up beside them. Most of them were Chinese. Other people came down towards them, smiling sympathetically and a little smugly because they had already completed the upwards trek. Giant dragons blustered in a faint wind, suspended over tents that dispensed drinks at ridiculous prices. One of the dragons had been tethered incorrectly and it swam upside down in the superheated air. Tom couldn't remember exactly, but he thought it was about thirty-five degrees, with not a hint of shade. Lucy skipped up and down ahead of them. The boys toiled behind. Tom turned and saw that Mary was wearing a thick pleated skirt and a green cardigan, quite unsuitable for the climate. His eyes widened in shock.

"Tom, ní xǐng le ma?" she said, although her lips moved as if she saying something else altogether. She leaned over him, her face full of worry. What was he doing on the ground? He must have tripped over one of those damned steps. What was Mary doing in China?

–Tom, are you all right? Tom? Tom?

He spasmed, and discovered he wasn't lying at the Seven Falls, in blistering heat. He was lying on a floor, in freezing cold. For long seconds he couldn't think who he was or where he might be. Then Ivy shifted and her face moved through bars of shadow and orange light from the streetlamp outside.

–I'm… all right, murmured Tom. He thought about it for a moment. –I've… been better.

–I've called an ambulance! wailed Ivy.

–Why am I down here?

–I don't know! wailed Ivy. –You must have fallened over.

Tom caught hold of the vestiges of his dream memory. What had he been thinking? There was meaning there, if only he could grasp it. He moved his legs and arms slightly, to check that they did move. They did. But he didn't feel that he wanted to go anywhere just yet.

–Cold.

–Oh! Oh! Ivy pulled at the duvet from the bed and almost smothered him with it. She lurched up, grabbed a pillow, and inserted it carefully under his head.

–That better? Tom?

But Tom had drifted back off to sleep. As a result, he didn't know that the ambulance turned up a scant five minutes later, that two burly paramedics lifted him onto a stretcher and expertly whisked him downstairs and out of the front door. He had no memory at all of Ivy standing at the front door, waving rather forlornly at the blue lights of the emergency vehicle as it backed off past parked cars, eased around a corner, and accelerated off in the direction of the hospital. Tom opened his eyes half way through the trip. Puzzlingly, he found a man with ginger hair looking down at him.

–What—?

–You're in an ambulance, mate. You'll be okay.

Tom looked alarmed.

–Ivy… Ivy's not driving, is she?

–No, mate, said the ginger-haired man reassuringly, without missing a beat. –Bert's driving.

–Bert? The director?

–No, mate. Bert the driver, said the ginger-haired man. –We'll be there in no time.

Tom's brow creased.

–Steps and dragons, he said.

–Right.

–No, really. I've got to remember that. It's important, said Tom. He tried to lever himself up, but the ginger-haired man put a hand on his chest to restrain him.

–Better not do that, mate. You're a bit wonky. Hang on.

He fumbled behind himself and produced a clipboard with a pen attached to it by a spiral coil. Tore off a strip of paper.

–Right. What was it?

–Steps and dragons, said Tom. He felt the ambulance slow and take a sharp turn.

–What, like snakes and ladders, eh?

–Something like that, murmured Tom. His grip on reality was fading again, but he saw the ginger-haired man fold up the piece of paper, and felt it when he tucked it into his pyjama breast pocket. Then the world turned black.

When he awoke, it had turned white instead. The ceiling was white. The walls were white. The bedsheets, on which his hands were neatly crossed, were white. There was a square, orange plaster on the back of his right hand and as soon as he saw it the skin underneath started itching. He turned his head, feeling a twinge in his neck as he did so, and caught sight of Ivy's legs in blue jeans. Further up, she was encased in a virulently purple jumper decorated with multicoloured horizontal stripes. Ivy herself was leaning back, sleeping. The window behind her was a rectangle of white light scarcely impeded by flimsy curtains. Which were also white, Tom noted.

He deduced he was in hospital.

He turned his head back to the right and saw a pole carrying various tubes and an empty, transparent plastic bag. He presumed that whatever had been in the bag was now in him. What was the matter with him? He twiddled his fingers, moved his arms, surreptitiously bent and straightened his legs. All appeared to be in working order.

–You awake!

–So—Tom coughed—are you.

–Let me… No, wait. Ivy stood up, leaned over him and pressed a red button at the edge of his vision. –Now you awake, I have to sum the nurse. Let me… No, wait. She pushed and pulled at his pillow and shoulders and Tom found himself marginally more upright. –Now, let me… She poured water from a jug into a plastic cup. Tom sipped at it thirstily. It struck him that he was hungry.

–What happened?

–You were on the floor.

Tom vaguely remembered being on the floor.

–In the bedroom, clarified Ivy.

Tom also vaguely remembered lying on steps in searing heat. Well, that obviously hadn't happened.

–I call an ambulance. You remember?

Now that she mentioned it, he did recall some guy leaning over him, telling him something about the hospital. His brow creased. There was something else he should be remembering.

–What time is it?

Ivy produced her mobile from somewhere.

–Two, she said. –In the afternoon, she added redundantly.

–It's the same day?

The door opened and a nurse came in. Tom recognised her. It was nurse Rosemary.

–Well, well, she said.

–Fancy seeing you here, said Tom.

–How are you feeling?

–All the better for seeing you, said Tom.

Ivy sniggered and nurse Rosemary rolled her eyes.

–The doctor's on his way. Give me your hand. She checked his pulse. –Mm, good numbers.

–Yes, said Ivy.

Both nurse Rosemary and Tom looked at her.

–The same day, said Ivy.

–Probably, said nurse Rosemary.

Both Tom and Ivy looked at her.

–What? We need the bed, said nurse Rosemary. –But it's the doctor's decision. Do you want tea? Toast?

Both Tom and Ivy's stomachs gurgled.

–Okay. Right. Nurse Rosemary, shaking her head, departed.

–I didn't have any lunch, said Ivy defensively. –I was watching you.

That couldn't have been very interesting, thought Tom. But still. He reached out, and Ivy held his hand.

–So, you found me on the floor?

–Yes, and the ambulance came to take you away. I got Xiao Xiao to school and then I came here. And you wake up.

–Is Xiao Xiao okay?

343

–I sent him a message to say you're okay.

–How's he getting home?

–Getting a lift from Mrs Someone, said Ivy. –You stop thinking.

–Yes, dear.

Ivy smiled at him fondly.

–Oh, and I just remember. One of your clever children rang this morning.

Tom sighed.

–You said I had to stop thinking.

–You can think a little bit, Ivy informed him. –Think slowly.

Think. Slowly, thought Tom.

–Is it abroad?

Ivy considered.

–They all are.

Damn, thought Tom. Technically, she was right.

–Is it overseas? he amended.

–Not allowed, said Ivy.

–What?

–Trust me, said Ivy earnestly.

–For goodness sake, grumbled Tom. –This is getting too hard for my poor, tired, overused brain.

Ivy was silent. Damn, thought Tom. She's on to me.

–Does it have more than one child?

–Ivy considered. Gave a small nod.

–No, she said.

Not John, then, thought Tom. But it could be either of the other two. Lucy had a daughter, who they had yet to meet; Adam no children yet. Tom pondered.

–Does it have less than one child?

Ivy scowled.

–That seems like a cheating, she complained.

–Just answer the question, said Tom implacably.

–Oh, alrighty then.

Tom winced. The door opened.

–Yes.

As usual, Tom had to work through the logic. Less than one child? Yes. Therefore no children.

–Luke!

The doctor who came into the room stopped in surprise.

–No, he said. –Gareth, actually. Doctor Gareth Lennox.

He stepped forward and showed Tom his name badge.

–Ah, said Tom, nodding. The doctor was an older man with white hair. Tom couldn't recall seeing him before.

–Well now, said Doctor Gareth Lennox. He picked up a clipboard fixed to the end of the bed, scanned it briefly, and put it back again. –The nurse tells me you are feeling okay.

–Not too bad, agreed Tom.

Doctor Gareth produced a thin implement and said,

–I'm going to shine this into your eyes.

–Okay.

Doctor Gareth peered into Tom's eyes, instructing him to look left, right, up and down, which Tom dutifully did, seeing for the most part different aspects of Doctor Gareth Lennox's visage.

–Is he all right? squeaked Ivy.

Doctor Gareth thumbed off his torch and straightened.

–Seems fine. No pain anywhere?

Tom shook his head, whereupon he was reminded of the pain in his neck. When he mentioned it, Doctor Gareth advanced, seized Tom's head and moved it gently this way and that.

–Hurt?

–A little.

–I don't think it's anything to worry about. Got a crick. Slept awkwardly, didn't you?

Tom acknowledged that he must have done.

–What were you doing before you went to bed?

Tom tried to think.

–On the computer, said Ivy helpfully.

–Oh yes, I was writing. I was—

A sense of urgency overtook him. Writing. *Mary.* Something he had to remember. A ginger-haired man leaning over him. Tucking something into his pocket.

–Frankly, we think you are here under false pretences, said Doctor Gareth.

Tom surreptitiously felt at his chest. Yes, he was wearing his own pyjamas. Yes, there was something rustling in his breast pocket.

–Judging by the reports from Mrs Bradley and the paramedics, you fell out of bed. We don't think you were standing up. No evidence for that. No bruising. No concussion.

–Right. Good, said Tom, distracted.

–What we think—Mr Bradley?

–Sorry. Sorry. Tom had pulled a scrap of paper out of his pocket and glanced at it.

–What we think, repeated the doctor severely, –is that you slipped out of bed during the night and lay there for, well, some time before Mrs Bradley noticed. And it was sub-zero last night.

Steps and dragons? What was that about?

–What are you meaning? squeaked Ivy.

–Oh, said Doctor Gareth hastily. –I didn't mean—

–Ivy sleeps, uh, quite heavily, said Tom. He closed his eyes. Memory was stirring. In the background he heard Ivy protesting that he, Tom, had slept on so late, until after lunchtime, and Doctor Gareth answering that it had been—what, five a.m. when she had found him lying on the floor. It was no wonder Tom had slept late. He was tired.

What had he been trying to tell himself? Suddenly Tom pictured colourful, flying dragons. And steps.

–What is it you are saying? squeaked Ivy.

–And a good thing you did, added the doctor hastily.

Lots and lots of steps. Mary had been on the twelfth floor. Dragons!

He opened his eyes to see Doctor Gareth Lennox peering at him anxiously.

–Are dragons bats? enquired Tom. –Are bats dragons?

–Mr Bradley?

–Tom?

–I'm absolutely fine, he assured them. –I just thought of something while I was asleep. When am I going home?

At last he knew how to start Mary's book. He should, he thought, fall out of bed more often.

> Beautiful. Beautiful and sad. I was in floods of
> tears at the end.

Well, no surprises there, thought Tom. Sometimes he felt that one of his main purposes in life was to make Monique cry. Beryl said it was a wonderful love story. Some of his friends said they would read it later, and he knew they wouldn't, because they didn't read books. The older children seemed unsure of whether they wanted to read it, and Ivy insisted that she would read it later, when the whole thing was finished. She had started her own writing, describing her thoughts and experiences when she came to the West for the first time. She called it *East Meets West*, and once, when Tom tried to extract a cup of tea from her, she complained, "Shh. I'm on the Muse." She had also started to teach herself to touch type, which Tom found mightily impressive given that English was her second language. Tom gave her some of his old typewritten stories to transcribe.

"See," he said. "All those years ago I used a Chinese quote. Is that fate or what? Have you heard of Zhuang zi?"

"Who?"

"Zhuang zi."

Ivy continued to look puzzled.

"The guy who wrote the butterfly quote."

"Oh. Zhuāng zi."

"That's what I said."

"No, you say Zhuang zi."

"Zhuang zi," said Tom.

"No, Zhuāng zi," said Ivy.

Tom gave up.

Now that he had kept his promise to Mary and written about their life together he felt an unexpected sense of peace. He wondered what she would have made of it. Would she approve of the choices he had made? Of his decision to write about certain incidents, but not about others, and to interpose fact with fiction? One afternoon, when heavy rain battered the windows under the influence of an icy Arctic wind, he shut himself in his study and read the whole thing through. Then he sat in front of his flickering computer screen, considering. Would Mary have approved? After thinking about it for a long while in the fading light, he decided that she would. She would probably say it was too much about her, and not enough about him, or the children, or almost anyone else. She was like that. But overall, he felt she would approve of his efforts.

Christmas came round again, together with a visit from Lucy and her daughter who, Tom was pleased to discover, showed not the slightest interest in rearranging his books. Lucy's husband Paul couldn't get away because he was involved in an important legal case, so he and Lucy spent ages WhatsApping to each other at peculiar times of the night and day. And what does that remind you of? Tom asked Ivy one night. 6715, she replied. Tom wrestled with this for a while and finally recalled that this had been his ICQ number, all those years ago when dating on the internet was new and slightly scandalous. Well remembered, he said admiringly, and Ivy had wriggled and blushed and admitted she had just been writing about it in *East Meets West*.

It did not take long to repurpose *Monique*, making sure it followed on properly from *Mary*.

> Oh yes. Good job. You have said all that can
> be said. I don't have that red car any more but I
> remember it well.

–I'll read it later, Ivy insisted.

Beset by an inexplicable sense of urgency, Tom scribbled and typed into the last section of the book. Neither of them could remember when Tom had proposed to her.

–I think it must've been on my visit. Otherwise why did we do all that travelling?

–All that, yes, agreed Ivy.

–Are you sure I proposed to you?

–Yes, sure, said Ivy. –Almost.

–And I can't remember the name of the ball thing.

–Xiùqíu, said Ivy, and spelled it out for him. –When I throw it to you, it means you are to be my husband. Over here, she added. –I remember it was hard to packing it.

–To pack.

–Yes, agreed Ivy.

Tom reflected that, given the start to her visit to Scotland, it was a wonder she ever gave it to him at all.

§

–Mmmmm andhoware you, MrsBradley?

Ivy's consultant, Mr James, had wild, unkempt hair, protuberant eyes, and a slight speech impediment that Tom thought of as an almost stutter. Mr James never actually stuttered, but every time he spoke he wound himself up before firing out words in staccato fashion and sitting back to observe their effect, as if he had cast them into a pool and was watching the ripples they caused.

Ivy worked out the opening salvo, and said,

–I'm fine. I was wondering—

Ivy's sole aim during these appointments was to get the level of her medication reduced. Mr James was well aware of this. Tom watched with fascination as he contrived to not answer the question.

–Aaaaaaahaha, MrBradley have youany er concerns?

–No, she's very well. Taking her medication.

–Gooo dgoodgood.

–I was—

–Norelapses?

Ivy paused, trying to work this out.

–No, said Tom.

–wondering—

–Aaaaand youaresleeping okay?

–Yes. About my—

–Aaaaand eatingokay?

–Yes.

Mr James and Ivy paused and stared at each other. Ivy was frowning and Mr James' expression was slightly alarmed.

–I was wondering—

–So eeeeverything seemsfine. Yes?

Mr James looked at Tom.

–Fine, assented Tom.

–But I was wondering about my—

–Weeeeee can talkaboutit again in—what? Six months? Every-thing seemsfine, Mrs Bradley. Includingyour er medication. Let'snot fixitifitisn'tbroken.

While Ivy was trying to work out what this last barrage of words represented, Mr James stood up and proffered his hand to Tom, who felt obliged to stand up and shake it. Once Tom was on his feet, Ivy realised the appointment had come to an end, so she stood up and also shook Mr James's hand. As they left the tiny consulting room, Tom wondered why consultants always shook you by the hand, as if they were businessmen, but doctors never did.

–Your medication works, he told Ivy. –Probably best not to mess with it.

–Probably, sulked Ivy.

–Leeeee tsgo out forameal, suggested Tom.

Ivy elbowed him and brightened up.

Tom's consultant appointments were less entertaining than Ivy's, if only because he seemed to see a different consultant each time. He remembered how that had happened with Mary, and how it had upset her. He didn't especially mind, although it was a little irritating to see someone going through his notes, making little satisfied noises of understanding and asking random questions for clarification, every time he turned up for an appointment.

–And who was it you saw last time?

How was he supposed to remember that?

–Oh, it was Mrs So-and-so, the current consultant would say, turning pages of Tom's thick and thickening file.

–Any problems?

–Not that I remember, Tom would say. Some consultants saw the joke; most didn't.

Tom's balance was still precarious and occasionally he had to report a fall. The consultant would nod and shake his or her head and make a clucking noise and add another note to Tom's burgeoning file.

–I just get up too quickly, grumbled Tom.

–Hmmm. Mm.

–Could happen to anybody.

–Not anybody has squishment.

–What was that, Mrs Bradley?

–Ask him about the clothes basket.

In the middle of the night it was hard to remember not to get up quickly. Tom climbed out of bed and threaded his way through darkness to the bathroom which, when he clicked on the light, swayed alarmingly and disappeared from view.

When he came to it was to see a stretch of floor at eye level. He deduced he was lying down. He didn't know where he was and couldn't for the moment recall who he was. Weirdly, he remembered this happening before, so he didn't worry about it. His location and identity would return to him in due course.

If he lifted his gaze slightly he could see that the stretch of floor ended at a cupboard, neatly made out of planks and painted white. His brow creased. He seemed to remember making a cupboard like that. In fact, exactly like that. To fit underneath the window in the bathroom. Ah yes. He was, for some reason, lying down on the bathroom floor. Ah yes, he was Tom, and had fallen over again.

He realised he wasn't actually on the floor. He was lying, coiled neatly, in the clothes basket. He was very cold and very stiff, but when he took a mental inventory, he thought all his limbs were responding to instructions. He realised that he'd been extremely lucky. If he had fallen a few inches to the left, he would have cracked his head on a radiator; a few inches to the right, and he would have crashed into the sink. Forwards, and he would have fallen against the ceramic toilet. Backwards, he would have hit his head on the open door. He concluded that he must have folded up in a vertical sort of way, similar to how a condemned tower block or giant outmoded chimney collapsed inwards and downwards into itself after a controlled explosion. He had seen it on the TV often enough. His brain had supplied the controlled explosion, and his collapsed body had ended up in the clothes basket.

Slowly, he eased one leg out, then the other, then both of his arms and the rest of himself. He assumed a crawling position. The door was still open and with a tremendous effort he executed an almost perfect three-point turn and headed through it, back to the bedroom. He didn't want to risk standing up again and in any case he wasn't sure that he could.

The bedroom was still in darkness and Ivy was still asleep. Tom crawled to the side of the bed and paused, panting. Then he reached up and tugged at Ivy's bedclothes. Dimly in the light from the bathroom reflected off various surfaces he saw her open her eyes and jerk in shock. Her eyes widened still further and she screamed.

"Tom!"

"I—" gasped Tom faintly, when he realised that Ivy wasn't addressing him. She was addressing the other side of the bed, which was, of course, vacant.

"Tom! There's an animal in here!"

The vacant side of the bed failed to respond. Ivy clutched the duvet about her as if it could act as armour against whatever creature had invaded the bedroom. She edged backwards. Tom painfully rebalanced himself on three limbs and stretched an arm over the bedside table. He found the light switch and flicked it on.

"Oh! Oh!"

Ivy covered her eyes, momentarily blinded. The duvet sagged and even in his delicate position Tom could not help but notice she wasn't wearing pyjamas.

"Oh! It's you!"

Ivy stared down at him, perplexed.

"What are you doing down there?"

"I—" Tom coughed "—fallen over. And I'm cold," he added.

"Oh!"

Ivy sprang into action, pulling back the duvet—which itself did wonders for Tom's temperature—and hauling him into the bed. Was there anything quite as nice, he thought, as climbing into the bed-warmth left by another person? He thought not, especially after lying, half-frozen, in a bathroom clothes basket for God knows how long. Ivy pulled the duvet over them and curled up against his side. Even her arm draped across his chest felt warm.

"You all right?"

"Mm-hmm."

"Shall I call ambulance?"

"I'll be fine as soon as I warm up."

Ivy cuddled up to his left side, not his right. She was lying in the vacant space on the side of the bed where he usually slept. They had swapped positions. It felt, thought Tom as he pulled Ivy closer to steal her warmth and his eyes started to close of their own accord, as if he was sleeping with a different woman.

§

More figurines slowly cluttered up the shelves and Tom finally got around to moving the horses to a separate display. His memory continued to improve. It would not be long before they would need a new shelf for the figurines. Ivy nestled back against him as they inspected the latest addition.

    –It's about the same size, Ivy said, meaning, as the last one.

    –I don't think you can get them lying down, said Tom.

    –Remember all the paperwork? asked Ivy.

    –There was an awful lot, agreed Tom.

They spoke their lines.

    –Have you got another man?

    –No, said Ivy sadly. –Have you got another woman? Apart from—you know.

    –Yes, said Tom.

    –Yes? squeaked Ivy. –Ooh, who is she?

    –I don't know, said Tom, –We only had one night together.

    –Ooh, I bet you were exciting.

    –Excited, said Tom. –You remember the clothes basket night?

Ivy nodded back against his shoulder.

    –Well, she got into bed with me, on the other side, you know, the window side.

    –The husky, breathed Ivy.

    –What?

    –Taking my man.

Tom thought for a moment.

    –Hussy, he said.

    –Yes, that.

    –But I never saw her again, said Tom gloomily.

    –Oh, what a shame, said Ivy. She wriggled. –But you never know.

She turned her head and looked archly up at him. He grinned.

    –Another year, then?

    –Another year.

–But you be careful, warned Ivy. –You don't want to meet this other woman again.

–Oh, I don't—

–Tom.

–All right.

–Good.

–I'll be careful.

–Good.

They sat quietly. Tom thought how lucky he was, that Zhang Lan had travelled all the way from China to become Ivy and stay with him. He wondered how many times he had thought this thought. He recalled the school geography teacher asking him to point out China on a world map. Which he had conspicuously failed to do. How could he possibly have imagined that he would end up sitting side by side with a Chinese woman, inspecting a long line of figurines that represented their many years together?

–I'll see if I can get her phone number for you, said Ivy.

§

And he did try to be careful. At night he swung his legs out of bed and sat on the edge, counting up to thirty—or sometimes he skimped to twenty, if it was unusually cold. Only then would he lever himself upright and head towards the bathroom. Ivy insisted that he turn on his bedside light when he made these forays, so sometimes he returned to the bedroom to find her still fast asleep, and sometimes he returned to find her gone altogether, but another woman, awake and giggling, lying in his vacated space.

It all worked perfectly well, until one morning, an hour or so before dawn. He had woken up feeling thirsty and decided to fetch a drink from downstairs. He kept to the protocol. Light on. Sit on edge of bed. Count. Ease upright and head out of room.

He found the hall light and clicked it on, since he was going downstairs and not into the bathroom, and that was where things started to go wrong. As he turned from the light switch towards the stairs one foot caught behind the other and he unexpectedly found himself launching into space.

Oh, this is not good, he thought.

A few other thoughts struck him as he continued out over the stairwell, failing to grab on to the banister as he went. The foot of the stairs seemed a long way off, and entirely in a downwards direction. He remembered Ivy trying to take the same aerial route, and Mr Right lurching upright to prevent her. But there was no Mr Right to stop Tom from sailing onwards and outwards. The cupboard over the stairs with its dangerous-looking silver handles was going to interrupt his progress, he noted. It was coming towards him at a tremendous rate and appeared to be aiming directly at his squishment. He doubted he would be able to turn his head away to avoid the collision, although he tried. He thought he shouted out to Ivy, to warn her that something was happening or about to happen, but he could not be sure because, in another instant, it happened.

§

He creaked open his eyes. It occurred to him, although he couldn't immediately think why, that he was surprised he could do so. He couldn't remember who or where he was—again—but it didn't seem to matter much. The ceiling was white. The walls were white. Oh yes: he had been here before. He was in hospital and his name was Tom.

His eyes tracked downwards and he saw Ivy. She was sitting by the bed, leaning forwards as if she was holding his hand. Perhaps she was, but he could not feel it. Her face was placid but her eyes were sad. Standing next to her was a blonde female nurse clutching a clipboard or some such thing. With infinite care and not a little pain he inched his head sideways to see who was standing on the other side of the bed. It was Monique, her silver hair falling to her shoulders and her eyes glinting with tears. He always seemed to make Monique cry. It was odd that she was there. He saw her lips move.

–He can probably hear, said the nurse.

Hearing might be the last thing to go. Nobody knows, it seems.

–I'm here, dear.

I'm coming, dear. That was Ivy. Did she say that? He inched his head around again. No. She was already here. Why would she say that? It made no sense although, he thought fondly, she so often made no sense. He closed his eyes and the genie returned, gently, to engulf him for the last time.

The world changing as he climbed to the twelfth floor. He could see it now. Rain slanted from a dark sky while he played tug of war with a dog and Mary doubled over with laughter. McEnroe and Borg slugged it out under the summer's sun. Mary told him that she was pregnant, watching his face anxiously. The family listening to his stories; Gus barking at their laughter. Faster. The cardboard city. The coincidences. Faster and faster. *I will always be part of you.* Blue sky and a warm wind blowing against his face. Rushing past now, almost too quickly to see. Maltese rain. *Our shield.* Making love to Monique, the little red car, the hotel room, Casanova parting. *I'm coming, dear.* Peking duck. *I have made a deciding.* The Xiùqui. Have you got another woman? One and one makes one. Another year, then? Another year.

So much, but when he opened his eyes he guessed he had only been remembering things for a few seconds. Ivy's sad smile seemed fixed to her face; the nurse was standing motionless, her pen stilled; the tears on Monique's face had halted in their tracks. All very weird. Imagine, though, Tom Are-You-Overtaking Bradley with three women clustered around his bed. No, four. He hadn't noticed the door open, but it must have done, because Mary stood at the foot of his bed. There was something not quite right about Mary being there, but he couldn't think what it was and anyway it didn't matter.

It didn't matter.

He moved forwards and, as usual, lost himself in her smile.

Postscript

Creating this book has been a long journey. More than twenty years, and an awful lot of words. It has been very hard to write and I hope that in places it has been very hard to read. But I also hope that some of the characters, some of the situations and events, have amused you too. If you haven't both laughed and cried on this journey, then I haven't have done my job properly.

I must take the opportunity to thank a few people who have helped me to produce *Three Into One Does Go*. My family and some old friends—a few of whom appear in the book—read early versions and gave me valuable feedback and even had the gall to point out typos. Sparsile's beta reader Alex Winpenny very kindly gave me such a wonderful review that I was tempted to print out lots of copies and paper my wall with them. Jim Campbell edited the book to within an inch of his life. My thanks also to Gerard Hill, one of the best proofreaders in the country and a long-time advanced member of the Chartered Institute of Editing and Proofreading. Any mistakes remaining in the book are, of course, entirely due to his missing them. Thanks to Lesley Affrossman who not only decided to go ahead with publishing *Three Into One Does Go* but also designed its splendid cover. Finally, I must thank you, whoever is reading these words, for taking the time to read the book: I hope that you find some satisfaction in reaching the end of Tom's story.

Mary, my dear, I hope you like your book. I hope you approve of the way I have depicted you, and Monique, and Ivy; and I hope you approve of the unexpected routes my life has taken.

Stephen Cashmore

April, 2022

Printed in Great Britain
by Amazon

42554706R00205